THE RAVEN NAELO SAGA
BOOK 1

ARCANE ASSASSIN
PATH OF ANNIHILATION

R. A. FISCHER

HELLBENDER BOOKS

an imprint of Sunbury Press, Inc.
Mechanicsburg, PA USA

an imprint of Sunbury Press, Inc.
Mechanicsburg, PA USA

For information about special discounts for bulk purchases, please contact Sunbury Press Orders Dept. at (855) 338-8359 or orders@sunburypress.com.

To request one of our authors for speaking engagements or book signings, please contact Sunbury Press Publicity Dept. at publicity@sunburypress.com.

FIRST HELLBENDER BOOKS EDITION: July 2024

Set in Adobe Garamond Pro | Interior design by Crystal Devine | Cover design by Sienna Rose | Edited by Sarah Peachey.

Publisher's Cataloging-in-Publication Data
Names: Fischer, R. A. author.
Title: Arcane assassin : path of annihilation / R. A. Fischer.
Description: First trade paperback edition. | Mechanicsburg, PA : Hellbender Books, 2024.
Summary: Raven Naelo's realm guardian dreams come true when her father sends her to Gideon's camp, where she meets four other trainees. Little does she know, a human necromancer plans to destroy Euphrasia while collecting undead souls. When Raven discovers a war has begun in Omlett City, she must return to join them. The final test for the realm guardians has arrived, and they must repel the attacks or face annihilation.
Identifiers: ISBN 979-8-88819-162-0 (softcover).
Subjects: FICTION / Fantasy / General | FICTION / Fantasy / Epic | FICTION / Fantasy / Dragons & Mythical Creatures.

Product of the United States of America
0 1 1 2 3 5 8 13 21 34 55

Continue the Enlightenment!

DEDICATED TO
Jarod Fischer and Austin Fischer
Kevin Fritsch and Addison Fritsch

IN MEMORY OF
Ashley Purnell, Charles Beaston, Dawn Hary, Earl Neidig,
Mary Mikula, William "Belushi" Markley Jr.

Euphrasia

Pangean Ocean

Fellswar

Fellswar Claim

Grey-Holg

Horcish Lake

Boars Blood

Zahgan

Vatur

West Euphr

Glimnok

Wheatland

Hag Swamp

Mystic Bay

Waterfront

Clea

N

Arctic North

Arctic Straight

The Gorge Mountain Range

Northern Euphrasia

Koport

Ebony Forest

Penn's Woods Village

Forest

Sattiir

Penn's Woods

Brindell

Sattiir

Gideon's Camp

Omlett City

River

Woods

Spires Hand

Armistice

River

Thistlebane

The Dryad Lakes

Central Euphrasia

Iron Cliff

Ril Zorn Mountain Range

Stone Forge

Thanorus

Iron Vale

Steel Ridge

ck

River

noemier

Sand Castle

The Hourglass Desert

PROLOGUE

he humans were right. Debris and body parts blasted past her, interrupting her thoughts. *This place is hell.* The voluptuous succubus plunged to her knees, covering her face with her hands. The shards of obsidian rocks and chunks of burnt flesh rained down on the small ledge where she and her master, Draklor, perched for the viewing.

Courtlynn quickly wrapped her garnet wings around her nude body to prevent any sharp objects from scratching her soft, ivory skin. She pulled her wings tighter as the crumbling rubble that echoed in the cavern dulled short screams of terror. Smokey gray dust invaded her nasal passage, tickling her throat when it reached her on the ledge. *What have I done?* She noticed tiny rips in the fleshy part of her wing, but the only thing that hurt was the burst of mocking laughter from her fire demon master.

Flexing her wings back, she slowly lowered her trembling hands from her eyes, still cupping her nose and mouth as tears swelled. The stories and warnings about floxes that her parents told her as a child were true: The demon foxes chew off their tails as a defensive mechanism. A shield prevents them from being a casualty except when it's their last tail. Even her imagination didn't prepare her for the extent of the destruction.

Courtlynn scanned the charred area, where the smoke from the fires mixed with the layer of fog in the limited sky. The grand Cubbis Town Hall was reduced to black stone rubble, all for her master's selfish plan. Piles of gravel covered the small gardens of rare fire-spinner flowers that decorated the entranceway—the air smelt of burning wood, mortar, and flesh.

The five elderly Cubbis council members were buried somewhere beneath the wreckage. Her master ordered her to trick them into attending an emergency meeting to discuss the idea of sharing the third layer with the fire demons. *Only fools would fall for that.* The feeling of betrayal should have consumed her, but she stood tall as a sense of retribution washed over her as she recalled all the succubi and incubi the council had forced to be fire demon tributes. *And for my parents!*

Her master's filthy loincloth pressed against the back of her head as Draklor moved closer, his eight-foot frame shadowing her petite stature. A long vorpal sword dangled from a leather sheath attached to his rawhide belt, reminding her of the prisoner he stole it from, still chained in her master's chamber. He placed his calloused hands on hers, pulling them away from her face and examining the dampness on her fingers, laughing maniacally again.

Seething with anger, she clenched her fists. Her long nails pierced her palms, drawing blood. *He probably thinks the tears are for my people, but that is farthest from the truth.* Her bond with Grimmly and Flixxes exceeded any bond with the council members who allied with the fire demons and sent their own to be concubines. The loss of the imp and flox stung more.

Her mind played the memory of her watching helplessly as the elderly Grimmly flapped his wings to hover, cautiously guiding Flixxes into the obsidian structure. Once at the entrance, Flixxes sat staring at Grimmly with complete trust as the imp's gray-skinned hand petted the demon fox's bright orange and spotted-yellow head for the last time. The image of Grimmly's weathered face glancing up at her one last time sent shivers down her spine. The imp dashed to the side of Flixxes with a dagger, severing the flox's last tail, triggering the devastating explosion. Warm tingles scattered across her body at the memories of the old imp comforting her on the first day she was assigned to Draklor.

Grim always watched over me. Why would Draklor do this to his beloved messenger? And knowing Flixxes was on his last tail, it would be fatal to his long-time pet. If he could do this to his faithful followers, what will he do to me when the time comes? She felt her master's thick legs between her garnet wings as she flexed them again. His strong hands ran through her red curly hair as he gripped her horns, forcing her to stand.

A blue portal crackled open at the gateway receiver next to them, and Draklor's deep voice echoed across the wasteland. "Now."

Courtlynn tilted her head, watching her balor master raise a leather cord. A stone pendant attached to it caught her eye; energy from it called out to her. She reached up and cupped the cone-shaped pendulum as the magic calmed her trembling hands. The crimson-colored crystal matched the drying blood on her palms. Specks of fire, peppered throughout the gem, blazed as a symbol of the spark of life. *The jewel looks like it was forged in the Astral Realm by the gods.*

Draklor yanked it from her hand, closed his eyes, and yelled, "𝒜missa 𝒜nima Mℯa." It pulsed with a dark red glow. Bright blue energy emerged from the smokey rubble floating in the air. Her master opened his eyes and unsheathed the prisoner's vorpal sword, pointing to the gateway. The orbs flowed toward the portal.

"What are you doing?" she asked with concern.

"Stealing souls," Draklor boasted, concentrating on the orbs of energy.

"How?"

"The Artifact of the Stolen Souls is one of the five forbidden artifacts that created the worlds we know today." Courtlynn followed the spirits as her master continued. "It can control souls from bodies that aren't properly buried."

She turned, glancing back at him quizzically as he sprouted an evil grin.

"Even if they are in pieces."

In the distance, she heard a mob of Cubbis villagers approaching. Their voices screamed in terror, calling out the names of the council members. Courtlynn's heart raced. *If they catch me, I'll be exiled to the ninth layer and chained wingless to the cliff for the dire rodents to feast on my flesh.*

"Don't worry, I'll deal with them," Draklor declared as his oversized hands pushed her through the portal, making her topple.

Glancing up, she didn't recognize the area. The space was a massive cavern with two tunnels leading from the main room. Strange, flesh-colored capsules lined the room, covered with a layer of mucus—the smell reminded her of the overflowing privies of the Mortal Realm.

A figure appeared from one of the tunnels, and Courtlynn was surprised to see a male ceredella, clad in his red High Council robe, inspecting the five pods. His bright yellow eyes contrasted with his rusty orange skin. Tessk's long squid-like mouth tentacles squirmed effortlessly, reminding her of the human bards' drawings of the sea monster, Kraken.

The council member represented the Abyss Realm for forty-nine Mortal Realm years. *The partnership between him and Draklor worries me.* Gracefully sliding to a tall, fleshy pod, the ceredella watched as blue energy entered an organic device, then closed his eyes as his tentacles frantically twisted. Like a human heart, the flesh-like pod pulsated in a stable rhythm. "The connection is made."

His harsh voice makes my skin crawl. It's— A loud *whoosh* interrupted her thought as Draklor appeared through the portal.

"Perfect," Draklor responded, entering the room as the gateway closed behind him.

The lump in her throat made it hard to speak. She wasn't fond of the council, but thought of her Cubbis friends, who could be in that crowd. *I hope Vanessa is all right. I miss my friend.*

"Did you kill the others?" she finally asked.

"Just one. The rest fled in fear," Draklor replied, cleaning chunks of bloody, gooey fluids from his sword. "I need you to request another imp messenger." She bowed her head in response. "Tessk will oversee the pod convergences. I need to hunt down and trap another flox." The balor reached his hand out. Courtlynn mirrored him as he kissed the back of her hand. "Wait for me in my bed chamber."

Courtlynn nodded again, watching her master exit the tunnel to the war chamber. After closing her eyes, she sighed with relief. An amused snort came from Tessk.

"What?" she asked curiously.

"My child of the damned, you will not find what you seek," Tessk responded, inspecting the seal of the flesh pod as fluids pumped from an organic pipe feeding the new demon.

I'm not too fond of their telepathic traits. Nothing is private. "And that is?" Courtlynn asked aloud.

"Freedom. Love. Acceptance. You spend too much time in the Mortal Realm. You're becoming weak." He adjusted the tubes around the slimy shell.

"But I have to—"

"Feed . . . feed off human males' sexual energy. You can't pretend that you belong in their world. Your people are peaceful. It was a miracle that the fire demons wanted an alliance. You must remain loyal to Draklor."

The truth hurts.

"I know, child," Tessk responded to her thought.

I really hate that they can read minds.

Tessk stopped and glared, flanges wailing, until all five pods began pulsating. "It's working!"

As she stepped cautiously toward the capsule, Courtlynn's heart raced. She braced herself and peered inside. Bringing her face inches from the outer membrane, she jumped back as the demon's six eyes opened. The succubus stumbled backward, bumping into Tessk.

The creature ripped through the lining of the pod, using the crown of bones protruding from its gray, spiky head. The newly created demon's eyes were the same color as the blue souls, and its mouth oozed black fluid. Tessk stepped up to the pod, spraying a mist into the demon's face. The monster leaned back, passing out in the pod.

"I would love to continue our conversation, but can you take your primitive, undisciplined mind somewhere else? I have work to do," Tessk chided.

Keeping her mind as silent as possible, she spread her wings, flying down the corridor, leaving the ceredella to celebrate on his own.

As Courtlynn entered Draklor's war chamber, she noticed the empty pen that had caged Flixxes. The half-opened bag of feed Grimmly prepared for the flox's dinner sat in the corner.

No need for that now. The succubus folded the bag, placing it inside the empty cage. Courtlynn was about to fly to her master's bed chamber when the prisoner's rattling chains caught her attention. His white, feathered wings were outstretched and pinned to the stone wall with iron spikes. Thick metal shackles hung from the wall, securing his arms above his head. His gold armor lay under his chained feet in an unorganized mess.

"Cubbis," the prisoner hoarsely whispered while yanking on the chains, "set me free, and I'll have the High Council show you mercy. I need to report Tessk for his betrayal."

"And be hunted by the balors and ceredellas in the Inferno-Plane forever?" Courtlynn snarked. "No thank you, Guardian."

"It's Tier," the guardian responded.

"Do you want to bond with me—Tier?" she asked, placing her hands on his thighs. "Too bad you're an elf and not a human. We could have bonded . . . vigorously."

"I have a companion."

"And are you in love, Tier?" Courtlynn asked with interest, sliding her hands further up his legs.

"Yes," he replied, gulping.

She dashed away laughing. "Fool," she mumbled as she sat upon a rock bench overlooking the Lava Falls. "I do like your wings."

"Thank you. It comes with the job."

Courtlynn huffed. "I know. I like the feathers compared to my fleshy-skin wings." Silence filled the chamber as if waiting for his compliment, but it never came. She spun on her seat to face the prisoner again. "Does it hurt? Your wings pinned out like that?"

"Uncomfortable, but no pain. But thank you for your concern."

"I'm not concerned—just curious."

"Cubbis listen—"

"It's Courtlynn."

"Courtlynn, I'll take you away from here—wherever you want."

"Why would I leave? The most beautiful creatures are here. Have you ever seen a team of Nightmares gallop across the fiery planes of the eighth layer? It's the most breathtaking sight. The Mortal Realm horses don't even compare."

"Have you seen the unicorns in the Fey Realm?"

Courtlynn shook her head. "What do they have in the Shadow Realm?"

"They have a shadow mane," Tier replied as she perked up. "They have a fluorescent green glow and flames like how the Nightmares have a red, fiery appearance."

"They sound magical," she said, looking back to the falls.

"You don't have to stay here. You can be free."

Tessk's voice rang in her mind—*You will not find what you seek*—and, momentarily, she thought about setting the prisoner free. *Draklor will kill me like he did Grimmly.* So, instead, she turned to the guardian with a wicked grin, preparing her most sarcastic voice. "So, I could, like, go dancing in the stardust of the Astral Realm or swimming in the crystal waters of the Fey Realm. Bask in the moonlight of the Shadow Realm. I've been to the cities of the Mortal Realm. Those guardians wouldn't allow me to stay." She climbed off the rock and sauntered over to him again. "Or maybe you could hide me in another plane in the Abyss Realm. Hydro-Plane's waters are nice this time of year, or maybe I could go gold-digging in the Metallic-Plane. I could plant some nice crops in the Petra-Plane or build a tree house in the Sylvan-Plane."

"No need for sarcasm."

"Was it *that* obvious?"

"My point is, I can take you anywhere for your safety."

Courtlynn huffed again, spreading her wings, and rose to face the elf. "That's interfering, and you'll lose your position as a guardian. You didn't want to risk that when you sat by while the fire demons wreaked havoc on all the layers." His blank stare proved she was right. *He had no intention of helping me.* "Tessk informed us about being a guardian . . . except the immortality ritual. So, Tier, if you want to see your love again, I would tell my master everything you know—for your sake."

CHAPTER ONE

THE FINAL TEST

"Beauteous," Raven Naelo whispered, staring at the sunset as it fell on the rustic orange and red leaves that descended from the oak trees. Shutting the doors of the Omlett Inn behind her, she stepped down the curved stone stairs, clad in ebony leather armor. The teenaged half-elf tied her long jet-black hair into a ponytail and strolled across the grassy patch of leaf-covered land. The sound of crickets filled the chilly air and merged with the rustling and crunching of the leaves as she kicked every pile in her path. She inhaled deeply, enjoying the aroma of wood-burning fireplaces and stoves as they mingled with the scent of decaying leaves.

Under the stable's wooden archway, Raven passed the groundskeeper, who glared at her and threw down his rake. Brugg was a tall, brawny, green orc cast out by the orcs of his village. Raven's father, Eugor, had saved him from a group of humans and sheltered him, eventually offering him a groundskeeper job at the Inn. Realizing she undid most of his hard work before he could bag up the mounds of foliage, she whispered, "Sorry, Brugg," in Orcish, the language he taught her as a child. "I'll rake it tomorrow."

"No," Brugg replied, struggling with the common language. "Tomorrow, you birthday girl." His communication skills were getting significantly better.

"Thank you," she responded in Orcish. *How flattering that he remembered.*

Raven watched Brugg pick up the rake and return to his work. Wanting to make amends for creating more work for him, she decided to help by lighting the torches that led to the horses' pens. She glanced back at him, smiling, remembering when she and her older sister, Carya, were young girls, and Brugg would swing them in his arms, calling it "orc swing."

Raven unlocked the short, wooden gate to Ghost's pen. "It's time! After four long years of my father's intense training, it's finally time to prove to him that I can do this on my own." The charcoal-gray unicorn offered a short, quiet neigh as if she understood.

Raven pulled her hand out of her dark purple cloak to pet Ghost's soft, silvery mane. "It's hard to believe we've been together for almost two years, girl." The memory of her sixteenth birthday came to her, when Gideon surprised her with the unicorn. Raven pulled the reins to guide Ghost out of the pen. "Equipment checks before we leave," she stated methodically, tugging on the black leather saddle. "Saddle secured, check. Ooh, and we match, double-check!" Raven brushed aside her long cloak and placed her palms on each gem-encrusted hilt. "Two daggers, check." She reached inside her cloak as her friend bucked with eagerness. "Finally, a treat for the road!" she giggled, pulling a sugar cube from the pocket. The impatient unicorn bobbed her head and devoured it. Raven placed her boot in the stirrup, swinging herself onto Ghost before trotting outside the stable, pausing to take in her surroundings.

The sun had already disappeared over the horizon, leaving a cloudy, starless night sky. A strong gust blew the leaves, and her cloak whipped wildly. "Looks like rain."

Brugg walked by, throwing the rake down again. "Me give up."

Raven checked the lockpick snuggled into her ponytail holder, then pulled up her hood, trying not to laugh as Brugg slouched and trudged to the main doors of the Inn until finally slamming the doors behind him. *Poor Brugg.*

Thunder echoed in the distance, and she wondered if it was possible to make it across town before the storm. "Here we go," she said excitedly, tugging on the reins. Ghost emitted a long, loud neigh before galloping across the grass onto the main dirt road. Their destination was on the westernmost side of Omlett, so they'd have to make haste through the city's heart if they wanted to stay dry.

The silent night was disturbed only by her cloak flapping in the breeze and the clanking of her daggers against the saddle. As they raced around the bend, Ghost's magical hooves made no sound as they passed the halfway point, where Maggie's Magic Shop and the church Carya attended were visible to the left. Storm clouds now completely hid the crescent moon. "Pick up the pace!" Raven yelled.

Ghost responded with a burst of speed. Images of the weapon shop, black-smith, and apothecary blurred past them as they approached the Cache Tavern. Raven halted the heavily breathing unicorn, checking the surrounding area for signs of trouble. All was quiet. Relief and disappointment collided at the thought of not being tested.

The fire from the torches at the entrance danced in the wind. Raindrops began to pelt Raven's hood, and a crack of thunder exploded above. She quickly dismounted and tied Ghost to a hitching post where five frightened horses mingled. "Looks like you're getting a bath tonight." Ghost snorted in response. Raven rubbed the unicorn's broken white horn in their shared tradition and whispered, "For luck." *Blade, watch over me.*

Cautiously, she stepped onto the broken stoop, touching the wooden door. As she slowly cracked it open, drunken voices flooded her ears. Her pulse quickened as a smile spread across her face. A gust of wind wrenched the door from her hand, and she winced, bracing herself as it smacked into the back wall. The voices stopped abruptly, and she opened her eyes to see everyone gawking at her standing in the doorway. *So much for being inconspicuous.*

The muttering resumed as she stepped inside and struggled to close the door behind her. Gathering her composure, she turned toward the long oak bar. Stale alcohol and tobacco smoke permeated the air, making her cringe as much as the floorboards that creaked under her steps. She scanned the room as she made her way through. The only patrons were a group of male humans on the far left, focusing on someone sitting in the corner. To the right was a table where three half-orcs sat. The four empty tables around the rough-looking half-orcs, half-humans, indicated no one wanted to be near them.

Raven navigated the maze of unknown stains on the floor until she reached the bar. The redheaded dwarf behind the counter appeared to be standing on a crate or box and was drying a freshly cleaned glass. "Prin—" the bartender began before Raven quickly put her finger to her mouth to silence him.

"Mister Keggs, I heard you have a Horck problem," she said in a low tone, nodding toward the rowdy half-orcs.

"Aye, milady," the bartender whispered as he placed the glass down, "and please, just Rusty. The dirty Horcks have been causing trouble for days." He leaned closer to Raven. "Robbed some customers, too."

She leaned in as well. "Any weapons?"

"I imagine so," he answered in a hushed tone, "but the only one I've seen is the long sword in the corner."

Raven pulled away from the bartender. "I'll take a dwarven ale," she ordered, keeping her eyes on the three half-orcs.

"Aren't you a little young for that?" Rusty asked nervously.

With a confused look, she returned her attention to the bartender. His eyes were on the front door. "He's here, isn't he?" she asked, agitated.

"Don't know who you're talkin' about." He quickly poured her a drink but continued to watch the far corner.

"How much?" she asked, pulling out her brown leather-hide coin pouch and peeking at the Horcks to ensure she had their attention.

"Compliments of the Cache Tavern," replied the bartender, waving his hand and shaking his head.

"Work with me, Rusty," Raven whispered, counting the coins in her bag. The pouch slipped from her hands, spilling silver and gold coins across the bar. After swiftly gathering the currency on the counter, she knelt to retrieve the single gold coin that had fallen to the floor. A worn, dirty brown boot suddenly obscured the bright gold sparkle as she reached for it.

"Finder's keepers," a deep voice said in Orcish. The bottom of his boot moved quickly to slide the coin backward toward the group of laughing Horcks.

The deep brown eyes of the tallest half-orc stared down at her. "Pretty eyes," he sneered. "They would look good on my mantel."

Raven stood, her head barely reaching his green, hairy chest, and secured the pouch to her belt. She turned her attention back to the tense bartender.

"Barkeep, drinks for my buddies and me," the half-orc shouted in the common language. A loud cheer erupted from his table. "This little elf is paying." The ruffian pulled back her hood, exposing her hair and semi-pointy ears.

"Half-elf," Raven mumbled as she reached for her drink.

The Horck attempted to intercept the glass, but a dagger quickly pinned his large hand to the counter. He cried out in pain, struggling to remove her weapon with his free hand, but a second dagger quickly pinned both hands together. The surprised half-orc glanced up as a glass of ale shattered against his forehead, and he dropped to his knees, unconscious.

Raven hated to waste good dwarven ale, but it was for a worthy cause. As she stared at the Horck's companions who watched from their table, her face warmed, and anger consumed her. Her voice hardened as she stated in Orcish, "You can touch my gold, you can touch my cloak, but do not touch my ale."

Furious, his two friends sprung from their seats and overturned the table. The shorter of the two charged her while the other grabbed the long sword.

Raven smirked and spun both hands in opposite directions to cast her elven spell. "Cessis Nar," she murmured, watching her hands emit a bright red glow that radiated heat as the smaller half-orc approached. She ducked under his sizeable green fist, positioning herself behind the off-balance attacker. Grabbing his arse, her hands burned through his cloth pants, searing his backside. He screamed in pain, hobbling out the front door, smoke trailing from his rear.

The scorched outline of her hands on his pants amused her until the smell of burning flesh made her gag and double over, dry heaving. Lightheaded, she turned as a female voice screamed, "Watch out!" A magical stream of water sailed over Raven, splashing the third Horck in the face.

The Horck bent over, spitting out water, wiping his eyes with his free hand. His face was bright red, and his black facial hair was soaking wet. Their eyes met.

Raven repeated the hand motions for the next spell. "Nissrɛ Nar." Electricity sparked from her hands as the Horck fearfully raised his long sword. Grasping his broad shoulders, she forced the voltage through his body. The long steel sword clattered to the floor as his bulky body collapsed, twitching. She turned to thank the stranger, but a clapping sound from the opposite corner drew her attention.

"Hail King Naelo!" shouted the bartender, smiling as the patrons knelt.

"Please, carry on," King Naelo responded as he approached Raven. The king lowered his hood, exposing the tips of his elf ears poking through long, white hair. As he pushed his robe aside, she noticed that he was wearing his black leather armor.

"Father!" Raven exclaimed, disappointed. "I told you I could handle this on my own."

"I trust you," he said, his arms encircling his daughter, "but I had to evaluate you on your final test."

"In your battle gear?" Raven huffed, gesturing to the dispersed group of humans. "And a hired hand!"

"I wish I had, but I have no acquaintance with that young lady," her father contested.

"What does that mean?"

Her father nodded toward the Horck's body, still lying in the small puddle. "You were about to taste the tip of that long sword."

Was he right? Doesn't matter! Her mouth uttered the first defensive argument that could come to mind. "I had it under control!"

"That was against three drunkards. Imagine if it were—"

"A fire demon from the Abyss that takes my head over a trinket?" *Did I cross the line?* Raven softened her voice to help ease the pain reflected in her father's expression. "I know your story. And I'm ready to face challenges like you and my brother. You two were guardians, and I want to be one, too."

"Gideon agrees that you should wait until the next class."

"You two are trying to delay the inevitable. Just hoping I'll find something else, like settling down, running the Inn."

"It gave you and your sister a comfortable lifestyle so far."

"Only because you became king. But look at poor Rusty."

Rusty dropped the rag and the Horck's unconscious head on the counter. "Hey!"

"No offense," Raven quickly replied as Rusty continued wrapping cloth around the dagger-pinned hands of the injured Horck. "I'm surprised you didn't have Buzz—" But the front door swung open before she could finish. Four cloaked dwarves entered the tavern to arrest the other decommissioned half-orcs. Her eyes narrowed when, outside, she noticed a dwarf with a patch over his eye. "Buzz, too?!" she exclaimed, throwing up her hands in disbelief. Buzz'diir Plunkett had arrived with a squad of dwarves. Her father's security detail dragged the smoldering half-orc from the mud puddle to a horse-drawn wagon.

"To take them to the prison," King Naelo innocently replied as Raven jerked up her hood and stepped out into the cold drizzle. "You did great!" he yelled from the doorway as she untied Ghost. "Even with those hocus pocus spells."

Raven rolled her eyes. *I hate when he calls them that.*

"You neutralized the threat—there were no casualties and minimal property damage," Eugor said with pride as he watched her prepare to leave. "I would say you passed the final test tonight, but—"

Raven sighed. "But what?"

"You remind me of my younger self."

"And?"

"That's dangerous."

She shot her father a smirk, whipped the reins, and dashed toward home. *Here it comes!*

"Don't forget TO LOCK UP!" her father called out as she lip-synced the words.

Raven entered the Omlett Inn through the front doors, tugging at them to ensure they were secured. *This is not my future.* The hall torches were out, but being a half-elf, she could navigate the unlit corridor with natural dark vision. Making a left down the hallway, she passed a couple of sleeping rooms. Following the hall to the right, she approached the double-sided doors across from the banquet room that led to the stables. *Locked.*

Raven peeked into the banquet hall to see if her party preparations were underway. *Any presents? Maybe an exotic gift from Gideon or one of my father's mundane but practical gifts.* The room was dark, though she spotted the Illusion Ball hanging in the center. She entered, strolling to the side door that opened to the courtyard, still scouring for bulky packages. As she expected, the doors were secured, too.

Returning to the main bar area, she walked toward her father's work chamber. On her way there, she spotted the magical painting of the ebony tree that hung in the hallway, and her thoughts turned to Gideon. She blushed, remembering standing there with a group of drunken bar patrons when she was seven years old as they all watched Gideon cast a naked dwarf out from the portrait. The same awe overcame her as she recalled him in his gold armor with those gorgeous white wings. *I wonder what it's like to be an actual Mortal Realm guardian working at the High Council in the Astral Realm.*

At the end of the hall were the doors to the arena, already padlocked and secured. She liked to think of it as a dungeon, but the stadium was for combat entertainment. Finally, she entered her father's work chamber and locked the door. Raindrops and fog obscured her favorite view from the two cathedral-style windows. *Damn it.* She turned from the windows and pulled open the bookshelf, entering a secret tunnel to her home's galley.

Mmmm . . . that smell. The lingering scent of missed dinner excited Raven's stomach as she escaped the tunnel. She leaned against the closed door, taking a deep breath and enjoying the candle-lit kitchen's quietness. She helped herself to a slice of fresh pumpkin pie from the pan, slowly making her way into the living area near the fireplace and watching the fire gradually burn out.

Raven continued upstairs to her bedroom, nibbling on the slice of pie. Her sister's room was across the top of the stairwell, and her parents' room was off to the right, down the hall.

Carya always had a rule about removing footwear before entering, which made Raven stop and glance down at her feet. "Oh, no," she muttered, staring in disbelief at the mud trail behind her. *How did I not notice it going back down the hall?*

Stuffing her mouth with the final bite of pie, Raven quickly slid off her boots and stashed them next to the door. She backtracked to discover that it led to the point where she entered the kitchen. A yawn caught her off-guard as her body ached. *I'm too exhausted to deal with it right now.* She followed the mud trail back to her bedroom. *I'll rise early and clean, or I'll never hear the end of it.*

CHAPTER TWO

A SPECIAL DAY

THUD! THUD!
Something slammed into Raven's bedroom door, waking her from a deep sleep. Rolling onto her back, she squinted at the ceiling through heavy eyelids. She anticipated another knock, but it never came. Turning to face Carya's old bed, she sat up groggily and stretched. Her body ached as if an owl-bear had run her over. Looking down at her hands, she saw spots of dried blood. Images of the fight the night before flooded her mind, and her eyes widened. *The mud!*

Raven threw her heavy woolen covers off, dashing to the door. Staring down at the oak floor, she tried to find the slightest trace of mud, but the mess was gone. Brugg exited Carya's room, sweeping the dust into the hallway. Like the rake, the broom looked tiny in his giant orc hands.

"Brugg, please tell me you cleaned up the mud," Raven implored.

"No . . . mud," Brugg answered, looking confused. "Where . . . mud?"

"Never mind, Brugg. No mud," Raven said with regret. "My mistake." She hurried halfway down the steps to find Carya in a white and gold-trimmed cleric gown, packing muffins and fresh fruit into her basket. Raven wanted to compliment her sister's celestial appearance—their mom, a human, would call them angels. Carya's long, curly, strawberry-blond hair glistened in the morning sunlight.

"Did you—"

"Nope," Carya interrupted, "Father did." She glanced up with a smirk. "You look like ogre poop."

The angel compliment quickly faded from her thoughts. "Thanks," Raven responded, jumping the remaining steps and approaching her sister.

Carya opened a cabinet, glancing inside. "Last night must have gone well. You're still in one piece."

"Look at that. My cleric sister became a comedic bard overnight."

Carya placed a jar of fresh honey on the counter. "Aspirant—I'm only an aspirant—but hopefully soon I'll be promoted to a cleric."

"Father promoted me, so—"

"To what? A rogue? What does that even mean?"

"Means whatever you want it to mean."

"You're a thief? An assassin? A courtless tavern wench?" her sister teased, spreading a thin layer of honey on a bun.

"I use magic, so a title of arcane assassin will be *just* fine."

"Mother was worried when you and father missed dinner. I was mentally preparing to care for you at the infirmary at the church today."

"Thanks for the confidence," Raven replied, tearing off a piece of her sister's honey bun, avoiding a defensive slap.

"So, will you leave with Gideon in a few days?" Carya asked, providing a stink eye.

"No . . . it seems that Father and Gideon feel I have an attitude that will get me killed." Raven waited for her sister to reply, but she didn't. "I don't have an attitude!"

Carya choked on her bread. "They think you can be reckless and egocentric."

Raven gasped with mouth agape.

"I heard them speaking a few weeks ago. You also don't work well with others."

"Wonderful . . . what else did they say?"

"That if anything happened to you, it would break Mother's heart. Also, they fear that Father and Gideon's friendship will break."

This is not fair. Raven seized her sister's hand. "You can always join me at camp and care for all the guardians."

"I'm not looking for adventure and danger. My place is here, caring for the people of Omlett and preparing to become queen one day." Carya pulled her hand from Raven's and finished packing the basket.

"Speaking of queen, where's Mother?" Raven asked, reclining back on the chair.

"She's out in the garden, tending to the herbs." Carya picked up her basket and approached Raven. "You might want to clean that dried blood off you. It can't be sanitary." Carya sniffed, wrinkling her nose and fanning the odor away. "You *smell* like ogre poop, too."

"Sorry, I'm not one to hide in a church or go rolling around in flowerbeds and dancing in the sunshine."

Carya's chuckle ceased. "And if you were to be hurt, young sis, guess who would have to mend your pompous head? Us, the flower-scented clerics." She pulled on a pair of white gloves. "Well, time to dance in some more sunshine."

Raven stormed back up the steps to her room, where she saw what had made the two thumps that woke her. A parchment was pinned to the door by her weapons.

Here are your daggers. I took it upon myself to clean up your mess. Meet me at the prison later.
Love, Father

"Dragon poop," Raven muttered as she pulled out her daggers and rolled up the parchment. She carried them into her bedroom, tossing the items onto her bed. After slipping into her black silk robe with gold trim, she had her bathing kit in a bucket and returned downstairs. On the way, she ran into her mother, Mara, at the front door.

"Are you going to your water hole again?" Mara asked, shuffling a basket of herbs between her hands.

Raven raised her bucket and towel, rushing past. *I don't need to hear another lecture about bathing at home.* When Mug created a new well in the front yard, they installed bathing tubs in the house, but Raven preferred to feel the sunshine and breeze as she bathed.

The morning air was cool and crisp as Raven walked outside, and she slowed her pace to appreciate the day's beauty. Following the leaf-covered dirt path, she headed north along the Suttiir River up to her watering hole as a slight breeze caressed the branches of the willow trees.

She found her secret path that bypassed the dense vegetation. At the trail's end, a pool of crystal blue water sparkled, where the sunlight shone through the rare holes in the canopy of leaves. Now that the leaves were scarce, the sunlight was more abundant. A kaleidoscope of magical butterflies danced through the last remaining flowers in the middle of the woods.

Removing her robe and nightgown, she slid into the warm spring, sinking below the water's ripple as her muscles relaxed. She closed her eyes to listen to the birds and the raging water of the Suttiir River. "Beauteous," she whispered.

After a moment of relaxation, Raven went to work on cleaning herself, running her hands over her matted hair and across her skin. Even with her mother's homemade soap, she had trouble removing the dried Horck blood. Once clean, Raven floated on her back, thinking about the battle the night before. She wanted to thank the person who had helped her, even though she had it under control. *I think I did well overall.* She held her breath as she dove under the water and swam toward a hidden cavern.

As Raven swam through the small passage, she entered the cave and emerged from the water, and a light orb appeared above her. The celestial sphere, a gift from Gideon to Carya on her eighteenth birthday, floated above the pool, filling the dark cave with light. Raven crawled up the rock wall and sat on the ledge where thick, mossy plants covered the rocky terrain. The pool shimmered coral blue in the light as she kicked, making waves—*my favorite place in all of Euphrasia.*

Raven laid back against the wall, staring at the orb. Light reflected off the beads of water still clinging to her body. As far as she knew, only Carya and she had swum down this far and discovered the cavern. They used it as their secret sister spot for the last five years, but it remained a mystery to them how they could hold their breath for that long.

I wonder what magical gift Gideon has in store for me today. The thought of all the gifts he had given her put a gentle smile on her face. It had become a contest between Gideon and her father to offer the best present.

Eugor gifted practical presents: books, daggers, and training gear. Gideon always found a way to bring magic and beauty into her life. Like the colorful glowing stones for her room when she was younger, a magical journal that only she could write in with invisible ink, and last year, a silk robe from the Fey Realm. She remembered her father's face when Gideon presented the unicorn on her sixteenth birthday. But her father must have known because he had a new black leather saddle made with pouches containing fifty gold coins.

I wonder what they'll have for my eighteenth birthday.

But Gideon's generosity and gift-giving was known to everyone. When bored, he would randomly teleport items to strangers or friends. Raven's mother once received a barrel filled with dirt from the Petra-Plane of the Abyss Realm, and the soil increased the quality and quantity of her crops. Another year, Gideon gave Eugor a wheelbarrow filled with metals from the Metallic-Plane of the Abyss Realm, which helped Mug create his iron golems that would help guard Omlett.

Raven's stomach growled. Returning to the pool, she resurfaced, dressed, collected her bathing items, and returned home.

In the kitchen, her mother was trying to finish cooking breakfast but abruptly stopped, grabbing her lower back in pain as she reached for a pan.

"Can I help?" Raven asked, noticing that her mother's perfect strawberry-blond hair was coming undone from her bun.

"It's fine, dear," Mara answered. Raven tried to suppress her chuckle. It was rare to see her mother, always prim and proper, covered in soil. She was the same height as Raven, but she meant business when she gave that motherly stare with her dark blue eyes. "What?" her mother asked.

"I didn't know you actually bake mud pies," Raven grinned, pointing to her mother's hands.

Mara clucked her tongue and quickly rubbed her hands on her apron before placing a plate of eggs and bacon on the table. "Here's some breakfast," she said with a smile, turning to wash her hands in the basin. "No mud pies—I promise."

"You know, plenty of gnomes would love to cook for us." Raven laid her bathing items next to her and began to eat.

"We are quite capable of taking care of ourselves unless you're implying that you don't like my cooking."

Raven just chuckled and kept eating.

Busying herself on filling two mugs with water, Mara asked, "I assume everything went well last night? You know I worry about you following in your father's footsteps."

Raven picked up a piece of bacon, snapped it in two, and stuffed both pieces into her mouth, mimicking her father.

Her mother shook her head. "You are two of a kind."

Raven responded with a mouth full of food. "I'm eighteen—"

"Where are your manners?"

After swallowing, Raven continued. "Father was younger than I was when he began his training."

"True, but I'm not his mother. I do have an adventure for you, though."

Raven's eyes lit up. "Really?"

"I need you to stop at the bakery." Mara placed a coin purse on the counter.

Unimpressed with the requested errand, Raven slumped over. "The bakery?"

Mara smiled. "Let Miss Crinkly know she can deliver the cake later today."

"Oh, a cake?" She finished her last piece of bacon. "Maybe a bacon cake?"

"You need to finish getting ready to visit your father." Mara carried the empty plate to the sink. "I know he has something for you."

"Is it his magical razor wire?"

"You'll never get that, dear," Mara laughed. "I think it's a new mop."

Raven scowled. "Doesn't matter," she said, rising from the table. "Gideon won't let me down."

"Don't get your hopes up," Mara warned. "Gideon has had his hands full lately."

Raven ignored her mother's warning and collected her bathing items. "But how do you suppose he'll top a unicorn?"

"I don't suppose you can," Mara answered, shaking her head. "You were obviously disappointed last year when you received the robe."

"I was not!" Raven protested. "I love this robe. It's the first silk thing I've ever owned. And didn't he say it was made from magical silkworms in the Fey Realm?"

"If you say so. Just make sure you're gracious no matter what—it's more than what many get in a lifetime."

"Always," Raven promised as she tossed the soap bar to her mother before picking up the change purse. "Make sure you bathe here and not at the watering hole. It could be *dangerous*."

"Mock me all you want, but one day you'll understand. In the meantime, please take the laundered robes to your sister's room for me."

Raven clucked her tongue, imitating her mother, dragging her feet over to the pile of clothes, then paused, sighing. "You know there are gnomes who would—"

"Raven Jade!"

"Just sayin'." After picking up the folded robes, Raven continued upstairs and opened Carya's bedroom door. On the left was a mahogany bed adorned with white blankets and red drapes. A small nightstand held an oil lamp and a stack of healing books from their mother's library. It appeared Carya had once again been up late studying.

Raven tossed the robes into the wardrobe and moved to the window. Pulling back the golden drapes to let the sunlight in, she sat on the window seat and gazed out, spotting a couple kissing by the river. *We have rooms for that.*

There was little time for a social life between her mother's life lessons and her father's rogue training. Raven used to make fun of her sister for frolicking with the guys. It was amusing when their father would lecture Carya on courting rules. The door suddenly swung open, startling Raven as Brugg held an armload of wood for the fireplace.

"Wrong room," said Brugg, appearing confused.

"No, Brugg, you're in the right place. This is Carya's room." She glanced at the couple one last time before standing and walking past him.

Returning to her room, she noticed the sun above the windowpane. *It's time to go.* She quickly dressed in chestnut-brown leather armor and sheathed her two daggers. She felt her cloak that hung by the fireplace to see if it was dry enough after last night's rain. There were damp spots, but it was wearable.

Rushing downstairs, she decided to go through the tavern first. *I wonder if anything interesting is happening.*

Raven opened the heavy oak door in the kitchen that led to her father's work chamber in the Inn. At the end of the dimly lit, damp tunnel, their family coat-of-arms hung by a rope to the right of the wooden blocked entrance. The prominent crest had four engravings on a heater shield with an interactive tavern mug in the middle. The four images included crossed double daggers on the top left, a wizard book and staff on the top right, an ebony tree on the lower right, and a bow and arrow on the lower left. At the top sat a crown between two inns on a tavern-style shingled roof stretching across the shield's top. A black dragon cuddled an egg on the shield's left side, and a gray unicorn appeared on the right. At the bottom was a wavy banner reading:

Omlett—Naelo's—Inn.

Raven reached up and twisted the top of the mug toward the double daggers. The sound of the lock mechanism clicked, and then she pushed on the back of the fake bookshelf to enter.

After all these years, her father's chamber still had the same old leather smell. She closed the bookcase and noticed a space where his desk always sat. *What the spell? Maybe he's getting a new one.*

Raven exited his work chamber and entered the tavern as Mug, the gnome tinker, walked by with a wicker basket of carrots. Ash and soot covered his gray beard and face except for the rings around his green eyes where his goggles had been. "This is a first," she said, helping herself to a carrot. "Usually, it's a basket full of junk."

"Take it," Mug urged, reaching up and shoving the container into Raven's arms. "It's for Ghost."

"Thank you, Mug."

"Don't thank me," Mug grimaced. "I repaired Miss Crinkly's oven, and she paid me in orange vegetables—so there you go."

Raven laughed. "Well, I'm sure Ghost will appreciate it." She bit into the carrot as Mug turned and stormed down the hallway. "Will I see you later tonight?"

He snapped the goggles back, raising his hand in acknowledgment.

He's definitely working on something for tonight.

Raven dropped off the basket of carrots at the bar as Cyndi Sharp, a human bard, was wiping down the countertops. *I'm surprised she's not singing.* The full-time barkeep was curvy, a bit taller than Raven, and had wild, short, ruby-red hair. Cyndi and her mother, Trixie, had come across Omlett many years ago, long after the bard's father decided to continue wandering as a musician. With no place to return, Eugor had taken them in and offered Trixie a job as a barkeep, and Cyndi had taken over when Trixie passed away a few months earlier.

"Hey, Cee, will you take care of these for me, please?" Raven asked.

"Sure, Rave," Cyndi replied, then sang, "*Lucky . . . it's your birthday!*"

As Raven rolled her eyes, she noticed a familiar scene. A group of men huddled in the corner surrounding someone, and that someone had their full attention. "Looks like you have competition today."

"Finally, I can get some work done." The bard picked up the basket of carrots and sang, "*Basket . . . full of carrots . . . beats a cage . . . of squawking parrots.*"

Raven quickly grabbed a couple of carrots for Ghost and shook her head. "See you later, Cee," she called out as the bard exited to store the vegetables in the pantry. The tune of Cyndi's song stuck in Raven's head, and she began whistling as she used her rear to push the tavern's front door open.

Her whistling halted when she spotted another leaf pile. Just as she raised her foot, prepared for a punt, she noticed Brugg raking the leaves again. *He said I didn't have to help today.* Cyndi's voice rang in her mind, *Lucky . . . it's your birthday.*

Instead, Raven scampered to the stable and greeted Ghost. "Good morning, girl. Did you rest well?" The unicorn nuzzled against her. "I'll take that as a yes." Raven dangled the carrots and fed her loyal friend. "Ready for a morning stroll? It's a special day—places to go, gifts to get, and coins to spend!"

CHAPTER THREE

Knight in Shining Aura

Thomas Wellington, a young paladin knight, finished packing up his camp. Everything was still a bit damp from the rain the night before. The sound of the water rushing in the Suttiir River was a relief—it meant that his four-day travel was nearly complete. Using a cloth to wipe the morning dew from his skin, he paused momentarily to view the orange and yellow sky breaking the horizon. The colorful light filled every gap between the trees. Thomas ran his hands over his smooth face to ensure he was clean-shaven. Moistening his hands in the wet grass, he used his fingers to style his short, dark brown hair.

"Have to make a good first impression, Grail," Thomas said to his white warhorse while wiping his hand. "This could be a permanent position."

Grail neighed as Thomas re-equipped the horse's armor and saddle. He secured his silver armor across his strapping chest and prepared to ride off. "We need to find breakfast," he said, gripping the reins. "I guess we'll just follow our noses."

The ominous sounds from creatures high above the trees did not seem so menacing now that the sun was rising behind him. He slowed his pace, trying not to kick up mud from the path, and released a sigh of relief as he approached the edge of the tree line. The view of Omlett was breathtaking. The city had existed for over twenty years but flourished as a central hub for more than five cities. For that reason, Omlett was quite diverse.

There were several dwarf and gnome cities about a four-day journey to the south. Suttiir, the oldest elf village, was a day trip to the north, and Grey-Holg, a half-orc town, was a two-day trek to the west. Brindell, a human city and Thomas's hometown, was a four-day journey to the east.

"We're finally here, Grail," Thomas said to his steed as he pulled on the reins. He unrolled a map of Omlett. "There's the bridge, so the church"—he pointed to the southwest—"is that way. But first, priorities." He rolled up the map.

As Thomas crossed the bridge and gazed upon the winding streets, he was amazed that the booming metropolis was only as old as he was. Passing the Omlett Inn, a majestic wood and stone tavern-style building, he watched a woman in a black robe skip with a bucket in hand, entering an attractive house attached to its rear. The descriptions he had heard of this Inn didn't do it justice. Two stained-glass windows glimmered in the morning sun. An embracing couple swayed on a balcony above, watching the sunrise, as Thomas steered Grail around to the front.

"Uh-oh," he moaned. "I don't think I brought enough coins for this place." A sizeable green orc exited the Inn as Thomas marveled at the impressive dwelling. "Good morning." The orc grunted in return, slowly strolling across his path. *They do just let anyone in, don't they?*

As the sun broke over the tree line, Thomas continued along the path to the north, where small shops were nestled together. An angry gnome mumbled to himself as he stomped by, hauling a basket of carrots. *This town is strange.*

The shopkeepers opened their doors and swept the stoops, welcoming the morning's first customers. The fishmonger's display of salmon and trout hung on display hooks in the window. The garden gnomes filled baskets with brightly colored fruits and vegetables, but Thomas had his eye on the shop at the end. A plump dwarf exited the brightly decorated shop and walked toward him, eating a delicious-looking pastry. Thomas's stomach growled. He dismounted Grail, tied his horse to a hitching post, and then pushed open the shop door.

"Can I help you?" a female voice sweetly inquired as he entered the shop.

Thomas inhaled the scent of the freshly baked bread and crossed toward the counter, where an elderly gnome struggled to stand on a box. "Need help?"

"I'm fine, dear. I meant to have this lowered. Bought this here shop from some human female," she grumbled, folding her arms on the countertop. "So, what can I get you, dear?"

"Everything!" he teased. "I'm famished."

"I just love you humans and your big appetites." She smiled and waved toward the baskets. "Please! Help yourself."

Thomas grabbed a handmade wicker basket and searched the shelves of baked bread. He turned around to see a shorter frame filled with different types of muffins and rolls on the other side. He began to fill it with some honey muffins.

"I'm Miss Crinkly," she introduced herself, readjusting her glasses. "If you need anything more, I've got some baking in the back, too. I just got that oven fixed again."

Thomas chuckled as he placed his basket on the counter. He noticed a plate of small slices of hard bread and containers of something creamy. "What's this?"

"That's pita bread with my homemade spread." Miss Crinkly held the plate up, offering him one. "I'm giving people samples before I begin selling it." She handed him a small container. "I call it the Crinkly Special."

Thomas dipped the pita in the greenish dip, smelled it, then took a bite. The spicy flavor kicked him from his tastebuds to his nostrils. He dipped the pita bread again, taking another bite. "Mmm . . . That's good. What's in—"

Miss Crinkly quickly held up her hand. "If I tell ya, I have to kill ya." She grabbed the empty container as Thomas tried to scrape the little dip stuck on the sides for the last bite of the bread. She placed it under the counter. "I'm glad you like it."

"Oh, I'll be back for that, but for now, I think this will be enough."

"That will be five SIPs. That's silver pieces."

"Of course—we use the same currency in Brindell," Thomas replied, setting down a gold piece. "Here's a GOP. Keep the rest."

"You are too kind, good knight," Miss Crinkly said, biting down on the coin.

"Any recommendations of places to stay for a couple of nights?"

"You could stay at the Omlett Inn," she suggested, placing the coin in her safe. "It's just south of here."

"I passed it on the way here, but I don't think I can afford a room there," Thomas replied hesitantly. "Maybe the church will have a spare room."

"You could try the Cache Tavern." Miss Crinkly's face soured. "It's not as nice. It's affordable, though you do get what you pay for."

"Thank you, but I'll try the church first," Thomas answered as he turned to leave, nearly bumping into a young elf. She glanced up at him, instantly captivating him with the most beautiful bright purple eyes he'd ever seen. "I'm sorry," Thomas apologized, "seems like I'm a klutz today."

"It's fine," the girl chuckled as his gaze stuck to her. She broke the awkward silence. "What?"

"Please forgive me if I'm being too forward, but you have the most spellbinding eyes. I mean, I've never seen that color before."

The girl blushed, apparently pleased with the compliment. "Thank you. I always hear words like 'beautiful' and 'mesmerizing,' but I've never heard 'spellbinding.' I like it." She nodded proudly and offered a grin. "I like your eyes, too, even though they're just *brown*."

"Miss Raven, this young man was inquiring about the Inn," explained Miss Crinkly.

"Is that so?" Raven asked, bemused.

"Would your father allow him to stay for a beggar's fee?" Miss Crinkly asked.

"Beggar's fee?" Raven responded. "That's some fancy armor for a beggar."

"Oh, no, I'm not begging," Thomas replied, trying not to appear desperate. "I just don't travel with a lot of gold . . . you know, with bandits and all."

"You look as if you could defend yourself," Raven replied, inspecting him.

"I didn't mean to insult you, dear," Miss Crinkly apologized. "The Naelos are kindhearted souls who will take care of anyone—"

"Naelos . . . wait, you're Princess Raven Naelo?" Thomas nearly dropped his basket.

"Yes," Raven answered cautiously. As Thomas began to bow, she pushed on his chest armor to stop him. "No, no, we don't bow here," she giggled. "Or at least to me. It's more of an honorary title."

"Yes, Princess," he responded.

"Call me princess again, and you'll sleep in the stables."

Miss Crinkly snorted. "That'd still be classier than staying at the Cache Tavern."

"Betty!" Raven laughed. "I'll repeat that to Rusty."

"Just saying, dear," Miss Crinkly said. "You should send Brugg over there to teach them how to clean."

"Maybe," Raven tittered, eyeing Thomas, "but we should have available rooms."

"Thank you," Thomas responded gratefully.

She raised her eyebrow, cueing him for his next word.

"Raven."

They both smiled.

"Great!" Raven exclaimed, turning to leave before she stopped abruptly. "Oh, Betty, I almost forgot to pay for my birthday cake."

"That will be two SIPs," Miss Crinkly said. Her eyes lit up when Raven flipped a platinum coin, or PIP, to her.

"I'm sure my mother would like it delivered by sunset," Raven told the gnome.

"Sure, sure," Miss Crinkly replied, biting down on the platinum coin.

"I'll take one of these, too," Raven said, helping herself to a cinnamon roll as she brushed past Thomas, who was lingering. "See you around, Brown Eyes."

Did she just flirt? "Happy birthday," Thomas said, blurting out the first thing he could think of as they exited the bakery.

"Thank you," Raven responded. They saw Grail and a gray horse being fed carrots by a gnome in overalls and an oversized straw hat.

Thomas grinned, admiring the two animals. "They look cozy."

"Too cozy," Raven huffed. "Gary! I already fed her!"

As Gary stormed off, mumbling, Thomas stepped closer to her mount. "What's that protruding from your horse's head? Is she all right?"

"She's fine. She's a unicorn," Raven responded, untying Ghost.

"A unicorn? From the Fey Realm?"

"Yes."

"You must have some powerful friends," Thomas said, impressed.

She smiled with a shrug, then mounted Ghost.

"But I thought unicorns were white."

"She used to be as white as—" Raven motioned toward his horse.

"Grail," Thomas answered.

"When unicorns break their horns, they lose their color and are discarded, left to die." She stroked Ghost's mane. "A friend saved her and gave her to me to care for."

He reached for Ghost's muzzle as the unicorn neighed softly. "She's enchanting."

"She's beauteous!" Raven replied confidently.

Thomas smiled at the word.

"I hate to be rude, but I really have to be somewhere."

"Honestly, so do I," he admitted as she rode toward the west. "See you around the Inn?"

She raised her hand and waved in response.

He stood momentarily, gazing at her light purple aura that sparkled with a swirl of yellow. As she vanished, he thought about this city's beauty and prayed that his stay would be permanent. Glancing at the sun, it suddenly dawned on him. "Holy smite! I'm going to be late!" he exclaimed, quickly mounting Grail to complete his journey.

When Thomas arrived at the church, he left his shield and sword with Grail but happily carried the basket of pastries. He stuffed a bite of the muffin into his mouth before greeting the elf high priest at the church entrance.

"Welcome to Blade's Freedom of Religion," the high priest said, trying to hide his disapproval of Thomas's apparent lack of decorum.

"Thank you, High Priest Carne," Thomas replied, wiping off his palms to shake hands with the elf. "But Blade's?"

"The church was established in honor of King Naelo's son, Blade Naelo. Now, this way." Carne turned to escort Thomas to the Instruction Room.

"Wait, as in the demigod Blade Naelo?"

"Indeed," the high priest answered.

"In Brindell, it's known as the Freedom Cathedral."

"The church was the third building established in Omlett after constructing the Inn and the golem factory."

"Omlett has a golem factory?" Thomas asked with surprise. "I heard of those constructs before, but no one could master the gears."

"Indeed. Mister Cogwheel is very close."

"It's not on my map."

"You won't find it on most maps. Mister Cogwheel doesn't like to be disturbed." High Priest Carne paused at the door. "Now, wait here one moment, please." He entered the room, leaving the door slightly open.

Thomas finished his muffin, brushing the crumbs from his hands before peeking in. The only things visible were some empty chairs and the backs of the heads of two people, but he could hear the high priest as he spoke.

"Cleric Stone-Prayer will not be here today. He traveled to the prison, and then he's going on to Iron Cliff," explained the high priest. "We do have a replacement until he returns."

A feminine voice asked, "Who's the replacement?"

A low, husky voice followed. "Probably some young dragon fodder who thinks he knows everything."

Then came one of the cutest laughs Thomas had ever heard.

High Priest Carne motioned for the paladin to enter. "This is Thomas Wellington. He will be your instructor until Cleric Stone-Prayer's return." He patted Thomas on the back. "They're all yours. And may Blade bless you with all the luck."

"Sorry I'm late," said Thomas, rushing in and placing his basket of pastries next to the podium. He glanced up and saw a female elf and male dwarf staring in awe as he frantically tried to open the book before him. "This it? Only two students? No matter . . . if you would, please turn to the section on detecting evil," he instructed, eyeing the two students.

"And who are you again?" the dwarf asked.

"I'm Thomas Wellington, paladin knight from Brindell, and I'm filling in for, um, Storm-Prayer."

"Stone-Prayer," the dwarf corrected sternly. "You're not even a cleric?"

"That's correct," Thomas replied. "Why's it matter?"

"We're clerics, not paladins," the dwarf retorted, irritated.

"A spell is a spell, Master Dwarf, no matter who casts it."

"I'm Shorte," said the dwarf.

"I see that," Thomas said without thinking.

The female elf laughed again but quickly stopped when the bald, red-faced dwarf turned toward her, so angry that his braided black beard seemed to quiver.

"My *name* is Shorte," the dwarf corrected curtly, putting his book away to pick up his war hammer and shield. "Not Shorty, just Shorte. But you can call me Cleric Stone-Grin."

"Where are you going?" the female elf asked.

"There's nothing this dragon fodder can teach me," Shorte answered. "I have better things to do, and besides, I was detecting evil before he was born."

"But Shorte, I haven't. Stay and help me," the female elf pleaded.

"He probably doesn't even have a sense of humor," Shorte scoffed, storming out of the classroom.

"Cleric Stone-Grin," Thomas called out, then looked over at the elf as she shrugged her shoulders. "For the record . . . I do have a sense of humor."

The curly-haired elf smiled sweetly, her strawberry-blond hair highlighting the color in her cheeks. "I'm sure you do."

"I guess it's just the two of us then," Thomas said. "And you are?"

"Carya."

"An elf cleric," Thomas assumed.

"Half-elf," Carya clarified.

"Excuse me, half-elf."

"Don't worry, I get that a lot," she said, flipping her pages to the Detecting Evil spell page. "And I'm not a full-fledged cleric yet. I'm only an Aspirant. But I'm ready, Sir Wellington."

Thomas was impressed that she knew the honor title of being a human knight. "As you may know, we paladins have a sixth sense and usually detect evil naturally. But we do have the capability to turn it on and off at will."

"I didn't know that," Carya replied, amazed.

"Can you imagine how annoying it would be if you could see everyone's aura all the time?"

"I don't know. It would be nice to see if people are as sincere as they seem or if they're hiding something."

"Believe me, it gets old quickly. It's always best to go with your instincts." Thomas paused and activated his Detecting Evil on Carya. It took everything within him to keep his jaw from dropping. The radiant light-blue aura around her sparkled like the moonlight off a calm pond.

"You just aura'd me, didn't you?" Carya blurted out, snapping him out of his trance.

"I'm sorry. I was beset by curiosity."

Carya laughed. "You need to teach me this now because it's only fair for me to aura you."

As Thomas laughed with her, he couldn't remember the last time he'd laughed like that.

"Nice dimples." Her compliment caught him off-guard. "I don't need the spell to see that your aura is turning red," she teased.

Thomas felt himself blushing. "Let's get to it, shall we?" he said self-consciously, changing the subject. He taught her the hand motions and the words Malum Depre. "The longer you concentrate, the more powerful the spell becomes and the more you can detect."

Carya turned to him. "Malum Depre." Finally, she grinned with pleasure. "As my sister would say, that's beauteous."

Beauteous? That's the same word Raven had used at the bakery.

The church bell rang. He must've looked confused because Carya answered his unasked question. "It's high noon. Time for physical exercise, and then we can retire for the day."

Thomas couldn't believe how fast the morning flew by as she pulled out a thin cloth strip and tied her hair into a ponytail. She approached a door in the back and then disappeared inside. Thomas followed, finding himself entering a training room.

The aroma of floral incense enveloped him as he crossed the threshold. *This beats the musty scent of the Paladin Guild's training chamber.* It reminded him of the stories his mother, a botanist at Waterfront, used to tell when lighting scented candles. She had specialized in exotic flowers and constantly compared Mortal Realm flowers with the Fey Realm flora.

On an ornate shelf near the door, Thomas spotted piles of cloth and a ceramic bowl with pale yellow ointment he recognized as aloe oil. On the floor sat a wicker basket with several soiled linens.

The sound of running water drew Thomas's attention to the rear of the room. A beautiful woven red rug with a yellow circular symbol representing Cenergy lay in front of a fountain topped with a tall statue of Natus. Water ran from the top of the figure, filling the cupped hands and overflowing into a pool.

"It represents the water of life," Carya explained. The intimidating ten-foot stone tribute to the first physical being was erected before five multicolored stained-glass windows. "Each windowpane represents a realm."

As he admired the craftsmanship, he glanced at the clear glass-dome ceiling that allowed the sun rays to highlight the fountain. Thomas stood in awe. "It's incredible." He finally managed to move further into the room. Three-tiered black iron racks filled with different types of weaponry lined the walls. "Preparing for a holy war?" he joked, taking one of the weapons from the stand.

"Your physical body has to be as strong as your faith and mind," she replied as Thomas rubbed the dull edge of a long sword. "But don't worry, it's practice equipment." She removed her robe and folded it.

It was hard not to notice her soft skin and toned arms appearing from her sleeveless white tunic. As she turned to place the robe on a side table, the paladin's eyes quickly traveled over her tight, crimson-colored pants tucked into white leather and gold-trimmed boots.

She glanced back at him confidently as she proceeded to the other side of the room. "I promise I won't hurt you."

Omlett City has some beautiful women—first Purple Eyes and now Carya.

He put the long sword back and picked up a golden dagger, twirling it with his fingers as a loud scraping noise caused him to fumble. He stopped the blade from rattling and rushed over to help.

Carya struggled to push a sandbag training dummy to the sparring circle drawn on the floor. Together, they slid the base toward the circle's edge.

She momentarily made eye contact with him as a flash of sunlight hit her blue eyes, and her face tightened, turning red. Then she giggled. "I'm not sure how Shorte does this by himself."

Thomas chuckled. "I heard rumors that dwarves need to roll a boulder up the Zorn Mountain Range before entering the mines."

"I'll find out." Finally, the target dummy passed the red line, but they noticed a trail of sand from where it originally sat.

"Looks like a flesh wound," Thomas said.

Carya huffed, grabbing the broom. "That's the second one this week."

Before she could walk away, Thomas gripped it. "Please, allow me." He swept up the sandy mess as she found a cloth and wiped the beads of sweat from her brow.

She pointed to the shelf, brushed her ponytail off to the side, and tilted her neck. "Do you mind?"

"Not at all." He hung up the broom, dusted himself off, and dipped his fingers into the aloe lotion. He gently applied it to her neck and shoulder, then massaged it.

Carya closed her eyes and moaned. After a moment, she rotated her shoulder blade. "Thank you. You're a natural."

"Well, you can thank Sir Booney. I had to apply it to George, my sparring buddy, all the time. Your back is less hairy."

She giggled, then snapped, "Great! Now take a shield—sparring buddy."

Thomas wiped his hands with a cloth, then moved to the weapons rack and picked up a metal buckler. *The shield is much lighter than mine.* He shook it as he moved toward Carya, who twirled a wooden replica of a mace in the middle of the circle. "You're making me nervous," he chuckled, raising the buckler.

"Stop acting like the Fey Realm fairies."

Thomas puckered his lips as if the words stung. "Ouch, that hurt more than any mace to the face."

Without warning, Carya swung her weapon, and Thomas braced the shield for the impact as a loud *CLANK* echoed. *That wasn't so bad*—until nine more slammed against the training shield. He lowered the buckler to peep over it, watching her sidestep him. She swung her mace while he lifted his shield. When she reached ten again, she turned back toward him, her weapon swaying like a pendulum.

Beautiful and dangerous.

As she advanced on him again, Thomas counted her strikes, but at nine, the sound of the door opening distracted him.

Carya tried to hold back her attack but staggered forward from the force she'd built. Thomas dropped his shield to catch her, but he slipped on the sand and fell, pulling her down atop him.

"I think I missed a spot," he joked, following her eyes to a woman gawking from the doorway.

Carya immediately raised her head and innocently uttered, "Hello, Mother."

"Mother?" Thomas repeated.

Her eyes dropped down on him. "Umm, yes."

Embarrassed, Thomas quickly scooted her to the side and jumped to his feet.

"Mother, this is Sir Thomas Wellington of Brindell," Carya announced, smiling as the paladin went over and kissed her mother's hand. "My mother, Mara."

"A knight and a gentleman," said Mara, impressed. "It's a pleasure to meet you."

"He's filling in for Cleric Stone-Prayer until he returns," Carya noted, placing the mace down and slipping into her robe.

"How nice. Welcome to Omlett." Mara turned to her daughter, who was using a cloth to wipe beads of sweat from her forehead. "Carya, I need you to pick up the dresses from the seamstress and a few other items for tonight's party." She handed Carya a list. "Thomas, you are more than welcome to join us tonight for her sister's birthday party."

A realization suddenly struck Thomas. *Birthday?* "Are you the Naelos?" he asked, barely disguising his surprise.

"That's correct," Mara answered. "Didn't Carya tell you?"

"Mother, you know I don't like telling anyone." Carya tossed the damp cloth into the hamper. "I want to be treated like everyone else."

Thomas bowed to both.

"See what I mean," Carya said irritably.

Mara turned to her daughter. "Should I send for a security team?"

Carya rolled her eyes and focused her attention on Thomas. "Sir Wellington, would you like to escort me on these errand quests?"

"Of course, I'd love to," Thomas replied.

"See, Mother? I already have a security team," Carya beamed, pulling Thomas out of the training room.

"Queen Mara," Thomas respectfully nodded before being dragged out.

CHAPTER FOUR

BIRTHDAY GIFT

R aven arrived at a castle-like stone building. The security teams gathered at the entrance and atop the towers were responsible for detaining all the lawbreakers at the Omlett Prison. Upon entering the great hall, a bald dwarf with a scruffy gray beard and an eye patch over his right eye greeted her. He was leaning back with his feet propped up on his desk, smoking a pipe.

"Miss Raven," Buzz'diir said, surprised. "Thought you would still be in bed after last night."

"Mornin', Buzz." Raven saluted him and placed a cinnamon roll on his desk. "I wish," she answered as she looked around. "It's a busy day today."

"Oh, that's right. Happy birthday, Princess," he replied as he sat up. "Eighteen, right?"

"That's right." She would've been annoyed to be called a princess by anyone else, but it was natural and sincere with Buzz. He used to call her a princess even before the family received the honorary title.

"Still a baby," Buzz'diir joked. "In elf years, that is."

"Well, my father must think I'm pure elf then," she said sarcastically.

"He's just being a protective father, like any other."

Raven shrugged her shoulders. "Where is the old fella, anyway?"

"I think he's in the training room. I'll escort ya there."

"No need," Raven replied, heading confidently down the newly constructed hallway.

"No, it would be my pleasure, Princess." Buzz'diir slowly stood. "Besides, it's this way," he added with a grin as he pointed with his pipe.

Raven turned around. "You really did change this place."

"We've had to make a few additions over the years. As you know, Omlett keeps growing."

Raven followed him down the left tunnel, where the three Horcks from last night were locked in a cell. In a wooden chair, the tall one she'd smashed with a glass mug sat hunched, his head bandaged like his hands. He grunted as he watched her walk past the cell. The second Horck was leaning against a wall, but when he saw her, he grabbed his damaged buttocks and scurried further away. The one she'd electrocuted was asleep on a cot.

"Any clerics visit them yet?" Raven whispered.

"Cleric Stone-Prayer is supposed to arrive soon," Buzz'diir answered. "He'll tend to them."

They walked past a few more occupied cells on their way to the end of the hall. *I never realized how much illegal activity took place in Omlett.* Finally, they came upon another locked oak door.

"Training room is off to the right," Buzz'diir directed as he unlocked the door.

Raven entered, scanning the training room from under the archway. She didn't see her father, but he appeared behind a training dummy as she turned to the mess hall.

Eugor thrust his dagger into the back of the sandbag and somersaulted to the next one, raising his other blade and slicing the throat marker.

Raven clapped mockingly, as he had done the night before. "Not bad, even without those hocus pocus spells." Her father waved off her comment as she continued. "All these changes to the prison, yet you still have the same old practice dummies?" Raven laughed, inspecting the closest target. "I've trained on these for years."

"I guess I'm sentimental." Eugor eyed her. "I see you have your weapons. Let's see if all that practice paid off."

Raven pulled her daggers from their sheaths, then moved to the center of the training ring, aimed, and let one fly. It went wide, hitting the object's head instead of its chest. *Damn it.*

"You have to aim—"

"I know!" Raven snapped back. "Aim, picture the dagger hitting the target, and follow through with the throw."

Eugor crossed his arms, lowered his head, and grumbled, "This skill is essential. It's the difference between disabling or killing someone."

Closing her eyes, she inhaled a deep breath. *I don't want to fight with him today.* She opened her eyes and stared into her father's gray ones. "I can keep practicing—at Gideon's camp."

He lowered his head again and closed his eyes. "I know I've been hard on you. It's difficult to accept that my daughter is choosing a life of danger."

"Father—"

"But I didn't call you here to argue." He placed his hands on her face. "Happy birthday, my dear."

Knowing the pain she caused him, her heart shattered, so she leaned lower for him to kiss her forehead, something she'd done ever since she surpassed his height. "Thank you, Father," Raven replied as he stepped back. "And for cleaning up the mud."

"It was all through the Inn, so consider it an early birthday gift," Eugor chuckled. "Follow me."

Down the hallway, she followed, past the mess hall and to his work chamber. Inside was a mahogany desk, precisely like the one in the Omlett Inn.

"You really like this style of desk, huh?"

Eugor grinned. "It's the same one."

"The same desk?" Raven asked, puzzled.

"It's magical. I acquired it during one of my many adventures."

"No way!" Raven exclaimed with shock, running her hands over the desk. "All this time and you never told us."

"Watch out," Eugor warned as he approached the desk. He held the golden owl emblem in front and twisted it to the right, and they watched as the desk folded itself down to the size of a copper piece.

Raven rushed over, taking it from him. "I thought you didn't like magic," she said, inspecting the tiny desk.

"I never said I didn't like magic. There's a difference between magical items and my youngest daughter wanting to learn magic to use in combat."

"To protect myself," she corrected him. "When you were a guardian, Gideon taught you to cast invisibility."

He snagged the desk from her hand, placing it back on the floor. "And it got me killed."

Any time he said it aloud, shock overcame her body, the same terrible feeling as hearing the story for the first time. She couldn't keep herself from gazing at the scar around his neck.

"N-Alta," he whispered, watching the desk return to its original size. "Raven, are you sure this is the path you want?"

She straightened her posture, eyeing him with total confidence. "Yes. I want to join Gideon's camp to become a guardian. It's all I've ever wanted."

"You're eighteen now, an age to choose your path. And after a long conversation with your mother—we've decided that we would be proud to have another Naelo guardian at Gideon's camp."

Raven's eyes widened, then rushed to her father, wrapping her arms around him. "Thank you! Thank you! And Gideon?"

"He knows our decision." Eugor pulled away. "But if you insist on following our foolish and dangerous family tradition, you'll need some tools to protect you."

Raven closed her eyes and crossed her fingers. *Please, Blade, let it be the razor wire.*

Her father walked to a cabinet, removed a box adorned with ribbons, and handed it to her. "Every rogue should have these."

"Magical razor wire?" Raven asked excitedly, shaking the box. She tore off the ribbons only for her excitement to alter into disappointment. It wasn't her father's epic gift from Gideon but simply a pair of purple boots. Raven pulled them out and held them up alongside her cloak. "They match," she said, disguising her displeasure.

"And yes, they are magical," said Eugor, grinning.

"They are?" Raven asked as her face lit up. "Do they shrink?"

"No, no, they're Boots of Stealth. They make no sound when you walk."

Raven sat down on her father's chair, swapping out her boots. "They fit perfectly." She sprung from the seat with a grin and slid across the ground but heard no sound. She kicked his desk and still heard nothing.

"They silence everything within a small area around them, so if you kick a stick into the grass, you will not hear the initial kick but will hear the stick as it hits the grass," her father explained.

"I love them!" She hugged her father again. "Just like Ghost's silent hooves."

"Exactly. Remember that your mother has been busy preparing for tonight's not-so-secret surprise party. So make yourself scarce till sunset."

"I will, Father," Raven replied, still trying to make sounds with her new boots. She left, strolling down the hall, where she overheard Cleric Stone-Prayer with the half-orcs. The dark-skinned dwarf was in a cell with four armed dwarves. With her new boots, no one heard her approach.

Raven returned to Buzz'diir, still relaxed, smoking his pipe as he nibbled on his cinnamon roll. "I'll see you later tonight," she said to the startled dwarf, watching him nearly choke on the pastry.

"I didn't hear you come in." Buzz'diir sat up, coughing. "I'll see you later, Princess, and thank you for the roll."

Raven left the prison and returned to the Omlett Inn to show off her new boots, but the house was empty. She went through the secret tunnel, entering her father's work chamber. His desk wasn't there, and she shook her head, amused now that she knew the magic behind it.

As Raven entered the tavern, she again noticed a group of guys huddled in the corner. "Cee, I'll have a dwarven ale," she ordered, "and since I'm of age, I'll take a real one."

"So, you finally found out," Cyndi chuckled, filling a mug. "It was ordered by your father to ensure you didn't have any alcohol till you were older."

"That's what Rusty said. I thought it tasted different!" She sipped her drink before continuing. "Have you seen my mother around?"

"*Noo, maaa'am*," Cyndi sung.

Loud cheers and laughter erupted from the back corner.

"What's with the crowd?" Raven asked. "It's been like that since I left."

A blond teen parted the group and approached the bar. The bronze-tipped ivory water horn strapped across her swayed as she made her way across the room, and Raven couldn't help but stare curiously as the perfect, long, curly hair bounced with every step.

Raven slowly turned to the bard. "Oh, Cee, I need to reserve a room for a paladin named Thomas."

"We're out of rooms for tonight," Cyndi apologized. "You know, for that special occasion."

"Dragon poop," Raven mumbled. "What can I do?"

"If he's cute, he can bunk with me," the stranger boasted, smiling.

Taken aback, Raven asked, "And you are?"

"Hello, Princess. I'm Izarra Lyte from Thistlebane. It's nice to meet you finally."

"Thistle-vain, home of the conceited"—Raven cut herself off, realizing that Izarra might be one, and changed her tone from snarky to sweet—"water nymphs?"

"I understand. They *are* so full of themselves. But I'm half-nymph. My father was human."

"I can relate. Except it's my mother who's the human."

"I know. We've heard all about Omlett and the Naelos."

"Word gets around, huh?"

"We've heard everything about the mighty elf, Eugor Naelo, who slayed and roasted a black dragon with his fire-giant friend . . . and then built the city using the bones."

Raven nearly spat out her drink. "One . . . he didn't slay a black dragon," she explained, wiping her mouth with a napkin. "Second, his friend is a gnome named Mug, not a fire-giant."

"Oh," Izarra said, disappointed.

"But they did eat a black dragon egg," Raven continued with a grin, trying to lighten the mood.

"That's crazy. Wonder what it tastes like."

"He told me it tastes just like a chicken egg," Raven said, remembering her father telling her and her sister the story when they were young.

"So . . . no dragon bones?"

"No, sorry," Raven confessed. "Mug collected some black scales of the egg but sold them to help build Omlett Inn."

"Black dragon scales. They had to be worth a fortune."

"It helped build this Inn and Mug's golem factory."

Izarra's expression changed to confusion. "Golems?"

"Mug describes them as heavy iron constructs to ensure the city's safety. But to me, they look like ogres in knight armor. I still haven't seen one function yet. I can only tolerate being in the shop for so long before the grease smell makes me nauseous."

"Well, I think the Inn is beautiful. May I have a tour?"

"Sure." Raven sipped the last of her ale. "It has to be quick, though, because they need to set up for my party and don't want me snooping around."

"Party?" Izarra's crystal blue eyes lit up. "I love a good party."

Raven jumped off her barstool and pointed to the group of men. "What about your friends?"

"Oh, them? I can always find more."

"Just like last night," Raven said, shaking her head, "at the Cache Tavern."

"Yes, those Horcks weren't very nice."

"So it was you who helped me?" Raven asked, finally hearing the similarity between Izarra's voice and the voice that warned her last night.

"Of course. Three-on-one wasn't very honorable." They walked together in silence, moving through the hallway past four rooms.

"These are the overnight rooms," Raven explained. "There are ten sleeping rooms, four downstairs, five upstairs, and we have a sizable royal suite."

"I'm right here in room four," Izarra said happily.

"Down the hall to the left is the stairs, and to the right is the banquet room. If you like parties, that's where they're held. It has an Illusion Ball."

"Illusion Ball? Sounds fun."

When they reached the exits to the stables, Raven turned, opening the opposite door into the banquet hall, where they found Mug with his tools, working on a strange mechanism.

"There's the mighty fire giant," Raven teased. "Hello, Mug!"

The gnome raised his goggles and waved, then remembered that she wasn't supposed to be there. He threw down his tools and charged, cussing all the way, but she slammed the door shut.

"Not sure what he's working on," Raven said innocently to Izarra, "but I guess I'm not supposed to see it." They returned to the bar area and moved to the arena entrance.

"I'm intrigued by this 'do not touch' painting," Izarra said, "the one with the list of names and numbers below it."

"It's a magical painting called *The Ebony Tree*," Raven explained, shooing Izarra's hand away as she reached for it. "When you touch it, you're teleported inside and enter in the buff."

"So maybe some other time."

Raven scowled at her. "The patrons have made a game to see how many times they can circle the tree before they're teleported out."

"How do you get teleported out?"

"The three knights in silver armor chase you in the painting," Raven replied. "The only way to get out is if a knight catches you or a wizard from out here casts a spell to pull you out."

"Rusty did it twelve times," Izarra read.

"He's the redheaded barkeep at the Cache Tavern."

"The dwarf? I always thought they were so serious."

"Not when they're drunk."

Once Raven opened the floor hatch to the arena, the two girls descended wooden steps that led into a massive dungeon with a circular stadium and a seating area for onlookers.

Izarra walked over to the weapons racks. "This is so barbaric," she exclaimed as she lifted a sickle.

"It's for entertainment," Raven clarified. "In all my years of watching these competitions, I've never seen anyone get hurt."

"I might have to see it for myself."

"Definitely. And now I'm old enough to enter."

Izarra gasped. "You wouldn't."

"Maybe." As they returned upstairs, Raven pointed to a door on the left. "That's my father's work chamber; not much to see in there." She noticed Brugg carrying a long table toward the banquet room. "Well, that's my cue to go."

"Where are we headed?" Izarra asked.

"*We?*" After a moment of hesitation, Raven added, "Well, I guess I can take you to Cache Tavern and introduce you to Rusty, the *Ebony Tree* record holder."

Izarra beamed. "That would be fantastic! But first, I need to take care of something. I'll meet you out front."

CHAPTER FIVE

SWEET DREAMS

Courtlynn sat on a boulder inside her master's lair, wishing the entrance was more prominent for her viewing pleasure or that the enormous, dreary cave had some windows. Her favorite spot gave her a splendid view of the magma waterfalls splashing into the vast lakes of fire. She tucked in her garnet wings and hugged her knees close to her chest, hypnotized by the hot lava cascading over the black, molten rocks. The bright red glow almost matched the color of her long, curly hair.

The prisoner's moans interrupted her thoughts, but before she could say anything, the Celestial Guardian's body fell limp again. His pristine, white wings were still outstretched and pinned to the wall, contrasting with the rest of his naked body. She followed the chains down, taking notice of the transition around his chest, where the skin was charred and flaky. *I warned you to talk. But I wonder why the High Council has not investigated the missing Abyss Guardian.*

Her thoughts focused on the giant cage across the room that housed her master's new pet. Floxy, a nine-tailed demon fox, was curled up in his tails. He was at least seven feet long with gold streaks throughout his matted, blood-red fur. Demon foxes, while rare, ran free in the Seventh Layer. *My master has excellent skills to acquire not just one, but another.*

It had been six mortal years, and the thought of the Cubbis Council experiencing the wrath of a flox still brought an evil smirk to her face. But she still missed Flixxes, which kept her from bonding with Floxy.

Courtlynn returned her attention to the entranceway, only to have the view obscured by a familiar silhouette of an eight-foot-tall, muscular balor with curved horns on his head.

He stopped to review the chaotic state of the war preparations below his balcony. The fire demon turned, tucking in his dark wings to enter his domain. Draklor smiled broadly.

Courtlynn sighed as her lips sagged, realizing his pleasure wasn't because of her presence. *It's wartime, the only time he smiles.* She flew off the rock, landing across from Draklor as he carefully unrolled a dirty parchment onto a round stone table. His intense gaze upon the map was one she wished he would turn on her.

Inscribed on the parchment was a battle map of the nine layers of the Fire-Plane, Inferno. Small markers were present, each representing the locations of his home in the Third Layer and his enemies—the insectoids—in the Second Layer. She couldn't help but look at his long, dirty nails as they traced the battle lines.

"We'll start here at Devils Fork and take a portal to get behind their defenses," he said confidently.

"Sounds great," Courtlynn responded as she flew away. "If they give you—"

"Command—they must select me! They must!"

"Of course, my lord," she replied, but the direction of her voice immediately caught his attention.

"Stay away from him!" the fire demon bellowed, watching the hovering succubus as she studied the unconscious Celestial Guardian.

She plucked a feather from the guardian's wing. The action brought no response from the prisoner. "Is he dead?" she asked, waiting for the slightest movement. She tried tickling his chest with the feather, but it flaked off pieces of burnt skin. "What was his name again? Terd? Tire? Tier?"

"I don't care about his name," Draklor said as he returned to studying the battle plan. "But he won't talk."

Face to face with the guardian, Courtlynn ran her hands through his coarse hair. "Maybe you should let me try," she said, hoping to evoke an emotional response from Draklor, but his attention remained on the map.

Gimp, a young imp messenger, flew into the chamber. The small-winged creature bypassed them and headed straight to Floxy's cage, waking the beast to feed it. Draklor and Courtlynn both stared impatiently, waiting for the vital message.

"Don't test my patience, Gimp," Draklor scolded. The imp's dark gray body tensed as he continued feeding the caged demon pet. "Do not make me ask twice."

"You were *not* selected, my master," Gimp answered, dropping the feed while the flox pounced to gulp it down. The messenger flew over to hide behind Courtlynn; the role reversed from when she hid behind the old imp messenger, Grimmly.

Draklor grabbed his fire whip, marched over to the prisoner, and cracked it, destroying a wing. The guardian screamed as scorched feathers rained down.

"Guess he's not dead," Courtlynn whispered to Gimp, who cowered behind her dark wings.

"He's immortal," the balor sneered, using a finger to raise the guardian's head to meet him eye to eye, though the guardian refused. Draklor scraped his nail along the prisoner's chin, drawing blood as he pulled it away, letting the prisoner's head drop. "But he can still feel pain." The fire demon managed a smirk and loosened his grip on the whip. "I don't understand." Her master's tone had changed. "I have acquired a vorpal sword from this Celestial Guardian, the Artifact of the Stolen Souls from the Mortal Realm, and a flox from the Seventh Layer."

"It's your size," explained Gimp. He closed his yellow eyes and again ducked behind Courtlynn.

"My size?!" Draklor mocked, standing up straight and tightening his hold on his whip.

"I overheard a demon lord say you were the runt of the clan," Gimp said, peering over Courtlynn's shoulder. "You are too small to command an army."

"A runt?!" yelled Draklor as he whipped the second wing, sending more burnt feathers into the air and producing another pain-filled scream from the prisoner.

Courtlynn strolled over to Draklor, placing her soft hand on his brawny arm. Her ivory skin contrasted with his maroon flesh. "Tell them how you captured a Celestial Guardian," she pleaded, looking up at the once again limp body of the prisoner. "They are supposed to be the great Realm Guardians, and one hangs like wall art—this alone would command great respect."

"I can't," Draklor responded. "It could cause an all-out war with the High Council if they find out. Even I am not ready for that . . . yet. Tessk is already putting us at risk by falsifying the Abyss Guardian's reports." He turned to face Courtlynn. "I'm going to need your help, child."

"Anything, my lord," Courtlynn replied eagerly.

"You saw the pods. I'm going to create my own army, but I need more souls," he said, deep in thought. He removed a loose rock from a wall and removed a stone amulet. "Without tipping off the guardians, we need someone from the Mortal Realm to use the Artifact of the Stolen Souls."

Courtlynn's voice cracked. "The Mortal Realm?"

"I cannot destroy that many lives in the Abyss, or the demon generals will banish me."

"But how?"

Draklor slowly gazed at Floxy as Courtlynn frowned. "That's where he will come in. Tessk cast an anti-scry on Floxy to protect it from the Realm Guardian's vision. The explosions from his tail will trap the deceased, and I can steal those lost souls through a portal and turn them into my personal demon army. Tessk increased our army from five pods to hundreds of thousands. But for this, you will have to find one *ugly* soul."

Courtlynn winked. "My specialty."

Draklor grabbed both of her dark horns, kissed the top of her head, and placed the artifact around her neck. "Protect this with your life."

She was thrilled to receive such affection from her master, but it was short-lived as he quickly flipped his attention to Gimp.

"Do not just flap around. Make yourself useful. Retrieve me an update on this war."

Gimp did not hesitate to dash out of the chamber.

Courtlynn reached the entrance and glanced back to see Draklor grab a handful of burning lava coals. She ducked behind the wall, peeping around the corner as a lump tightened her throat. *Talk, Tier, talk.*

Draklor grabbed the guardian's neck and dumped the coals over the prisoner's exposed skin. There was no reaction at first, but as the fire demon ignited the coals, the flames quickly climbed from Tier's feet to his knees, forcing a wild scream. Draklor closed his eyes, swaying to the painful wails and crackling flames. "Are you ready to tell me the secret?" he asked, increasing the heat of the fire. "This ritual—how does it make you immortal?"

Tears from the immortal's eyes hissed as they immediately evaporated.

Courtlynn wished again for the guardian to answer, to end the suffering, but the prisoner fell unconscious again.

Draklor noticed her. "What are you gawking at?"

She wanted to respond, but for once, she was at a loss for words and flew off.

Courtlynn, the ambitious succubus, traveled to the Mortal Realm, where she knew she could dominate most men in their dreams. Her goal was to find someone evil to help her win her master's heart. She traveled in men's dreams night after night, searching for that perfect *ugly.*

After arriving in an elderly cleric's dream, she viewed a young knight presenting a chest of gold and trinkets to the religious leader to help people experiencing poverty. But the cleric stole the collection and used it to pay brothel workers for sexual favors.

I like his style, but he's too old.

As that dream faded, another one emerged and showed a middle-aged alchemist stirring white powder into a vial. Then, the scene changed to the corpse of an older woman foaming at the mouth. A broken glass lay near her hand, the rim coated with powder. The man happily whistled as he stuffed jewels into a sack and ran out the door.

What a coward. Anyone can poison an older woman. What we need is a true warrior.

Courtlynn shook her head before entering another dream where she witnessed a young bandit watching two of his older crew attack a couple with a child. The female victim screamed out, "Run, Tommy!" The dream shifted to the same man but older, leading the others to slaughter a group of gnomes.

It's getting uglier.

His dream changed again to the same group of men facing an army of the undead. "Bob, behind you!" the balding man called out. But it was too late. The undead swarmed Bob and their other friend, Stanley.

My master could work with this—undead bodies are useless for the souls!

"What a brave man!" Courtlynn called out, startling him. The landscape of the dream changed to a quiet clearing in a forest. "And you are?"

"Astrick," the man replied, baffled. "Am I dreaming?"

"Indeed," she said, touching his chest.

"But you feel real."

"That means you can enjoy yourself. But first, I'm here on a mission. So, tell me more about this encounter."

Astrick sighed. "We thought it was just a myth."

"A myth?"

"The haunting story of the Undead Shade Knight protecting Fellswar's Claim. Bob and Stanley insisted the myth wasn't true. They wanted to ransack the castle for the treasures."

"And?" Courtlynn asked, intrigued.

"It turns out it's just a man."

"But no ordinary man."

"No, this Aushade has an undead army roaming the island. I have never seen anything like it. It's creepy." Astrick paused, then continued, "Now, where were we—" He leaned in for a kiss as the forest faded.

Courtlynn pushed him away and kissed his cheek. "Thank you."

"Will I see you again?" Astrick asked as she faded out of his mind.

"Soon."

CHAPTER SIX

ASTRICK'S AMBUSH

A busty redhead woman kissed his cheek as her angelic voice whispered, "*Soon.*" Sadness washed over Astrick as she faded, but his mind managed to recall the image of her face. *I knew you couldn't get enough.* He could feel her soft lips touch his as her hands explored his body as she moaned, *Oh, Astrick.*

"Astrick!"

The redhead pulled back, placing her hands on his shoulders. She slowly leaned her head closer but stopped and shook him. *What are you doing?*

"Astrick!"

Astrick's eyelids stuck as morning crust covered his eyes. He pried them open as the smell of stale beer and a loud burp washed over him. The beautiful soft face of his dream woman transformed into the shape of his associate Butch. Her sexy red curly hair formed into Butch's long, shaggy red hair and matted beard. Scars from knife wounds decorated the man's face, but his missing teeth drew the most attention when he opened his mouth to take another rancid breath. Disgusted, Astrick brushed Butch's arms off his shoulders and sprang to his feet, then bent over, retching. He stood, running his hands through his receding hairline. "What the hell?"

Butch trembled in rage, "Oh no, you tried to *kiss* me. You're lucky I didn't cut your tongue out trying that trunk-on-trunk elf shite with me."

Wiping vomit from his mouth, Astrick surveyed the rest of his clan of human misfits. Already awake and perched in a tree across the road sat his scout, Bo, the youngest and most professional-looking of the bunch.

Bo was the perfect scout because no one expected him to mark a location for the next target. His crossbow was slung over his back as he sat perfectly still, a sign of a well-trained ranger. He nodded at Astrick and returned to his watch.

Butch bent over, trying to wake another one of their associates, Ax. Hammer, his fourth partner, was asleep in a camping bag. The older, dark-skinned man moved, exposing his butt crack from his stained brown pants. Rolls of dirty flesh hung over his belt.

Astrick grabbed a bucket filled with last night's rainwater and hovered above his men before dumping the cold water over their heads. "Wake up!"

The two men jumped up, cursing. Ax wildly swung his blood-stained axe, almost slicing Hammer.

"What the hell, man!" Ax yelled, wiping water from his frizzy brown beard. Pieces of dead leaves were still visible in his long brownish hair. His short, stalky frame always reminded Astrick of a dwarf, which repulsed him.

"It's almost daybreak!" Astrick stated. "Why is Bo the only one up and ready?"

"He's a donkey lover," Butch mumbled.

"Get into your positions," Astrick ordered.

Butch grumbled, "I'm not sure why I'm taking orders from a thespian."

Astrick quickly placed his elbow on Butch's chest and pushed him against the tree, pulling a dagger and resting it under Butch's chin. "Think I'm acting now?"

Butch placed his dry, crackled lips together and blew Astrick a kiss. "Gonna try and kiss me again?"

Astrick lowered the dagger. "I participate in Omlett's silly fall play to pay for a decent room and food."

"Speaking of food, I'm hungry," Ax complained, packing his sleeping roll.

"Find something on your way over to Bo," Astrick responded as he lowered his head while Ax smashed through the tall plants and trudged across the road. "Why doesn't he just hold up a sign?"

"What's the purpose of a sign?" Butch asked as Astrick exhaled in annoyance and slapped him on the back of the head. "What?"

Idiots! Stiff from the night before, Astrick stretched his tall, thin body. He noticed traces of blood on the cuffs of his dark green wizard robe. *It must be from the fight with that necromancer.* Reaching for his canteen, he poured the warm water over his face, feeling it drip from his beard.

He and his four associates hid in the Dark Woods along a southern road between Omlett and Iron Cliff, the dwarf city. He knew this would be a perfect spot to ambush travelers; everyone had thought the idea was insane since it could draw the attention of King Naelo, but Astrick merely laughed at the thought of a filthy elf besting him.

The three knelt by a tree beside the road, hidden from view. The sun was barely over the tree line when a small carriage with two dwarves passed by.

"Now?" Butch asked eagerly.

"Patience, Butch," Astrick responded as he raised his hand in the air, a sign to hold back.

Butch sneered. "C'mon, we've waited all night!"

"I'm feeling lazy today, and dwarves are too much of a hassle," Astrick replied. "Remember when we lost Randy to a dwarven caravan?"

"Randy was weak," Butch said. "He was better off dead."

"It's just two of them," Hammer pleaded, spinning his hammer. "We can take 'em."

"Impressive—you know how to count." Astrick's words dripped with sarcasm. He took a deep breath. "There are only two, and the carriage is too small. It's not worth it." He looked across the path to see Bo waving his arms to attract attention. Astrick motioned for him to stand down.

Bo must have been as disappointed as the others because he shook his head and slammed down his crossbow before relaying the hand signal to Ax a few feet away. Ax lowered his head in frustration.

"You guys have to trust me," implored Astrick.

Butch watched the carriage as it got smaller and began to laugh. "I don't trust anyone, not even the voices in my head. Like right now, voice number one tells me to chase them down, but voice four says we need breakfast, and voice nine—"

"You scare me sometimes, Butch," Hammer said, shaking his head.

"Talk about something else. Take our minds off this waiting," Astrick suggested, leaning back against the tree and stretching out his legs. "What about that barmaid in Brindell from a fortnight ago?"

"What about her?" Butch asked.

"She seemed to like you, Butch," Astrick teased. "As hard as that is to believe."

"Not my type," Butch said. "I don't mess with women who could snap me in half while I sleep."

Astrick and Hammer laughed.

Hammer chuckled. "I didn't know you could afford to be picky."

"Watch it, Ham," Butch warned. "Voice six didn't like how you said that."

Hammer glanced at Astrick, who just shrugged his shoulders.

"What can I say?" Astrick joked. "You have to respect voice six."

"Speaking of women, I'm going to nap," Butch said as he laid his head against a boulder. "I keep having this dream—a beautiful redheaded woman."

"Me too," Hammer said with surprise. "Beautiful long, red hair—"

"Yeah, yeah," Butch agreed excitedly. "Real curvy."

Astrick threw a stone at Butch to make him sit up. "Boys, a succubus has visited you," he informed them, picking up another rock.

"How do you know?" Hammer asked.

"Because I've seen her, too," Astrick replied, "in my dreams."

"What's a suck-a-biz?" Butch asked.

"Suck-yuh-bus," Astrick repeated slowly. "It's a demon who possesses men's minds while they sleep."

"A succu—what?" Butch pondered. "No, no, this woman was the woman of my dreams. She did *not* look like a demon."

"She's searching for something or someone. I told her about that necromancer we ran into at Fellswar's Claim, and she vanished," Astrick recalled.

"That nightmare," Butch said. "I have never seen so many undead in one place."

"Back when we had Bob and Stanley," Hammer reminisced. "Now they're mindless bodies wandering that cursed land."

"They were weak, too," Butch snorted. "They're better off dead."

"Bob nearly ripped my head off," Astrick said, glancing at the blood on his sleeves again. "I barely got away. We should have never trespassed on his territory."

"That place scares me more than Butch does," Hammer stated, getting the chills.

Butch huffed. "Even I'm not crazy enough to go back to that place. We might have been capable of owning that island if Astrick had completed the eight years at Waterfront."

Astrick shot Butch a cold stare. "You really want to be on my shite list."

Butch shrugged. "I'm just saying you're not operating at your full potential. Imagine if you didn't quit—"

"I got thrown out," Astrick corrected him. "My third year. I guess the institution disapproved of using the Alter Self spell when I visited the women's hall of residence, appearing as their significant other." They stood in silence for a moment, staring down the road. Astrick's face morphed into a cocky half-grin. "I didn't hear the women complain, though."

They all laughed.

Astrick perked up when he heard wagon wheels and the neigh of a horse coming down the path as the sun brightened the day. He glanced across to see Bo signaling that it was one gnome and a delivery carriage.

"Get ready, boys," Astrick warned Butch and Hammer. They looked like two hungry hellhounds ready for chow.

"Rotam Clauditis," Astrick whispered, locking the wheels in place as the carriage came to a sudden halt and tossed the gnome forward. As the driver untangled the reins and got off to inspect the wheels, Astrick yelled, "Now!"

Butch and Hammer ran toward the carriage, screaming. The frantic gnome scurried up to the driver's side and tried to grab his single-hand crossbow. Astrick cast Projectilis Magicus to create a magic projectile that slammed into the gnome's back and knocked him off the other side of the carriage.

The gnome appeared dazed when a bolt pierced his thigh, trying to find his footing. Astrick glanced up to see Ax charging the carriage as Butch grabbed the injured gnome by the hair and dragged him into the middle of the road.

Astrick slowly approached and dallied over the gang's prey, grinning maniacally while the others ransacked the carriage. "You are a brave soul, traveling alone with this much cargo," he snarled, kneeling. The gnome didn't say a word but held his leg with the bolt protruding from it.

With a broad grin, Ax brought Astrick a parchment he'd found in the carriage. "We hit a dragon lode."

Astrick smirked as he rose to review it. "I'm surprised you can read."

"I can't," Ax replied, "but I can tell it looks like a long list."

Astrick read it out loud. "Six barrels of dwarven ale . . . destination Cache Tavern, yada yada . . . destination Suttiir, boring shite."

"Anything else?" Bo asked.

"Oh, get this, boys," Astrick replied. "Fireworks, bags of flour, decorations. Destination: Omlett Inn."

"Fireworks!" Hammer exclaimed.

"That's funny. I didn't get any invitation to a performance after-party," Astrick said, glancing up from the list. "Boys, did you get one?"

They all shook their heads.

"We can have our own party now!" Butch said happily.

Astrick continued to read, *"Gus, please get the signatures of Rusty Keggs at Cache Tavern and Cyndi Sharp at Omlett Inn."* Astrick knelt again. "I guess that makes you Gus."

"Omlett will track you down, and you will rot in prison," Gus said, huffing in pain.

"So, Gus can talk! I thought maybe I had to know Gnomish or whatever your stupid language is," Astrick replied.

Gus spat in his face.

"You know what, Gus . . . I liked you better when you didn't talk." Astrick eyed Butch and gave him a nod before returning to the carriage, wiping the spit from his face. He smiled at the sounds of the butcher knife repeatedly hacking at the gnome and the pained screams that filled the air. The others watched Butch shred the gnome with his knife while Astrick locked the back of the carriage and made his way to the driver's side. He sat on the box, grabbing the reins.

"Let's go make some deliveries, boys," Astrick declared. "We're gonna sell this load—you know, at a high finder's fee—and then we can go back to Koport and rest for a bit." Ax, Hammer, and Bo jumped into the back of the carriage.

"It's been a while since we were home," Bo said.

Astrick glanced at Butch, who was splattered with blood and grinning. "C'mon, Butch, why didn't you pull him off to the side first. Now it's a big ol' mess in the middle of the road." Astrick rubbed his forehead, exasperated with the reckless mess.

"What? Animals will take care of it." Butch's grin faded as he prodded the gnome's remains with his boot.

"And if someone sees it before then?" Astrick asked. The others grunted and began cutting open some flour sacks, emptying them over the sides, then tossing the empty bags to Butch.

"I'm going to need some help," Butch requested, holding the flour sacks.

"Hammer and Ax, help him," Astrick ordered.

"Why us?" Ax asked. "Hammer and I always have to help clean up his mess."

"You want your cut? Do as I say," Astrick commanded. "Bo has his job, and you have yours. That is unless you want to end up like poor Gus."

"No," Ax grunted as he grabbed a sack. The three men started stuffing parts of Gus into the flour sacks.

"That's disgusting, guys," Bo said, mocking them. "Have the decency to wear some gloves."

"I think you missed a toe," Astrick joked.

"You have a spell to make that disappear, don't ya?" Bo whispered to Astrick.

"Yes! It'd be so much easier, but they don't need to know that." Astrick winked, laughing.

The men stuffed the sacks until they were full. "Now what?" Butch asked.

"Stuff him in the carriage," Astrick ordered. "We'll sell it to the butcher as—"

"Roadkill?" interrupted Bo.

They all laughed as Astrick snapped the reins, moving the carriage forward as the crew loaded the flour sacks.

"What about your play in Omlett?" Bo asked.

"I think this will be my resignation," Astrick replied. "Step one, sell the ale to the Cache Tavern; Step two, Omlett Inn. I may have special plans for those fireworks. Perhaps we go out with a bang."

CHAPTER SEVEN

CACHE TAVERN CHAOS

arried by Ghost, Raven and Izarra arrived at the western end of Omlett, near the Cache Tavern. Raven dismounted and helped her new friend down.

Izarra giggled excitedly as Raven tied Ghost to the hitching post. "That was amazing! I've never ridden a unicorn before."

Raven flashed a smile. "She's the best," she gloated, stroking Ghost's mane.

"How did you get her? Because I want one."

"A friend of mine rescued her in the Fey Realm. He gave her to me as a birthday present."

"And the guardian allows her to stay—" Izarra stopped with wide eyes and grabbed Raven by the arm. "Wait—are you telling me you're friends with the Realm Guardian?"

"I'm leaving for his training camp in two days." Raven coyly smiled as they walked toward the Omlett Outfitter shop.

"He has a training camp?" Izarra asked in awe.

"Yes, he selects a handful of trainees to help defend our realm against domestic threats."

"That sounds dangerous." Izarra paused. "I want to help. But before you tell me no, I can care for myself." She continued walking toward the outfitters, admiring the dresses that hung in the shop window. "I mean, I traveled from Thistlebane to meet you."

Raven motioned to the shop next door. "Here, Izarra."

Izarra's smile of pleasure at viewing the pretty dresses quickly faded when she saw the frightening-looking armor in the window of the adventure shop. "Only if you promise we can go there afterward."

"Sure, why not? I have a lot of daylight to kill." Once they entered the shop, the girls navigated the maze of armor stands displayed in light, medium, and heavy categories. Raven stopped in front of a bulky chest plate. *How the spell does anyone function in that?*

A large rack had different types of shields arranged by size, while a circular table held used adventuring supplies on sale. Raven rummaged through the backpacks and then turned to Izarra, who admired the shield artwork.

"I'm not sure why you wanted to meet me," Raven stated.

"There aren't too many princesses my age, and besides, I'm half-human, so I can relate to you being half-elf." Izarra lifted a small buckler decorated with roses. "No offense, but your sister seems too serious for my taste." She posed with the shield. "What do you think?"

Raven shook her head, then turned back to the pile. "She can be sometimes." She strapped on a torn leather bracer. "How much do you know about my family?"

Izarra sat down the shield, turning to the armor on a stand behind her. "We get visitors from Omlett," she explained, holding up a silver chainmail tunic. "Shiney . . . Uh, my mother told me my father was a soldier in the Omlett Army."

"What was his name?" Raven asked. "I might know him."

"Brian Lyte," Izarra answered, amused by the chainmail's jingle as she shook it.

"No, sorry, doesn't sound familiar."

"They named me Izarra, which means star," Izarra explained, gravitating to a tall tower shield decorated with three giant stars. "So, my mother called me her starlight, and they believed I would help guide my father home, but he never returned." She struggled to lift the shield but quickly walked away as if the attempt had never happened, joining the rogue at the table.

"I'm sorry," Raven softly responded, a frown falling across her face. "Maybe I can ask Buzz or my father if they know him."

"I would appreciate that," Izarra said gratefully.

"Here we go." Raven held up a black leather backpack. "This will do." After inspecting the bag, Raven watched as Izarra picked out a crazy pink and white one. "Ummm . . . no." Raven held up a light blue bag. "How about this one."

"Boring," Izarra responded as she counted the pockets on the pink backpack.

"It's blue, like water," Raven said, handing it to her new friend. "My treat for splashing the Hork last night."

"Fine," Izarra finally agreed, dropping the bright bag and taking the one Raven handed her. "But it's *your* birthday."

"So?"

"Only if you let me buy you a dress for your special day."

Raven frowned. "I don't know. I really don't wear dresses." They strolled to the counter, where the rogue paid for the two items.

After securing the bags to Ghost, they wandered to the next-door outfitter shop. This place made Raven more uncomfortable than fighting three half-orcs. Izarra glowed like she was in the Astral Realm, rolling around in stardust.

"I want to buy them all," she said gleefully, then suddenly stopped.

"What's wrong?" Raven asked, only to be met with silence.

Izarra reached up and pulled down a bright purple backless party dress, holding it up against Raven. "It matches your eyes. The guys will melt."

Guys? Raven's thoughts went straight to Thomas, the handsome paladin she'd met at the bakery.

"Gideon Grindal would lose his wings over this." Izarra draped the gown over the rogue's shoulder, snapping Raven out of her thoughts.

"Gideon?" Raven snapped with a puzzled look.

"The Mortal Realm Guardian, the one who gifted you your unicorn, right? He's *very* popular amongst the nymphs in Thistlebane. They purposely break realm rules so he'll show up. It's embarrassing sometimes."

"He's just a longtime family friend," Raven replied firmly.

"Can you believe he had to stop a losta-lotus flower trade? The sneaky Bane-Wenches were trafficking the banned Fey flowers to Waterfront."

"I haven't thought much about what he does."

Izarra stopped rummaging through the dresses. "Oh, I see. I hate to inform you, Princess, but the world is much bigger than you think." She continued browsing. "Besides, he has to be breaking some kind of rule allowing you to keep Ghost in this realm." After scrutinizing the last garment, Izarra turned to Raven and searched for the tag on the purple dress. Her eyes grew wide at the price; her head dropped in disappointment, and she returned the hanger to the rack. "Maybe I won't buy them all."

Raven sighed in relief. "Just pick out your dress. I'm going across the road to get a drink."

"I'm sorry, Raven," Izarra replied. "Omlett is a little more expensive than Thistlebane."

"You can buy me a drink," Raven suggested.

"Deal! Can we stop by the church later?"

"Sure, I guess. Is there—"

"I heard there's a cemetery there for fallen soldiers. I thought maybe my father might be there."

"I was thinking about stopping there, too," Raven said shyly.

"For—?" Izarra replied, seeming to try to pry for more information.

Should I tell her? "Fine, fine. All your talk about guys reminded me about a cute one I ran into earlier—I'd like to run into him again."

Izarra perked up. "Really! Do tell."

Raven groaned. "I met him this morning at the bakery and overheard him say he might stay at the church since Omlett Inn is too expensive."

"Oh, the paladin—Thomas," her new friend teased. "I signed him into room nine."

"You what?!" Raven asked with surprise.

"I have room four, and room nine was for my mother," Izarra explained. "But Thomas seemed like he needed it more, and besides, getting my mother out of Thistlebane is nearly impossible. You can tell him when you see him again, and don't mention me. You can be the hero."

Raven blushed—*room nine.*

"I'm going to pay for my dress," Izarra stated. "I'll meet you at the tavern." She walked over to the shop clerk, carrying the light blue flowy dress.

Raven exited the shop, her head still buzzing about Thomas. *Maybe I should visit room nine tonight after the party.* A cold sweat dampened her forehead, and butterflies swirled around in her stomach. *Could I get my first kiss?* A long smile stretched from ear to ear as she untied Ghost.

Raven guided her unicorn to the Cache Tavern's hitching post, but her smile faded as a strange gaze followed her. A short, stout guy sat on the box of the carriage, eating a meal using his hands as utensils. Food particles dangled in his frizzy beard as he brushed his long hair to the side. She eyed the horses attached to the carriage. *I know those horses from somewhere.*

Raven entered the tavern and waved at Rusty, who was already filling a mug with ale. "Make that two!" she called out.

Rusty chuckled. "Rough day?"

"I have company."

"Male?"

"No," Raven answered awkwardly, noticing the blood stain on the bar counter from where she pierced the half-orc's hands. *Maybe Miss Crinkly was right about their cleaning habits.* "Make that three ales."

"Don't mind that." Rusty quickly threw down a cloth to cover it. "Blood is so hard to get out. Maybe I'll just paint the bar red."

Raven forced a half-grin. *I can't tell if he's joking.*

Rusty lined up the three drinks. "That will be three GOPs."

"Three gold pieces?!" Raven asked, shocked.

"Aye, sorry, milady, but with the new delivery charge, the cost was triple what I usually pay," Rusty explained, pointing at the four men sitting in the corner.

"Where's Gus? Isn't that his horse and carriage?"

"They said he retired and got into the flour business. So, I guess he's baking now? But apparently, they bought everything from Gus."

"That doesn't sound right," Raven muttered, staring at the men. "Gus loved his job."

Rusty's head tilted as he looked past her. "Izarra! Welcome back."

"My company," Raven said, nodding toward the half-nymph. "At least I don't have to make introductions."

Izarra sat on the stool next to her. "Hello, Rusty. How do you know my name?"

"Or maybe I do," Raven quipped as she sipped her drink.

"It's my business to know everyone." Rusty chuckled. "Especially someone who brings in crowds of young, thirsty men. Speaking of which, where are they?"

"She left them back at the Omlett Inn," Raven answered into her mug before the liquid hit her mouth.

Rusty gathered empty mugs from the bar. "I guess I can forgive you this time."

"You own *The Ebony Tree* record, correct?" Izarra asked before taking a sip.

"Yours truly." Rusty bowed, then held his finger to his lips. "But shh, no one can know I drink at my competitor's establishment. It's bad for business."

Izarra wiped her mouth. "I'm going to break that record," she declared, slamming down her mug.

"Ha! I'd like to see that," Rusty teased.

"I'm sure you would," Raven mumbled under her breath. "I still can't get the image of your butt and . . . other parts . . . out of my head."

"Ha!" Rusty snorted. "I was younger, though, and in better shape."

"It was only eleven years ago," Raven snickered, waving her mug.

Izarra leaned in and whispered, "So, you *do* lose everything when you go in?"

"Not everything—it can't take away your pride," Rusty proclaimed, puffing up his chest.

"That's what you call it?" Raven asked. "Well, Izarra, pay up so I can get my pride on."

Izarra pulled out her coin pouch. "How much is it?"

"The drinks are three GOPs," Raven answered, waiting for Izarra's response.

"What?!" Izarra exclaimed, digging into the bottom of her pouch.

"Forget it," Rusty said. "On the house. After all, it's your birthday. And Happy Dragomas!"

"Thank you, Rusty." Raven toasted him with her mug. "I think I'll chat with the new delivery boys for you."

"It's no problem," Rusty responded nervously. "I can manage."

"But can your patrons' pockets manage?" Raven asked. "Poor Izarra was about to teleport out of here."

"No, I wasn't," Izarra responded, "but I do have my portal scroll to Thistlebane."

Raven wrapped her arm around her friend. "I was jesting, but keep it handy if this doesn't go well." She grabbed her drink and approached the vagrant-looking men as Izarra followed closely behind.

The bald man nudged the blond guy as the two girls approached. "Look, boys, the entertainment has arrived. Butch, Hammer, show the women some courtesy."

A scrawny redhead and a heavy-set guy rose from their chairs as the girls promptly occupied their seats. The redhead quickly moved between them, dipping his fingers into the mashed potatoes. The guy's body odor made Raven cringe as her eyes followed his hand. He licked his fingers clean. She quickly turned away when he attempted a flirtatious head nod, but it came across as creepy and repulsive.

"I'm Butch," he said.

Raven froze with her hands on the hilt of her daggers as he grabbed his plate.

"Sorry," Izarra apologized, watching Butch with disgust. "We aren't bards."

The bald man laughed. "That's all right, sweetheart. We can find something you're good at."

The blond guy sorted through his pieces of chicken and then glanced up. "To what do we owe the pleasure?"

"Why did the delivery cost triple?" Raven asked sweetly.

"Ah, boys, it turns out to be a business meeting." The man slumped back in his chair. "Lucky for you, it didn't quadruple," he said menacingly, "or should I count that in Elvish?"

"Common is fine," Raven answered as she noticed his green eyes matched his wizard robe.

"There are five of us now, so the prices went up. I'm sure you'll be old enough to understand how business works one day."

"Maybe you're underestimating me," Raven warned. "I do know Gus and how his family business works. And those are his horses out there."

"Oh, you know my buddy Gus?" the mage asked. "Well, you know he retired and left the business to me. Last we saw him, he was at the butcher." Cackles rippled around the table, but the mage kept a straight face. "I'm Astrick, and this is my delivery team, so get used to it."

"I'm Bo," the blond said, chewing on a chicken wing and holding a greasy hand to shake. He quickly withdrew it when they ignored him.

"You already know Butch, and that's Hammer." Astrick pointed at the guys who were standing. "Ax is out on the box guarding the rest of the cargo. You can't trust anyone nowadays."

Raven kept her eyes on Astrick the whole time. "I'm going to talk to Gus and verify your story, so either I'll owe you an apology or—"

"Or what, elf?" Astrick shot up from his seat threateningly. "You have no business in my business. And I'll charge whatever I feel like. You know what? I think there will be an elf tax now."

"Have a good day, gentlemen." Raven rose, and Izarra followed her to the front door.

"HAVE A HAPPY BIRTHDAY, PRINCESS!" Rusty yelled.

Raven paused, closing her eyes and raising her head to the ceiling. *What the spell? Rusty!* She reached for the door handle and heard Izarra whisper, "Raven." She turned to watch the four men raise their mugs and start singing, "*Happy birthday to you, happy birthday, dear Princess . . .*"

"Make it a royal tax, too." Astrick grinned while toasting her with his mug.

Raven eyed Rusty as he mouthed, "I'm sorry."

Something about this group of men bothers me. Church bells rang in the distance, signaling midday, as the girls hopped back onto Ghost, taking off at full speed.

They approached the butcher stand to find Bernie, the butcher, chopping up meat on a crate. "Hey, Bernie," greeted Raven, glancing down from Ghost. "You see Gus today?"

"No, sorry," Bernie answered in his deep voice. "The delivery came by some other men, which was odd because I wasn't expecting any deliveries today."

"What did they bring?" Raven asked.

"They sold me a couple of sacks of meat. My apprentice, Sebastian, inspected and paid for it, and then they headed west."

"Anything unusual?" Raven asked, guiding Ghost over to the stack of sacks.

"Just the fact that the meat was stuffed into flour sacks and hadn't been kept on ice, but they said it was fresh, so I didn't think anything of it."

"Bernie, don't sell that meat," Raven said, concerned. "Something doesn't feel right."

The butcher walked over, opened a flour sack, and winced at the smell. "This isn't an animal carcass. I'll send for Buzz right away," he urged as he shook his head. "Sebastian!"

"Oh no," Izarra's voice shook as her grip around Raven tightened. "Do you think it's Gus?"

"I'll pray to Blade it isn't," Raven responded, "but poor Gus if it is." Her thoughts went to the men at the tavern. *Do I go back and confront them?*

"Is there anything we can do to help?" Izarra asked nervously.

Can I handle a fight with a mage and four others? Raven swallowed her pride and blurted, "I think it's best to leave this to Buzz and the guards."

"Do you think we could still stop at the church?" Izarra questioned. "I would still like to visit the cemetery."

"I guess. There's nothing more we can do here."

Raven snapped the reins, and they headed southeast to the church. The front of the church seemed deserted. *Everyone probably vacated for lunch.*

"We'll make this quick," Raven said, dismounting before turning to help Izarra, "then we return to the Inn."

Raven pushed open one of the double doors. She paused, listening for anyone in the prayer boxes before calling into the empty foyer. "Hello?" Statues of other demigods seemed to watch them as they crossed into the prayer chamber.

"This place is creepy," Izarra stated before taking a whiff. "If death had a smell, I would imagine this would be it."

Raven snickered. "What are you talking about? It does not."

"Sure," Izarra responded slowly, following behind the rogue. Raven glanced back, watching the half-nymph's eyes scan every pew as if something would jump out at her.

They moved slowly down the aisle. "I thought they would have this place decorated for tomorrow."

Izarra hesitated as if embarrassed to ask. "What's tomorrow?"

"Blade Day, the celebration of his birth."

"You'll have to tell me all about that sometime."

They continued through the prayer chamber, into the hall, and to the Instruction Room. It was also empty except for Carya's food basket and what Raven assumed was Thomas's pastries by the podium. "They must have left in a hurry," she surmised, "or maybe I'm just being paranoid."

"I'm sure they're just busy setting up the party," Izarra reassured her.

"Come this way . . . we must go through the bell tower." They quickly passed the spiral metal staircase in the particularly dark chamber. The urge to yell at the bell for her voice to echo like she did as a child quickly faded as Izarra stepped on her heels.

"Sorry," the half-nymph whispered, coming to a dead stop.

They passed by storage boxes until they reached a heavy door that Raven pushed open, leading to the courtyard. As they followed the stone path, Izarra admired the tall white gazebo hugged by green hedges.

They finally reached the cemetery at the rear, where a white fence penned in the headstones. "I'll try here on the north side if you want to start on the south side," Raven stated.

"Sure," Izarra hesitantly replied.

Raven made a conscious effort to keep an eye on her new friend as she read some names before she came across one she knew—Cyndi's mother, Trixie Sharp, had passed away from a heart condition.

With mothers on her mind, Raven wandered toward the middle of the graveyard, where a stone fountain with four carved stars—a tribute to the Astral Realm and memorial for the Fisker family sat. Raven's mother tended this area daily, keeping the water clean and fresh flowers on her uncle's, his wife's, and her two cousins' graves. *They died in the unprovoked orc attack at Fellswar, so the story goes.*

Trudging toward the graves near the tree line, Raven noticed the names of the fallen soldiers who had fought in battles. Before calling to her friend, Izarra cried out and then dropped to her knees, weeping. She dashed over, putting her arms around her friend and glancing at the tombstone. "Captain Brian Andrew Lyte of the Omlett Army." Raven paused for a moment before continuing. "Day or night shines my Starlight." The thought of her father cheating death and the fact he was still with her hit like a magic arrow. She quickly wiped her wet cheek.

Izarra sobbed. "I wish I was old enough to remember him."

"Did your mother tell you anything about him?"

"When I was younger, she always told me she loved how he could make us laugh, even when I was fussy. And he would help anyone in need. His eyes were as blue as the ocean, and hair as blond as the sand."

"So, he resembled you," Raven said, gently helping her friend stand. "I'm truly sorry for your loss."

"Thank you," Izarra replied. Her giggle broke the sadness, and they each wiped tears from the other. "Look at us. We should freshen up for your secret birthday bash."

The two girls somberly followed the stone path to the front of the church, arm in arm, until the sound of racing horses made them turn down the road.

"Hey! It's the birthday princess!" voices called out. The driver halted the animals as the wagon came to a halt. It was the new delivery team from the Cache Tavern. The men whistled, calling out vulgar innuendos and making rude gestures.

Raven didn't have to remember their names because each had a corresponding weapon in their hands, but Astrick shot her a look sinister enough to make her body quiver. She rushed to untie Ghost and then handed Izarra the reins. "Return to the Omlett Inn and retrieve help."

"Come with me," Izarra pleaded, gripping the reins tightly.

"Izarra, do as I say, please," Raven implored as she unsheathed her daggers.

"It appears you ladies could use some comforting," Astrick yelled as his four henchmen hopped off the wagon. "We offer that service free of charge."

CHAPTER EIGHT

THE PARTY PALLY

Thomas delivered the sixth heavy oak table to the banquet room, dropping it near the presents and stretching his back. He was glad he'd removed his metal armor because he was already dripping with sweat. The courtyard and main doors were open to the breeze, but the air still felt stagnant. The stuffiness seemed to disperse as Carya entered with colorful tablecloths and a water pitcher.

"Thank you," Thomas said gratefully as he filled a mug and gulped the cold refreshment. He noticed an orc enter the hall, heading to the corner. *The same orc from this morning?*

Carya smiled at the shock on his face as Thomas watched the orc hoist up a petite female elf to hang a banner. "That's Brugg," she said, placing some wrapped gifts on the table.

"If I saw him walking my way in a dark alley—"

"Don't worry," Carya laughed. "He's harmless."

"The only orcs I've seen were in battle, and none of them wanted to be my friend."

"That's why his tribe cast him out. He refused to fight. As he wandered from city to city, a group of humans captured him, tied him up, and threw him off the Suttiir Bridge."

"I'm sorry. Humans have been fending off orcs and bugbears for a long time."

"My father knew it was unusual for an orc to travel alone, so he dove in and rescued him. Brugg's like—well, he's family now."

"Dragon dung!" a voice yelled from the middle of the room, followed by clanking sounds as an angry gnome threw his tools and continued yelling in Gnomish.

"What's his story?" Thomas asked with concern.

Carya glanced at the gnome, who was now deep in thought, scowling at the broken mechanism. "He's the co-founder of Omlett and one of my father's best friends. Come on. I'll introduce you." Taking Thomas's hand, she led him to the frowning gnome. "Mug, this is Thomas."

"Nice to meet you, sir," Thomas said, offering his hand as Mug uncrossed his arms. He shook the gnome's oily hand. "What are you building?" he asked, discreetly wiping the grease off.

"It's a riding device," Mug replied. "It's supposed to move when you mount it."

Thomas studied the design. "Sounds interesting."

"Oh, it gets better," Carya said, activating the Illusion Ball hanging above them. "Pick an animal."

"A black bear," Thomas answered with a smile.

Carya chanted something in Elvish, and Mug's riding device transformed into a giant black bear. Everyone in the room turned to gaze at the spectacle.

"That's amazing," Thomas responded, examining the illusion more closely. "Why isn't it moving?"

"That's what I'm working on, genius," Mug snapped as Carya's eyes widened and her cheeks flushed.

"Mug, that wasn't nice," Carya scolded, glancing at Thomas in apology.

The gnome huffed. "Sorry, Gus still isn't here with my parts from Glimnok, and I'm hungry!"

They watched as Mug stormed out. Carya shook her head. "He's usually more pleasant. I guess he wants everything to be perfect."

"If someone had told me this morning that I would be decorating a room with an orc, petting a black bear in the middle of a tavern"—he paused—"and spending my time with a beautiful cleric, I would have told them they were under a madness spell."

Carya blushed. "I'm not a cleric quite yet. But one day." They both watched Queen Mara enter the banquet room and approach them.

"Thank you, Thomas, for all your help," Mara said sweetly. "How can we repay you?"

"I could use a room for the night," Thomas stated eagerly.

"Done," Mara responded. "We will make sure you have one."

"Thank you, Queen Mara," Thomas replied. His eyes scanned the room, then landed back on Carya. "By the way, everything looks beautiful."

They heard Brugg grunting by the walls. The elf helping him must've had to leave, and the orc struggled to hang the lanterns alone.

Thomas scanned the room. "Is there a ladder?"

"Mug might have one, but usually, Brugg *is* the ladder," Carya joked.

"It's fine. I'll help," Thomas offered nervously. He felt their eyes on him as he approached the orc. He pointed to himself with both hands. "I . . . will . . . help. . . ."

Brugg eyed Thomas up and down, looking suspicious. Then the orc shoved a lantern into Thomas's hands and lifted him into position.

Mara and Carya laughed at the spectacle, but Thomas ignored them as he reached for the hook. "I can see my house from here," he teased.

"Hurry—you stink," Brugg said, pinching his stout nose.

"What?" Thomas sniffed himself as the orc bellowed with laughter. *An orc just outwitted me.* "Good one, Brugg."

The two women continued laughing as Brugg bent over to retrieve another lantern.

"Who needs a riding device?" Thomas joked to the amused women as he fought to keep his balance. Carya whispered something to her mother, causing Mara to smile broadly. *What did she say?*

Carya approached the two as the little elf that had been helping returned, and Mara left. "Brugg, I need the human back now."

The orc grunted as he lowered Thomas to the ground, and the young elf replaced him. "Bye . . . stinky human." Brugg grinned, and the little elf giggled.

Thomas smirked at them, returning to Carya. "That's another first," he said breathlessly as his face tingled from exertion. "He's a real character."

"That's Brugg," Carya agreed as she retook Thomas's hand. "My mother asked us to find Gus. He's late with the party supplies."

"Sure. I could use some fresh air. Maybe there's somewhere I could clean up?"

"No problem," Carya said, playfully putting her arm through his, "stinky human."

Thomas grinned as they returned to the bar area, where Mara was paging through a book.

"Someone already added you to the log," Mara said, smiling as she read. "Room nine is reserved for Thomas, the cute paladin."

They all glanced over at Cyndi, who was wiping down a table. She must have felt their eyes on her because she responded, "Wasn't me. Last time I checked, all the rooms were occupied."

A warm feeling flushed to Thomas's cheeks. "Well, I'm flattered."

"Looks too neat to be Raven's handwriting," quipped Mara, studying the entry.

"You know, I've been meaning to ask you, Carya," Thomas said. "Remember when you said 'beauteous' earlier and mentioned it was your sister's birthday?"

"Yes," Carya answered suspiciously. "Why?"

"I met Raven at the bakery before church. She was kind enough to offer to help me, but I never heard from her to find out if she could get me a room."

Carya's gaze shot to the floor and went silent, fidgeting with her hands.

Mara snapped the ledger closed. "That sounds like something your sister would do."

A stern male voice behind them yelled from down the hall, "Halt, Sir Knight." Thomas turned as an elf and dwarf approached them. "Mister Plunkett, please cuff him and return what belongs to me," the white-haired elf demanded sternly.

Thomas raised his hands. "I'm sorry, sir, but I don't know what you're talking about."

Carya touched her forehead as if trying to hide her embarrassment. "Buzz'diir, Father."

Thomas quickly glanced at Carya and back at the elf. "Father?"

The dwarf with a patch over his eye approached more aggressively, raising his fists as if ready to fight. He faked a swing but tapped Thomas on the thigh with his knuckles, then laughed as the paladin flinched, bracing for the impact.

Thomas realized the prank and tried to save face by quickly bowing. "King Naelo."

"You are now free to go, Sir Knight," Eugor pronounced.

Is he serious?

Carya walked over and gave her father a hug and a kiss on the cheek. "His name is Thomas Wellington, and he's replacing—"

Eugor smiled. "I know who he is, dear. I approved the request from the church on Cleric Stone-Prayer's replacement."

"I traveled to Brindell to interview all his human peers," Buzz'diir explained. "He's a paladin—just another young do-gooder."

"Thanks," Thomas responded suspiciously, "I think."

Carya returned to Thomas's side. "We're about to go find Gus."

"No need—we got a report from Bernie," Eugor said. "Buzz sent a squad to investigate. Meanwhile, your mother and I will supervise the banquet room." He held out his hand as Mara walked over and grabbed it.

"Do you need any more assistance?" Thomas asked.

"Do-gooder," Buzz'diir coughed, then he cleared his throat. "I need to prep the security team to watch over the children collecting their sweets tonight for

Dragomas. I'll see you all at the party." Buzz'diir walked past Thomas. "I'm keeping my eye on you—and yes, my good eye," he joked, leaving the group laughing.

"You two can relax and freshen up for the party," Mara said. "I'll keep this old elf from harassing you."

"Carya, make sure you're not late for your sister's party," Eugor instructed.

"Don't worry, Father." As her parents headed toward the banquet room, she turned to Thomas. "If you want, I can show you where room nine is."

Thomas knew he could figure it out but didn't want to leave her company. "Sure," he responded eagerly, "but I need to wash up first."

"All the rooms have water basins, but if you want to get really clean, I'll show you my sister's favorite bathing spot tomorrow. It's a natural spring that stays warm all year long. You can go early in the morning since Raven will probably sleep in. She's going to have a late night tonight."

"That sounds wonderful," Thomas replied. "Let me grab my gear from my horse." They opened the Inn's front door as a stranger on a gray horse galloping at full speed darted toward them. As the frantic duo got closer, Thomas recognized the steed. "Wait! That's your sister's unicorn."

"Yes," Carya replied. "But that's not Raven."

CHAPTER NINE

AN ACIDIC ABILITY

Raven noticed the blond guy, Bo, advancing toward her, making the fatal mistake of loading his crossbow too slowly. She used the opportunity to throw one of her daggers, aiming at Bo's chest, but it lodged in his forehead. As he collapsed, she and Izarra gasped at the sight.

"Bo!" Astrick screamed. He dropped the reins and stood to cast a spell.

"Echye An-Ala." Raven quickly cast the Cause Fear spell to spook the horses, knocking Astrick off balance before he could finish.

The mage frantically grabbed at the reins as the horses bucked and galloped away at high speed from the church. The other, slower men froze before Hammer finally charged at her.

Izarra quickly uncorked her magical water decanter, blasting him with a geyser.

Disoriented and enraged, Hammer shouted, "Water? You plan on drowning me?"

Raven instantly somersaulted over to him. "Not quite," she said, putting her hand in the puddle. "Nissre Nar."

His body shook violently from the Shocking Grasp spell, then he dropped his hammer, collapsing face-first into the pool of water.

Raven held her breath and the spell as long as she could until the breath bubbles quickly subsided. As Ax charged at Izarra, attempting to mount Ghost, Raven promptly tried to stand, but her legs buckled, forcing her to lean on one knee, taking a whiff of the electrocuted body. She gagged and helplessly watched as Ax grabbed Izarra with both arms behind Ghost. But the slippery half-nymph dropped to the ground as the gray unicorn kicked the attacker in the stomach. The man doubled over, and Ghost finished him with a fatal second kick to his forehead. *Ghost's combat trainer was worth every coin.*

Raven slouched, using her knee as support, and held up her only dagger as a last-ditch effort to intimidate the red-headed man, but he raised his superior butcher knife in return.

"Mine's bigger," Butch drooled demonically.

Exhausted from using all her power in the electrocution spell, Raven glanced around, then staggered onto the church stoop while Izarra tried to summon water again. A short blast hit Butch, but it turned into a light stream as the crazed man cackled.

"Izarra, go, now!" Raven yelled, hunched near the front door.

Izarra mounted Ghost and circled Ax, crushing his skull as they dashed toward the Omlett Inn.

Raven entered the church, leaving the door open, hoping Butch would follow her instead of her friend. Spotting a prayer box, she ducked inside to catch her breath. The cushioned seat provided a quick comfort as she laid her head against the wall. Butch cackled again, scraping his knife against the church doorway, causing her to sit straight up. Peering through the door's latticework, she saw him wandering the foyer, eyeing the gold candle holders.

"Come on out, Princess," Butch said nastily, randomly opening a prayer box on the opposite side. "We got a lot of coins from the butcher for Gus. I wonder how much we could get for the tender meat of a princess, but it seems like you're out of tricks. Astrick will return any moment now. Maybe I'll wait for him." He passed under the archway, and she heard him flop into the rear pew.

"You're sick," Raven replied, "and you will pay for what you did to Gus." *But the ogre shite has a point. I have a chance to run out the front door, or I must attack now.*

She took a deep breath, gripping her dagger tighter. *Watch over me, Blade.* She burst out from inside the box, directly charging Butch. She swung at his exposed head just above the pew, but all her training seemed futile as emotions gained control.

He dodged the violent swings and quickly rose. "I like this," he sneered. "My turn." He swung more aggressively as Raven jumped over and rolled under the pews. As she was about to jump another, he snagged her cloak and pulled her close enough to grab the back of her neck. He shoved her against the wall, forcing her to drop the dagger. "How appropriate to die in a church," Butch taunted maliciously. "I would love the ransom, but you killed three of my friends."

"You're next," Raven uttered into the wall as he gripped her neck tighter.

"I can't hear you, Princess," Butch said, bringing his head closer as she struggled to turn until her eyes locked onto his bloodshot ones. "Look at those eyes. I think I'll cut those out first. They've gotta be worth at least one hundred PIPs each."

"It's the last thing you'll see," Raven promised, gathering saliva.

"Oh, so you plan to spit—" The saliva splattered his face, causing him to drop Raven and the knife as his eyes blistered. Bringing his hands to his face made him scream as they burned, too. "What the dragon balls did you do to me?!" Butch collapsed onto a pew, his hands shaking, resisting the urge to raise them to his face again. His head dropped between his knees as he rocked back and forth. "You think I'm a monster?" Butch whimpered. "No, Princess, you are!"

Still in shock, Raven watched him suffer as his skin continued to blister. *The spit was pure instinct.* But Butch's words still lingered. *I'm a monster!*

Raven picked up her dagger and silently stalked Butch. She tried to think of something clever to say along the way, but she just wanted his cussing to end. After she drove the dagger into the back of his skull, he collapsed onto the floor as she walked around to inspect his face. Nausea washed over her when she saw his dark, empty eye sockets and the scarring around them. His hands reminded her of the same scar tissue Carya had.

"I am a monster," Raven whispered, trembling as the sweat poured down her body. She sat down on the pew, pulling her knees up and wrapping her arms around them. The church doors swung open and she reached for her dagger, expecting Astrick, but it was High Priest Carne.

"What in Blade's name is going on?" the high priest asked, standing in the doorway. "Princess Naelo, did you kill all these men?"

Before she could answer, a fiery projectile ripped through Carne's chest and hit the wooden pew in front of her, shattering it into charred splinters. Raven grabbed a tapestry from the wall and ran to the fallen priest, smothering the flames on his robe. His blank eyes stared into hers as the crackling of burning wood grew louder and fire engulfed the foyer. Black smoke quickly filled the air as a menacing voice yelled, "You elf bitch!"

Raven glared at Astrick as he stormed toward the front door. The hate in his eyes took her aback, but before she could stand, she heard him yell Projectilis Magicus, and then a magic missile knocked her down, dazing her.

The foyer ceiling filled with smoke as it began to spin. Raven shut her eyes and reopened them, hoping things would be clearer. A loud ringing hummed in her ears, drowning out the sound around her. As she tried to focus, his hand yanked her ponytail, wrapping it around his fist. She struggled to move her arms and feet, but nothing responded—it was as if her body had shut down. Her vision blurred as the scene of the smokey ceiling converted to the blue sky as she slipped in and out of consciousness.

Father.

The smooth stone tiles of the church floor changed to coarse dirt as the angry wizard dragged her out and onto the road. Her captor tightened his grip on her hair. "You will pay dearly for this, Princess," threatened Astrick. "I'm taking you to Koport . . . where I will kill you . . . slowly."

CHAPTER TEN

A CALL FOR HELP

"HELP!" the girl screamed as she approached Thomas and Carya. "Raven's in trouble!" Her curly blond hair was windblown, and her cheek had a prominent scratch. A blue aura appeared around her as Thomas quickly activated Detect Evil.

"What happened?" Carya asked urgently, petting Ghost's mane.

After a moment of gasping, the stranger replied, "We were attacked at the church."

"I'll go help," Thomas replied, gazing into Carya's eyes before heading to the stable.

Carya rushed to the front door. "And I'll inform my father. Be careful!"

Thomas nodded, hurrying to the stable to retrieve Grail as the blond girl followed him. "Lead the way," he said, gripping his shield and leaving his long sword in the leather sheath attached to his war horse. When he glanced back at the front doors, Carya had already returned inside. He pushed Grail's speed, but Ghost remained several paces ahead. *That's one fast unicorn.*

In the distance, black smoke rose into the midday sky. A wave of urgency rushed over Thomas as he snapped the reins.

When they arrived, he raised his shield as the girl on Ghost swung her decanter around. A tall, bald man in a green wizard robe dragged an unconscious Raven by her hair toward a carriage. Billowing smoke poured from the church, flames licking the walls.

Raven's friend screamed, drawing the man's attention as a jet of water shot out from her decanter, pushing him away. The frightened girl dismounted, grabbed a hand axe lying near a man's lifeless body, and proceeded to stand in front of Raven. She gripped the handle tightly, poised to fend off further attacks.

The soaked man tried to climb the driver's side of the carriage, but Thomas rammed the man with his shield, knocking him to the ground.

Thomas dismounted Grail, but before he could retrieve his long sword, the wizard summoned a creature from the flat of his back. The eight-foot, hunchbacked demon snapped its enormous oval head around. Bright red eyes stared out while exposing its sharp teeth. It then charged on all fours at the paladin. *A dretch!* The Abyss creature's red aura was almost blinding. *These creatures are fouler in person than in our study books.* It scared off Grail.

"Watch out!" the girl called out.

Thomas swung his shield as the creature's forearms slammed down, and the paladin watched feebly as the wizard scurried back to his feet, escaping by summoning a magical steed. Recognizing that his armor was still at the Inn, Thomas stepped back, raising his shield. *Oh shite!* The sword—his divine focus, his magical source—was stuck on Grail.

The creature raised its two burly arms, striking the shield again, making the steel vibrate and sing out. Thomas crouched and rolled away as the beast's left arm swung wildly. *I can't keep this up much longer.* As he began to stand, the monster charged, knocking the paladin over and pinning him down. The foul breath of the dretch filled Thomas's nostrils.

The girl helplessly watched until she called out, "Over here!" A rock bounced off the creature, barely missing Thomas's head. Saliva dripped off the dretch's fangs as it came face-to-face with the paladin, ignoring the pleading girl.

The front claws gripped Thomas's shield tighter, but having no armor left him vulnerable to the creature's rear talons, which were trying to pierce his sides. He sweated profusely, using all his upper strength to hold his shield while his lower half twisted and dodged the flurry of strikes. Thomas gripped his shield tighter, digging his shoulders into the ground and pushing upward. The creature's long, dirty nails grabbed the top of the shield, dropping all its weight onto the target as Thomas's arm muscles shook. Suddenly, a sharp pain ran down his side as a rear talon grazed him. "Shite!" he yelled, connecting a kick to the beast's leg.

Taurus Robur, Taurus Robur. But he knew the Bull Strength spell wouldn't work without his sword, so he relied on adrenaline to keep up his might. Thomas glanced at his long sword hanging in its leather sheath attached to Grail, who frantically paced back and forth with Ghost. As Thomas reached an arm toward his war horse in desperation, the creature swung a claw, and he quickly returned his arm to the safety of his shield.

Suddenly, a red portal appeared, and a blond elf with white wings emerged, wearing gold armor, combat-ready and wielding a vorpal sword. Thomas noticed the guardian's rare golden aura, which represented pure goodness.

"Gideon!" yelled the girl who straddled over Raven.

The creature's weight vanished with a leap off Thomas's shield, charging the new arrival. He heard Elvish chanting as he rolled over to his side, watching the dark silhouette of the animal burst into dust. Particles of what remained of the demonic creature rained down like confetti.

Gideon rushed to Raven and her friend. "Thank Blade, she's still alive," he said as he picked her up and laid her on the back of the carriage.

"Thank you," the paladin said gratefully, reaching to shake his hand. "I'm Thomas."

"Gideon," the guardian replied as he shook Thomas's hand. "And no, thank you."

"Thomas, you're hurt," the young girl said, pointing to his scratch.

Thomas inspected the wound. "I'll be fine. I know a good cleric. And what's your name?" he asked the trembling girl.

"I'm Izarra," she answered, holding back tears as she dropped the axe. "Thank you both for your help."

"Do you know who summoned the creature?" Gideon asked as he created a red portal. "It came from the Abyss Realm."

Izarra nodded. "The same mage who attacked Raven. I think his name is Astrick." Her face shifted to concern. "Are you going to teleport her back to the Omlett Inn?"

"I'm truly sorry, but I can't," Gideon responded sadly, glancing at the incapacitated rogue. "But I will find out the source of this realm breach."

Thomas pulled a blanket from Grail's saddlebag and covered Raven with it. He grabbed his sword, placed his other hand on her forehead, and cast Detect Poison to verify it wasn't in her system.

Her eyes opened briefly. "Thomas?"

"I'm here," he whispered, sliding his hand from her forehead to cup her face as she uttered something incoherent before losing consciousness again. "I'll escort her back to the Inn." He pulled himself onto the carriage and was about to ride off when King Naelo and Carya arrived on horseback.

"Gideon?" Eugor asked, fearing the worst.

"She's alive," Gideon reassured him, standing by his portal.

"Thank Blade!" Eugor said as he dismounted his horse and dashed to the carriage to see his daughter as Carya did the same.

"The coward headed west toward Grey-Holg," Thomas stated.

"Raven will be all right," Carya said, feeling her sister's forehead. "But the church."

"The church can be rebuilt," Eugor replied.

Izarra tried to extinguish the fire, but only a few drops of water came from her container. "My decanter isn't recharged yet." She watched the flames as the other clerics and monks gathered.

"I'll find out what's going on," Gideon said, placing his hand on the king's shoulder. "Don't go after him alone." The guardian moved beside Izarra, casting a small rain cloud over the church. The downpour doused the flames as the half-nymph smiled at him. "But if the council asks, the dretch caused the fire," he instructed, then stepped through the portal.

Izarra watched the king take a deep breath, surveying the mess. "Aren't you angry that Gideon wouldn't portal her back?"

"He can't," Eugor responded as he approached the dead men. "He almost lost his wings trying to help me. I think he knows she will recover. As you saw, he must pick and choose his battles with the council. I'll have Buzz'diir send a squad or two after the mage."

Carya joined Thomas on the box as the king removed a dagger from one of their skulls. A piece of the church ceiling collapsed loudly behind them, and they noticed another body beneath the rubble.

High Priest Carne.

"You're hurt, too," Carya said, placing her hand near Thomas's injury.

"Just a demonic scratch," Thomas responded, stopping her soft hand from touching it, "nothing a paladin can't handle."

"But the demonic infection spreads quickly," Carya replied concernedly. "I can help with that."

Eugor eyed the three. "Hurry now and return Raven to the Inn. I must deal with this."

"May I help?" Izarra asked.

"Stay with my daughter," Eugor responded. "I can manage this, and I'm sure Buzz is en route."

Izarra secured Ghost's and Grail's reins to the back of the wagon, then sat in the rear, resting Raven's head on her lap. She glanced up at Thomas and whispered, "Let's go."

CHAPTER ELEVEN

PARTY CRASH

hree-year-old Raven stared at her reflection in a copper mirror, a gift her mother had received from Mug. She was marveling at her bright purple eyes for the first time when her sister's reflection suddenly appeared behind her.

"You're a monster," Carya mocked, pushing Raven through the mirror.

The light blurred into slow-moving streaks as Raven fell through a gold buckler and landed on her rear. But it was four years later, the sisters were in the arena, and Carya was kneeling.

"You can't catch me," her sister taunted.

Raven dusted herself off and chased Carya around the workbench where Eugor and Mug burned holes into metal.

"Girls, go outside and play. You shouldn't be running around down here," Eugor said sternly before returning his attention to Mug. Raven stopped and climbed onto a stool at the other end of the bench, picking up one of the colorful green flasks before her.

Carya rushed over and tried to wrest it free. "Father!" she whined, struggling with Raven.

Exasperated, Eugor reached for the flask, but before he could take it away, the acid inside spilled onto Raven's right hand and Carya's left. Carya began to scream in pain, waving her burnt hand as the acid seared her flesh.

Mug rushed over with a container and poured its contents onto her hand while Eugor frantically inspected Raven's hand, where there were no signs of trauma.

As Mug bandaged Carya's hand, the older sister glared at the younger through tears before tossing a full glass of liquid at Raven. "You're a monster!"

Suddenly, five years had passed, and the sisters were underwater. It felt like a long time since they'd come up for air. They swam downward through a tight channel until it opened, and they saw the light on the surface.

"I found it yesterday," Carya said, floating on her back. "I never knew I could hold my breath that long, but apparently, you can, too."

Raven jumped out of the water to inspect the incredible cavern as the last torch began to burn out. "Our secret sister spot, but we'll need a better light source." The cavern plunged into darkness. "Carya! Where are you?" Raven stumbled in the dark, moving toward the water where her sister had gone missing but then fallen in. Raven swam to the surface, splashing and crying for her older sister.

An orb lit Carya's face as she screamed, "You're a monster!"

Raven awoke, sat straight up, covered in a cold sweat, and yelled, "A monster!"

"Don't worry," Izarra said in a calm voice. "Thomas and your father are searching for the monster that did this."

After a quick moment, Raven realized she was back in her bedroom wearing her lazy day tunic and cloth breeches. Carya, Izarra, and Mara gathered around her bed, staring at her anxiously.

Carya sat down and replaced the icy cloth on her sister's face.

Raven pushed it aside and hugged her sister. "I'm sorry."

"For what?"

"I never said I was sorry for burning your hand," Raven cried, clinging tightly to her sister.

"It's fine," Carya replied lovingly. "That was long ago, but you need to keep this ice on your swelling."

Raven replaced the cold cloth on her face and glanced up at her sister. "Your freeze spells finally coming in handy?"

"You warm my teas. I cool your swelling head," Carya teased. "Isn't this how it's supposed to work?"

Raven managed a grin as she noticed her mother in tears. "Did I miss the party?"

"No," Mara answered with a faint chuckle, placing an ointment in a basket. "We should probably cancel it."

"No, no, I'm fine," Raven reassured everyone. "I just might look like ogre poop," she joked, drawing a giggle from her sister. She tried to move. "I definitely *feel* like ogre poop."

Carya and Izarra helped Raven stand.

"Do you want to get ready?" Mara asked.

"I forgot to pick up our dresses," Izarra realized. "I wanted to surprise you."

"I'm just glad you saved my life," Raven answered, hugging Izarra. "That's worth more than any dress."

"Can we get a wizard here to ensure she's not a doppelganger?" her older sister joked.

"Carya," Mara scolded.

Carya laughed. "One more hug and Euphrasia will explode."

"That will change," Raven said, "I promise. But let me freshen up, and I'll be right down."

"Do you want some help?" asked her mother as Izarra and Carya finished packing the healing supplies.

"I'm fine. I want some privacy," Raven replied. It was more curtly than she had intended, and the three women scurried out of the room. She walked to her water basin and tried to make out her reflection in the still water. The battle damage was a black and blue eye. *They must have had ice on it for a while because the swelling has significantly decreased.* She splashed some water on it and moaned slightly at the pain. She washed up as best she could and dressed in the comfortable black, gold-trimmed robe she'd received from Gideon on her last birthday.

There was a knock on the door. "I'll be down shortly," Raven responded, but there was a knock again. "Mother!" Annoyed, she wrenched open the door, but to her shock, it wasn't Mara.

Gideon, clad in his Celestial gold armor, his hands and white wings tucked behind his back. "How are you feeling?"

"As well as can be expected after a five-on-one fight, I guess."

"Impressive." Gideon inspected her eye more closely. "I can't imagine what the others look like."

"Four of them are dead, so not too good."

Gideon stood, rocking and smiling as if waiting to shout something.

That's not a typical response after telling someone you killed four people. "Please, come in."

"Happy birthday, Raven." He handed her a black box with a purple ribbon tied around it.

"Thank you, Gideon, but shouldn't you be watching over our realm?"

"I am," he assured her as he held up his gauntlet, and the inlaid red gem blinked.

Raven frowned. "Do you have to go?"

"Give it a moment," he replied as they watched it stop. "Probably the nymphs in Thistlebane again."

"Shouldn't you check it out?"

"If it were something serious, it would blink and then turn to a glow," Gideon explained. "After all these years, I've learned when to check. Otherwise,

I wouldn't have a life." He noticed the look on Raven's face. "But don't worry, I'll keep an eye on it."

"Good," Raven said, swept with relief. "Can't let the realm fall into chaos—at least not tonight."

"I see you like the robe," Gideon smiled, changing the subject.

"Of course! I don't want to sound like a greedy hobgoblin, but I look forward to your gifts. Don't get me wrong—you don't have to get me anything. I would be just as pleased to have you here." Raven removed the lid from the box as he flashed a smile. "Wow! It's beauteous!" she exclaimed as Gideon removed the silver circlet from the box, placing it on her head. The black onyx in the middle gleamed in the light. "Is it magical?"

"Of course! I know you love your magical items. And as a bonus, the onyx matches your bruised eye."

"Funny," Raven responded sarcastically. "So, how does it work?"

He handed her a piece of parchment. "Chant these words, $Visus\ Verum$, and it will activate True Seeing."

"Meaning?" Raven asked as she studied the parchment.

"It means you can see through illusions, see things or people that are invisible, identify secret doors, and even see in a spell of Darkness."

"So, I can finally prove that Carya has been an ogre all this time!" Raven quipped. "But seriously, I can't wait to test it out." She set down the scroll and hugged him.

"But we need to get you to the Inn," he said. "I volunteered to be the one to tell you that everyone has returned."

"Did they catch him?"

Gideon shook his head. "Not yet . . . but we will."

They walked downstairs and into the kitchen as Eugor entered the secret passage. When he saw his daughter, he ran over for a hug.

"I'm fine, Father," Raven assured him as Eugor admired the circlet on her head.

"That's one more Gideon gift to add to your collection." Eugor glanced at the smirking guardian. "I'm not sure when this became a competition."

"That's just part one," Gideon said proudly.

"No," Raven retorted, "this is more than enough."

"He's just rubbing it in," her father said scornfully.

Gideon shrugged.

"But Father, I'm still wearing your—" Raven stopped when she realized she was barefooted. "See, those boots are so comfortable and quiet, I thought I was still wearing them!"

Her father put his arm around her as they walked through the passage and exited his work chamber into the bar. Raven glanced across the room, watching Brugg hand out treats to the children dressed as dragons at the front door. Cee was behind the bar, filling a mug as Thomas waited patiently for the drink.

"Excuse me," Raven uttered to Eugor and Gideon as she rushed up to Thomas and hugged him tightly. "Thank you, Brown Eyes, for saving my life."

"Just doing my job, Princ—Raven," Thomas said, smiling broadly.

Cee exited the bar area past Carya, who was strolling down the hall with an odd expression. Raven wasn't sure why, but suddenly, there seemed to be a wagon full of tension in the room, so she backed away from Thomas just before her sister arrived.

"He's been so helpful today," Carya said, wrapping her arm around his.

"Not again," Raven replied impatiently, deducing that Carya was wearing her heart on her sleeve.

"What?" Carya asked.

"We should go," Eugor chimed in.

They all walked to the banquet hall together. Raven hung back with Gideon while Thomas and Carya chatted in front. She noticed her sister grabbing the paladin's arm, touching his shoulder, and giggling.

Carya only giggles when she's making fun of me.

Thomas didn't seem to be responding. Eugor led the pack, as always, but his steps were slower than usual, and he kept glancing back to ensure Raven was still with them. What had happened today must have worried her parents greatly, but she wasn't a child anymore. They had to understand that there would always be danger. Gideon interrupted her thoughts by nudging her with his elbow, trying to keep a straight face.

Eugor, Carya, and Thomas broke off to the side of the open doors as all the guests greeted her with "HAPPY BIRTHDAY!"

Cyndi and her merry-bard band struck up some music, and Mara approached Raven and embraced her. "Happy birthday, my darling," she said, a slight tremor in her voice.

Raven's elf grandparents from Suttiir then greeted her. It was rare that they came down from the elf city to Omlett. They bombarded her with questions about her eye and the attack, but her father interjected, much to Raven's relief.

"No more talk about the events earlier today," Eugor commanded. "Let us just celebrate this special occasion." He handed her a drink, winked, and diverted the conversation with his parents to stories of their recent travels.

Raven excused herself and walked around the perimeter, surveying the room. A tall, sharply dressed elf followed the local magic shop's owner, Maggie McGee, who stopped and inspected Raven's eye.

Raven flinched. "It could have been worse if it wasn't for the spells you taught me."

The tall elf huffed. "Unauthorized spell training."

Maggie bit her lip.

The elf straightened up, hands behind his back, clad in an elegant black robe with gold trim. His gray hair was slicked back, showing off his piercing green eyes. "I thought I taught you better, Miss McGee."

"I didn't train her in anything over level two," Maggie responded. "Raven, this is Waterfront's Headmaster, Gavan Taiker."

Raven reached out her hand. "It's such an honor that you would attend my party."

Headmaster Taiker ignored the gesture. "I'm sorry, Miss Naelo—I can't risk touch spells. After glancing around awkwardly, he spat out, "But your family has a lovely tavern."

Maggie handed Raven a long, thin box. "I hope it comes in handy, like my spells."

Raven opened the box and saw a scroll tied with a ribbon, "Maggie, you didn't have to—"

"Nonsense," Maggie interrupted. "Home should always be a scroll away."

"It's a portal scroll to Omlett?" Raven asked with delight. When Maggie nodded, Raven hugged the woman tightly and excitedly said, "Thank you, Maggie! I'll have Gideon teach me how to activate this."

"A guardian attending the party, too," Headmaster Taiker stated. "Fascinating."

This paranoid elf gives me the creeps.

"All Omlett scroll portals will open up at the church, so you may need to make travel arrangements." Maggie hugged Raven again, then left with Taiker as Shorte and Buzz'diir approached.

"Man, all I got was a drink named after me," Shorte complained. "Guess it wasn't too bad because it pissed off an entire gnome village—Castle Light Wolf."

"Shorte," Buzz'diir chuckled, "let her enjoy her night."

"You know, gnomes are short," Shorte continued. "I guess they're sensitive about their stature."

"I get it," Raven mused. "You're not much taller."

"Indeed"—he puffed out his chest—"but I'm an adventure bag packed full of confidence."

"Of course you are," she said, smiling as she glanced around. "Have you seen Thomas?"

Shorte released the air from his chest and asked, "The clean-shaven dragon fodder?"

Raven eyed him sternly.

Shorte sighed. "The last I saw him, your sister had him cornered by the food table. Those two have been inseparable since this morning."

"Really?" Raven asked, trying to hide her disappointment.

"He's replacing Stone-Prayer at the church," Buzz'diir said.

Shorte grunted. "Temporarily, I hope."

"Speaking of which, Princess," Buzz'diir interjected. "Cleric Stone-Prayer wished you a happy birthday, too. But with what happened at the church—"

"I'll thank him when he gets back. I'm glad you both could make the party," Raven replied, trying to avoid the subject. "Will you excuse me?" She walked over to the feasting table, where Gary and Miss Crinkly replenished the food. *Thomas and Carya aren't here.*

"Happy birthday!" the two gnomes exclaimed together.

All the attention Raven was getting made her uneasy. Placing down her scroll, she made herself a plate of food from the buffet: boar meat, pumpkin, apples, squash, and fresh bread. "Mmmm . . . delicious," she said, biting into a roll.

"You're too kind, my dear, but make sure you save room for your cake," Miss Crinkly said, smiling.

"I will." Raven turned and walked away, leaving her plate and scroll behind. She noticed Gideon and Brugg in the corner with some children, the orc entertaining them with his famous orc swing. Those who waited admired and touched Gideon's wings with expressions of awe on their small faces while the guardian inspected the dragon costumes of some who ended their special night early.

Raven witnessed Izarra chugging a mug of ale near the drink bowls with Rusty and his cousin Pixie from Iron Cliff. *That looks like trouble.* As she made her way through the crowd, she glanced toward the middle of the room and saw Mug controlling a massive device. The Illusion Ball started to spin, and the mirage began. The young dwarf sitting atop the apparatus was now riding a giant, gray elephant.

"Wow!" Izarra exclaimed, startling Raven. The tipsy half-nymph dropped her chin on the rogue's shoulder.

"Izarra! Some warning next time."

"The Illusion Ball?" Izarra asked, ignoring Raven's scolding.

"Yes. Are you drunk?"

"Maybe a little." Izarra grinned, turning her empty mug upside down.

"RAVEN!" Mug yelled. "Come on, birthday girl! Your turn."

As a young dwarf slid off the mechanism, Raven hesitantly approached the machine. *If a child can do it, how scary can it be?*

"Go on! Hop up and take a seat," Mug encouraged as he fiddled with the controllers, appearing proud of his new contraption.

Raven took a deep breath, climbed into the saddle, and strapped herself to the mechanism. The leather seat felt warm between her legs as she adjusted her feet in the stirrups and grabbed the reins. *It's not so bad—it's like taking Ghost on a joy ride to Suttiir.* The vibrations tingled her thighs as cogs began to spin inside. The tickle sensation moved higher. She sucked in her lips. *All right, maybe not!*

"Pick a creature or animal," instructed Mug.

Shorte raised his tankard and called out, "A dragon!" which drew everyone's attention to the middle of the room.

"A black dragon," Mug smiled. "Ahhh, that brings back memories. How appropriate for Dragomas." He activated the Illusion Ball, and the crowd cheered in unison as the ride transformed into a magnificent black dragon.

"I'm next, I'm next," Izarra shouted, taking Shorte's drink out of his hand.

Shorte froze agape. "Did she just take a drink from a dwarf?" he asked incredulously to anyone within earshot.

Izarra bent over to be eye level with Shorte and teased, "You are so cute when you're angry."

Raven ceased laughing when the dragon sprung off from the ground and soared through the sky as the Illusion Ball transformed the room, white clouds the only thing visible. "This is amazing, Mug," she called out, assuming he was still nearby. She wondered if the Illusion Ball blocked sound because she didn't hear any response. "Can it go faster?"

The dragon picked up speed, taking a nosedive toward the ground, and flew back up, launching Raven's adrenaline to an all-time high. The excitement triggered something inside her, and she felt her body cast an involuntary spell. Suddenly, she was sitting in complete darkness and heard people panicking, trying to find their way to the doors. She listened to her father yelling for Mug.

"It's not the device or the Illusion Ball," Mug answered.

Raven struggled momentarily to recall the words of the True Seeing spell that activated her new circlet, "Verbis . . . Virbum . . ." but finally, she got it to work. "Visus Verum." She jumped off the machine and screamed out in pain as her chest burned, then stumbled out the courtyard door, crashing into Thomas. People scurried for the exits; others stood or sat still, waiting for the chaos to end.

"Carya?" Thomas asked as he held her in his arms.

"No," Raven cried as she hugged him in the darkness. "It's me."

"What's going on?" Thomas asked nervously. "You're trembling. Are you all right?"

Her breath intensified as she sobbed in Thomas's arms. Gideon's voice echoed through the courtyard door as he cast a spell to counteract the darkness.

"Sounds like it was just a Darkness spell," Thomas whispered to her reassuringly as they watched rays of sunlight fill the room.

"Where's Raven?" someone called out.

Then Gideon entered the courtyard and asked, "Are you all right?" but his voice seemed colder than usual.

"I'm fine." She wiped away her tears and pulled away from Thomas. "Where are my parents?"

"I saw them and Carya tending to the guests," Gideon answered curtly. "Most of them are leaving."

"It's my fault." She began to cry again, and Thomas embraced her.

"I'll tell your father you're out here in good hands," Gideon said grimly.

Raven heard the courtyard door close. She wasn't sure why, but she felt even worse.

"He didn't seem too pleased," Thomas observed.

Raven glanced up at him, confused.

"Is there something between you two?"

"Gideon? He's a family friend."

"Are you good to return to the party?"

Raven nodded and Thomas extended his arm to escort her back into the banquet room. The ballroom was empty. She couldn't help noticing the mess—upended tables and chairs, food and gifts sprawled all over the floor. Mug appeared confused, alone in the middle of the room, cursing as he kicked and beat the machine.

"Let's go get something to drink," Thomas suggested.

Raven nodded, and they went to the bar. Rusty and Pixie were chanting excitedly at the *Ebony Tree* portrait, where Izarra's garments were lying on the floor. In the nude, Izarra ran around the tree, teasing the knights.

"It's her second time around the tree," Rusty said, laughing and pointing.

"Izarra!" Raven yelled.

Distracted by Raven's voice, Izarra stopped running long enough for the knights to catch her and expel her from the painting. "No fair," Izarra slurred. "I want a re-do."

Raven removed her robe, put it around Izarra, and then gathered the drunken half-nymph's clothes from the ground. "Rusty, Pixie, we'll discuss this later."

The dwarves' faces became serious. "We're sorry," they slurred in unison.

Raven placed her arm around Izarra. "Thomas, I'll have to pass on the ale. I need to get her to bed."

"Of course," Thomas agreed. "I'm in room nine if you need me any more tonight."

"Room nine," Izarra repeated. "That's my room. Let's make our way to room . . . nine."

"No, Izarra, you gave that room away, remember?" Raven explained as if talking to a child.

Izarra shook her head and then nodded. "I'm in the room . . . four." She held up three fingers, but Raven folded them down.

"You can bunk with me tonight."

"Oh, I get to stay at the castle," Izarra said, bringing her head closer to Ravens, "with the princess."

Raven flinched when the alcohol breath hit her, and her nose wrinkled. "There's no castle," she responded, shaking her head as Thomas laughed.

Leaving the festivities to the others, Raven helped Izarra to her bedroom and placed the tipsy half-nymph on Carya's old bed. While pulling up the covers on her friend, she wondered if Izarra might be all right alone. *Room nine.* The thought quickly faded as she realized how exhausted she was from all the crying and an overall rough day. She glanced over and noticed Maggie's scroll box sitting on top of another enormous box that almost filled the entire surface of her bed. She eagerly opened a card resting on top and read:

> *Part two, just for you. New Year, New Gear.*
> *Happy birthday! —Gideon*

Opening the box, Raven shook her head and stared in disbelief. "Gideon!"

CHAPTER TWELVE

AN UGLY SOUL

After an extensive search, Courtlynn arrived in the mind of Aushade, who lived on Fellswar's Claim, a small island between Fellswar and Euphrasia's west coast. She sat back and watched as he dreamed of himself as a boy, surrounded by war orcs as he screamed for his father and brother. The fearful paladin boy raised the dead around him to help fight off the orcs, contradicting the beliefs of the paladin class. Suddenly, all the creatures in the dream turned to ash, and he became the tall, dark-brown-skinned man with short, black hair and a stubbly beard—his present appearance.

"Who are you?" Aushade asked as the nude redhead approached. Courtlynn wore only the stone amulet necklace Draklor had given to her.

"I'm Courtlynn."

"Am I dreaming?" he asked as she circled him.

She assessed every inch of his nude body. "Of course."

"You're a succubus, I imagine." He grabbed her hand as she moved to touch him. "Where are your wings?"

"So, you've heard of us," she said, impressed. "Then you know we can take any form we want." In the blink of an eye, her wings and horns returned. As quickly as hers had appeared, Aushade himself was in armor. "You have very good mind control for a mere human."

"What do you want with me?"

"Straight to the point—I like that." Courtlynn was face-to-face with him. "Very direct. Anything you want from me?"

"State your business, or find some drunkards looking for a cheap thrill."

"Fine," she retorted irritably. "To the point . . . my master has a plan and needs a great army, and I'm here to help him get it."

"Go on," Aushade said with interest.

Pulling back her hair, she lifted the artifact. "See this necklace?"

"How can I not? It's the only thing you're wearing."

"Maybe you were distracted by other things," Courtlynn teased, letting her hair fall back down, "but it's the Artifact of the Stolen Souls. It takes the souls of the dead who are not properly buried."

"Intriguing, but my undead armies have no souls," he replied. "I can't help you."

"But imagine," she said, placing her hands on his chest armor, "increasing the size of your army while helping us increase ours. You take the bodies—we take the souls. It's a win-win."

"It doesn't matter who dies?" He rubbed his chin in deep thought.

"Nope, it doesn't matter. Souls are souls."

"So you could help me wipe out the orcs?"

"Anyone . . . you . . . want," she stated, moving in for a kiss. Their lips locked. "I knew I could win you over," she whispered coyly.

"Not doing this for you," Aushade smiled, yanking the necklace off her. "It's for my family."

Courtlynn ran her hands around her bare neck. "Typical dumb human. This is just a dream." The necklace disappeared from Aushade's hand and reappeared around her neck. "Don't worry. I'll get you the real artifact. Just meet a bald mage at the tavern in Grey-Holg very soon."

"You won't bring it yourself?"

"Maybe if you ask nicely," she said, seductively blowing him a kiss, "because I hope I get to flirt with you again, my dark pally."

"In your dreams," Aushade replied as she began to vanish.

Courtlynn grinned. "No, dear—in yours."

CHAPTER THIRTEEN

UNDEAD DREAMS

strick was doubled over on his magic steed, holding his shoulder. The ache radiated from the area, hit by the paladin's shield. The mount vanished as they came across the clearing, and Astrick dropped onto the dirt path below. Wincing in pain, he got to his knees and glanced around, discovering he was just outside Grey-Holg. *This haven should be a safe place for now. They wouldn't dare search for me here.*

Holding his left arm steady, he stumbled over to a tree and slid down the trunk. Pausing to take a deep breath to prepare himself, he slammed his shoulder against the tree to pop it back into place. Grunting in agony, he reached inside his wizard robe and pulled out a Demon Blood whiskey flask. He popped the cork and gulped down a few sips.

As he closed his eyes, he envisioned that damn elf and her friend in his mind's eye. Hatred burned inside him like a raging fire as he fantasized about all the evil things he would do to that princess for killing his friends. *Well, I know what Butch would say. They're better off dead!* The thought made him smile, and he eventually relaxed and dozed off.

Astrick's dreams began replaying the moment at the Omlett church. He had the young princess by the hair, dragging her to his wagon. *Until that ass decided to play hero and ruin everything.* A beautiful woman with fiery red hair wearing tight black leather armor approached him. The image of the shield flashed before his eyes, and he flinched into a cowardly stance. He straightened up, embarrassed, not knowing how much she had just seen. "You look familiar," he stated, glancing around in confusion.

"Don't be afraid," she said, placing her arms on his shoulders and wrapping them around his head. "I've visited you before. How did you think you were able to summon a dretch?"

"I'm just that good," Astrick retorted snidely.

"Not *that* good," Courtlynn responded. "I planted some spells in your sub-conscious the last time I visited you, but I didn't expect you to cast any so soon. The spells are meant to help protect you when you deliver an artifact for me."

"What other spells have you planted?"

"You'll find out all in due time."

Astrick grunted. "Well, I probably have the Realm Guardian hunting me down now."

"You'll be fine," Courtlynn assured him. "I have something to hide you from the guardian."

"Why don't you deliver this artifact yourself?"

"The anti-scry on Floxy isn't powerful enough to continuously keep this much power hidden from the Realm Guardian. His vision would eventually detect us."

"Anti-scry? You must know what type of scry spell the guardian uses."

Courtlynn grinned mischievously.

"You figured it out," Astrick said. "Amazing! You're beautiful *and* smart."

"You're too kind," Courtlynn responded as she kissed him. "But enough with the flattery. I don't have much time and we need to discuss your quest. A demon will soon visit you and hand you the artifact. You must deliver it to a man named Aushade, who is—"

"Aushade! Oh, hell no! That creepy bastard killed two of my men."

"Please, Astrick," Courtlynn interjected, batting her eyelashes. "For me."

Astrick rubbed his beard in thought. "Will you give yourself to me if I complete this?"

"Anything you want. My master will make you powerful and rich."

"Powerful, rich, and you by my side—fine, fine, let's do this before I change my mind."

"A demon will open a portal to you and give you the artifact, and Floxy will remain at your side."

"Where is Aushade?"

"The Grey-Holg Inn," Courtlynn answered, then vanished.

How convenient. Astrick remained in the empty void of his mind. His dreamscape was fuzzy with images that flashed through his mind as he began dreaming again. Courtlynn draped across a throne inside a gorgeous palace, rubbing her thigh as she smiled at him. "Welcome home, my love," said the beautiful illusion. He approached her just as another Courtlynn shimmered into his consciousness.

"Typical male," Courtlynn teased, suddenly bringing his current dream to a halt.

"What?" Astrick asked, confused as the exotic dream of the succubus faded away.

"You are one heavy sleeper. The artifact is already hanging around your neck," Courtlynn said. "And I left you my master's pet to keep you company. Make sure you take care of Floxy for me. He's an extraordinary pet. Now—WAKE UP!"

Astrick jolted awake, startled. He glanced down to see he was covered and thought about how considerate the demon had been until he realized the blanket was crafted from flesh. A stone amulet thudded against his chest as he yanked the skin cover aside. He removed the charm from around his neck and studied it. It was a cone-shaped pendulum made from a crimson jewel—with specks of fire. He had never seen a gem like this before. A low growl came from behind him. He jumped up and saw an oversized, nine-tailed fox creeping toward him. Holding out the amulet, he yelled, "Heel, Floxy!" The fox stopped and sat obediently.

Astrick summoned his magical steed again and headed into Grey-Holg with his new pet. The half-orc city was empty and dead quiet. He placed his head on a swivel as he tightened the reins, bringing his mount to almost a tiptoe as they traveled toward the inn. Upon their arrival, he dropped to his feet and dispelled the magical steed. He stepped onto the porch of the dilapidated inn. Shingles had fallen from the roof, and years of aging had yellowed the window treatments. The smell of old garbage filled his nostrils. "Wait," Astrick commanded. The demon fox obeyed and kept guard at the foot of the steps, facing out toward the city.

Astrick slowly pushed open the moldy black door and entered. In the far corner, three patrons moved gradually. The bartender licked and chewed on a glass mug. The wizard quickly realized something wasn't right and turned to leave, but the door slammed closed, and a tall person with black and silver armor stood staring down at him.

"Aushade?" Astrick asked, bowing nervously.

The mysterious knight nodded.

"A succubus is searching for you," Astrick said, raising his arms in a feeble attempt to hold back the dark knight.

"I know," Aushade responded, tapping his helmet. "I won't grant her access to my thoughts again."

Astrick surveyed the inn to avoid staring at the menacing figure.

"You have something for me?"

"No, I don't. As a matter of fact, I should be going."

"Did she visit you?"

"Yes, but only in my dreams."

Aushade clenched his fist, but before Astrick could duck, the fist caught him on the side of his head, knocking him out cold.

A vision flashed of a dagger piercing Bo in the forehead. The dread rushed back as Astrick stared at that damned elf holding up her other weapon, casting a spell. The horses from his carriage kicked and dashed off as he lost his balance and fell back into Aushade's arms. "How the hell are you in my head now?"

"You're a wizard. You figure it out." He paused. "Who's that?" he asked, eyeing the dark-haired elf.

"A professional arcane assassin from Mizzendale," Astrick lied in response. "She followed us to Omlett from the Dark Forest and killed my men." His mind betrayed him as the words echoed through his head—*I cannot admit a princess murdered my boys.*

Aushade chuckled. "A princess . . . interesting—well, call out to the succubus."

Knowing the necro would confront the demon, Astrick admitted, "Yes, yes . . . she did give me an artifact."

"I'm glad I could knock the truth out of you," Aushade said, smiling maliciously.

The beautiful redhead appeared again, surprised to see Aushade with Astrick in the dream world. "My dark pally!" Courtlynn exclaimed. "Where have you been?"

Aushade tapped on his helmet again.

Courtlynn folded her arms. "Tsk, tsk, that's not very nice. I know you don't sleep with that thing on."

"Why didn't you just give it to him?" Astrick huffed.

"He's been avoiding me, plus I needed someone else's help," the sweet-talking succubus explained.

Astrick shrugged his shoulders. "Lucky me."

"We have the issue settled, so I'll be going now," Aushade said as he vanished.

"Playing hard to get," Courtlynn replied with a smirk.

"What about me?" Astrick felt like a fool. "I thought we had a deal!"

Courtlynn ignored him and disappeared, too.

Astrick woke with a gasp as cold water splashed onto his face, and he immediately checked his neck to find the artifact missing. Glancing up, he saw Aushade facing away from him, placing the artifact around his neck before sliding his helmet back on. A loud moaning came from outside, and Astrick peeked out the inn door to see Aushade's massive army of undead orcs and half-orcs falling into formation.

"Let's go. We've got work to do," Aushade said, lifting Astrick by his collar.

"Where are we going?"

"South. I'll grow my army with more dead orcs."

"What about the guardian?"

Aushade pushed him through the doorway. "He can't interfere. I'm not from a different realm." Flox growled as Aushade approached.

"But the artifact and that . . . *thing* . . . are," Astrick said, pointing to the oversized flox.

Aushade held up the artifact as Floxy brushed against him. "If Courtlynn said the flox would block the guardian's vision, then he will block the guardian's vision."

Astrick watched the undead soldiers gather, searching for his old buddies Bob and Stanley.

"But you will return to Omlett and handle your *assassin* problem."

Astrick's face dropped. "Do I have to?"

"There's a shop with scrolls down the road. Grab one for Omlett. I don't want any loose ends interfering with our operation. Then we will meet up with Courtlynn outside the village of Yatur. The next step will be known when the time comes."

Astrick felt a large lump in his throat. "I'll take care of it."

"And if you cross me," Aushade warned, "you will join *my* ranks . . . just like your associates."

CHAPTER FOURTEEN

CRAZY TIMES

Raven lay still as her black eye throbbed with the beat of her heart. Her back muscles ached as she rolled to her side. Images of the church fight raced through her mind. *Where are my daggers?* Her eyes shot open when she heard a groan. She'd forgotten Izarra was sleeping in Carya's old bed.

"Am I a lich?" Izarra moaned. "I feel like I was stepped on by a frost giant and then raised from the dead."

I feel the same way.

The half-water nymph struggled to untangle herself from the heavy covers, eventually conceding defeat and sprawling in the middle of the bed.

Raven sat up slowly and glanced at her friend, amused. "You're not a powerful wizard. Last time I checked, you weren't immortal either. So no, you're not a lich." Raven whipped her covers off, watching Izarra finally pry the sheet and blanket. "I'm sure it had nothing to do with the twelve pints of ale you drank last night. You really should learn to pace yourself."

"Yes, *Mother*," Izarra joked, freeing herself from the fabrics. Her robe fell open, exposing the sides of her breasts as she ran her fingers through her curly hair. "Rusty and Pixie kept filling my mug. I lost track."

"Never try to outdrink a dwarf," Raven warned as she rubbed gunk from her eyes.

Izarra circulated her fingers across her temples. "Now you tell me."

Inspecting the dirt on her hands, Raven rose from the bed. "I need to freshen up."

"Me too." Izarra sat up. "I smell like the Cache Tavern."

"You can use the washroom down the hall."

"Great!" Izarra said, sliding out of bed as the sides of the robe split open completely.

Raven quickly turned her head. "You might want to secure that first."

"You're right," Izarra said, grabbing the tie string. "I don't want to blind anyone accidentally."

Raven didn't know if her friend was serious, but there were rumors that water nymphs could blind people with their beauty. "It would have been nice to know that last night."

"I'm jesting," Izarra said playfully, rubbing her hands over the material. "I love this robe. It's so soft."

"It was a gift from Gideon."

"I should have guessed. The guardian certainly loves to shower you with presents." Izarra moved toward the door but paused to point at the long box on the floor beside Raven's bed. "What's that?"

Raven bit her lip. "Birthday gift from—"

"Gideon," Izarra blurted out. "Where can I find a handsome guardian to surprise me with lavish items? Am I not worthy?"

"He's like family." *Why do I have to keep explaining this to people?*

"So? He's still handsome."

"Do you know how old he is?" Raven asked incredulously as she climbed out of bed.

"He's an *elf*. He could be one thousand, and I'd still court him. Do you even know how elves age?"

"Kinda. My father explained it when I was younger."

"Answer me this. Would you court a twenty-one-year-old elf?"

Raven carefully answered as if it were a trick question. "I suppose."

"Wrong!" Izarra spat. "The elf would be mistaken for a three-year-old human toddler."

"Eww . . ."

"Exactly. For an elf to be as mature as us, they'd have to age one hundred and twenty-six years."

"My father always mentioned Gideon's age stuck at one hundred and forty-seven after the ritual."

"That's why he appears to be around twenty-one human years. And you, my friend, are one year closer to his maturity level."

Raven rubbed her temples. "This is giving me a headache. It's too early for a math lesson." She turned away, embarrassed, and retrieved a fresh towel from the side table.

"Just be glad your birthday falls on Dragomas Day. Mine's on Trickster Day."

"Sounds fun."

"Not really—my mother once pretended she forgot and scared me with a surprise party in Mizzendale. It's not the safest place to have everyone jump at you. I dowsed the crowd with my decanter, which extinguished the candles on the cake. It isn't my fault they insist on using the dwarven tradition with the torches."

The story made Raven smirk. "We should get ready for the day."

"So, what shall us ladies be doing today?" her friend continued, changing the subject.

"Are you my personal shadow now?"

"Of course," Izarra agreed. "Will you show me more of the city?"

Raven cringed. "I don't know if it's safe. That mage is still out there."

"You can't hide in your room forever. You're leaving for camp tomorrow."

"I know. I'll probably face more menacing things than an angry mage."

Izarra stepped out into the hallway and peeped her head back into the room. "Like living with Gideon for three years."

Ignoring the innuendo, Raven continued, "I've been waiting to train with him since Maggie taught me basic cantrips and spells when I was fourteen. I'm just excited to learn advanced spells."

"Unh-hunh, exciting . . . stimulating . . . we all have our preferences."

Throwing the towel at her friend, Raven then pointed down the hall. The simple movements made her bicep ache. As she rubbed her arm, Izarra popped her head back in.

The half-nymph whispered, "Someone tried to murder your door."

"What?" Raven grumbled as she staggered to the opening. This time, a dagger stuck in the door without a note from her father. *Not again!* It was the weapon that struck the blond archer's head. *What was his name again?* She grabbed and tossed the dagger near the washbasin while stretching her sore limb. *Bo?*

In the still water, the reflection of her bruised eye and now-puffy cheek reminded her of the assault. Astrick's voice rang in her mind: *I'm taking you to Koport, where I will kill you slowly.*

Raven shuddered and glanced back in the basin. *I think I'll hold off on the bathing hole for today, or am I hiding?* Grabbing her hair tie, she styled her hair into a ponytail and splashed her face one last time. The small cut on her lip stung again. *But if I ever run into that guy again, he'll pay.* Moving toward her wardrobe, she picked out her clothes for the day. After dressing, she gazed down at the box that held her new armor. The dragon scales were smooth against her fingers. She closed the box and slid it under the bed. *Wait till my father sees this! Gideon outdid himself this year.*

Loud voices from downstairs interrupted her thoughts as she drifted out to the hallway. Raven descended the stairs to find her mother and Shorte at the kitchen table and Carya in front of a sizzling pan.

"You must flip'em," Shorte explained, "before you burn'em."

"Will you quit worrying," Carya snickered, inching the spatula near whatever she was cooking. "I won't burn them."

Shorte stopped crushing the stuff in his stone mortar. "If you wasted my grapeseed oil, I'll—"

"What the spell?" Raven interrupted from the bottom of the steps as her mother approached.

"Morning, dear," Mara replied, holding her daughter's chin and inspecting her eyes. "How are you feeling?"

"Sore, but I'll survive," Raven answered, pulling away.

"I'll make you some peppermint tea," her mother said, hurrying to Carya's side to get the kettle.

"I wish I were there," Shorte grunted, grinding even harder. "I would have—"

"It smells good," Raven exclaimed, changing the subject. She walked toward the skillet and then peeped over Carya's shoulder. "What are you *trying* to cook?" The smell of fried batter made her stomach rumble with hunger.

"Shorte's flour-jacks," Carya responded, flipping the last one. "Golden brown perfection."

Shorte chuckled. "That's my girl."

Raven joined him and plucked a berry from the bowl in the center of the table. The dwarf held up the mortar filled with a brown paste, and she stuck her finger in, slowly bringing it to her mouth.

The dwarf gave her a confused look. "It's for your eye, silly."

Carya and her mother glanced back and laughed.

"It's arnica ointment. It should help with the swelling," Shorte said.

Raven grabbed the bowl and used her finger to apply the paste around her eye and cheek. Instantly, a cooling sensation settled over the puffy skin. She handed the extra back to Shorte. "Thank you." Her mother placed the mug of piping hot tea on the table. The smell of peppermint tickled Raven's nose. She gently blew on the steaming liquid as Carya brought over a plate with hot flour-jacks.

"Don't get used to it," her sister joked as she turned to clean off the pan.

Shorte squinted at the food as if giving it a final inspection. "Not bad, Carya, but you forgot the maple syrup."

"I'll get it," Mara replied, quickly turning to the counter and placing the clay pitcher on the table next to the tea.

Raven poured syrup on the hot cakes, then took a bite as they watched her. "Mmm," she moaned, shoving another bite into her mouth.

Shorte snatched a knife and added butter to her flour-jacks. "Can't forget that either."

"Aren't you two supposed to be at the church?" Raven said with a mouth full.

"Raven, manners," Mara scolded. "Finish chewing first."

"You don't know?" Carya asked as she paused to wipe the pan.

"The entryway was torched," Shorte explained, cleaning up his area of the table. "Your father has a crew there now." The dwarf tossed the excess arnica roots in a bin and poured himself a mug of tea.

The image of the fiery projectile piercing High Priest Carne gave Raven the chills. "Where's Father?"

"His work chamber, but you should be resting today," her mother recommended. "You leave for Gideon's camp tomorrow."

"Mother, I'm fine. I have things to do today." Raven finished the last sip of tea and set down the mug. Footsteps from the stairwell made everyone at the table stare. Izarra reached the bottom of the stairway, still wearing her robe, but it was apparent she had nothing underneath.

"I hope you don't mind," Izarra said, with her wet hair dangling. "My clothes are covered in—oh! Flour-jacks! May I have some?"

Carya huffed and prepared the pan for more. The dwarf raised his eyebrow at Raven as the half-naked water nymph moved to join them at the table.

"Shorte, no," the rogue whispered as Mara placed a chair at the table for Izarra.

The dwarf split a roll with an innocent expression and began buttering it. "I didn't say anything."

"Hello, I'm Izarra."

Shorte tensed up. "I know." He cleared his throat and stared at the roll basket. "You stole my drink last night."

"Hmm . . . it's all a blur." Izarra grinned. "I'm sorry."

Shorte nodded as he stuffed the last piece in his mouth and excused himself, continuing to avoid any eye contact.

"What's wrong with him?" Izarra whispered to Raven.

Raven shrugged and stood. "I need to speak with Father. I'll return shortly."

"One moment, you two. Don't forget the family dinner is tonight," Mara called out. "Gideon is attending, and Izarra, you are also invited—"

"Thank you," Izarra replied, pulling the bowl of berries toward her as Carya delivered a plate of flour-jacks.

Mara continued. "Shorte, don't forget to mention it to Buzz." The dwarf raised his hand before exiting the kitchen area. "And Raven, if you see Thomas, please extend the invitation."

Carya gritted her teeth and whispered, "Mother, that's been taken care of."

"Why are you so far up his shite hole?" Raven snapped as Carya gasped and Izarra dropped her utensils.

"Raven Jade Naelo, watch your language," Mara scolded.

"Izarra, I'll meet you at the Inn." Raven dashed toward the secret entrance. She hurried down the passageway, holding her side as a wave of anger rushed through her. *What's wrong with me?*

As Raven approached the door, she took a deep breath, twisted the mug toward the double daggers, and prepared to push it, but she stopped when she heard her father talking to someone. She opened the secret bookcase just enough to poke her head in. Her father and Gideon were sitting in tall leather chairs facing the fireplace. A massive, crackling fire filled the hearth. Raven watched the dark liquid slosh in the glass as her father toasted the portrait hanging above the mantel.

The oversized, two-century-old parchment had seen better days. The colors had faded, and small tears on the edges peeked out from the frame. The portrait was a gift given to Eugor before Celeste—his beloved then—and Gideon departed for Waterfront for eight years.

Gideon had hired a bard to paint the image of the three friends early in the morning to immortalize their friendship. Raven had heard the story a million times about how hard it was for her father to watch them leave for the institution.

Even though Raven had passed the picture millions of times, she paused to study it this time. Gideon stood with an ear-to-ear grin, relaxed in his dark blue robes, hands gripping the backs of the chairs, casually leaning forward between his seated friends. *And he's actually smiling.* Celeste was radiant in light blue robes that matched her eyes perfectly, and her face beamed, eyeing Eugor with her hand on his lap. Her father's jet-black hair was a mess, his face full of befuddlement. He sat on Celeste's right, wearing a black leather chest piece and short black braies.

As Raven approached, they turned to eye her.

"Happy Septi-Di," her father toasted. She was baffled by the term.

Gideon explained, "It's the elven birthday celebrated every seven years."

"I regret not teaching you and your sister more elf traditions." Eugor clanked Gideon's glass with his own while Raven mentally calculated—again. Her head still ached from Izarra's earlier conversation about the aging system.

"The math is off," Raven said, shooting him a half-grin as he refilled his glass.

Gideon rose, offering his seat. "Please join us." The fire reflected off his eyes as he conjured a small, gilded chair, and she sat, trying to ignore her pain. The comments Izarra had made about him flashed through her mind, making her blush. *Gideon is attractive.*

"Showoff," her father teased his old friend, pulling Raven back from her thoughts. "All that hocus-pocus for a chair. What you need are tools. *Real* tools."

"Magic *is* a tool," Gideon replied with a grin, taking a sip. She was witnessing what they must have been like in their youth. *Gideon looks precisely like the portrait, though maybe a bit more mature.*

"You should try this," her father said, handing his glass to her. "This is better than that dwarven ale you love so much."

Raven took a whiff, scrunched her nose, and then slowly sipped it. She pulled it away with a sour look. "What is it?"

"Orc whiskey from the exotic land of Fellswar," Eugor answered. "I've had it for a couple of decades. It was an I'm-glad-you're-alive gift from your uncle before the Fellswar Castle was invaded. I also have the vase your mother gave me for my recovery room."

Raven glanced up at the flue. Along the sides were artifacts, souvenirs from all his adventures, and a longbow belonging to her half-brother, Blade.

"That vase—" Eugor began, getting choked up, ". . . once held the most beauteous flowers . . . imaginable." He swallowed another mouthful of his drink.

"But isn't it early to be drinking?" Raven asked, disappointed.

"Not if you haven't slept yet," her father replied as she noticed his bloodshot eyes.

It's either from lack of sleep or alcohol. Even with her father trying to hide behind the liquor, she felt his pain.

"It's been a very long day," Eugor continued.

Raven glanced back at Gideon, who was staring at the portrait with a concerned expression. She was hoping the guardian, Eugor's friend, would step in to offer comfort.

"So, what can I help you with, dear?" her father asked.

I honestly forgot what I wanted to ask.

An awkward silence filled the room. Raven was about to speak when Gideon interrupted. "I still think that portrait captured your bony knees well, Night Breeze."

Raven let out an unexpected chuckle. She always thought it was silly that her father's childhood nickname was just the Elvish translation of Naelo. *Gideon*

99

always has a way to lighten the mood. As the two eyed her, she took a deep breath. "You never asked how I'm feeling."

"You told me you were fine last night, but I'll leave the coddling to your mother," Eugor said, taking another sip. "Because I know how you feel. Bruised eye and ego." Her father slumped back in his chair. "Gideon, remember when my eyes were swollen shut?"

"I sure do," Gideon answered with a playful grin. "But I did warn you! Wear eye protection."

"What happened?" Raven asked in amusement.

"Sand fleas is what happened." Eugor chuckled, then finished his drink. "Searching for a stone tablet with special runes near the Pyramid Dunes of Sand Castle."

"It was their graduation test," Gideon said, leaning close as the smell of fresh-cut pine wafted toward her. "It was over a century ago, and he blames me for everything."

Her heart fluttered as Gideon pulled away.

"I still believe a colony of those fleas resides behind my eye socket," Eugor replied, pouring another drink. He sat the bottle back on the mahogany end table.

"Don't forget about the time you almost severed Mug's ear," Gideon said, leaning back in his conjured chair.

Her father almost choked on his drink as he chuckled. "Poor Mug." Eugor ran his hand over the rim of his glass.

Raven tilted her head. "Do tell."

"Rapier plus bad timing plus sunlight"—Eugor combed his hand through his messy hair—"equals disaster. Besides, it was just a flesh wound."

"Un hunh," Gideon mocked. "Imagine your father running around camp frantically screaming, 'CLERIC!' just for a flesh wound."

"Anyhow," Eugor said, stretching, "I think it's time for us elders to retire."

Gideon snickered. "Speak for yourself, Night Breeze. I haven't aged a day since—"

"Yeah, yeah," Eugor interrupted, downing his drink. "I have that painting to remind me how you and Celeste are practically frozen in time, and I'm growing old."

"Eugor, my friend," Gideon pleaded. "You know what I meant."

Raven's heart sank. Her father's aging faster than regular elves always put him in a funk. *I guess watching your friends stay young takes a toll.*

A knock came from the tavern side door. "Enter!" Eugor yelled as he slowly rose from his chair.

Buzz'diir opened and entered. "We found Gus, and it isn't pretty."

Eugor huffed, leaned over, and kissed his daughter on the forehead. "I'm glad you're all right and safe. I wouldn't know what to do if I lost you or your sister. Now, if you'll excuse me."

Gideon puckered his lips. "What? No kiss for me?"

Eugor tossed his empty glass at the guardian.

"Father, please get some rest before our dinner tonight," Raven pleaded.

Her father nodded and escorted Buzz'diir out. As the door shut, she saw Gideon's face turn somber as he stared intently at the fireplace. When he realized she was eyeing him, he smiled and sat the empty glasses down.

"Do you think they'll catch that Astrick guy?" she asked.

"I'm sure they will," Gideon responded. "Even if he has to hire mercenaries."

"Gideon, that armor . . ."

"You're welcome. You'll need it for your training."

"But—"

"Remember the sand fleas!" Gideon snickered as the stone in his gauntlet glowed. He stood, eloquently waving his hands. "Opus Porta." He cast a red portal and walked toward Raven, staring into her eyes. "I'll see you at dinner tonight."

Raven bit her lip and nodded.

He turned back before entering the portal. "Sand fleas."

"Sand fleas." Her heart pounded and her palms were sweaty as he smiled, then vanished. *What the spell?* She wiped off her hands on her tunic, exiting her father's work chamber, and headed toward the bar area. Gathered around the barkeep were three people. One was a male elf with short auburn hair. He had his arm wrapped around a petite female human with chestnut brown hair pinned up in an elaborate twist. Standing before them was a teenage half-elf, who played nervously with her long, braided chestnut hair with auburn highlights. *They seem familiar. I've seen them around town.* The couple hugged their daughter and exited the Inn as Raven moved closer. Cyndi instructed the girl to gather baskets from the pantry. When the bard turned around, she locked eyes with Raven.

"I'm fine," Raven announced, walking closer to the bar.

"That's a nice shiner," Cyndi said before returning behind the counter.

Raven motioned to the back room. "New assistant?"

"Indeed," Cyndi replied, wiping down the bar. "Lilianna Spriglockett, half-elf about five years younger than you. She could use a friend. Her father says she can be hotheaded and stubborn. You have a lot in common."

"Funny," Raven responded. "Does her father work for Mug?"

"Yes. Mivaro has been working with him since Omlett was founded," Cyndi answered, "and her mother, Yulnea, owns the hide tanning shop near Miss Crinkly's bakery."

The teenage half-elf returned with several fruit baskets and sat them on the tables.

"Lilianna," Cyndi called out, "this is Princess Raven Naelo."

Raven huffed. "Cee."

The bard shrugged.

The new help stopped and curtsied. "Princess." Her smile highlighted the freckles on her cheekbones.

"Nice to meet you," the rogue responded. "You can call me Raven."

"Lilly," she replied. "Only my parents call me Lilianna."

Cyndi's words echoed in Raven's mind: *She could use a friend.* "Would you and your parents like to attend our family dinner tonight? After the show?" She surprised herself by offering the invitation.

"That would be wonderful, thank you," Lilly responded, then lifted the empty baskets. "But if you don't mind—"

"No, please, you can return to your duties," Raven replied.

Lilly returned to the pantry but turned back and beamed before entering. "We'll be there by sundown."

Raven nodded and went behind the bar.

Cyndi proudly stacked the last glass. "She's a good kid."

"I'm sure she is," Raven replied, flipping through the ledger. "Still at max capacity, I see." She scrolled her finger down the page until it came across the name in room nine. *Thomas Wellington. He did say I could stop by.*

"Do I need to bring anything for tonight?" Cyndi asked, interrupting Raven's thoughts.

"I can't think of anything," Raven murmured as she walked past the bar in a trance-like state. "I'll see you later." She could feel Cyndi's stare behind her.

Raven climbed the stairs and paced in front of room nine's door. Behind her, she heard her grandparents' voices coming from the royal suite. She took a deep breath and knocked as quietly as possible.

A deep voice called out, "One moment." The door cracked open, and Thomas stood shirtless, staring at her. "Raven," he said, sounding surprised. "To what do I owe the pleasure?"

"You said I could stop by if I wanted . . . *needed* . . . anything."

"Of course," he responded, widening the door. "Please."

Raven hesitantly entered. Once inside, she casually moved her eyes around the room. His paladin armor expertly hung on the armor stand, and his boots sat near the foot of the bed. On the vanity was a small coin pouch with his sword propped against it. The bed had blankets strewn across it, the undersheets balled up in the middle. She heard the door to the wardrobe open and turned to face him as he slipped on his tunic. Raven averted her eyes to the floor as her cheeks reddened. A deep desire inside created a vision in her head of her ripping the shirt back off.

"How are you—"

"Don't," Raven interrupted, glancing up at him. "That's what everyone keeps asking me."

"My apologies," Thomas replied, raising his hand in defense. "It just shows that everyone cares."

"It's true, I suppose." She crossed her arms as Thomas sat on the edge of the bed and patted for her to sit next to him. His rucksack filled the only chair in the room. Giving in, she sat beside him. "I wanted to invite you to our family dinner tonight."

I already know my sister did.

"Thank you," Thomas said politely, "but Carya—"

"I know," she muttered.

"But if you already knew . . . then why are you here?"

"I remember glancing up at you at the church. I never thanked you for saving my life," Raven responded, touching his knee. Her face inched slowly toward his.

He placed a hand on hers and cupped her face with the other, brushing his thumb across her cheek. His hand felt more rugged than expected. "You're welcome, but it's Gideon you should be thanking."

Raven pulled back, puzzled. "What?"

"It's true. I delayed the attack, but that wizard summoned a demon from the Abyss that pinned me down. Gideon vaporized the creature and put out the church fire."

"I just saw him, and he said nothing about interfering."

"It's probably just another workday for him. I don't see the guardian as the bragging type."

Raven quickly shot from her seat and faced the door as she went to leave. She felt Thomas's hand on her shoulder and pressed against her back.

He whispered in her ear. "What do you want, Raven?"

She turned to face him, her back against the door, his dark brown eyes gazing into hers. "I don't know what I want."

His lips formed a frown in disappointment. "Don't know, or too frightened?"

They stared at each other as if playing a mental game of tag.

"What about Carya?" Raven whispered.

"What about her?" Thomas asked in return.

"She likes you," Raven answered. "I—"

"Who do *you* like?"

She shrugged, lowering her eyes to the floor.

He pulled her away and reached around to open the door. "Well then, just let everyone know I'll be happy to attend tonight."

Raven paused momentarily, then rushed downstairs to find Izarra in fresh attire. Lilly and Cyndi accompanied the half-nymph, sitting at a small table near the fireplace.

"Room nine, I assume," Izarra called out. "You sneaky wench."

"Isn't that the paladin's room?" Cyndi teased.

Raven ignored the question and addressed Izarra. "Did Gideon save me?"

"Yes . . ." Izarra responded cautiously, then quickly added, "but he saved Thomas, too—probably all of us."

Raven pulled out a chair and collapsed into it, staring at the flames while she tried to remember the attack. *Why didn't Gideon tell me? Does he think I'm weak now? Am I good enough for the training camp?*

"I must head to the stage for the fall festival rehearsal." Cyndi turned toward Lilly. "Will you handle the Inn until Brugg arrives shortly?"

The younger half-elf nodded.

Cyndi placed her hand on Lilly's shoulder. "I'll return by the mid-sun."

"May we watch the rehearsal?" Izarra asked Raven as Lilly returned to the bar.

"Sure," Raven answered as they followed Cyndi out of the tavern and across the road.

The crew had decorated the amphitheater with dragon banners for the holiday. With each gust of wind, the pendants flapped in celebration. The grass changed colors from vibrant summer green to a dull, withered brown, the sign of winter's approach only a month away. Soon, fresh snow would blanket the ground. *I love the seasons.*

The land sloped upward from the stage to the royal box with four separate sections of a hundred granite benches embedded into the earth. Raven despised those seats for the longest time—as part of her training, her father would have her jump from bench to bench. The main stone stairs led to the royal box, giving them a perfect view of the stage. However, when she and Carya were children, Eugor would take them to sit in the grassy area near the music pit so they could see the performers up close.

"What's it about?" Izarra asked the bard as they approached the stage.

"Dragomas," Cyndi replied, "how that magical day came about. It is the only month to have thirty-one days. We perform it every fall."

Izarra's face lit up. "And—"

"My birthday, I know," Raven responded as Cyndi appeared on stage inspecting the instruments. "I go through this every year." The two girls sat and watched Cyndi's band take their spots in the music pit.

Cee's band was the most eclectic group of performers. An elderly female elf played the lyre, and twin gnome brothers played the lute, mandora, and gittern. The half-orc with green-streaked black hair made the harp sound unique, and a male dwarf with long brown hair that covered his face played various cowbells. Cyndi mainly sang but was known to beat out a few tunes on the timbrel.

"What's the band's name?" Izarra asked.

"The Cee Sharps," Raven answered as they began playing a high-energy fairy tune.

Izarra sprung up and danced. "Join me, Princess!"

"I would rather traverse the waters on the Hydro-Plane of the Abyss," Raven responded, watching her friend dance. "Where are you getting this energy, especially after last night?"

"Us water nymphs have a high metabolism," Izarra responded, still moving to the beat.

"That's crazy."

Izarra giggled. "Why do you think we draw crowds—we're known for our crazy-good times."

CHAPTER FIFTEEN

EMPTY DRAGON'S NEST

As more people arrived for the rehearsal, Raven dragged Izarra away from the stage. They left the amphitheater and crossed the road to the stables. Ghost bobbed her head excitedly as the rogue attached the saddle, and Izarra helped with the reins. "I thought we could visit Miley's Bookshop. I'd like to acquire some things," Raven stated.

"Sure! May we visit Rusty at the Cache Tavern later?" Izarra asked.

Raven felt a knot tighten in the pit of her stomach. *What if Astrick is there?* She knew the fastest way to that tavern would be to travel past the church, but a cold sweat broke out on her skin. "Do you mind if we stay close to the riverside?" Raven asked, "I'm still a bit—"

"Understood," Izarra responded with a tone of sympathy. "I'm your shadow . . . so lead the way."

Raven used a stirrup and the saddle to pull herself onto Ghost, then reached down to help Izarra settle in behind her. Ghost galloped from the barn and headed north toward the shop.

"Is that the prison?" Izarra asked, pointing to the left at the enormous compound.

"Indeed, not only the prison but Buzz's quarters and the barracks for the Omlett Army and the local security squad."

Izarra let out a playful purr. "All those men."

"And women, too," Raven responded proudly.

"I suppose . . . if you're into that."

"Izarra," Raven snapped, blushing, as they dismounted and tied Ghost to a hitch.

Izarra pushed through the front door of the fancy elven bookshop. "Rumor has it that elves are."

Raven brushed past her. "Good for them."

Following behind the rogue, Izarra perused the leather spines on the shelves. "Are there any spell books?"

"No, Maggie has the only spell shop in Omlett."

Izarra returned a book to the shelf. "Why?"

"It was part of the deal my father had with her," Raven answered, studying the inventory, "to train me to cast some low-level spells."

Izarra giggled.

"What?"

"Like how you almost fried that Horck's arse?"

Raven slipped a half grin. "I did, didn't I?"

After finally picking out some books, they approached the counter. Most titles were copies of ancient elven texts containing the tales and history of Euphrasia and the five realms. Raven dropped her last two PIPs on the counter for the two books. The shopkeeper swept the coins into his hands and nodded as she placed the books under her arms.

Izarra smiled curiously and asked, "May we stop at Miss Crinkly's for a blueberry tart?" But her face quickly changed into disappointment as Raven turned her coin pouch upside down, exposing the emptiness.

"Unless you're treating," Raven responded as Izarra dug through her coin pouch. "Outfitters?"

Izarra shrugged with a smirk. "Outfitters," she repeated as Raven untied Ghost from the post. "Can we walk? I want to take in the scenery a bit more. It's just a blur from the back of Ghost."

Raven pulled Ghost's reins to follow. "If you insist."

They made their way down the road, briefly stopping at the wagon shop, where the owner flagged them down to apologize for missing the birthday party. The rest of the walk was peaceful and quiet. Further down the path, Raven noticed Lilly's mother working on a fresh carcass at The Tanning Pit. *I think this is the first time I've appreciated the citizens of Omlett.*

"I'm going to miss you," Izarra whispered, breaking the silence between them.

"We just met," Raven responded, confused.

"I know, but this has been the most fun I've had in a long time." Izarra grabbed the rogue's hand. "Nymphs don't get along—very competitive nature."

Raven felt slightly uncomfortable but continued holding her friend's hand. "Will you return to Thistlebane?"

"No, I like it here," Izarra answered, proudly swinging the held hands. "Maybe Rusty would hire me at the Cache Tavern as an ale taster."

Raven smiled. "He's going to lose so much gold." The two friends chatted more about family, traveling, and men until they were at the front doors of the Omlett Inn. Holding Izarra's hand had become more comfortable.

A voice called out from behind them. "Raven!" Cyndi called from across the road from the amphitheater. "Over here!"

Raven released Izarra's hand to investigate what the bard needed.

"I'm glad I caught you."

"Caught me for what?" Raven asked.

"We decided to have an early run-through of the fall festival's annual play. It's my first year directing it, so I really want you to see it."

I haven't missed a fall play since it began a decade ago. "That's so kind, Cee, but you know we have a family dinner planned."

The bard smiled and pointed. "You mean them."

Raven turned to see her family and friends making their way over to the stage. "I don't understand—"

"It's simple, my dear," Mara stated, leading the group to the royal box, "change of plans. Now, let's take our seats."

Raven's parents settled in their thrones, with Raven's seat to her father's left and Carya's to her mother's right. Anger stabbed her heart as Thomas got pulled into her sister's guest seat. In front of them, her grandparents, Izarra, Buzz'diir, Shorte, Mug, and Lilly, filled the bench in the general seating area.

Lilly glanced back at Raven's father. "Thank you, King Naelo, for allowing me to sit with you all."

"You're welcome, and don't worry about Brugg. He'll be fine running the tavern. He never liked this play anyway. The dragons scare him," Eugor teased.

"Will your parents be attending?" Raven asked, contemplating offering her guest seat since Izarra was now conversing deeply with Buzz'diir.

"Soon. Mother was finishing up at the tannery," Lilly replied.

Mug glanced back. "Her father is on an errand for me but should be arriving soon."

Raven was about to offer, "If you would—"

"Am I late?" asked a familiar soothing voice.

"When are you ever punctual?" Eugor teased. "Have a seat. The show is about to begin."

Gideon, clad in his gold armor, dismissed his wings, sat beside Raven in her guest seat, and gave her a friendly smile. "Greetings."

"Sure, you can sit here," Raven mumbled. *Who does he think he is?* "Taking a break?" His armor filled the entire seat, bumping her arm and ratcheting her frustration. "Maybe wear something more comfortable."

"I'm always working," Gideon replied, placing his gauntleted hand in his lap, but then he quickly leaned over to Izarra and whispered, "I need to speak with you after."

Izarra glanced back at the guardian and nodded; her eyes widened at Raven as a panicked Cyndi appeared, leaning over to Gideon and whispering frantically in his ear.

What the spell is going on?

When the upbeat music filled the arena, Raven leaned forward to escape Gideon's armor and watch the performers take their spots on the stage. She tried to focus on the play instead of eavesdropping.

Cee rushed down the steps to center stage. The bard amplified her voice over the intro music as it faded out. "Over six hundred years ago, our world was alive with dragons and magic. These beautiful beasts . . ."

On stage, a curtain lifted to reveal a gorgeous replica of the Waterfront Academy of Arcane. A replica of the marble steps led up to the back wall. The Illusion Ball projected the transformed area around the actors to match the institution's exterior as Cyndi's voice bellowed, "The Dragon Wars—a dark time in our world. The dragons try to befriend the humans even after they steal magic from them to become more powerful. The human magic users were now known as wysards. After years of peace, everyone thought the humans and dragons had found a way to coexist. The dragons experimented on creatures to create protectors. The wysards were not thrilled with the news and nicknamed the half-dragon breed 'Gooners.'

"The dragon protectors heard that the school's headmaster had imprisoned a blue dragon in retaliation, planning to drain its magic slowly. The dragons sent two Gooners, who insisted on searching the castle. The headmaster graciously agreed and asked them if they would like to feast first since they had traveled far."

The Illusion Ball scene changed to show the dining chamber. "The dragon protectors sat and drank with the wysard students at the round table."

A female bard, clad in a blue robe portraying a Waterfront wysard, announced, "We have the greatest respect for dragons, and history has shown us how dangerous greed can be."

A dwarf bard, clad in fur armor portraying a dragon protector, asked, "What of the rumors that a creature is being tortured in the dungeon by this institute?"

"It's just students making up stories," a male wysard replied. "If it were true, Lora would know."

"Who's that?" the elf asked.

"She's the head of our defenses," whispered one of the students.

"Is her word to be trusted?" the dwarf bard bellowed.

The students stared at each other, and one replied, "Lora is faithful to the school and follows orders. But I don't think she would lie."

Cee returned to the stage. "The visitors continued questioning the students as the sun began to set. The Gooners insisted on searching the lower levels of the chamber as the students showed them the way; the headmaster ambushed the protectors with fatality spells." The two performers dramatized overdramatic deaths as the headmaster spat on the ground. "Death to all the Gooners."

Raven noticed a tall elf in the front row abruptly rise from his seat. As he turned to exit the seating area, she realized it was Headmaster Taiker. And he wasn't pleased. Raven felt her father's eyes turn toward her, as did Gideon's. The two eyed each other as she became caught between the gaze crossfire. *Something's not right.*

"Someone is going to get an ear full," Gideon whispered bluntly to himself as he and Eugor returned to watching the show.

"Hunh?"

"It was the headmaster's grandfather who *supposedly* started the dragon war. He *is not* going to be happy."

Cyndi finished the first act by stating, "This unforgivable act was the beginning of the Dragon Wars." As the same upbeat music began, the actors cleared the stage.

"Damn, they aren't holding back, are they?" Shorte asked, pulling snacks out of his canvas bag and handing them to everyone. "But intermission!"

Raven heard Gideon huff softly. She glanced over, and his leg was twitching slightly. "Are you all right?" she asked, touching his thigh. His eyes shifted down and then back up to the stage. *Was it something Cee said, or was it about the headmaster?*

"I'm fine," Gideon responded as her hand lingered momentarily before he shifted in his chair. "But you're right—sitting in this armor for long is unpleasant."

Mug huffed. "I better check on my structure and the Illusion Ball." He hurried down the steps to the stage as Lilly's parents arrived and sat beside their daughter.

Gideon stood, dropping his gauntlet in Raven's lap. "Find me backstage if this even thinks about glowing. The fate of the realm is in your lap."

"The fate of the realm is in your lap."

"Wait—" she called nervously, worried she'd break his gauntlet if she touched it.

Her father snickered. "All my years, I've never seen him trust someone with that thing."

Raven's head was on a swivel, glancing around the theater as if Gideon would miraculously appear to take it back. Cyndi and Mug talked animatedly on stage until the Cee Sharps played a melancholy tune called "Ode of the Dragon." Raven tried to get her friend's attention, but Izarra conversed deeply with Carya and Thomas.

"Jerky?" Shorte called out, handing Raven a piece of dried deer meat.

"No thanks," Raven answered. She clutched her chair with both hands, praying to Blade that the gem wouldn't glow.

Shorte watched her for a moment. "You have the same look the deer had when I—" Raven shot him a death stare.

"Never mind," Shorte replied, his body turning toward Izarra while his head faced the stage. "Here," he said, reaching behind him, randomly waving the jerky stick.

"What are you doing, Shorte?" Mara asked.

"I don't want to go blind," Shorte replied, signaling her to take the meat.

Izarra shook her head, grabbing the meat stick from his hand. "It doesn't work that way, silly. I'm only half-nymph. My powers are a lot less potent. I would have to really want to harm you. So, don't make me angry." She returned to her conversation with Carya and Thomas.

"Great," Shorte huffed, returning to his seat as his Uncle Buzz'diir shrugged. The music tempo changed, indicating the next act.

Gideon!

A hooded figure ran across the stage as a female voice spoke.

"Draconia, the goddess of dragons, hear me. For five years, the wysards have hunted your children and us. Their fear and greed have blinded them. The headmaster only wants the dragon magic for himself and his human kin. I've watched my friends and protectors perish for pure selfishness." The mysterious figure fell to her knees in defeat. "My village was destroyed for nothing more than power. As a Gooner, I hid among the very things that hate me, the wysards. I was pretending to be just a common moon-elf with the powers of the Shadow Realm." She paused briefly before continuing. "But Krea, they have imprisoned one of your children here at the institution. I've sensed her calling out for help. But I am not strong enough to stop them from torturing the young one."

The curtain slowly opened, revealing a massive dragon with a rider—an actress dressed as Draconia. A loud, guttural feminine voice rang through the theater. "Then I shall free her."

The figure in the middle of the stage lowered her hood. A moon-elf with dark skin and long, curly, silver hair turned and faced the back of the stage. The moon-elf bowed and spoke. "Draconia, tomorrow is graduation at Waterfront. Everyone would be distracted by the festivities. It would be a perfect time to attack."

"You have done well, Caddie. For too long have my children been hurt and hunted by the humans of this realm. We will free my child, and I'll provide you all asylum away from this realm."

The Illusion Ball changed the stage's image to a blue sky, and the great dragon spread her wings and took flight. The cloaked figure cast a gust of wind at the audience, and Raven heard Izarra gasp as she clung to Shorte. The dwarf's eyes were wide, his mouth agape, as he clutched the half-nymph's arm, bracing for the forceful air's impact.

The scene on stage changed again, showing wysards in robes at a graduation ceremony. The headmaster lingered at a podium in the middle, chatting animatedly with the students. Then, the sound of dragon wings grew louder and louder. On stage, illusions of dragons dove and fought the groups of wysards. As the battle continued, more and more dragons fell. The undergrads reinforced the graduates.

Cyndi's voice bellowed, "The dragons became overwhelmed until—"

A mighty dragon roar shook the benches as Krea's image flew over the box seats where Raven and her family sat. Izarra screamed and covered her eyes. A long pillar of fire shot from the dragon onto the stage. As the smoke cleared, the audience clapped as the crew changed the set on stage.

Now, there were steep steps and three people hurrying down.

"James . . . hurry!" Caddie cried. She pushed open the door to a war chamber. They frantically searched the room.

"I found it!" the human male yelled, stashing an oversized book into his satchel.

"We need to go!" a new voice yelled, running on stage—a young female dwarf dressed in white.

"What's wrong, Krystal?" James asked nervously.

"Krea has joined the battle, and I'm unsure how long this structure will hold," Krystal replied.

"Move back!" Caddie called out as the palms of her hands ignited.

The two actors moved to the edge. James and Krystal cast the Fireball spell into the war room, destroying the table. The red-hot flames set the ancient tapestries on fire and quickly climbed the walls, setting the room ablaze. The thick smoke filled the space, hiding the stage from view.

The audience began to clap, but Raven felt only chills as the burning image of Blade's Church spread through her mind as fast as the fire. *Don't think about it!*

The mumbling of the audience grew louder as they waited for the next scene when Raven heard her mother whisper to Lilly, "James Fisker is an ancestor of mine. He kept a journal of this event and passed it on for generations but never named the moon-elf. We know it starts with a 'C.'"

The stage transformed into a long, stone, underground bridge. The group quietly made their way across when Krystal asked, "Do we have all the artifacts?"

"Yes," Caddie replied, "now we need to make our way to the Dragon Prisoner."

As the three actors reached the end of the stage, the illusion of an old blue dragon burst from the water with a magical bind around its leg. Caddie stepped forward and gazed into its eyes. The ancient creature seemed to calm down and called out with a growl, making a young blue dragon appear from the pool, too.

"Two?!" Krystal asked in surprise.

"I—" Caddie started; the ceiling above rumbled, and pieces fell into the water. "Quick, give me the artifacts." Krystal poured water into a white bowl as James pulled out a knife and the book taken from the war room. Caddie uncovered a necklace that hid under her tunic. "James, put the knife in the bowl."

"Can we save both?" Krystal asked, her voice unsteady.

"I don't know," Caddie replied as she studied the spell. The chamber shook again. She pulled out the dagger, calling "ᚪinu ᚾᴇhtar."

"The Cenergy Blade," James breathed. "Are we sure this will be strong enough to break through the headmaster's Binding spell?"

"It's supposed to cut through any magic," Caddie responded. "It even executes immortals." They moved to the chains binding the prisoned creature, but the mother dragon blocked them. "I think she wants her child freed first." She proceeded to the youngling and, with one swing, cut through the chains—the young dragon dove under the water.

"Thank Natus," Krystal exhaled. They hurried to cut the other magical chains when the adult dragon moved before them. An arrow bounced off its hide and fell to the floor.

"Stop!" yelled Lora. On either side were two of her guards. "Come with me now, or I will have no choice but to kill you."

"How can you stand by and watch what the headmaster does to these creatures?" Caddie asked.

"You know this is wrong," James called out.

"It's my duty to protect Waterfront, the headmaster, and all its secrets." Before she could notch another arrow, Krystal and James cast Magic Missiles, knocking Lora and the guards out cold, but more footsteps echoed from the catacombs. The baby dragon burst from the pool of water once more as the elderly blue dragon flooded the chamber, collapsing the bridge.

"This way!" Caddie called, splashing toward the baby dragon and crawling on its back as James and Krystal followed. Taking one last glance at Lora and the guards' bodies, Caddie cast a levitation spell, and they rose out of the water toward the ceiling. She heard James cast a Water Breathing spell, and they all dove into the pool. The illusion of a wave rising from the stage washed over the box seats as the audience screamed. The stage went dark, then lit again as the actors ran on stage, bowing.

Everyone laughed and applauded—except Raven, still sitting nervously with the gauntlet in her lap. Gideon lowered his hood on the stage and walked up the stairs as people clapped. He smiled and waved dramatically, entering the royal box.

"Where did you go?" Raven asked, shoving the gauntlet back at him before she decided to smack him with it.

"To help a friend," the guardian replied, re-equipping his gauntlet. "I'm assuming all is well in the Mortal Realm." He must have noticed her expression because his tone changed. "I'm sorry. But you helped save the play by allowing me to fill in for the effects wizard."

"That was you? Is that what Cee wanted?"

"It took every ounce to fight my conscience because the High Council wouldn't approve of me performing for a mundane festival show."

Raven inhaled slowly. "Maybe I overreacted."

"But I should have asked first or handed it to your father. I am truly sorry. Forgiven?"

"Yes," Raven responded with a half-grin as Mug rejoined the group.

"Mug, the Illusion Ball was spectacular this year," Eugor praised.

Mug grunted. "Hmff—most of it was Gideon and his spells."

"Raven, dear," her mother interrupted, "everyone must be starving. Shall we head home?"

Raven paused momentarily. "May we join the cast and crew in the banquet hall?"

Mara smiled broadly. "I think that would be a wonderful idea."

Raven went to push Gideon out of the way, but he halted in front of her guest seat until he motioned to Izarra as she passed by. "Miss Lyte, May I speak with you?"

Izarra glanced at Raven with a caught-with-a-hand-in-the-cookie-jar look. "I suppose."

"I was so impressed with how you protected Raven at the church."

"Thank you," Izarra responded, eyeing the rogue again with relief. "But she would do it for me."

"In a heartbeat," Raven responded, placing her hand on her friend's shoulder.

"And Eugor also tells me you were brave enough to intervene at the Cache Tavern during Raven's battle with the Horcks."

I had it under control.

"I would be honored if you joined us at my camp," Gideon offered.

What the spell? I trained my arse off!

Izarra gasped as Raven quickly folded her arms. "But Raven explained everything she went through to prepare for this. I—"

Thank you!

"You demonstrated great courage at the church and the Cache Tavern."

"Only if I have Raven's blessing."

Both sets of eyes focused on Raven as she contemplated the decision. *She was there for me. But is it fair? I worked hard for this.*

Izarra's face drooped in defeat as she waited for what must have seemed like an eternity.

Raven bit her lip, tapping her foot. "Fine."

Izarra's face beamed. "You sure?"

"Yes, I'm sure," Raven smirked. "I'll still have my shadow."

Izarra grabbed Raven's arms, bouncing up and down. "Thank you, thank you! You won't regret it."

Gideon slowed his speech to ensure Izarra understood what he was saying as she stopped bouncing, trying to focus on him. "It's a ten-year commitment, three years of which you'll attend camp to learn new spells and work as a team. It will be physically and mentally demanding." Izarra continued nodding her head throughout the explanation. "And you will be on call whenever there is a need for the following seven years."

"I'm so excited!" Izarra finally screeched, hugging the rogue. "Wait . . . what should I wear? Oh my, I need to pack." Then she pulled away and ran excitedly toward the Inn.

Raven whispered to the guardian, "Thank you."

Gideon nodded. "Anyone willing to be that brave to protect you that fiercely deserves to be a guardian."

CHAPTER SIXTEEN

DEPARTURE DAY

Raven gathered her bathing supplies and cautiously followed the tree-lined path. The whistling of the wind through the branches sounded like an ominous warning. Grasping her bucket tightly, she hurried down an uneven trail. A loud crack from a mulberry bush made her jump. The hairs on her neck prickled. *Is someone following me?* The shrubbery rustled again as her bucket dropped, dumping out her bathing supplies. Throwing her head back, she felt like a fool reaching for her daggers. She searched frantically for a fallen branch, taking a defensive stance against the source of her terror—which turned out to be a snow rabbit. *This is ridiculous.*

Dashing down the path, Raven picked the dirt off her soap bar. Once at the water, she glanced back again. *Something feels different.* She disrobed and waded into the frigid water as paranoia replaced her usual admiration of the scenery. *Astrick is probably long gone by now.*

As she bathed, the visions of her birthday party from the other night filled her head. *Astrick, the dragon ride, the darkness—what's happening to me?* She dove under the water, thinking a few laps might distract her, but it didn't help. She swam to shore instead. As she broke the surface and opened her eyes, a nude male was knee-deep at the edge of the water.

"Raven!" Thomas exclaimed, startling her as he retreated from the water.

Her heart pounded as Thomas grabbed his shirt and covered his lower half. She ducked back into the water, her head just above the surface. "What the spell, Thomas?"

"I'm so sorry—I didn't know you were here."

"How did you know about my bathing hole?"

"Carya told me about it at the cast after dinner party," Thomas responded. "She said you wouldn't be here this early."

"Normally, I wouldn't be, but I think Izarra drank enough for the both of us."

"She was definitely intoxicated again. I'll leave you to fin—"

"Or you can join me," Raven interrupted in her most flirtatious voice. "It's a sizable watering hole, after all." She rose from the water just as Carya came through the thick bushes.

Raven and Carya's eyes locked. At that moment, something felt like it broke between them. Her sister bit her trembling lip. *Is she going to cry?*

Carya averted her eyes from the naked figures, staring at the sky. "What's going on here?" Her hands fidgeted at the hem of her sleeve.

"Thomas came to pay me a visit," Raven said, causing unnecessary trouble.

"I didn't know your sister was here," Thomas explained as he struggled to put on his clothes. "I just wanted to bathe quickly."

Carya crossed her arms. "And you decided to stand around in the buff, having a lovely chat?"

"Carya, what is wrong with you?" Raven asked. "This has nothing to do with you."

"You're out here naked with him"—Carya motioned to Thomas—"and you don't even know him."

"It was just bad timing," Thomas chimed in, trying to make peace. "An accident."

"Well, I was getting to know him before you interrupted," Raven said. As she waded back into the water, a thought struck her. "Wait a spell, what are *you* doing here?"

"What?" Carya answered, feigning confusion.

"You don't bathe out here, but you knew Thomas—Ah . . . now I see. You're jealous. You wanted to be here with him . . . *alone.*"

Carya turned red. "I would never! I have morals, Raven, unlike you."

"Oh, I see. Like the morals you had with that elf Sarven? That relationship turned out to be one-sided, too."

"Ladies, please," Thomas interrupted.

"Oh, and this would work out for you. You're leaving for Gideon's camp for a couple of years!"

"So what, Carya? Do you think I'll do to him what that wandering elf druid did to you?"

Carya scowled. "Raven, don't—"

"What was his name?"

"—go there."

"Erlax? No, no, Erlar, yes, Erlar," Raven stated. "He left when? A couple of days after the relationship started?"

Carya began to sob.

Maybe I've gone too far.

"You're a MONSTER!" Carya screamed as she turned and ran away.

Thomas eyed Raven. "I'll go talk to her."

Raven felt the color drain from her face as she stared blankly at where her sister had disappeared from the brush. "Sure, good, thank you."

"You all right?" he asked gently.

"Never better," Raven lied.

Thomas followed Carya's path, disappearing into the brush as Raven released an exacerbated huff. *It's too early for this!*

Raven folded her arms against the bank and put her head down. The grass beneath her arms felt dry, and a smell of rot filled her nose. She glanced up as darkness spread across the bank, killing the water hyacinth and marsh marigolds. In the distance, she watched a cluster of baby rabbits scurry deeper into the woods.

Confused, she pushed herself back toward the middle of the pool. Small fish floated dead to the surface as the water under and around her turned to mud. She swam as fast as she could to the low end, slipping, sliding, and falling into the dirt. She threw on the robe and raced back to the house, her heart racing. *What just happened?*

As she followed the trail, she spotted Thomas wandering ahead of her. He turned back as he heard her footsteps, opening his arms at the last moment to welcome her for a hug.

"Where's Carya?" Raven asked, pressing her head against his chest and hugging him tightly. Thomas didn't respond. She felt his hands slide from her upper to lower back, then caress her arse cheeks over the robe as he began nibbling on her neck. "Thomas?!"

Thomas whispered, "Royalty and no security." She pushed away, staring into his *green* eyes. He beamed with a creepy expression. "Hello, Princess."

"No, it . . . it can't be," Raven stuttered, slowly backing away.

"I'm here to collect my royal tax," the imposter threatened. "You owe me four men and a carriage." He reached out to grab her arm as the illusion wore off. She dashed past him as he called out in his normal voice, "YOU OWE ME, PRINCESS!"

When Raven reached the rear of the house, she bent over, out of breath, as she saw her mother, Izarra, and Shorte standing around talking.

"Raven!" Mara exclaimed. "What in Euphrasia happened?"

"Why are you covered in mud?" asked Izarra as Raven's hands trembled.

"Bah, it's just a mud bath," Shorte added. "It helps cleanse the pores." The three women just stared at him. "What? My mother taught me that. After a long day in the mines, it helps the complexion eliminate all the dust particles."

"You use dirt to clean dirt?" Izarra asked, laughing.

"Well, if you put it that way." Shorte shrugged. "Does sound crazy."

Tears rolled down Raven's face as she shook her head and pointed back. "Astrick!"

The dwarf didn't hesitate—he sprinted off down the path.

"Shorte!" Raven called out.

"Are you all right?" Mara asked, hugging her daughter. "Did he hurt you?"

"No," Raven replied. "Carya—fight—Thomas."

Mara sighed softly, patting her daughter's head. "Calm down, dear. You'll be fine."

"I'll get Gideon," Izarra said as she went and knocked on the front door.

Muted voices explained what happened, and then the guardian walked out, flexed his wings, and flew down the path.

Raven cursed under her breath. "I'm going to use the house tub to clean up."

"Even better!" Izarra exclaimed, swinging around her water decanter as Mara stepped back.

"Izarra, no," Raven pleaded, getting a mouthful of water.

"Spin for me," Izarra ordered.

Raven closed her eyes and spun around in a slow circle. When she opened them, Eugor stood there laughing. *Perfect.*

But her father's joyful face flattened out after Izarra whispered something. He dashed out, staring down the path.

"I'll be right back." Raven stormed up the steps to her room, leaving muddy footprints behind, and passed Brugg in the hall.

"More mud!" Brugg complained.

"I know, I know, more mud," she said as she slammed her bedroom door. *How could this morning get any worse?*

Mortified, she finished washing with the water basin in the corner. After tossing items into her backpack, she approached her new dragon armor. *How the spell do I put this on? Knowing Gideon, there must be a special trick to it.* Her hand shook as she picked up the note and reread the back. "Wearing the circlet, chant these words to activate the suit." She placed the circlet on her head and chanted, "Tolth-Armis." In an instant, the black dragon armor encompassed her body. *Impressive!*

The shaking in her hand stopped as she gazed into the copper mirror. She'd been waiting for this moment since turning thirteen when she first overheard Gideon tell her father that he would be recruiting guardians for the realm in a few years. She'd exercised daily, studied magic with Maggie, performed intense rogue training with her father, attended strategy planning with Buzz at the barracks, and learned how to handle medical emergencies from her mother. So many people helped her get here. *I won't let them down.* After straightening up, she felt a burst of confidence. "So, this is how Shorte feels?" she said aloud, not realizing that the door to the bedroom had been cracked open.

"Wow, you look amazing," Izarra said, inspecting the armor.

"Thank you." Raven smiled. "It feels amazing and very comfortable, too."

"I've traveled a lot and never seen armor like that before."

"Well, you spend most of your time in dress shops."

"Guilty," Izarra snickered. She picked up her backpack and waited for Raven in the hall.

Glancing one last time to ensure she hadn't forgotten anything, Raven grabbed her bag and closed the door. Brugg mumbled under his breath as he swept the hall. "Brugg?" she whispered in Orcish. "I'm really sorry for the mud."

He looked at her with concern.

"I'm going to be gone for a while. Take care of yourself and everyone else for me, all right?"

"Be . . . safe," Brugg said in Common as he gave her a crooked grin.

Raven hugged him around his waist, noticing a rolled-up parchment.

"Just stop," Izarra said sadly. "You're going to make me cry."

Brugg unrolled the parchment and dabbed it under Izarra's eyes.

"What's that Brugg?" Raven asked, taking it.

"Elf wizard," Brugg replied. "For Raven."

Raven read the note as her stomach churned.

I know what you are. I'll be watching.

What the spell? Astrick? "Do you know this elf?"

"No," Brugg responded, grabbing the broom and continuing to sweep.

"What does it say?" Izarra asked.

Raven rolled up the parchment and tossed it in her backpack. "Best wishes from a friend."

Once outside, Raven walked up to her parents, who were in conversation with Buzz'diir and Mug.

"Buzz is alerting security—" Eugor eyed her new armor. "What in Euphrasia are you wearing?"

Raven suddenly noticed that when it hit the sunlight, the black armor had a purple shimmer to it.

"Part two," Gideon flaunted as he and Shorte returned empty-handed. Her heart sank at the thought of Astrick escaping as the guardian continued, "Think I won again this year."

"Are those the black dragon scales?" Eugor asked.

Mug grunted as he pulled down his magnifying glass from his headband. "So that's what you did with it, hunh?"

Looking back and forth between Gideon and her father, Raven blurted, "I need to talk to you two—alone. It's urgent."

They both eyed her with alarm. "Of course," Eugor answered, leading them back into the house.

"You haven't changed your mind, have you?" Gideon asked, sounding disappointed.

"Yes!" Raven snapped, fidgeting with her gloves. *They're going to think I'm insane or a monster.* "It's—" She bounced her head back and forth between her father and Gideon, fighting the urge to run off. "I think I'm cursed." As they stared at her, a heavy weight lifted off her chest, and the words rushed out of her mouth. "I spit acid in a man's face, I created a darkness that ruined my party, and now, I turned my watering hole into a muddy pit. I have other people chasing a wizard around for me. I should be able—" She took a deep breath to calm her nerves, waiting for them to respond as they eyed each other for a moment.

Eugor turned to her. "Don't be silly, my dear. For one, Mug reported it was probably a glitch with the Illusion Ball and the Animated Object spell at the party."

Gideon offered a comforting smile. "And two, as for your watering hole . . . there is nothing supernatural about the earth shifting and releasing mud into pools."

Raven huffed. "And the acid?"

"And thirdly . . . bad breath," her father teased as Raven tilted her head, flashing an irritated expression at the remark. "I don't believe it was acid. I saw the man. The fire made him unrecognizable. The mind can play tricks on you."

"But it happened before the fire," Raven replied, feeling discouraged. "You don't believe me." Everything around her blurred as tears formed in her eyes. *Don't you dare cry in front of them!* "I don't . . . it felt . . . I *am* out of control." She finally spat out the words.

"You're of age, dear," her father said calmly. "Things will sometimes feel uncontrollable. I promise you, if you were cursed, Gideon, your mother, and I would know."

"Father, you know you shouldn't have passed me on my final test. I left my daggers behind and tracked in a mud trail that a blind ogre could follow."

Gideon cut his snicker short, changing the subject. "Remember—your father had both eyes swelled shut on his final test. And wizards can be tricky to defeat. That's why I'm training a group of guardians and not just one. But we will find this guy. Sometimes, it takes a team effort. If you're up to it, I would love for you to attend."

Raven nodded and hugged her father. *Do I tell them about the cryptic message?*

"You'll be fine, and I love you very much," Eugor said. He kept his arm around her and guided her out of the house as Gideon announced to the others that it was time to depart.

Raven hugged Buzz, then turned to Mug and then her mother.

"You're in good hands," Mara said, wrapping her arm around Eugor's. "We are so proud of you."

Gideon created a blue portal from a scroll and stepped through, followed by Shorte and Izarra. Raven glanced back one last time for any signs of her sister and then followed them through the magical gateway.

CHAPTER SEVENTEEN

MAKING AN OMLETT

Thomas exited the rear door of the church's mess hall, approaching a white gazebo in the center of the courtyard. He noticed Carya's strawberry-blond curls hung loosely down her back above the wooden rail. Following the freshly cut hedges to the opening, he leaned against the archway pillar, observing her head bowed and hands pressed together. "Who are you praying to?"

"Blade," Carya answered with her eyes closed, "to watch over Raven." She glanced up at the paladin with eyes red from crying. "How did you know I was here?"

"Lucky guess . . . I guess. Or it could have been the two SIPs I paid to get the info out of that weird monk eating grass in the mess hall."

Carya burst into that cute laugh he liked so much.

"So, Blade . . . Isn't he . . . a demigod?"

"Yes, and my half-brother," Carya replied, lowering her head again. "But my father conceived him over a century ago."

"That's right—they age more slowly than humans."

"Even me," explained Carya. "I'm half-elf, but I age like my human mother."

Thomas was intrigued. "Really? So, you'll be old and gray when I am." Carya laughed again as he continued, "Will your father outlive you and your mother?"

"No," Carya answered. "But it's a complicated story."

"Try me."

Carya eyed him momentarily, then tucked her hair behind her ears and sat on the floor, appearing angelic in the morning sunlight. "I'm sure you noticed the scar around his neck."

"Indeed," Thomas said, pushing his back off the pillar and sitting on the gazebo bench.

"He and Mug did Gideon a favor by retrieving an artifact," she said as she rose to sit on the bench beside him. "A fire demon came searching for the artifact, decapitated my father, and stole the amulet."

"Wait, a fire demon—an actual balor—beheaded your father, and he's still alive today?"

"It gets better," Carya continued. "Before the fight with the balor, they came across a black dragon egg."

"A dragon egg?" Thomas asked excitedly, leaning forward like a child listening to an adventure tale. "They were extinct centuries ago!"

"That's what they thought."

"Don't tell me you have a pet dragon," Thomas joked as Carya laughed again. The giggle he heard the first day of the class still made him feel warm inside like her laugh had its own healing power.

"No, they ate it."

After a brief hesitation, Thomas's eyes widened as his voice became louder. "They ate the dragon egg?!" Several clerics and monks in the courtyard turned to look at the commotion as he mouthed, "Sorry."

Carya shook her head and continued. "The mission for the artifact left my father and Mug starving. When they came across the egg, some humans were trying to figure out a way to haul it away but couldn't figure out how. Once the humans left, Mug found a way to remove the black scales so he and my father could tap into it. My father said the humans returned, shouting at him, 'You turned our fortune into an omelet!' So, when he retired, he returned to where he found the egg, creating the Omlett Inn. People settled around him, eventually growing it into a city."

"That's crazy," Thomas said, then chuckled.

"What?"

"Omlett City, Omlett Inn . . . I get it now. But it's spelled wrong!" Thomas flinched as something flew across his nose.

A ladybug landed on his shoulder. Carya reached out, allowing it to travel across her fingers. "Well, my father's an elf who had never heard the word before, so he and Mug did their best to spell it. When my mother corrected them, they shrugged and decided to leave it." They both watched as the ladybug flew off.

"But how did your father return?"

"Resurrection spell."

"No way. That spell is obsolete because you need dragon's blood for it."

"Gideon teleported my father to my uncle—well before he was my uncle," she explained. "Ausharz was a cleric and a friend at the time. They attempted it because he had eaten the dragon's egg, and luckily, it worked."

"I can't believe that. It's like a miracle."

"Some say Blade had something to do with it, but that's where my father also met my mother. She's Ausharz's sister, and she nursed my father while he was recovering."

"So, his aging sped up because of the Resurrection spell?"

"Yes, it somehow changed his aging process to be more like humans. He used to have black hair like Raven's, but the spell turned it pure white."

"So you became a cleric like your mother and uncle?"

"Yes, they saved my father's life, and one day, I hope I can do the same for someone else."

Thomas was silent for a moment as he took it all in. "And your sister?" he asked cautiously, aware that it might be a sensitive subject.

"Out of all the professional classes, barbarian was too barbaric. Bard was out because Raven can't sing or play an instrument, even though she can play a fool sometimes."

Thomas shook his head. "Be nice."

"I am," Carya replied, then continued. "Monk, paladin, and cleric are too religious and need one hundred percent dedication."

"Oh, I know," Thomas chimed in.

"The ranger and druid had to deal with too much nature. A tinkerer—she bruised her own hand with a hammer."

Thomas's face winced. "Ouch."

"She's lucky she has two healers in the house. She didn't want to attend Waterfront for eight years, eliminating wizardry. So, she chose to be a rogue, like my father," Carya explained. "Even though she always fancied slipping around in the shadows and picking the lock of the sweet bins, she always had a fascination with magic. She learned some minor spells from Maggie, so now she's leaving to learn more complex spells from Gideon. She thinks she's some kind of arcane assassin."

"I thought to be a spell caster, you were required to attend Waterfront?"

"My sister does nothing by the book. My father hired Maggie, an ex-professor with a decade of tenure there."

"Will you miss her?"

"Maggie?"

"Your sister." Thomas shook his head as she snickered.

"Of course," Carya responded, now frowning. "We've been inseparable most of our lives."

Thomas faltered but knew he needed to ask. "Is it true? You've been hurt in other relationships?"

Carya hesitated, fidgeting with the belt of her robe. "I guess you could say that," she admitted, lowering her head.

"I can't imagine why," said Thomas, pausing. "You're beautiful, smart, and compassionate."

"And a princess," Carya added.

"And a princess," Thomas repeated. "How did that come about, anyway? Your sister said something about it being an honorary title."

"When I was about seven years old, the city appointed my father King of Omlett, so we became princesses . . . naturally."

"Naturally." Thomas grinned.

"What about you?"

Thomas chuckled nervously. "After that story, you'll find mine really boring." He glanced around to find the courtyard now empty.

Carya slowly turned his head toward her, drilling her eyes deep into his, and said, "Try me."

"For starters . . . umm . . . bandits killed my parents when I was thirteen."

Carya gasped and grabbed his hand. "I'm sorry."

He flashed her a look of appreciation. "I entered a paladin guild, sweeping floors, cleaning horse stables, and taking classes to slowly work my way up until three years ago when the King of Brindell knighted me."

"My father forbids us to travel to Brindell," Carya interjected. "He said humans can get very disorderly, very quickly." She batted her eyelashes and smiled. "No offense."

"None taken. I get it. I used to do security for the city until I decided to patrol to protect travelers from bandits."

"Because of your parents?"

"In honor of them, yes," Thomas answered. "And to protect other children's parents."

They sat for a moment and stared at each other. Thomas got up and held out his hand to help her. "We should return so you can say farewells to your sister before she leaves."

"You're right," Carya said, taking his hand. "It'll be a while before I see her again."

"In the meantime, I hope you will enjoy my company."

"I'm sure I will," Carya said, glancing at him shyly.

Thomas reached out and tucked a stray bit of hair behind her ear, then, without hesitation, he leaned forward and kissed her lips. Gently moving his body closer, he embraced her as her hands lightly caressed his back. Her lips were soft and tasted of sweet berries. With great effort, he pulled away and beamed. "Now, let's get you to your sister."

They rushed out of the courtyard and around the church to Grail. He felt her arms wrap tightly around his waist as they high-tailed it out of there. But when they reached the house, they could only see Raven's back through a blue portal.

Carya dismounted Grail and called out to her sister, "Raven!" She ran toward her parents but watched as the gateway closed. "May Blade watch over you," she whispered, rubbing her necklace.

"Carya, she'll be fine," Mara said comfortingly.

"I know. I just wanted to say farewell."

"I'm returning to the church," Thomas announced, turning Grail toward the road. "I want to help them rebuild from the fire."

"Do-Gooder!" Buzz'diir called out, nudging Eugor.

"May I join you, Mister Do-Gooder?" Carya asked, glancing up at the paladin.

Thomas smiled sweetly, extending his hand to help her onto the horse. "No need to ask."

CHAPTER EIGHTEEN

FIRST IMPRESSIONS

Raven heard her name just as the portal was closing, but when she glanced back, she stumbled into Izarra, who had come to a dead stop. "What the spell?" Raven asked irritably, pushing Izarra forward toward their new home at the training camp.

To their left was dense, green woodland. A raging waterfall surged from the rock walls to the right, swaying the rare coral reefs with mini waves. In front of them was a massive lake with a white, sandy beach and crystal-clear water.

A handsome, slender male human rummaged through a bag near his tent. He had short, light brown hair and a scruffy beard—his cloth pants and tunic appeared filthy like he had been rolling in the dirt. Three practice dummies that reminded Raven of the ones in the prison's training chamber sat across from his living area in an open field. The far-left target's leather cover was slashed to shreds, the middle one was scorched, and the one on the right was drenched in some fluids. The guy postured in a spellcasting stance with his arms cocked back, then, in a single fluid motion, he unleashed a firebolt at the middle target, then proceeded to cast a swarm of purple daggers around the far-left dummy.

"Who is that?" Izarra asked, pointing toward the lake.

"I don't know," Raven replied, impressed, "but I guess we're about to find out."

She spotted Gideon's covered wagon near the campfire in the middle of the encampment. Off to the left, near the tree line, a slender female elf with short, wild red hair snapped her drawstring, releasing an arrow that hit a bull's eye on the target. The archer glanced at Raven and reloaded another arrow. While keeping her gaze locked on the rogue, the elf fired again, hitting the target just below the first arrow. She stayed posing, flexing her toned arms.

Am I ready for this? Is my dagger accuracy that good?

The archer dashed and placed her longbow against the tree with the target, then gracefully swung on a vine and began to climb to a platform that overlooked the camp. Shorte placed his gear beside a giant boulder near the forest's edge.

Izarra was preoccupied with the human by the lake and dragged her belongings toward him. She was unpacking her bright, sea-green tent near her new crush in no time.

Raven shook her head. "Izarra! Really?"

"I'm part water nymph," Izarra yelled back, "of course I want to be by the water."

Raven placed her backpack halfway between Izarra's camp and the boulder Shorte had chosen. The area had several practice targets for ranged weapons that resembled Gary the garden gnome's scarecrows. *I should work on my dagger throw later.*

The dwarf popped his head out from the other side of the rock. "Hey, neighbor," he said with a silly grin. "I hope this stone blocks out my snoring. If it's bad, wake me up."

"Will do," Raven agreed as she glanced toward the tree line. The nosy elf archer was lying on her stomach, propping her head up with her arms, eyeing Raven back.

Gideon approached the campfire. "Everyone, gather around," he yelled, gesturing with his arms.

The elf in the tree swung down using a vine, landing gracefully on the ground. Izarra and the young man came over from the lake while Shorte untangled himself from the pieces of his tent before joining the others.

"I should just find a cave," Shorte said, discouraged. "This nature stuff is for the elves."

"I'll help you," Raven whispered to him, "after the introductions."

Everyone gathered and encircled the campfire, watching and evaluating each other.

"Welcome all," Gideon began. "As most of you know, I train a select few to help defend this realm from internal problems."

"Isn't that against your guardian code?" the elf archer asked.

"No, Avalann, it's not," Gideon answered. "My job is to prevent other realms from invading. This is to help maintain order in our own realm."

"Now we're the Gideon Guardians." Shorte chuckled. "But I've been around for a while, and things seem pretty peaceful except for those annoying war orcs."

"Many cities are well equipped to keep those orcs at bay," Gideon agreed. "They have calmed down a bit."

"They don't deserve peace," the young human sneered. He appeared tormented when he spoke. Izarra shot Raven a worried expression, then shrugged.

"Jarz, we are here to protect," Gideon said, "not avenge."

"Yes, sir," Jarz replied dryly.

"This is a ten-year commitment. If anyone wants to leave now, feel free." Gideon paused as everyone glanced at each other. "Good. Let us introduce ourselves. I'll begin. I'm Gideon Grindal, Celestial Guardian of the Mortal Realm." They noticed Avalann roll her eyes. "I'm here to ensure you can fight at your full potential."

There was a long pause before Avalann adjusted her dark green leather armor and announced, "I'm Avalann Greenorr, an archer from Suttiir. The *best* archer."

"Confident for an elf," Shorte noted. "I like that."

"She's also my niece," Gideon added, surprising everyone.

"I don't like that," Shorte whispered to Raven. "No favoritism there?"

Avalann lowered her head. "Thanks, Uncle," she mumbled sarcastically, then stared coldly at Shorte. "And I heard that, dwarf."

Raven was surprised that Gideon had never mentioned any family to her. *Maybe I need to get out of my bubble.*

"I'm Izarra Lyte," the water half-nymph said happily. "I'm from Thistlebane; I love the water, dark starry nights, moonlight swims, long romantic walks in the forest—"

"Thank you, Izarra," Gideon interrupted.

"I love bards," she continued, ignoring Gideon, "especially the comedic ones. Are you a bard?" she flirted, gazing at the human as Jarz shook his head. "Anyway, I love—"

"Talking about yourself," Avalann interjected under her breath as Izarra fell silent, lowering her head. The rest of the group stared judgmentally at the archer. "What? We were all thinking it."

"No, we weren't," Raven retorted. "At least she's honest."

"Well, go ahead . . . Princess," Avalann said with a smirk and a mock bow. "Let's hear yours."

All eyes turned to the rogue. "I'm Raven Naelo. I'm from Omlett. I'm a rogue like my father. I'm here to enhance my magic skills and become a guardian."

"Don't hold back," Avalann sneered. "Where did you get the fancy armor?"

Raven glanced at Gideon and whispered, "It was a birthday gift."

"From?" Avalann asked with an evil grin.

"Avalann, enough," Gideon warned impatiently.

"Gideon gave it to her," Izarra chimed in. "Sorry, I read the note."

"It's fine," Raven replied.

Avalann snorted. "Keep going—"

"Enough," Gideon fumed. "Next."

"I'm Jarz Fisker," the handsome human male said. "I'm from Waterfront . . . well, originally Fellswar."

"Fisker? That's my mother's maiden name," Raven said with surprise.

"He's your cousin," Gideon explained. "He survived the orc attack at Fellswar and was rescued by a wizard and taken to Waterfront."

"They offered to take me to Omlett, but I chose to stay at Waterfront," Jarz explained. "I wanted to train to be the first human selected as a Celestial Guardian. So I chose the path of a swordmage."

Raven, baffled, whispered, "But we have a grave marker with your name."

"I'm Shorte," the dwarf announced, redirecting everyone's attention. "And I'd better not hear any height jokes," he said as he waved his fist.

He continued, but Raven zoned out. She eyed Gideon, who watched her with concern and then returned to the conversation.

"—how I became a cleric," Shorte finished. "I know—boring—no drama here."

"Everyone, please settle in, and we'll meet back here later tonight," Gideon instructed. "We'll see if we can't get this fire raging."

"Yay, camp stories," Avalann said sarcastically. "Can't wait."

Jarz dashed for the pond and splashed water on his face.

Why hide from the family he still had in Omlett? Why go to Waterfront?

Gideon was about to approach Raven just as Izarra rushed over.

"You have to help me with your cousin," the half-nymph implored.

"I don't even know him," Raven responded, watching Gideon stop and retreat to his wagon.

"I'll go talk to him." Izarra rushed toward the water.

As Raven turned to ask Shorte a question, she noticed Avalann glaring at her before climbing back up the vine to the tree platform.

"Friendly, isn't she?" Shorte commented, then hurried down to his campsite.

Raven walked to the spot she'd picked out earlier and unpacked. *No tent.* She unrolled her sleeping bag onto the ground. *Right, I offered to help Shorte.* When she made her way over to the dwarf, he was kicking his tent pegs. "Give them to me."

With the tent pitched in no time, Shorte, covered in sweat, collapsed against the boulder.

"You all right?" Raven asked.

He waved his hand, signaling her to leave, then crawled over to the tent and began snoring.

Izarra and Jarz were in the lake, swimming toward the waterfall. *That water must be cold.* Grabbing her daggers, she lined up to the nearest training dummy and began to throw. The first toss hit the target's left arm and the second embedded itself in the target's abdomen. She pulled her weapons out and lined back up again. *Now aim for the head.*

After a few more misses, she finally landed one in the head zone. *Not good enough!* Her mind was so focused on the target and how fast she could retrieve her weapons and throw them again that pain from her right palm made her glance down to find blood. *I may have overdone it.*

Raven tossed her daggers to the side of her bag and then grabbed a cloth to wrap her hand. "Armis-Awaui." Her armor was suddenly on the ground next to her. Slipping on her favorite robe, she stared at the sky, contemplating her techniques for keeping her daggers from dropping to low. *Maybe I have to aim higher?* Checking the bandage to see if the blood soaked through, her eyes felt heavy as she reached her able hand for the parchment she'd managed to ignore.

I know what you are. I'll be watching.

Blood dripped on the parchment. "Ah damn it," she grumbled to herself, reaching for a new cloth. As she replaced the bandage, she continued her thoughts. *Should I return home? What if Astrick attacks my family? What if—*

After drifting off, crickets chirped, and the crackling of a fire flooded Raven's ears as she yawned, rubbing her eyes. Izarra stood over her, reading the parchment, then waved it in front of Raven's face. "What is this? Whose blood? Is this the 'best wishes'? Why did you lie to me?"

Should I have shared the message with her?

"I didn't want you to worry." Raven frowned as she noticed the dark sky behind her friend. She raised her bandaged hand to see if it needed a new wrap. "What did I miss?"

Izarra huffed. "Raven," she whispered, rolling up the parchment and placing it back in the rogue's backpack. "Come check out the fire Gideon built. Everyone's there now."

When the girls arrived at the bonfire, Avalann was crafting arrows as she sat in a chair, her feet propped up on a footstool she'd made from branches and vines. Izarra abandoned Raven to sit beside Jarz. Shorte sat on the end of the same log, roasting something on a stick.

Shorte glanced up at Raven. "You woke me up with all that snoring."

"*I* was snoring?" Raven asked, still groggy, rubbing her sore hand.

"Nice robe, Princess. Very nature-ish," Avalann blurted out.

Pulling her robe tighter as Shorte scooted over, Raven sat beside him at the end of the log. "Where's Gideon?"

"Where else?" Avalann answered. "In his wagon meditating."

"He has an important job," Jarz said in Gideon's defense. "I studied everything about the High Council and the Celestial Guardians. I'm surprised he has any life at all; the rules are so strict."

Avalann snorted derisively. "Can't be too strict," she stated as she motioned toward Raven. "He lets her parade around on a unicorn."

"What is your problem?" Raven snarled.

"Uh, oh," Shorte said quietly, withdrawing his stick from the fire.

"The problem," Avalann repeated, "is that ever since you were born, I've had to hear about how precious Raven is—the purple eyes, blah, blah."

"You have purple eyes?" Shorte interrupted as he turned to inspect her eyes. "Hunh . . . never noticed."

"I know jealousy when I hear it," Izarra pointed out, "and it's not flattering."

Avalann offered her familiar eye roll. "Who do you think recommended your father to become King of Omlett?" the elf questioned, ignoring Izarra. "Now his precious Raven is a princess."

The others sat quietly, staring at the fire. Shorte leaned over and lifted his leg to let out a loud fart, and they all began to laugh. "Nature's laughing gas, I always say," he chuckled as Raven held her nose and rushed to sit beside Izarra.

Gideon approached the group. "I'm glad to see everyone's getting along."

"Come here," Shorte said to the guardian, holding the meat on his stick. "Can you smell it and check if it is cooked properly?"

"No, thank you, Master Dwarf," Gideon responded. "I fell for it once when your Uncle Buzz'diir treated me to nature's laughing gas."

"Ha!" Shorte guffawed. "That's who taught me!"

"He got me by saying he came up with a new spell," Gideon chuckled as Raven watched his face light up with the memory. "Nature's laughing gas, he called it. I was confused because Captain Buzz'diir Plunkett was a fighter, not a wizard or a spell caster, but he told me to stand there and wait for it. I stood there waiting for some puff of smoke or something when it hit me." He paused. "I had never smelled anything so wretched in my entire life."

Everyone at the fire howled with laughter. Shorte laughed so hard that tears streamed down his face.

"I wasn't sure what was funny about it until I saw everyone around me laughing." Gideon shook his head at the silly memory, smiling sheepishly.

"Reminds me of a joke," Raven cut in. "A donkey and a pirate enter a tavern—"

Izarra and Shorte focused on Raven, but Gideon and Avalann tried to get her attention by shaking their heads.

Jarz angrily threw his stick into the fire and rushed to his tent.

"That was his late father's joke," Avalann said softly.

"I'm so sorry. I didn't know," Raven pleaded. "Maybe I should go and apologize."

"I'll go talk to him," Izarra said, rising and putting her hand on Raven's shoulder. "You didn't know."

Shorte extracted the meat from his stick with a cloth and threw the stick into the fire. "Well, this dwarf has had about as much drama as he can take." As he headed for his tent, he called out, "Night all."

"I need my rest," Avalann said as she headed toward her tree.

"Why do you sleep up there?" Raven asked.

Avalann glanced back. "I hate bugs," she replied as she climbed the vine.

Raven wasn't sure if Avalann was referencing her or the insects, but she let it go. Now, Gideon was the only one left with her at the campfire.

"You all right?" he asked with concern.

"I feel so out of place like I've been in my own world all this time, and now I'm experiencing a whole new one where I'm a step behind."

"Understandable," Gideon responded as he approached. "You're all grown up and on your own for the first time."

"On my own? You, Izarra, and Shorte are here."

"When I finish training you, you can go wherever you want and survive—alone. But what fun is that?"

"I'm not here for fun. I'm here to be the best guardian possible."

"And you shall be. But remember, if your father didn't have friends he could rely on, he wouldn't have been saved."

"But his friend is the one who put him in that situation." When Gideon turned pale, she dropped her head with regret. "I'm sorry." She quickly changed the subject. "I love the dragon armor. As gifts go, it's right up there with Ghost."

"I'm glad you like it," Gideon said, turning toward his wagon. "It's getting late. You should get some rest. You'll need it."

Raven grew worried. "What about my family, or that Astrick may be still roaming around in Omlett?"

"Your father knows what he's doing. They'll place down security measures for Alter-Self spells. It's not the first time we've faced a shapeshifter."

Raven nodded. "So, why didn't you tell me about Avalann and your family in Suttiir?"

"You never asked," Gideon replied as he continued to walk away. Shame washed over her as he continued, "Oh, by the way, I'll have Avalann instruct you on how to craft a shelter."

CHAPTER NINETEEN

TRIAL PAINS OF TRAINING

Wearing only his brown breeches, Gideon sat on the floor and dangled his legs from the open back door of the wagon. Watching the rising sun, he reflected on how quickly six months had passed since they'd arrived. It was the fourth of Vrrar; spring had sprung once again. In the moment of peace before gearing up, he closed his eyes and entered deep meditation. Using his vision power, he carefully scanned for any signs of abnormal portal openings or creatures from other realms.

The cart began to rock back and forth, and waves of yellow energy from his aura broke him from his trance. He burst barefoot out of his wagon, brandishing his vorpal sword as he investigated around his wagon. He couldn't find anyone but heard giggling from underneath. Extending his hand, he cast Levitation on the wagon to find Izarra, Shorte, and Raven laughing and staring at him.

Izarra stared at the shirtless elf. "Beauty-ex," she whispered to Raven.

"It's *beauteous*, Izarra," Raven corrected.

Gideon noticed Raven's flushed cheeks turned redder. After six months of holding back his feelings for her, he wanted to tell the world, but "Good morning" was all he managed to squeak as the trio rolled out from under the cart. "I see that even after a five-mile run, you're all still full of energy," he commented as he lowered the wagon, "so why don't we make it five more?" Izarra's smile disappeared while Raven's eyes were transfixed on him.

Shorte tried sucking in his stomach in a feeble attempt to impress someone. "It's getting there," he said proudly, patting his abdomen. "Six months of this grueling physical exercise—you'd think it would be rock hard by now."

Gideon smirked. "We can always do more crunches if you'd like." He looked over at the other two trainees at their camps. "You can join them, too!" he yelled to Avalann and Jarz.

The young elf threw down her backpack and glared at Gideon from her tree platform, but he was immune to her wrath. Jarz set down his water canteen and joined them. All five reluctantly headed out on another run.

Gideon returned his weapon to the wagon and then bathed in the lake. Today's training would push his limits and those of his students. *I hope they're ready.* He splashed his face one last time before trudging out of the water.

As he finished his breakfast by the campfire, his students returned from their run. As usual, Raven and Avalann were competing to see who would come in first. Avalann ran backward to taunt Raven. *Why can't they get along?* Suddenly, Shorte picked up speed and bypassed both girls, beating them to the finish line. The stubby cleric fell over, holding his chest.

Shorte laughed as he tried to catch his breath. "I'm dying!" he struggled to say as Avalann and Raven doubled over by his feet.

Raven kicked his boot. "What the spell, Shorte!"

"I didn't know I had it in me," the dwarf snorted as Jarz and Izarra ran up, hunched over, gasping for air.

"Would someone like to share the joke?" Gideon asked.

"We got tired of those two . . . always winning," Jarz said, taking deep breaths. "So, I cast the Haste spell . . . on Shorte."

"He's so witty," Izarra said, impressed. "You sure you aren't a bard?"

"Jarz, my friend, that was amazing!" Shorte said, gasping for air. "Why don't you . . . cast that more often? We could all finish . . . the runs quicker!"

"Because that would be cheating," Jarz responded, glancing at Gideon.

"I know, but can you teach me?" Shorte whispered to Jarz.

"I'm glad to see everyone in such good spirits," Gideon said over the trainees' chuckles. "Because today's task will be to learn an advanced spell."

"Finally!" Raven exclaimed.

"Everyone, grab breakfast, clean up, and I'll meet you by the falls. Make sure you bring your gear and weapons," Gideon instructed.

While the others resumed talking about Shorte's run, Gideon left the group. He gathered some magical components from his wagon and went to the falls. It was close to mid-morning when his students joined him.

"For the last six months, we've worked on physical conditioning and fine-tuning the skills you had before you came here. Today, we begin advanced spell skills. Over the next six months, each of you will learn three new spells. Miss Greenorr, your spells are Wind Wall, which allows you to deflect objects such as arrows; Tree Shape, which transforms you into a tree; and—"

"Wow," Shorte interrupted. "Guess I'll start relieving myself on bushes instead of trees."

Gideon continued. "—and since your biggest weakness is your fear of bugs—"

The group snickered. "I guess she was serious," Raven whispered to Shorte.

Avalann shot them a deadly glare. "Thanks, Uncle," she said snarky.

". . . since you dislike bugs, I'll teach you the Repel Vermin spell. It will let you keep all vermin, including insects, ten feet away."

"Great, that means Raven will stay ten feet away from me at all times," Avalann mocked vengefully.

"You don't need a spell for that," Raven mumbled.

Gideon turned to Jarz. "You're a strong wizard, but since you desire to train as a swordmage, I've chosen Teleport Defense, which allows you to teleport to any ally in trouble. Sword and Board will allow you to summon a magical sword and shield, and Sever Gravity will allow you to fly briefly."

"No fair. I turn into a tree, and Jarz gets to *fly*?" complained Avalann.

"Miss Lyte," Gideon said, ignoring Avalann, "your genealogy as part water nymph gives you strong water spells. You will learn Cleanse Water to help purify any contaminated water, Water Control, which can help you raise or lower pools of water, and Water Elemental, which will allow you to create water creatures. You can summon a varying selection of golems."

Izarra clapped with glee. "I can create my own water babies."

"Mister Stone-Grin, your clerical skills will be enhanced with the Stone Skin spell, protecting you from enemies by turning your skin to stone. Shield Others, a protective shield cast around a single target or a group to protect them, and Searing Light, a beam of light that will explode undead creatures."

"Great!" Shorte exclaimed. "I get to blow dead shite up . . . well, dead, then reanimated, shite."

"Miss Naelo, your rogue skills are top-notch," Gideon complimented Raven as Avalann scowled.

"As you know, I had a great teacher," Raven said.

"Your father was, and still is, one of the best, but we will focus solely on your sorcery spells. I want to teach you Invisibility, Blink, and Lesser Gaseous Form."

"Ha!" Shorte snorted. "I cast gaseous form naturally all the time!"

"Not that kind, Master Dwarf," Gideon said, restraining a smile. "Miss Greenorr, you will be first, and the rest of you will have some free time to continue practicing your melee skills." The other four armed themselves with their weapons and moved to the wagon near the campfire. "All right, Miss Greenorr, let's start with the Vermin spell."

They moved away from camp toward the opening of the woods.

"Uncle, it's just you and me here," Avalann said, following him. "Can we stop with the formalities?"

"Miss Greenorr," Gideon sternly replied while reaching into a pouch on his side, "you must have either mistletoe or holly to perform this spell." He handed her a branch of mistletoe and held another in his hand. "Focus your energy on the branch and rotate it circularly."

She extended the dark green plant, twirling it in a small circle.

"Good," he said as he stopped moving his branch. "Now, the incantation is *Vermin-Awaui.*"

"Got it," she replied, gripping the mistletoe.

Gideon noticed her hand shaking. *Why is she nervous? Her hands are always steady on the bow.* He placed his hand on top to help steady her. "Focus on the w—"

"I said I've got it."

Gideon stepped back, throwing his hands in the air as if surrendering. Then he gestured for her to begin. *I wonder why she's always cold toward me.*

She whispered the words, trying to memorize them as she lifted the branch to begin.

Gideon heard Jarz yell from behind, "Raven, watch out!"

The guardian turned and saw the rogue patting out the hem of her cloak. He shook his head and turned back to Avalann, who was doing circle after circle, chanting. "*Vermin-Thi.*"

"No, stop, stop! You're casting the Vermin Appear spell!"

He heard the others scream as Izarra jumped onto the log. Raven and Jarz froze, mouths agape as a massive army of spiders, ants, and countless other insects invaded their camp from the forest line. Shorte immediately smashed some with his mace as vermin scurried through the tall grass, heading straight for Avalann.

The archer screamed, ran over, and climbed onto Gideon's wagon. She made a giant leap for her tree vine, then climbed up to her platform.

"*Vermin-Awaui,*" Gideon yelled, waving the mistletoe as the vermin swarm retreated into the forest. "Are you all right, Avalann?" he called to her as the others laughed.

The young elf swung down and replied, "I'm fine. But maybe if you'd been paying attention to me for once instead of precious Raven, I wouldn't have messed up." She stormed off.

Gideon lowered his head as the rest of the group stared. "Mister Fisker, you're next," he sighed.

Jarz, clad in dark blue leather body and leg armor with a light blue cloak, the standard Waterfront-issued mage gear, adjusted his leather utility belt with little pouches. As he got closer, he dropped his cloak and cast blue illusion water wings. They weren't as big as the guardians' wings but weren't half bad for an illusion.

Gideon nodded. "I see why you want to be a guardian. It's the wings."

Jarz chuckled. "It's not the only reason, but they have fascinated me since I was a kid."

"This will probably be simple for you," Gideon said. "Hold out your arms and chant, Magol-a-pein."

Jarz did as Gideon instructed, and white magical sparks crackled from his hands. Energy moved up and down his arm as images slowly materialized. Moments later, Jarz held a white, beveled-edge shield and sword. Pale light trailed as the swordmage swung his weapon side to side.

"You can cast other spells but then lose the items. They will remain if you focus your magic on them."

"That was easy," Jarz replied as the items disappeared. He repeated the instructions, and the sword and shield reappeared. After a moment, the sword ignited in flames, and the shield grew sharp spikes.

"I think you've got the hang of it," said Gideon, impressed. "If we have time when I finish with the others, we can move on to your second spell."

"Great," Jarz responded, playing with his new sword and shield. "Thank you, Master Guardian." He then walked toward Izarra, who watched him manipulate his latest spell.

"Miss Lyte, your presence is required," Gideon called.

"Yes, sir," Izarra replied, skipping over to Gideon after whispering something to Jarz.

"I know you don't have much magical experience," Gideon noted, "but as a half-nymph, there is some somewhere inside you. So, we'll start with something easy." He guided her to the edge of the lake.

"Easy, I like easy."

"Take a pinch of dust or dirt, then hold out your hands and lower them while chanting the words, Nen-tovon."

Izarra picked up some dirt and tossed it into the lake. She held out her hands and lowered them as she chanted. The water in the lake receded inch by inch from the banks. "It's working!"

"Great job," said Gideon. "Now we'll do the opposite. Add a drop of water to the lake, hold out your arms, and then raise them as you chant Nɛn-ɛri."

Izarra tilted her water decanter over the lake, spilling a drop. She raised her arms and chanted, "Nɛn-ɛri." Amazingly, the water began to rise. "I'm doing it, Raven! Jarz, look!"

"Focus," Gideon commanded as the water overflowed onto the bank and submerged their boots. "You don't have to do anything special—just focus on it to make it stop."

"Gideon, it won't stop!" she said, panicking as the water flooded her tent and Jarz's.

"Focus, Izarra," Gideon instructed as the water moved closer to his wagon wheels. He quickly tossed in a handful of dirt, extended his arms, and lowered them, chanting, "Nɛn-tovon!" The water receded into the lake. Laughter sounded from above, and everyone looked up to see Avalann applauding. Embarrassed, Izarra stormed off to her flooded tent. Gideon shook his head at his niece in disappointment.

"Master Dwarf, you're up!" he yelled.

Shorte had been helping Jarz unpack his tent, which was now soaked. "I wonder how I can screw this up."

"I'll show you how to cast Stone Skin on yourself to help protect you from any stabs, cuts, bites, and claws."

"I could have used this one in that wench tavern in Brindell," Shorte snickered, elbowing the guardian, but Gideon was not amused and handed Shorte a pouch. "I get it." Shorte winked. "Those youngins makin' you wanna go drink, huh?"

"I believe Avalann is older than you."

"Bah, but she's still a baby in elf years," teased Shorte.

Gideon pointed to the pouch. "Take out some diamond dust and apply a little to your skin in a circular motion as you chant Sarn-Sɛrni-Riv."

"That's a mouthful," Shorte said, opening the pouch and rubbing it onto his arm. "Sarn—" He paused, forgetting the words.

"Sɛrni-Riv," Gideon corrected.

"Sɛrni-Riv," Shorte repeated. Small pieces of cobblestone formed across his skin, spreading to his arms, chest, face, and legs. "Holy smite!" he exclaimed as he patted his stomach. "Guys! Guys! I have rock-hard abs!" Everyone stopped what they were doing, and even Izarra couldn't help but laugh. "Sarn . . ."

"Sɛrni-Riv," Gideon finished.

"Sarn-Sɛrni-Riv, Sarn-Sɛrni-Riv—" the cleric repeated as he clunk-clunk-clunked back toward his tent in his new stone form.

"Miss Naelo," Gideon yelled, using his pointer finger to summon her.

Raven strolled down with two long side bangs over her onyx circlet and the rest of her hair tied back in its usual ponytail. A purple cloak topped the black dragon armor. She fiddled with the hilts of her daggers as she approached him. *She's definitely dressed for battle. Yet so beautiful. How do I tell her how I feel?*

"GIDEON!" Shorte yelled in alarm from the bush.

Gideon rushed over with Raven following, but the Mortal Realm Guardian stopped abruptly and looked on with a bemused expression while he suppressed laughter.

"I look like a fountain!" Shorte exclaimed as urine shot out of his stone groin.

Raven laughed uproariously. "Oh, we have to call the others."

Gideon grabbed her arm and shook his head. "It'll be fine, Shorte. Just say the words, Mo-Riv," he instructed. Shorte repeated the spell as things returned to normal, and the dwarf sighed in relief.

Gideon could still hear Shorte mumbling behind them as they returned to the training area. "Today, I'm going to teach you the Invisibility spell. I've applied it to your circlet, so all you need to do is chant the words Ed-Osite."

"Ed-Osite," Raven chanted and completely disappeared. "Did it work?"

"Yes, those beautiful eyes have vanished." There was silence. "Are you still there?" He reached into the air where she had been a moment before, and his hand brushed against her soft cheek. He followed the curve of her face and removed the circlet. "There they are." He smiled as Raven blushed.

"What happens if I'm not wearing it?" she asked, staring into his eyes.

"Cross your arms over your chest and repeat the spell."

She followed his every word, and parts of her body began to disappear. "Did it—"

"Raven!" Shorte called out. "Holy smite! What did you do? You have more holes in you than my underpants."

"What?!" Raven panicked, losing focus and causing her body to become whole again.

"As you can now tell, Miss Naelo, you must be focused without the circlet. It'll come to you with practice."

Gideon turned toward camp and yelled for the others to join them. "You all did well today. Even with the errors, you surpassed my expectations. I suggest you spend the rest of the evening practicing your spells. Mister Fisker, we will work on your other spell tomorrow."

Gideon pivoted to return to his wagon, but Raven stopped him. "Will you work with me a bit longer?" she asked. "Please!"

He felt overpowered by the innocent look when she said, "Please."

"Certainly, Miss Naelo. How can I be of assistance?"

"Come on, Gideon,"—Raven elbowed him—"quit the formalities."

"You're beginning to sound like Avalann."

"Umm, thanks a lot. I want to practice the Invisibility spell without the circlet."

"You may, but first, you must focus enough to feel the spell coursing through your body. Stand here, close your eyes, and cross your arms." Raven did as instructed. He stepped behind her and reached around, pulling her close to his chest. "Tighter. The spell's power comes from your body and mind working together." Her ponytail tickled his nose, making him shift his head to the side. Gideon inhaled the scent of Mara's homemade lavender soap in Raven's soft black hair. He snapped back to reality. "Now focus on your core. Imagine your body becoming lighter and the warmth spreading." He felt her pulse racing inside her wrist.

Is she nervous about getting the spell right, or is it because I'm holding her?

"Now repeat the spell," he whispered. Raven obeyed and vanished from sight, but he could still feel her body against his.

"Did I do it?"

"Yes," he said softly, still holding her. "You can release your arms at any time now." She didn't move for what seemed like an eternity. He held her a little tighter, feeling her chest rise with each breath. Raven pulled away, still invisible, and whispered, "Thank you, Gideon—for everything." Her soft lips brushed his cheek. Butterflies filled his stomach, and, for the first time in a long time, a spark of passion he'd suppressed since taking on the role of Mortal Realm Guardian exploded within.

"GHOST!" Izarra yelled.

Gideon felt a breeze as Raven reappeared, running toward her unicorn. *Eugor's going to assassinate me.* He greeted their guest, Pixie, as the dwarf dismounted from the carriage.

"Mister Keggs, it's nice to see you, my friend. Thank you for bringing the animals." Gideon watched his students' joy at seeing their companions.

Raven and Izarra fawned over Ghost while Shorte fed his plump, black miniature horse, Stubby. Avalann whispered to Krit, her black stallion, then whistled for her wolf pup, who jumped out of the wagon.

Izarra joined Avalann. "He's so cute."

Gideon was happy to note that Avalann didn't push her away.

"Everyone," he called, "please take the evening off. We'll begin again in the morning." As the trainees dispersed with their pets, Gideon overheard Izarra ask

Jarz where his companion was. Jarz summoned a Kelpie, a magical water horse, as they returned to the fire to continue drying their clothes. The young mage stripped down to his undergarments.

"Beauti-ex," Izarra called out.

"It's beauteous, Izarra! If you're going to steal my word, use it right," Raven joked, then shuddered. "You make me sound like my sister."

"Gideon, sir, if it's all right, may I stay overnight?" asked Pixie, yawning.

"Of course, and please help yourself to the rations as well," offered Gideon.

Pixie and Shorte made their way to the rocks near Shorte's tent while Avalann tied Krit to her tree and escorted her wolf pup to her platform. Jarz grabbed Izarra by the hand as they walked toward the lake. Pulling Ghost along, Raven followed. She looked back at Gideon, and the two exchanged quiet smiles.

Raven sat on the grass, avoiding the sand, watching Jarz and Izarra enter the lake. It was almost a full moon, and the moonlight's reflection danced on the water's surface. Gideon strolled over and sat beside her.

Jarz cast his Kelpie again, but this time, it was in the water and had fins for the front hooves and a mermaid tail for the back end. After lifting Izarra onto the horse, he pulled himself into the saddle. Izarra glanced back, beaming at Raven and Gideon before taking off around the lake.

"That looks like fun," Raven said, stretching her neck.

"It does," replied Gideon, watching her stare at the couple. He quickly rose and chanted, "Armis-Awaui." His wings folded in and disappeared as his gold-plated armor dropped to the ground next to him.

Raven giggled. "What are you doing?"

Gideon held out his hand. "Let's go."

Raven hesitated.

"What's wrong?"

"Do you remember when I told you what happened to my bathing hole back home?"

"Yes, I believe you mentioned it became swamp water."

"I'm afraid it will happen again," she said, frowning, "and I don't need Avalann teasing me about it."

"I'm here—I won't let anything bad happen." He leaned in closer, his hand still extended. Raven glanced up at him, smiling, the moonlight reflecting off her bright purple eyes.

Taking his hand, he helped her stand. Then she chanted "Armis-Awaui" to remove her dragon armor. She placed her circlet around Ghost's broken horn and retook Gideon's hand, interlocking their fingers.

Her skin is soft. Raven moved closer beside him as they walked together toward the lake. Suddenly, Gideon noticed a red flash on the sandy beach, and he swiveled his head to see the red gem in his gauntlet blinking. He raised his head and prayed to Blade that it would stop, but instead, it stretched into a constant glow. "I'm so sorry, Raven. I must check it out."

"It's all right," she replied. "I understand." She watched him call for his armor again.

Gideon summoned his wings. "Maybe we'll try this again tomorrow night?"

"Depends on if my instructor gives me the night off."

Gideon glanced back as she dove into the water and swam toward Jarz and Izarra, cozied on a giant rock in the middle of the lake. He entered his covered wagon and slammed the door. *This had better be damn important!*

CHAPTER TWENTY

ANOTHER YEAR

Raven wandered out of her makeshift tent. The chilly morning air made her rise later than she wanted. Stretching her tense body, she counted to ten, then stood from the toe touches as the crew, except Avalann and Gideon, gathered around her like the fallen leaves.

"Happy birthday!" they yelled in unison. Izarra hugged her, and Shorte handed her something that resembled a small cake with a candle stuck in it.

It feels like the thirty-first of IrAsil arrives way too fast.

"It's an oatcake," announced Shorte. "My great G-Ma taught me to make these if I was ever in a pinch. Don't mind the candle. It's a tradition for miners to have extra light."

"Izarra, don't douse it," Raven joked. She accepted the oatcake and blew out the candle, cautiously taking a bite. "Thanks, it's delicious," she said politely, trying not to gag. "Why don't you take it and cut it up so everyone can have a piece?"

"No need," Shorte replied. "I can make more."

"Fantastic," Raven mumbled as she forced another bite.

"I had to use natural ingredients," Shorte explained. "I was going to take some spices from Gideon, but he has that wagon secured better than the Omlett Prison."

"Why didn't you just ask?" Raven questioned.

"Never thought of that," Shorte answered as he walked away.

"So . . . nineteen?" Izarra asked.

"Yes, a year's gone, and it still feels like we just got here, doesn't it?"

Jarz hugged Raven and handed her a piece of blue quartz. "You can make it into some kind of jewelry."

"As I did," Izarra said happily, lifting her blue quartz necklace.

"It's beauteous," Raven replied, "thank you."

"Just keep it with you," Jarz said. "It helps me teleport to you if you're ever in trouble."

Raven smirked. "Well, let's hope it doesn't come to that." She glanced up at Avalann's tree fort and saw the elf staring out the window. It was awe-inspiring how she had made her platform into a small house. *And I'm still in a small tent.*

"Happy birthday . . . Princess," Avalann said snidely, closing the window shutter.

"Thank you," Raven yelled, returning her attention to Izarra and Jarz. "Where's Gideon?"

"No idea. We haven't seen him all morning," Izarra answered. "We let you sleep in because it's your special day."

"Is something wrong?" Jarz asked.

"Things have been awkward the last six months since our first spell training at the lake," Raven explained. "He's always so formal and never wants to be alone with me."

"We've noticed the tension between you two," Jarz confirmed. "But the High Council—"

Izarra slapped his arm. "Enough with the regulations. I think it's romantic."

"I mean, there might be something there," Raven stated unsurely, "but maybe I'm misreading his friendly intentions."

Izarra wrapped her arm around Raven. "I see how he looks at you, and trust me, being part nymph, I've seen it a million times."

Raven stared at the tall grass at her feet, torn between thoughts. "Izarra . . . but he's like family. It would be—"

"Weird?" Jarz interjected, eyeing Izarra as if he were still dwelling on the half-nymph's comment about the gawks.

"You're not helping," Izarra snapped, displaying a sour look as she placed her hand on Raven's lap. "Is it because of Thomas?"

Raven's brows dipped, and she tilted her head, but before she could answer, a blue portal opened, and Gideon stepped through.

"Gather around!" he called out as her stomach fluttered. She watched him inspect the area in his gold armor and white wings. He gracefully summoned seats for each of them and a floating map of Euphrasia. With each beckoned chair, she caught herself with a selfish urge for a gift. *Knock it off!* The others grabbed their seats. She was the last one to sit, still eyeing the guardian.

"I have reports that a group of bugbears is planning to attack some small human villages between here and Brindell, and a group of kobolds are occupying an old Dwarven mine just northwest of here." He pointed to a spot near the Gorge Mountain Range near the Gorge Lake. "Miss Greenorr and Mister Stone-Grin will go northwest to the Dwarven mine." He then pointed to a spot in Penn's Woods. "Miss Naelo, Miss Lyte, and Mister Fisker will head east to protect the human village against the bugbears."

"Ewww, bugbears," Izarra moaned. "Those tall, furry, humanoid, bear-like things?"

"Yes, Miss Lyte, those tall, furry, humanoid, bear-like creatures," Gideon answered.

"They are twice as strong as humans," Izarra complained.

"They are twice as strong but twice as foolish," Avalann replied with a snicker.

Izarra shrugged the comment off and continued, "I'm just implying, why don't we all stay together and do one mission at a time?"

"We don't know how long it will take for either mission," Gideon explained, "so I'm sending two groups to keep the attackers from increasing their numbers. I feel the groups that I assigned are capable of handling each task. So gear up and prepare to leave by sunset." They all stood as the map and chairs vanished. He left in a hurry and entered his wagon.

Avalann patted Raven on the shoulder and whispered, "Try not to kill them all."

"Ouch," Izarra responded, watching Raven's face sour.

"Avalann has said worst," Raven responded, still watching the guardian's wagon.

"I'm talking about how Gideon left without acknowledging your birthday. But maybe he's preoccupied with the missions," Izarra said comfortingly.

Raven shrugged and returned to her tent to pack her backpack for the two-day mission. She folded up her silk robe, a gift Gideon gave her on her seventeenth birthday. Running her hand over the smooth material, she glanced at the dragon-scale armor he gifted her that was currently in a pile in the corner. *It's not right for me to expect anything from Gideon.* After packing her gear, she stared at the circlet—yet another gift. She placed it on as the memory of opening the box last year flooded her mind. All that was left to do was to summon her armor, and she would be ready to go. Ghost loudly neighed, reminding her of her sixteenth birthday present from the guardian. *Am I being selfish?* Gideon's voice rang out, calling her name.

Raven exited her tent and trudged over to his wagon, where she found him sitting on the back steps. "Yes, sir," she said sarcastically.

"I need you to repair the front right wheel," he said. "I believe Mug taught you how to fix the spokes."

"You want me to fix your wheel?" she asked, irritated. "You're over three hundred years old. I thought you would have learned that by now."

"Theoretically, I'm still one hundred and forty-seven. I stopped aging when I swore the oath as a Celestial Guard."

"I know," Raven huffed, "Izarra and I already did the calculations."

"Is that so."

"That makes you equivalent to a twenty-one-year-old human."

"You're catching up to me."

Did he remember my birthday? Raven's pulse picked up. "I've been thinking about us down by the lake."

Gideon's eyes widened. "Oh, the training, yes, yes. The training by the lake."

"No, no, when we were going to go swim—"

Gideon gritted his teeth as he awkwardly nudged his head toward the back of the wagon. "Could you please inspect the wheel?"

Raven glared at him. The rejection felt like a backstab to the heart. His eyes shifted to an apologetic warmth as he saw right through her tough facade. She huffed and stormed around to the side of the wagon.

"Happy birthday!" two voices said in unison. Raven jumped, and her eyes lit up at the sight of her mother and father. She ran over to hug them.

"Did we teach you to argue with your instructor?" Eugor asked jokingly.

"No," Raven answered sheepishly, glancing back at Gideon as he smiled and disappeared behind his wagon. "I thought Gideon would be in trouble if he teleported people?"

"I guess he wanted to surprise you," Mara answered, handing her a box. "It's from your sister."

Raven carefully opened the box. "How is Carya?"

"She's doing well," Mara replied. "She misses you . . . a lot."

Eugor laughed. "I can't seem to keep her from pursuing Thomas."

"How's he doing?" Raven asked. *Does he miss me?*

"He helped rebuild the church, and now he serves under Stone-Prayer," Eugor told his daughter.

From the box, Raven removed a silver chain with a matching sword. A tear ran down her cheek as she dangled the charm.

"Raven?" Mara asked, concerned.

"It's Carya's favorite necklace. Her lucky Blade charm. She never takes it off," whispered Raven.

"I know," Mara said sweetly. "I was there when she decided to give it to you."

"Tell her I said thank you." Raven cried more tears. "And I will wear it always!" She hugged her mother again.

"I haven't been here in four decades," Eugor said, reminiscing. "I see the falls are as beautiful as ever."

"Let me introduce you to the rest of the Mortal Guardians," Raven said excitedly.

"Mortal Guardians?" Eugor chuckled. "Mug and I never had training nicknames."

"It was originally Gideon's Guardians, but Gideon thought that might bother the High Council."

Raven grasped her mother's hand, and Eugor followed them to the campfire. Gideon had already gathered the rest of the troops. "Mother, Father . . ." Raven glanced around and began the introductions. "That is Avalann."

The archer bowed.

"Gideon's niece," Eugor beamed. "It's a pleasure to see you again."

"You know, Shorte."

The dwarf bowed.

"Buzz sends his best," the king relayed.

"And, of course, Izarra."

The half-nymph bowed.

"I can never thank you enough for helping my daughter," Mara said, hugging her.

Izarra giggled. "That feels so long ago. But she would have done the same for me."

"Mother." Raven paused. "Jarz Fisker."

The young mage bowed respectfully. "Aunt Mara."

Mara's eyes welled with tears, then faced Eugor in disbelief. She ran over to Jarz and hugged him tightly. "You're so tall now," she chuckled, "you look so much like your father. I have so many things I would love to discuss with you."

Gideon put his arm around Eugor. "See, I'm taking good care of them."

Her father grinned. "I would like to know more about the training by the lake."

Raven overheard the comment, glancing at the guardian as he humorously deflected the question. The age difference was apparent, but sadness flooded her when a revelation hit.

Gideon has been taking care of the Mortal Realm for over a century. Who's there for him? Have we taken him for granted?

"I heard their first true mission is coming up soon," Eugor stated loudly for the group to hear.

"Indeed," Gideon replied. "They're leaving first thing in the morning."

The group gasped.

"I thought we were leaving tonight!" Avalann said with surprise.

"Happy birthday, Raven," Gideon said, smiling the same playful grin captured in her father's portrait. The guardian shook Eugor's hand and kissed Mara's. "Enjoy your stay, King and Queen Naelo." Then he left for his wagon. Raven's gaze remained locked on the guardian.

Avalann retreated to her tree shack. Izarra sat with Jarz and Raven's mother, absorbing every detail discussed regarding Jarz's past. Eugor sat with Shorte, most likely to talk about Shorte's Uncle Buzz'diir.

Raven debated whether she should talk to Gideon but realized she didn't have much time to spend with her parents before her first quest, so she sat beside her mother.

"I'm sorry for not finding you or sending you a message," Jarz said apologetically. "The headmaster suggested I begin my training right after we visited the aftermath of the orc attack."

"I thought I lost everyone at Fellswar," Mara said sadly. "No sign of your brother?"

"We found my father's body," Jarz explained, "but no sign of my brother."

"I can relate," Izarra cut in. "I found my father a year ago."

"How's he doing?" Mara asked.

"He's buried in Omlett Cemetery. He was a captain in the army," Izarra said with tears in her eyes.

"I'm so sorry," Mara replied. "What was his name?"

"Brian Lyte."

"Eugor, dear," Mara said, getting her father's attention. "Do you remember Captain Brian Lyte?"

"Yes, I do," Eugor recalled. "He liked his privacy, but before every battle, he always said, *day or night*—"

"—*shines my starlight*," Izarra finished.

"Izarra is his daughter," Mara said.

Eugor came over and shook her hand. "Your father was a brave man," he told her. "He died protecting Omlett from the half-orcs of Grey-Holg. They tried to take more territory, but we held them off."

"He died over land?" Izarra asked, shocked.

"He died saving the citizens on the outskirts of Omlett," Eugor explained. "He helped save lives, not just land." He placed his arm around a tearful Izarra. "We had no idea his family was still in Thistlebane."

Izarra sobbed. "My mother won't leave."

"What's her name, dear?" Mara asked.

"Dawn Hari Lyte," Izarra answered, her voice shaking, "but thank you. I've finally received the answers I've been searching for all this time."

A lump formed in Raven's throat as tears welled in her eyes. *How horrible it must be to lose someone you love before they have time to live truly.*

Mara slowly rose, dusting off her gown. "Well, this has been an emotional trip." Colorful fireworks exploded over the lake, causing her to jump.

The sound got Avalann to open her window shutters. Everyone walked over and gathered at the water. Jarz put his arm around Izarra as she leaned against him. Eugor did the same with Mara and his daughter.

Raven glanced down at Shorte, standing alone, so she knelt and put her arm around him. She looked up at the tree house and saw Gideon sitting with his niece, watching the fireworks through the window. *I wish this moment of peace, camaraderie, and love to last forever.*

With the last crackle of the biggest firework, everyone clapped. Gideon flew down from the tree and approached them.

"I believe that is our cue," Eugor said to Mara. "Take care of our daughter," he said, shaking his friend's hand.

"Always, Eugor." Gideon handed Mara a scroll. The parents hugged Raven one last time as her mother cast the portal back to Omlett.

Raven watched the gateway close. Her eyes followed Shorte's route to his tent, stretching and exposing his hairy stomach. The dwarf ducked into his shelter as Izarra and Jarz passed by hand-in-hand, moving closer to the lake.

They make having a relationship look so easy.

"Happy birthday again, Raven," Gideon said, awaiting a response. When none came, he mocked, "Thank you, Gideon," in a high-pitched tone before switching back to his normal voice. "You're welcome." But still no response from the rogue. She stood there like a statue, deep in thought. As he continued, her nerves had her frozen like a freeze spell. "Well, I'm going to retire for the night."

Raven stared momentarily as her heart raced while watching him walk away. The guardian glanced back.

It's now or never! She rushed to catch up as he opened the wagon door.

"Raven," Gideon said as her breath paused and her heart pounded against her chest. She gripped his tunic. "You all ri—" he tried to ask as she pulled his face closer. He tensed as their lips touched, then softened after placing his hands on her hips, pulling her closer.

Her mouth caressed his lips, tasting the sweetness of the blackberry tea, his favorite drink. A tingling sensation filled her stomach as the nerves in her body enhanced the pressure of his touch, sending uncontrollable shivers throughout her body. The fear of this moment quickly subsided in favor of how comfortable he made the experience. Their lips danced in sync. The passion of his embrace blocked the millions of doubts that threatened to invade her mind. They pulled apart, trying to catch their breath, staring into each other's eyes.

Raven whispered, "I wish this moment could last forever."

Gideon's face was flushed as he raised his left arm. "Prohibere Tempus." A white glow surrounded his lifted hand, and the sound of the waterfall silenced, as did every creature singing in the evening.

Raven glanced over the lake to see the waterfall, which remained perfectly still. The bats froze in mid-flight. "What the spell?"

"Time stop," Gideon replied, never releasing his gaze from her.

"Is there nothing you can't do?"

Gideon paused. "I can't sing."

Raven snickered and hugged him as the white light faded. The sound of the waterfall seemed more thunderous than before as it rushed back to life. She gently lowered his head and then whispered in his ear. "I think I can live with that."

She pressed her forehead against his chest, holding him tighter. *Am I dreaming?*

"What does this mean?" Gideon asked.

"I don't know," she answered, gazing into his eyes, "but like everything else, we'll figure it out." The sound of footsteps made her quickly pull away as Avalann lumbered around the corner, holding a piece of parchment.

The embarrassed rogue made a beeline for her tent as Gideon called out, "Raven!"

How much did Avalann see? Raven dove into her tent and onto her sleeping bag. *Does it even matter?* Taking deep breaths to slow her racing heart, she rolled onto her back, gripping her pillow tight. *What does this mean?*

CHAPTER TWENTY-ONE

MORTAL GUARDIANS

The pressure of a palm caressed her cheek. Raven's heavy eyelids struggled to open as a blurry image faded in and out. As her sight focused, so did Gideon's ice-blue eyes, staring down at her. They were alone in her tent. *You were my first kiss.* Her pulse quickened.

"You're a—" Gideon began, but Raven darted straight up to receive her second kiss before he could finish his words. Something wasn't right—it didn't feel like the night before. His warmth, smell, and taste were gone. Excessive saliva filled his mouth as he pulled back. His face swelled bright red as he struggled to breathe.

She quickly crawled backward against the tent as a corrosive liquid spilled from his lips, melting the flesh around his mouth. The acid continued burning through his skin, exposing his jawbone.

Her hand trembled, trying to reach out to touch his cheek. "Gideon! I'm so, so sorry!"

As the guardian collapsed in front of her, Butch's voice echoed in her mind. "You're a monster."

Raven scrambled out of her tent on her knees, colliding with someone's legs. She glanced up to see her father's horrified expression.

"You can't take care of him." Her father's face shifted to a murderous look. "He's a guardian. Your relationship will be the Mortal Realm's downfall."

Standing behind him was her mother, weeping. "Jarz doesn't love us! He abandoned his own family." *Something still doesn't feel right.* She glanced around the camp as a dome of darkness descended on the alcove. The trees wilted and died. Mud slushed over the waterfall's edge. The smell of decay and rot filled the air as she noticed the ground softened into wet earth. Brugg grabbed her by the ponytail, dragging her to the mud-filled lake, screaming, "You're a monster!" in Orcish. He shoved her into the sludge where Carya and a shirtless Thomas waited.

"Rise and shine!" Carya teased, wrapping her arms around Thomas. "How's that pompous head of yours since I stole what you wanted?"

"What the spell is going on?" Raven quivered.

They both laughed, then Thomas replied, "Did you really think I would fall for a demon?"

Carya held up her scarred hand. "My dear sister, you hurt me. I'm just returning the favor, and besides, no one wants to love a hideous monster."

Raven struggled to speak. "Carya—"

"This isn't my first," Carya smirked, then pulled Thomas in for a passionate kiss.

Raven gasped, rapidly sitting up in her sleeping bag as sweat beaded on her forehead. *What a nightmare!* She ran her hand across her brow, wiping away the sweat. Her hands shook as "monster" echoed in her head. She grabbed her canteen, downing warm, stale water. Tossing the empty container aside, she stood, stretching her sore arms. Trying to steady her nerves, she closed her eyes, counting to ten, before greeting the others.

Raven parted the tent flap and gazed out. The rays of sunlight radiated on her face, temporarily blinding her. The sky was a bright blue as a gentle breeze blew through her hair. *What a beauteous day!* Birds sang when they weren't flying back and forth from the trees, searching for the morning worms. The smell of fried eggs and bacon wafted nearby, making her stomach rumble.

In the distance by the fire, she overheard Jarz explaining that the theatrical powder wasn't necessary for battle. *The mission!*

Raven grabbed her already-packed backpack. She released the straps, opened the flap, and inspected all the compartments to ensure all the contents were there. *Rations, blanket, bandages, ointments that mother sent, disarm trap kit, and fire starter.* After taking inventory for the third time—*I feel I'm missing something*—she tossed the bag onto the ground, sinking to her knees. *Or am I stalling?*

Anxiety hit again as she took a deep breath. *Is it about the upcoming mission or the night terror I just had?* She placed her hand on Blade's necklace, which rested above her pounding heart. *Blade, watch over me.* Picking up the empty water canteen, she strolled down to the lake. She knelt, staring at her reflection while filling the jug. After securing the cap, she splashed cold water on her face, closed her eyes and inhaled the crisp fall air before returning to her tent.

Raven placed her circlet on her head and chanted, "Tolth-Armis," to equip her armor. Sheathing her daggers, she picked up her backpack, took a deep breath, and opened the tent flaps. *At least I get to try out my new spells.* The thought kept her mind on the task and not the horrible dream.

Raven approached Izarra and Jarz, who were finishing their breakfast at the campfire. She wanted to wish Shorte good luck, but it was odd for him not to be there telling crude jokes or releasing nature's laughing gas. She glanced toward Avalann's hut and noticed the door and windows secured with wooden cross bars. Near the makeshift animal pen where they kept their pets, Krit and Stubby were gone. Ghost was lazily eating hay. Oslo, the wolf pup, was sleeping in the cool shade underneath Gideon's wagon, chewing on an animal bone.

Poor Shorte, probably forced to leave so early. I'm glad I'm not on her team.

Raven grabbed a red apple from the ration basket. "Are you two ready?" she asked, taking a bite of the crisp, juicy fruit.

"Not quite," replied Jarz. "I need my armor. I'll return in a moment."

Izarra placed her hand on the rogue's shoulder, fully clad in the new, midnight-blue leather armor her mother had sent with Pixie in last week's delivery. "You all right? You look like you've seen a lich or something."

"I'm fine," Raven responded, instinctively trying to hide the shaking apple she held. "Are you nervous?"

"A little," Izarra admitted. "You?"

Raven placed her other hand on her friend's shoulder. "I've been waiting for this opportunity since I was thirteen. I want to test my new spells."

Izarra nodded unsurely.

"You'll be fine. Have you seen Gideon?"

"Why?" Izarra asked, eyes gleaming. "Need a good luck kiss?"

"What? No!" Raven snapped, almost choking on a chunk of her breakfast.

Izarra giggled. "Your cheeks are turning the same color as that apple. He's in the—" But before Izarra could finish, Gideon exited the forest.

Butterflies rose in Raven's stomach. *I can't believe I kissed him—my first real kiss.*

Gideon's face beamed as he yelled, "Good morning, Miss Lyte, Raven!"

Raven's blush grew as if this was the first time she saw the real *him*. Not as a realm guardian, not as a friend she took for granted, but something different, something more. No longer just a mere family acquaintance. Even though one eye was narrower than the other, and his battle-worn scars from magical weapons now notably stuck out, he was more handsome than ever. His ruffled hair seemed more golden than blond and his lower lip occasionally quivered. She realized the mental image she always had of him was gone. *The perfect aura surrounding him vanished, and I don't care.*

Izarra winked, nudging the rogue with her elbow. "You sneaky wench."

Gideon approached them, sounding chipper. "A beautiful morning, wouldn't you agree?"

"Of course, sir," Izarra agreed, with a high-pitched voice, nudging the rogue again.

"Beauteous," Raven mumbled awkwardly, her mind still racing.

Jarz returned clad in his Waterfront issue armor and cloak, stating, "We're leaving now, sir."

"Remember your training, and you'll all be fine," assured Gideon. "Good luck and may Blade watch over you."

Raven stared at Gideon, watching for a reaction, deciding whether public affection was appropriate. *Why not? I mean, Izarra and Jarz are in a relationship.* But she shyly turned away and rubbed her sister's necklace before throwing on her backpack and grabbing Ghost's reins.

Jarz summoned his water horse, and Izarra climbed on behind him. The three trotted out of camp, heading east toward Brindell.

Raven trailed behind her partners, glancing back to see Gideon watching. His expression triggered a memory of how Eugor always looked at Mara. *Carya and I used to call it "the twinkle"—or am I imagining it?*

They traveled to a human village named Penn's Woods. It took a day's ride, so night had fallen by the time they'd arrived. The trio dismounted and stretched before hiding in the dense trees surrounding the village.

Jarz set up a couple of torches around the perimeter before the three protectors settled against the trees, removing rations from satchels. He flopped down next to Izarra after handing out beef jerky.

Famished, Raven snagged the meat and then sliced her dagger into a loaf of oat bread Shorte had baked. The rogue noticed Izarra scrunching her face. "What?" she asked as she spread the slice with autumn olive jam Carya had taught her how to make.

"That dagger was *lodged* in someone," Izarra responded, placing a canteen in front of Jarz.

Raven stopped chewing, shrugged, and replied with a full mouth. "I clean'em."

Jarz snickered, almost blasting water out his nose, as Izarra nodded slowly, placing a strawberry in her mouth. He wiped his mouth and chin. "Do I even want to know where the dagger was lodged?"

"Head," Izarra responded bluntly, leaning back against the swordmage as she fed him a strawberry. "One of Astrick's henchmen."

Raven stopped chewing again. "To be fair, I was aiming for his chest." She glanced at the scar on her palm. "It won't happen again."

Izarra plucked a few grapes from the stem. "Doesn't matter. It's still gross."

As the trio finished eating, Izarra snuggled against Jarz, who placed his arm around her as they listened to the nightlife in the woods. The couple grew unusually quiet.

Raven pictured herself cuddling like that with Gideon. The thought of security in his arms triggered a warm sensation throughout her body. She finished her last bite, brushed the crumbs off her hands, and finally broke the silence. "But I do clean them well."

Izarra's head rested on Jarz's shoulder. "How do we plan to stop the bugbears from attacking Penn's Woods? Will they negotiate with us?"

"I don't think so," Jarz replied solemnly, gently sitting Izarra up to place the rest of the beef sticks inside his pouch. "I think we'll need to fight." Jarz moved back into position. When Izarra laid against him, he tenderly touched her trembling hands.

Izarra intertwined their fingers in response. "I never had to fight at this level and with new spells, what if I—?"

"You'll do fine," Jarz responded, kissing the back of her hand. "I'll protect you if need be."

"So will I," Raven added, trying to stay confident for her friend. "It'll be easier than swallowing Shorte's oat cake."

Izarra whispered to Raven, "If you were a bugbear, where would you hide?"

"My father faced them before. He told me they like to shelter in caves," Raven answered. "They're diurnal, so they should be sleeping. Now would be the best time to search."

The others nodded in agreement before standing and adjusting their gear. Jarz and Izarra grabbed the lit torches as Raven untied Ghost's reigns. "Follow me." The protectors moved to a prominent hilltop nearby. She scanned the area, noticed a cloud of smoke, and spotted a cave entrance on the side of a mound across from them. "Lights out," she ordered as Izarra and Jarz extinguished the torches.

Jarz pointed to an overgrown bush near the mouth of the cave. "I think that is our best option."

"Agreed," Izarra responded. "I just wish we knew how many there were."

Raven turned to her friends. "I think I have an idea, but you won't like it."

Izarra frowned. "I know that look."

"I'll sneak down there and try to get into their lair."

"No!" Jarz and Izarra declared simultaneously.

"Listen," Raven pleaded, "I have my boots and the invisibility spell. They won't hear me or see me." She turned to Jarz. "Watch my back, and if anyone approaches from behind, teleport with Izarra to the top of the mound where the smoke is."

"Then what should I do?" Izarra asked.

"Set up a perimeter to make sure no wandering scouts sneak up. If they do, hit them with your geyser. Bugbears hate getting their fur wet."

Jarz and Izarra glanced at each other and then nodded in agreement.

"Wait here," Raven instructed and moved toward the cavern. *Thank you, Father, for the new boots.* She chanted "Ɛd-Ơƨitɛ," the Invisibility spell, and vanished. As she made her way across the small clearing, she felt the quarter moon follow her till she reached the entrance. *No guards?*

Raven scanned the area. The fall leaves were vibrant colors scattered on the ground. *These creatures would never leave their home unguarded unless they have security somewhere.* She cautiously searched for traps among the vines that twisted to the slimy rock entrance. Patches of Toxicodendron Radicans almost rubbed against her hands. *Poison Ivy. Thank you, Carya, for the lessons on poisonous plants.*

Two small piles of rocks, perfectly placed at each side of the entrance, caught her attention. *That is not a natural formation.* She carefully stepped closer. *I found the traps!*

Foliage covered the explosive containers snuggled in the rocks, and Raven located the thin trip wire that ran between them at ankle height.

Memories of Mug explaining different types of powders flooded her mind. With her father's experience with the bugbears, he had her disarm this exact type of trap plenty of times. But during practice, flour exploded, covering her when she was unsuccessful. *I can't fail now, or I'll be the ingredient for their cakes.* She reached into her pouch, removing a pair of wire cutters. Jarz was probably staring at her, screaming, *Don't do it!* Carefully, she reached down and cut the wire. *Well, I'm still alive.* After stowing her tool, she quickly wound the wire up and placed it to the side of the explosive. *I might need that later.*

Raven crept further inside, carefully keeping her back against the wall. Her hands slid across the mossy stone as her right hand pressed down, crushing a giant mushroom. A foul-smelling odor filled the space. *Gross. Now, they'll smell me a mile away.*

As she crept closer to the bugbear den, she noticed the floor and walls covered by thicker tree roots. Wooden support structures helped shape the hollow hill. She crouched, peering between two massive guards. By a pool of water sat a tree trunk converted to a makeshift altar with carved markings.

A massive firepit for cooking sat under the hole the tree had created through the cave roof, which the bugbears used to vent their smokestack. Raven took a deep breath, crawled further inside, and then gasped. *There must be at least fifty bugbears.*

Many were asleep, but others were tending to the injured. *What the spell?* At the far wall, they had human prisoners shackled with chains. An elderly man lay crumpled on the floor while three young women huddled together, trying to protect two children.

Raven turned quietly, returning to her partners at the tree line. She knelt beside them, becoming visible again.

Izarra jumped. "Some warning next time."

"Disarming explosives!" Jarz exclaimed in disbelief. "Are you insane?"

Raven waved him off and then updated them. "Looks to be around fifty-ish bugbears. And they have six human prisoners."

"So, we're too late—they've already attacked," Izarra blurted out.

"Yes, and we need to act now. A few of the captives don't look well," Raven stated.

"The first thing to do is distract the bugbears so we can rescue the people," Jarz said confidently. "We need something big."

"What about Baby?" Izarra asked as her face appeared deep in thought, trying to remember her spell to call up the giant water elemental.

"Izarra, you're a genius," Raven replied. "Jarz, you've been practicing the Dark Vision spell with Gideon, right?"

He nodded.

"Good, because I have another plan." Jarz and Izarra groaned as Raven smiled. "Trust me."

"Always," Izarra replied.

"I'll relocate the explosive boxes above the opening. If any bugbears follow us, their foreheads—"

"Will set off the charges," Jarz finished.

"Exactly." Raven faced Izarra. "Jarz and I will go inside the tunnel for the prisoners. We need you to keep Baby at full strength for as long as possible. Tie Ghost further back in the trees so she's safe."

Raven returned to the cave entrance and quietly dug out the two small explosive boxes underneath the leaves and dirt, replanting them at the top of the mound. Her father had told her how he and Mug rigged their traps like this. *He would be ecstatic to know that I listen to his stories.* The thin tripwire stretched above her head as she carefully reattached it to the charge. She signaled to Jarz for him to teleport over. After a brief moment, her friends appeared from thin air. "Izarra, cast Baby just beyond the trip wire," Raven instructed. "Have him snuff out all the torches."

Jarz smiled. "I think I know where you're going with this."

"Jarz, you'll evacuate the prisoners," Raven continued. "Izarra, you go to the other side of the hill. There's a water source entering somewhere near the top. It's supplying them with a water pool. Once I seal the entrance, flood it."

Izarra gulped. "Umm . . . sure."

"Let's do this," Raven said, cheering them all on enthusiastically.

Izarra ducked under the tripwire and poured out a drop of water. She chanted, "N̲ǫn-Ūạn." The bead of water expanded in size, forming a giant water golem. It barely fit inside the cavern when it sprung to life. Izarra, still crouched, exited the cavern while Jarz planted his torch on the ground at the mouth of the cave and lit it.

Jarz dodged the tripwire and cast Dark Vision.

Raven activated True Seeing on her circlet, then glanced at the half-nymph. "Now, Izarra!"

The water golem marched forward, extinguishing every wall torch along the tunnel. As the passageway grew darker, Raven and Jarz followed. Baby must have reached the main camp area because the sound of chaos ensued, filling the cave. Once Raven reached the opening, she saw panicking bugbears knocking things over in their rush to grab weapons as Baby's splashing continued, slamming them around with the power of its hydro-fist.

Raven cast Arcane Step to appear behind the guards at the entrance, backstabbing them as Jarz summoned his water wings and cast his magical sword and shield, slaying a pair of bugbears as they reached for their swords. The rogue and swordmage met at the back wall where the prisoners were chained.

Jarz decapitated the bugbear guard surrounding the humans. A young girl screamed, flaying her arms as the bugbear's head rolled.

While Raven picked the lock of a child's shackles, the child accidentally smacked her upside the head. *Dragon poop!* The rogue removed the Invisibility spell. "Calm down. We're here to help. You're being rescued," she said, pointing in the direction of the exit as a head rolled from another decapitated bugbear.

The prisoners formed a line behind Jarz as he rushed them out of the cave to safety, but the older man fell behind the group. While Jarz guided the women and children under the tripwire, Raven guarded the gentleman until the swordmage returned. They raised their heads and froze in response to a massive splashing sound.

"No!" Izarra's voice echoed through the cavern. Baby exploded over the central campfire, drenching everything. The bugbears roared in triumph once the watery threat became a puddle.

"Jarz, I'll hold them off," Raven said as the swordmage returned. "Make sure she floods this place."

"Yes, ma'am," he replied as he teleported the older man and himself to Izarra.

Raven whispered, "Ed-Osite," and became invisible again. She unsheathed her daggers and flattened herself against the wall as heavy footsteps approached. The first bugbear ran by, but she stuck out her leg to trip the second one. The hideous humanoid fell, creating a pileup of the ones behind him. The first bugbear's forehead pressed against the trip wire, and two explosions collapsed the entrance. She couldn't see any signs of the torchlight outside, so she prayed to Blade that the cave would seal the water. The bugbears wandered in the dark as a few struggled to dig out the first bugbear from the rubble.

Raven returned to the enemy's camp area. The bugbears frantically rubbed sticks together to spark another fire, but to no avail. She nervously waited by the water pool. "Come on, Izarra," she whispered, wondering if her friend would fill the cave with her inside. The cold water flooded her boots just as the rogue finished her thought.

The bugbears stopped as the water washed over their feet. They panicked, running into each other, searching with their hands, trying to locate a wall. Some cowered in the wrong direction, while others spun in circles in confusion as water rose to their waists. "Keep going, Izarra," Raven whispered.

As the water rose above her head, her armor made it easy for her to float on her back as some bugbears struggled to stay afloat. She couldn't watch as some gasped for their last breath. She quietly chanted to dispel True Seeing before going underwater. Still, it enhanced the sound of gargling filling the cave, making it almost unbearable, and she pretended she was at her bathing hole, humming a tune to drown out the sound of death. The water rose enough to where she could touch the ceiling, and she cast True Seeing again before the water filled the cavern.

Reaching up with her hands, she guided herself along the ceiling until she found the opening of the smokestack. The stone chimney filled with water, which meant the entrance to the cave must've been immersed, too. Finally, the water receded down the stack shaft until it reached her shoulders. A silhouette appeared above her, and a rope was dropped for her to grab. She caught it, trying to pull through, but her shoulders wedged in the rock. "I won't fit," Raven yelled. She recited the incantation for her armor to drop off. "It's still going to be tight."

Jarz chanted something, pointing at her.

Raven's grip on the rope loosened, surprising her. She held on tighter as she watched her hands shrink. The hole in the ceiling seemed to be further away.

Wrapping her legs around the rope, she began to climb again. This time, her body cleared the gap in the rocks. A tug on the rope flung her out of the hole and over the hollow tree stump. Jarz stood over her, holding the other end. He appeared to be ten feet tall.

At that moment, she realized that he reduced her to the size of a gnome. "What are you—" she began to ask but stopped when her voice was weirdly high-pitched. Her friends snickered as Jarz ended the spell.

Raven returned to her original size as he tossed her a towel. She chanted to reclaim her armor, which immediately appeared on her. "Let's set up a camp for the people," she instructed, "then Jarz can fly to Brindell and have them bring a carriage with armed guards."

One of the female prisoners approached them, full of gratitude. "Thank you so much."

"You're welcome," replied Izarra. "Just rest. We'll be here until help arrives."

"Who are you?" asked another, hugging the children.

Raven smiled. *Oh, I've been waiting to say this*! "The Mortal Guardians."

The next day, after the Brindell guards had picked up the prisoners, the group returned to Gideon's camp. The ride was quiet as the Kelpie kept pace with Ghost. Izarra's arms wrapped around Jarz, and her head rested on his back as she fell fast asleep.

Raven's eyes felt heavy, and every time they closed on their own volition, the images of lifeless bugbears drowning in the water jolted her awake.

As the sun sank below the tree line before them, Jarz called out, "Shall we stop for the night?"

"No," Raven replied, sitting upright. The thoughts of Gideon kept her motivated. "Let's get back before nightfall."

As the last sunlight vanished, Raven saw the opening to camp just ahead, and she urged Ghost to gallop. Upon entering the camp, they watched Gideon carry a pile of firewood.

When the guardian glanced over, his expression changed from worry to joy. He dropped the wood and rushed over to them as Raven dismounted and tied Ghost to the back of the wagon. "How did the mission go?"

Killing creatures isn't exactly an enjoyable mission, but if we hadn't, the bugbears would have destroyed the human prisoners. "It went well," Raven stated. "I suppose."

"Well?" Izarra balled her fists, placing them on her hips. "I would describe it as exhausting, emotional, dangerous, and insane." Everyone eyed her in surprise. "When do we go again?"

"So . . . it went well?" Gideon teased, and then Izarra spat out every dramatic detail of the task.

Jarz interrupted. "He already knows, Izzy. Wizards can scry."

"True, Mister Fisker," Gideon replied, "but not this time." He turned to Raven. "So, how long were you submerged for?"

"It was longer than I can stay under," Izarra shared. "I was terrified that I had waited too long to lower the water, but then we saw her head pop up under the smokestack. I was so relieved!"

Gideon provided a strange look.

"What?" Raven asked. "Carya and I have been able to swim underwater for long periods ever since we were kids."

"Have the others returned?" Jarz asked, glancing around.

"Not yet," Gideon answered, "but don't worry, Avalann and Shorte should return soon. Meanwhile, go rest up. You deserve the night off."

Izarra and Jarz returned to their tents as Raven followed, but Gideon grabbed her hand, leading her to the back of his wagon. He kissed her gently, taking her breath away.

"I'm pleased you've returned safe," Gideon said, caressing her face. "I missed you."

"Is this the way you greet all your returning students? Shorte will be ecstatic."

"Beards tickle my nose," he teased, then his smile faded. "Are you all right?"

"I won't lie—taking a life isn't easy. But this is my chosen path, and I'll do what needs to be done." As she pulled him closer, she felt his heart beating through his tunic. "I've been thinking about us since we left."

He stroked her hair. "Would you like to spend some time together tomorrow? There's a lot we need to figure out."

"I would like that," Raven answered, smiling shyly. "I just don't want the others to know yet."

"I understand. I figured since you left without even a hug."

"I'm sorry, I'm still figuring it out."

"Don't apologize. I am, too."

Izarra ran up to Raven as Gideon returned to his wagon. "What were *you* doing?" she asked with a grin.

Raven beamed, ignoring her question. "Where's Jarz?"

"Bathing. I promised I wouldn't peek this time."

"I'm surprised you're not in there with him."

"I know, right?" Izarra giggled.

Raven noticed Shorte's empty tent. "Should I be worried? They had a shorter distance to travel, and Avalann was very strategic. They should have returned by now."

"They're fine," Izarra assured her. "If Gideon isn't concerned, you shouldn't worry either."

"Izarra, I'm done!" Jarz yelled up to the girls. "The warm water spell should last for a bit yet."

"I'm going to go soak in a long, warm bath and dream of Miss Crinkly's chocolate mint cakes," said Izarra as she dashed to the lake.

Raven called off her armor and dove into her sleeping bag. Being so exhausted, she didn't have the energy, even for nightmares.

As the morning sun lit up the sky and the early birds sang, she tried shaking off the grogginess. She moved to the campfire, striking the flint with her dagger to light it. *They must still be in bed, and I'm sure Gideon is meditating.* But she couldn't shake her concern for Shorte and Avalann. Following her instincts, she summoned her armor, grabbed a few pieces of fruit, jumped onto Ghost, and dashed off to help her friends. *Gideon will understand.*

After what seemed to be a quick day's travel, the evening was falling rapidly as Raven carefully approached the mountainside. The only obstacle between her and the mine entrance was a narrow stretch of woods. After tying Ghost to a tree, she searched for Shorte and Avalann. She saw the opening to a mine shaft a few hundred feet before her. The torches along the shaft opening were the only light in the darkness.

Raven quietly navigated through the woods toward the two bright spots off in the distance. A couple of small green humanoids with gator-like jaws were gathered around a cart, seemingly waiting for someone or something. Another kobold, wearing a feathery headpiece, exited the mine. Hurrying toward a giant rock to hide, she stepped on something hard hidden in a leaf pile.

"Ouch!" Avalann shouted as she shot a bolt that narrowly missed the kobold king.

"Wha . . . What's going on?" Shorte mumbled, half asleep. "Raven, what are—?

The kobold king sounded a horn, alarming his minions as Avalann rolled out of the leaves. The rogue jumped back, removing her hand from Shorte's stomach. His stone skin had allowed him to blend with the boulder, so it looked like a piece of cobblestone had emerged from the larger one.

Avalann pulled down the camo net that hid their weapons and rummaged through the sack. "Shorte, you were supposed to watch my back. You fell asleep again."

Raven noticed the guards circling the king as the sounds of battle drums vibrated off the forest floor.

Shorte stretched. "Sorry, I've been sitting against this rock for two days," he whined as Avalann handed him his mace. "I think my arse fossilized into that boulder."

"Uh, guys—hurry," Raven warned, drawing her daggers and kneeling behind the actual rock.

Avalann adjusted her crossbow. They all glanced up, frozen, as the kobold army approached. A group of angry creatures rushed from the mine and up the hill. The king paced behind his guards, shouting orders to his other followers.

The archer cursed in Elvish and dropped her crossbow, turning to Raven. "Why are you incapable of following orders? You're going to get us killed one day." She quickly equipped her quiver, readying her longbow. "Shorte, we need to take out the king."

"I'm on it!" he shouted, then he shuffled down the side of the hill, swinging his mace at two approaching kobolds.

Avalann climbed onto the boulder and then surveyed the battle scene. "Do you plan on helping, Princess, or will you just hide?" the elf sneered, releasing an arrow that pierced a kobold in the forehead. The small creatures raised their shields higher as they advanced while others continued to attack Shorte.

Raven noticed a kobold near the wagon, brandishing a spear aimed at Avalann.

The rogue gripped her daggers tighter, chanting "Kant-Osp" as she touched the elf. Avalann transformed into a gaseous form as a breeze came through the trees, blowing the green cloud closer to the mouth of the mine.

"Ogre poop," Raven mumbled as she rotated her hands counterclockwise. "Arcanus-Perambulo," she chanted, casting Arcane Step to appear behind a kobold. She pierced its neck as she blinked from kobold to kobold, stabbing them in the back. Following the gas cloud approaching the king, she noticed Shorte had also taken down two kobolds nearby.

Just then, the spell wore off, and Avalann returned to normal at the front of the mine. The archer pulled back an arrow and shot the kobold king point-blank. The king's head snapped back, distracting Raven enough to allow one of the kobold soldiers to sneak up behind her.

Blue sparks of energy formed around the rogue as Shorte cast a protective shield. A kobold swung his weapon, creating a spark as the iron sword shattered.

Spinning her dagger around, Raven slammed the pommel into the kobold's temple, knocking it out. The remaining kobolds retreated as their king's lifeless body lay there on the dirt path.

Avalann, enraged, stormed toward the rogue. "You! This was *my* mission. Why are you here?" she screamed, brushing by.

Raven sheathed her daggers. "I wanted to help."

"We had everything under control. All we had to do was take out the king, and the rest of them would have returned to their homeland," Avalann explained, "but now we've killed more than necessary."

"This one is still alive," Raven responded, eyeing the unconscious kobold by her feet.

"Being a guardian means saving lives, not taking them unless necessary. You are not slaughtering an entire race because you can! Your problem has always been that you need to show everyone how great you are. I have news for you, princess. You are not." Avalann turned in a huff, stomping through the woods to untie Krit. "I hope you're happy with all this bloodshed."

"What's your problem with me?" Raven asked. "It's more than some slaughtered kobolds who would have returned with a new king anyway."

"Princess!" Avalann sneered. "All I hear about is how precious the princess is, the princess with the purple eyes who can do no wrong. How she is becoming a better rogue than her father."

"This is about Gideon? You're jealous?"

Avalann snorted. "I've been working so hard on becoming the best archer in Suttiir, and you would think I would at least hear one—just one—compliment." She mounted her horse. "But you didn't even know who I was."

"That wasn't Gideon's fault," Raven replied. "It's true. I was stuck in my own little world, but that's changing. If you give me a—"

"I think Gideon loves you," Avalann interrupted. "Sometimes I think more than his own family."

"But Gideon has always been close to my family and me."

"Are you blind, Princess? He love-loves you."

Speechless, Raven stared at the angry elf. *I think she's right.*

"Ladies, can we settle this back at camp?" interrupted Shorte, already settled on his horse.

"Shorte, I'll see you back at camp," Avalann replied, eyeing the dwarf. "You fought well today." She then glared at Raven before dashing off.

Shorte huffed, shaking his head. "I should have fought well"—he paused then shouted—"TWO DAYS AGO." Avalann gave no response as she vanished down the path. "Come on, Princess. I'll escort you back to Ghost."

Raven walked beside Stubby as they headed north. Ghost was tied there, eating wild berries. "I'm sorry I ruined your mission," she said apologetically, mounting her horse. "I was just worried."

"My sore arse is glad you arrived. I swear that elf would have lay there for a month straight waiting for that king, but she'll be fine," Shorte said comfortingly. "And Gideon is like family to us all."

They began the journey back to Gideon's camp. After a moment of silence, Shorte snickered. "Besides, if you think she's angry now—wait until she realizes you would be her aunt."

Raven's eyes widened as the dwarf howled with laughter. *Avalann and I would be related?*

CHAPTER TWENTY-TWO

DESTRUCTION DEMONSTRATION

After the long trek from the orc city of Yatur, Aushade tossed his great sword and duffel bag onto the grassy hill, dismissing his magical mount. He grabbed the ration pack just inside the bag, then removed his helmet before laying under one of the only cypress trees on the prairie. Propping his head against the back of his helmet, he faced away from the rising sun. His undead army scattered and lowered into the tall grain stalks remaining out of sight.

One of the benefits of having an undead army is that there are no complaints of fatigue or hunger as we march through the night. He snacked on dried fruit, welcoming a slight breeze as his eyes grew heavy.

His recurring nightmare invaded his sleep. Fifteen-year-old Aushade hurried up the steps of his home in Fellswar, navigating around the piles of soldiers' and town folks' bodies. "Father!" He climbed over the wall of corpses until he reached the top, where his father's corpse lay. He dropped to his knees, sobbing next to the half-packed duffel bag. With trembling hands, he pulled out the broken wings made of blue cloth.

Aushade quickly stood and turned frantically, searching for his younger brother. The weight of fear slowed him amid his search through the dead, looking for any remains. The battle cries of the orcs alerted him to find a weapon. He grabbed a sword from one of the fallen soldiers. *ENOUGH!*

He'd gotten good at redirecting the nightly horror by redirecting his thoughts to more pleasant memories. The nightmare transformed into a vision of him sitting on his throne at Fellswar's Claim. Courtlynn, in nude human form, entered the room with her hips swaying.

Aushade tapped the arm of his throne. "It's time."

Courtlynn approached seductively. "I know." She smiled as she used the armrest of his throne to brace herself. "Have you been taking good care of my pet?" Moving her face inches from his.

Aushade laughed. "Astrick or the fox?"

"The fox is the key to everything, my love," she said, adjusting to sit on his lap. "You must keep him close."

"I don't see the need. I've spent the two years since we met destroying every orc city, town, and village. My army has tripled in size."

"Yes, I know," she cooed, stroking his hair, "and so has my master's. He is very pleased with you. But we must approach the gnomes and dwarves more cautiously."

"Why?" Aushade asked as her fingers traced his hairline, sending tingles down his neck. "My minions can slaughter them quickly."

"First, no one cares if townfuls of orcs get slaughtered. Second, the gnomes, dwarves, elves, and humans are more advanced and have more defenses. It would be best if you caught them off guard. With the demon fox, no one will have a chance to sound any alarms, unlike if you send in your army. We will destroy them quicker and make sure there are no survivors to alert the next city."

"Where do we begin?" Aushade asked eagerly.

"I've instructed Astrick to create a portal scroll and a receiver. Once the sun goes down, he will enter the city's center and place the receiver. This will mark the spot for the fox. Once that imbecile returns, I will join you both and show you what Floxy can do."

"Of course," agreed Aushade. "But will the anti-scry cover the fox and us once he's in the city?"

She hopped off his lap and began to walk away. "Yes. I'll meet you on the hilltop overlooking Grimlok at dusk." She blew him a kiss and vanished.

Aushade awoke, pissed on the tree, packed his bag, and summoned his magical steed. The mount was an illusion of a Nightmare, a pure black demon horse from the Abyss Realm with a mane, tail, and hooves engulfed in red and orange flames. He would have preferred a real one, but the guardian would not allow it.

After a two-day travel, Aushade arrived at the edge of the gnome city. Astrick approached him on the hilltop, and the two kept Floxy company while observing the town. The green grass danced as the wind picked up. The gnomes were busy going about their daily lives: They shopped at the local shops, a couple of gnomes worked in a cornfield, and a group of children played with wooden toys. Horse-drawn carriages moved along the streets, past the little huts with thatched roofs where the gnomes lived. All were unaware of the danger lurking on the outskirts of town. *This feels completely different than raiding an orc village.*

The absence of revenge exposed him to the true nature of this assault. His doubt of attacking came as the sky changed to a deep orange and golden yellow when the sun set behind the horde. "This is flat-out murder," he whispered to himself.

"Excuse me," Astrick responded, "I didn't catch that."

"Is your *princess* problem dealt with?"

Astrick cleared a lump in his throat. "Yes."

"Do I need to knock the truth out of you again?" Aushade grumbled, glaring down at the wizard. Astrick faced the city as Aushade stiffened his back and cleared his throat. "Do you have the portal scroll?"

"Of course," Astrick replied. "I'm the one who got stuck creating the spell."

"Go to the center of town and place the portal receiver," Aushade ordered. "Once it's dark, you'll open the portal."

"Please," Astrick mocked.

"Don't test me. Not tonight."

Astrick grunted and summoned his magical steed.

"Leave the fox here," Aushade commanded.

"Stay," Astrick ordered as he raised his palm, and the fox sat. The mage rode into town on his mystical horse to place the receiver.

Aushade leaned forward, patiently waiting, when he heard wagon wheels. He sat up, worried that his plan was about to be foiled. One of the two boys in the back of the carriage shouted, "Look! Look!" The children stopped clanking their wooden toy swords, their mouths agape, admiring Aushade's fiery steed. The adult gnome steering the carriage stopped whistling, and his relaxed face tightened as they locked eyes. As they passed, the children poked their small heads out the carriage windows, raising their toys in a knightly salute. The setting sun glared off the royal coat of arms on the rear of the carriage.

I wonder if they're brothers. His blood ran cold at the thought. *I'm now the orc in their story.*

As darkness approached, Astrick returned, his dark green robes billowing behind him. "It's done."

"And you're sure you placed it in the dead center of the city?"

"Yes, I placed it out of sight behind the weapons shop. The roads are oddly quiet tonight."

Aushade watched the gnomes lighting torches across the city. "Perfect. Now we wait for Courtlynn."

"Won't the guardian—" A bright red light interrupted Astrick.

Courtlynn entered through a portal, wearing a leather corset, shorts, and thigh-high boots. Her dark red wings reminded the necromancer of the fire bats that lived in the caves near his home.

How can a demon creature look so intoxicating?

Her proper form didn't bother Aushade as it did Astrick, who scurried over to the army, keeping his head down. "You're looking lovely," said Aushade, staring at Courtlynn.

"Is that a compliment?" she asked.

"I'm beginning to enjoy your company. It's better than that coward's over there." Aushade motioned to Astrick.

Courtlynn glanced at the bald mage, who seemed to avoid eye contact.

"But you shouldn't have shown up. You're a lot more powerful than a portal. You're going to get us detected," Aushade warned.

Courtlynn rubbed the snout of the fiery steed. "It's hard to believe this isn't real." She tickled the steed's chin and mocked like talking to a baby, "Tell your master to let me worry about Gideon, the precious guardian."

"I see you've been doing more homework," Aushade stated, sliding off the saddle. "I just don't want him to scry on me."

"When are you going to trust me? I told you that if everyone is within his range, Floxy's anti-scry will keep us and the portals hidden," she said with an evil grin. "You wiped out the orcs without a peep, right?"

Aushade returned to her side. "How do you know how the guardians operate?"

"We've been tortur—" She paused and corrected herself. "We've been studying a guardian for about a decade. Like you said, doing homework." She smiled proudly.

"Really?" Aushade said, impressed. "And you weren't harassed by the High Council?"

"Let's just say our representative on the council is fully aware of the situation." Courtlynn grinned again. They stood still, watching the town torches dance with the breeze as the wind carried the eerie moaning of Aushade's army. After a moment, she broke the silence. "Do you have the artifact?"

"Of course," Aushade answered, pointing to his neck. "But we could just return to Fellswar's Claim—my mission is complete."

Courtlynn's playful attitude changed. "Are you having cold feet?"

"No, I'm just saying we can leave this place and rebuild my home. Live a peaceful life."

"If I don't finish my task, my master will kill me," Courtlynn grumbled sadly. "He will hunt me down."

May the Astral Realm have mercy on my soul, but I can't lose her. Aushade finally mumbled, "Fine. We will complete your task."

"Good, now watch this." She turned to the wizard. "Astrick, create the portal." She then leaned over Floxy and whispered instructions. The fox rubbed against her affectionately and dashed into the gateway.

Aushade waited patiently. He watched Courtlynn as she stared down the road, her gaze shining with anticipation.

She glanced over at him. "Now, equip one of your undead minions with something sharp and order it to sever one of Floxy's tails."

Aushade glanced at her, baffled. "Yes, ma'am." He was thankful his helmet hid his reaction as he randomly picked the unlucky volunteer. "His claws will do just fine." Casting a spell on an undead gnome, he sent it through the portal.

A moment passed by.

"How do I know—" A massive explosion interrupted his question. "What in the Ninth Layer was that?"

"Oh, my favorite part," Courtlynn said gleefully. "Wait for it."

Aushade froze, shocked by the magnitude of the explosion, when several additional, minor explosions erupted from alcohol barrels and other explosive materials. *Her favorite part?*

Courtlynn swayed back and forth. "It's like music to my ears."

Did I make a deal with a devil and not a succubus? Floxy came sprinting back with one less tail and sat beside Aushade, still recovering from the aftermath. "How did he survive that?"

"If a tail is dismembered by any means, they cast a protective shield," Courtlynn said, petting the demon fox. "Your minion that you sent, on the other hand—"

"It's fine," Aushade replied as he mounted the Nightmare. "I have more where he came from." Once settled, he cast Desecrate on his entire army. "Feroces." The undead army let loose a feral scream and sprinted toward the city.

Courtlynn flew beside Aushade as he rode, and the fox raced alongside them. The horde of undead orcs bit and clawed at the gnome survivors. Courtlynn opened a red portal. "Activate the artifact."

"I know the procedure," Aushade retorted, holding up the necklace. "Amissa Anima Mea." The artifact pulsed with a dark red glow. Blue souls rose from the rubble and ashes, and more stirred from the dead gnomes in the open. All the souls funneled through the open portal to the Abyss Realm. Aushade cast the Reanimate spell, "Reanimatus," and the lifeless bodies rose to join his ranks.

"That was fun," Courtlynn said triumphantly. "Draklor thanks you, and I thank you." She batted her eyelashes. "You're saving my life."

Aushade nodded curtly, patting his magical steed and eyeing Astrick, who kept his distance by digging through some rubble.

"You know I can get you a real Nightmare from the Abyss Realm," Courtlynn offered sweetly.

"I'm sure you could," Aushade responded. "But you know the guardian wouldn't allow it to remain in this realm."

"What a hypocrite!" Courtlynn snorted. "Astrick told me he saw someone riding a unicorn, and we all know those hideous creatures aren't from this realm."

"I'm sure it's the evil, demonic stuff they tend to keep out."

"That's just a matter of perspective. You can always stay with me." When Aushade didn't respond, she continued. "Well, at least you didn't say no. Just something to think about." She winked as she moved toward the portal. "Not sure how you blocked me all these years. You can't sleep with that helmet on all the time."

"It's amazing what a human body can adapt to."

"I'll meet you at Wheatland, my dark pally." She blew him a kiss and exited through the portal.

Astrick pulled out a map and approached Aushade. "That was—"

"Pure evil."

"The fox only has eight tails left," Astrick reminded him. "If we attack the next two gnome cities to the east, we can make our way to the Ril Zorn mountain range. Once the four dwarf cities are conquered, only Omlett and Suttiir will remain in the path of annihilation."

The necromancer had wiped out almost an entire race of orcs and he'd been filled with rage all these years, but this was more vicious—the innocent gnomes had simply been going about their day. After a long silence, Aushade nodded, and the two strolled through the burning city to collect the remaining bodies and souls.

Near the outskirts, they passed a carriage where the horses and coachman had absorbed the shrapnel. Aushade watched as the reanimated coachman crawled toward the back of the carriage and clawed at the door. Spotting the coat-of-arms dangling off the rear, Aushade dismounted his Nightmare, ordering Astrick to continue. As he peered over the coachman's shoulder, two young boys attempted to fight it off with their wooden swords.

Aushade drove his greatsword upward, piercing the rotting head of his new minion. As it dropped by the carriage door, the boys pointed their fake weapons at the necromancer. He opened the door and retrieved a box of rations from his bag. Popping open the storage area of the carriage, he glanced around, waving to the boys to move. They ran past him and curled up together, shaking. He tossed provisions to the children as they stared at him, frightened. "You'll survive. I did."

CHAPTER TWENTY-THREE

OVERCOMING OLD OBSTACLES

R aven crawled out of her tent as a warm breeze swept across her face. After another romantic night with Gideon, the morning sun rising from the eastern side of the camp seemed brighter. The bird chirps were louder and more cheerful as if singing a love song. It was a beauteous first of Fogah—*the first day of spring.* After six months of wintry weather spent cuddling with Gideon, it was finally nice to plan things for a warmer season. *Maybe we can go for a long hike today.*

She sheathed her daggers and grabbed her canteen. In the distance, she noticed her friends huddled together, staring at something at the lake's edge. She wandered over, gulping water, and immediately spat it out when she saw what the others were gawking at.

A short, elderly woman with matted gray hair, splashed barefooted, in ankle-deepwater. The frayed hem of the hag's ragged brown dress dangled over the surface. Mug, wearing his usual work coveralls, was sitting cross-legged in the white sand, tinkering with a strange crossbow. The gnome kept pulling random tools out of his many pockets. Maggie absentmindedly adjusted a strand of silver hair that the wind blew out of place from her updo, then resumed reading a book under a tree.

But nothing braced Raven for the horror she was about to witness. Her father was doing lunges, and an elderly dwarf with an eye patch followed close behind. The burly dwarf mimicked her father's movements. He reminded her of Buzz but with more muscles and grayer hair. The deafening silence broke when Shorte asked, "Did someone burn down the retirement quarters?"

"No, my friends," Gideon said, approaching the group. "Those are your opponents."

"Opponents?" Jarz squeaked out.

Raven noticed her father glance up, waving at her. Blood rushed to her cheeks as his pale legs, matching his tunic and breeches, reflected the sun, almost blinding them.

The elderly dwarf smirked, raising his arms to show off his biceps. The black leather vest raised a few inches, revealing his hairy, burly abs.

"That's my Uncle Ray'diir!" Shorte shouted, shaking his head. "He hasn't changed."

"EWW," Izarra stated innocently.

Raven gasped. "Izarra!"

"What?" Izarra shrugged. "We've heard of his tales in Thistlebane."

"EWW is right," Shorte responded. "They call him Euphrasia's Wonderful Wanderer—EWW for short. He travels across all of Euphrasia, helping everyone who needs it. I can't believe Gideon found him."

"Wasn't easy," Gideon replied, casting spells.

Raven watched in awe as the guardian, like a band conductor, orchestrated objects into existence. Pieces of rock and stone formed a wall; the lake swirled in a cyclone; vines slithered together like snakes, creating ropes in the trees; and logs and planks stacked into a tall wooden structure—a climbing barrier.

Avalann positioned herself next to her uncle. "What's this?"

"An obstacle test," Gideon replied, conjuring a ten-foot spider as Avalann slowly backed away, hiding behind the group. "The Mortal Guardians versus the e'XP'es."

Shorte snorted. "HA!"

"What's so funny?" Jarz asked, stretching for his toes.

"That's Dwarvish for 'the experienced ones,'" Shorte answered, watching his team mirror Jarz's moves.

Izarra stood, pointing toward the hag on the beach. "And who's that? Is that—"

"Rull Thistle," Gideon finished.

Raven raised her head from a toe reach. "Rull Thistle?"

"She's the founder of Thistlebane," Izarra answered reverently.

Shorte focused on the elderly woman enjoying the water. "She's a water nymph?"

Izarra nodded. "When we reach a certain age, our magic withers away, and we relocate to Hag Swamp."

Shorte snickered, nudging the young swordmage. "That's your future, Jarz."

Raven and Izarra instinctively slapped the dwarf.

"It's a great honor to live that long," Izarra responded. "Besides, Jarz will be long dead when I experience the metamorphosis."

Jarz and Shorte eyed each other as Gideon continued casting spells, placing the finishing touches on the racing lanes.

"Is this the same obstacle course my father and Mug ran?" Raven asked.

"The exact same one," Gideon answered.

"How's that fair?" Avalann asked, irritated. "If they know it already—"

"It's been a long time," Shorte stated. "I'm sure they forgot."

Eugor popped up behind, startling them. "I remember it like it was yesterday."

Shorte grasped his chest and asked, "Are you trying to give this dwarf heart failure?"

The rest of the e'XP'es approached, forming their squad around Eugor.

Raven eyed her father as the Mortal Guardians surrounded her. The two groups entered a serious staring contest as if the realm's fate were at stake.

Gideon stood before the teams, intentionally coughing, drawing everyone's attention. "We will have five contests," he explained. "One from each team will be required to complete the task for the next leg of the course to begin."

Ray'diir cracked his knuckles. "It should be easy work against these infants." The elders laughed as the dwarf raised his eye patch, exposing the empty socket, and blew them a kiss.

Instantly, Raven froze in a trance-like as images of Butch's empty eye sockets, burned away by acid, flashed through her mind. The sound of groans snapped her out of it as Avalann and Izarra rolled their eyes in disgust.

"Is that your future, Shorte?" Jarz asked, teasing his friend, who shot him a you-better-be-careful-what-you-say gaze. "Just seems like it runs in the family to be one eye *short*."

Shorte took a deep breath, paused, slapped Jarz on the back, and howled as the others followed in on the humor. "Still not as funny as nature's laughing gas."

"Settle down," Gideon ordered with a grin, casting a blue portal. "Princess Naelo and King Naelo—"

"Please, Gideon," Eugor interrupted, placing a satchel over his head. "I'm Night Breeze for today."

Raven and her father headed toward the portal as the rest of the e'XP'es chanted, "NIGHT BREEZE! NIGHT BREEZE!" She lowered her head, sighing as everyone laughed.

The father and daughter duo went through the portal to a chamber with two locked chests.

The damp room, barely lit by two wall torches, smelled weird and stagnant. *Is this what magic smells like?* Two mahogany doors faced opposite inside the stone room, each with a symbol scorched into its surface. An outline of a raven marked one entrance, and the other was painted three-wavy lines for a wind symbol.

"You must wait here until one of your team members joins you," Gideon explained. "Then your first task is to open the chest by any means necessary. Then, escape the room to the next, which is the dagger throw. You must lodge a dagger in the red circle to proceed."

"If I remember correctly, you just need one dagger?" Eugor asked.

"Correct," Gideon replied, "then it's off to the finish line."

Raven's mind shifted to a vision of her dagger piercing Bo's skull instead of his chest. She flipped her right hand over, peeping at her scarred palm. *It won't happen again.*

Eugor grabbed the hilt of his dagger. "I hope you were practicing, dear."

If you only knew. Raven sighed. "I'm sure you know what's waiting for us at the end."

"Of course," her father responded cheerfully. "Even if I didn't, it's like taking gold from a baby dragon."

"At least I didn't *eat* a baby dragon." She felt the tension drop like a ton of bricks. "Besides, that doesn't even make sense."

Gideon snickered and stated, "Your portion of the course *is* the last section, so this means the first one to make it to the finish line wins it for the team."

"No pressure," Raven quipped as Gideon cast a blue portal. She quickly pulled away as he instinctively leaned in for a kiss. Their eyes widened as they slowly glanced at Eugor, who was thankfully preoccupied, scanning the room. *I don't think he noticed.* Gideon quickly rubbed her arm, then exited the portal.

After Eugor surveyed the room, he bounced on his toes. "This is so exciting," he said as she inspected the doors. "There's no tricks."

"Unh hunh," Raven mumbled. "You brought your razor wire."

"And?"

Raven ignored her father and investigated the scene. It was a simple room with no windows or exits other than the doors. The floor was a type of red dirt and clay mixture. "Gideon knows I can do this with my eyes closed," she mumbled, kneeling in front of a chest with a raven engraved above the keyhole.

"If Gideon keeps the course the same," Eugor began, swinging his satchel around before sitting on the chest, "Jarz will cast a portal to you, and Maggie will cast one to me."

"Is *that* so," Raven responded, preoccupied with examining the chest. She ran her hands across the lid, searching for secret latches.

"You're not supposed to begin yet," Eugor declared. "That's cheating."

Raven tapped on the top of the container with one of her daggers. "I'm just looking."

Her father pitched his voice, mocking her. "Is *that* so—"

She held back a smirk. "Besides, you already know, so how's that fair?"

"Have a plan?"

"Maybe," she replied, moving closer to the door. "I'm pretty sure there's a trap."

"Interesting," her father replied, rubbing his chin. "Anything else?"

Raven raised her hand to touch the door, and a shock ran through her fingers. Her father's snicker escaped his gritted teeth. "I know, I know," she began to quote, "always be aware of your surroundings." She knelt before the door and carefully brushed away the dirt, searching for a trip wire.

"Cheating . . ." Eugor reminded her.

She moved back to the chest and sat on top. Her father rummaged through his bag, which allowed her to peek over and notice he didn't have his thief's tools. It seemed odd not to bring those when you knew part of the task was to break into a treasure box. Raven mumbled, "You seem to be missing a few key items in your satchel."

A blue portal opened before he could answer, and Maggie appeared. Her dark blue and gold-trimmed mage robe billowed around her like a windstorm. Once the gateway closed, the mage touched Eugor on the shoulder. "You're up, Night Breeze."

Eugor hopped off the chest and smiled.

Raven stared intently at her father. "Well, what are you waiting for?"

"I think I can delay a bit longer," he replied, shooting a wink at Maggie as the mage responded with a nod and half-grin.

A portal opened, and Jarz appeared, winded. He exited the gateway as smoke billowed from his light blue robe. Burn marks peppered his sleeves and hem.

Raven gulped. "Are you all right?"

"I'm . . . I'm fine," Jarz responded, tapping the rogue on the shoulder. He then collapsed against the wall and propped his foot up on the chest, exposing a charred leather sole.

The smell reminded her of the Horck's burnt arse on her final test a year ago. She tugged on the clip that secured the short obsidian lock pick from her ponytail, then knelt in front of the chest. After pulling the thinner rod out of the thicker piece, she fidgeted the two pieces into the keyhole. *Come on! It's a basic chest lock.* Jarz's feet kept tapping against the wood of her target as he shifted from side to side. "Do you mind?" she asked, frustrated.

"Sorry," Jarz replied, returning his feet to the ground and sitting up more. He glanced over at Maggie. "You're good."

Raven glanced up at her father and Maggie, who were curiously watching her. She removed the pick from the lock and peered through the opening. After pausing to work out the problem, she tapped her tool against her thigh nervously. *This doesn't make any sense.* She tried to reinsert the pick and maneuvered the hook around inside again, cursing silently in Orcish. After a moment, she huffed. "There doesn't seem to be a lock mechanism."

"Are you sure?" Eugor asked.

"Now I know why you're not bothering to try," she responded.

"Clever," her father stated.

Frustrated, Raven wedged her lock pick back into her ponytail, then tried to lift the chest lid, but it didn't budge. "Jarz," she called as the swordmage slowly rose, "can you detect magic on it?"

"Is that allowed?" Jarz asked as the other team shrugged.

Raven snapped, "Gideon said to open by any means necessary."

"Sure, I suppose," Jarz said, waving his hand, "Curu Tuku."

After a moment, Raven asked impatiently, "And?"

"And nothing," Jarz responded. "It's just a chest."

Raven slumped to her knees in defeat. *I can't do this.* She looked at her father, who had crouched down at eye level. The corner of his mouth twitched from holding back laughter. *What the spell?!* In her head, she ran through all the spells she'd studied the last few years. *Shocking Grasp, Burning Hands, Arcane Step.* Then it hit her.

"You may need to help me if this goes wrong," Raven commented to Jarz, who stared, confused. "Kant-Osp." She felt the mass of her body lessen and dissolve into a gas cloud. Willing herself to move, she entered the keyhole. Once inside the box, she knew something was off. Raven tried to focus, recasting the spell, but nothing seemed to work. Her body tingled and burned as pieces started to reform. First, her head popped out of thin air, slamming into the top of the chest. *Ouch!* Looking down, she watched a shimmering light cover her body. Her neck started to expand, then the torso down to her rear. Two arms and, finally, two legs materialized out of thin air. As a reflex, she planted her feet and pushed, but her legs protruded from the inside while the chest still covered her head. "There's . . . no . . . bottom?!"

The top of the trunk magically popped open and slid down the length of her body. *I'll strangle Gideon for this.* Raven watched in slow motion as her father kicked over his chest and grabbed the key.

Maggie covered her mouth for a moment. "A dead magic zone inside the chest protects the lock. That's why your form ended so soon."

Eugor hurried to the door and ran his hand across the frame, revealing a thick vine. He pulled his razor wire out and sliced the rope. "I'll be waiting at the finish line for you," he said jokingly.

Finally coming to her senses, Raven stepped out of the chest and grabbed the key. She reached around the door frame, cut the rope, and opened the door with the raven symbol. Jarz followed her as she approached a white line marked on the floor, scanning for traps.

Across the room was a rotting wooden wall with a small red dot painted in the center. It seemed about twenty yards away. She gripped the dagger and gave it a good throw but missed the target; her blade clattered to the floor. *I need to calm down.* She quickly retrieved it and ran back to the white mark. Lining the blade's tip with the red dot, she took a deep breath and held it as she threw again.

The dagger hit the dot dead-center before bouncing off the wall again. *What the spell?* She lowered her head in defeat.

Jarz chanted something as she returned to the starting line. "It's an illusion," he stated.

"Hunh?" Raven responded as she prepared to throw the dagger.

"It's not a wooden wall," Jarz replied. "It's a stone wall. You'll never get it to stick." The rogue and swordmage paused there in silence for a moment. "But I think this is why Maggie and I were the ones to portal here. We were meant to help. Sarn-Serni-Na Mud."

Raven watched the target sink with the wall as the wood illusion wore off and the stone transformed into soft, dark mud. "That sounded familiar."

"That's because it's very close to the verbal component of Shorte's Stone Skin spell. But only turning stone into mud."

Please, Blade, I need a little luck. Raven wiped her sweaty hand on her breeches, gripped the dagger's tip, and flung her weapon at the target. This time, it went through and wedged into the mud. "Works for me," she blurted out as another door opened.

Jarz followed her. "Well, I'm proud of you, win or lose."

Raven stepped across the threshold to the outdoors. "Thanks, but I have a feeling they're already at the finish." She glanced to her left and saw her father exiting his room. His red face contrasted with the rest of his pale skin and white hair. He glanced over at her with an irritated expression. *He's not smiling any longer.*

They both sprinted down the marked lanes. Raven's father had the lead as she pushed herself to move faster. *I could use Jarz's Haste spell.* She hoped the mage would surprise her with one last magical gift.

Ahead of them was a twenty-foot wooden structure with planks attached in the middle. Raven was about to grab the first board when she noticed a gap between the planks. Her father had already climbed halfway up.

"Oh, I hope I don't get stuck," she mumbled. "Kant-Osp." Raven became a gaseous form again, squeezing through the gap. When she re-formed to her physical self, she patted her body and then glanced up—her father, who had cleared the top log, used a rope to repel down. He was dangling halfway when his eyes widened and mouth gaped.

Raven waved and continued running again, quickening her pace as she reached the next bend of the race. When she turned the corner, she froze. Her stomach rolled as she caught the smell of burning timber. A flaming building with fences engulfed in ten-foot flames stood in the center of the path. In her mind, she saw a fireball burst through High Priest Carne. She stumbled as a projectile flew down her father's lane, barely missing him as he evaded it with ease.

Eugor ran past her as she became paralyzed. He tucked his knees in and slid under the fence without hesitation.

You need to move! Sweat dripped from her brow. Raven warily moved closer to the structure when she heard a voice cast a spell. A fiery object aimed at her face made her duck as a firebolt grazed her hair. She placed her hands on top of her head, quickly dropping to her knees, trembling as she covered her ears to muffle the sounds: Butch's taunting, the crackling of flames, the high priest's shout of pain as the fiery missile penetrated his chest, Izarra's voice calling out, Astrick's voice as he pulled her by her hair. "Stop! Stop! Stop!"

Raven wrapped her arms around her knees, pulling them tightly to her chest as her body quivered, remembering sitting at the pew after ruining a man's face. *What's wrong with me?*

A gentle pair of arms wrapped under her armpits and pulled her up. She embarrassedly met the concerning eyes of her father. Raven couldn't hold back the tears as she lost muscle control in her face and sobbed, wrapping her arms around him.

"I'm here, Nightbird," he assured her, pressing his head firmly against hers.

She pulled away, wiping tears from her cheeks. "Nightbird?" She noticed the others standing around. Shorte looked at her with concern. Izarra's eyes were watery, and she mouthed, *Are you all right?* as Jarz had his arms around her, eyes wide with shock. While Avalann scowled, as usual, shaking her head.

"I'm fine now," she said, avoiding eye contact with the group. She knew her puffy red eyes gave away that she wasn't being honest. A lump formed in her throat as she swallowed back tears. *I will not cry in front of them.*

Gideon dispelled the illusion of the fiery wreckage. "I apologize, Miss Naelo. I should have known better." The sorrow in his eyes made her heart melt as she glanced up.

I want to run into his arms! "I'm fine, Gideon," she reassured him, shivering, wrapping her arms around herself. *I'm not sure if it's the shock or the chilly air.*

"So who won?" Shorte and Ray'diir asked in unison, which caused everyone to laugh.

Raven observed that Shorte's skin still seemed to have the glitter of pebbles from his spell. It made her grin.

"It's a draw," Gideon announced, not taking his eyes off her. "Everyone, please rest and prepare for tonight's celebration."

Eugor escorted Raven to her tent, mumbling, "That damn stone wall. I hit that target at least twenty times."

"New?" Raven asked.

"Of course," Gideon replied before Eugor could answer, placing his arms around both. "I couldn't let them have all the advantages."

"But it wasn't me," Raven replied. "It was Jarz."

Gideon sighed. "That wasn't an individual test—it was about how well you could collaborate with a partner and their strengths. I knew Jarz and Maggie had prepared those spells because I had given them a list. Transmute Stone spell is a Waterfront fourth-year spell. But I do apologize for the evasion test. I—"

"I'm fine, Gideon," Raven interrupted. "I needed it."

"I have a spell that will shield you from Magic Missiles," Gideon responded. "I can show you tomorrow."

"And if you want to talk about it," Eugor replied, "I'm here and can relate. It took me a long time to make peace with my resurrection."

"I think I'll take you two up on your offers," Raven replied.

"You may use my wagon," Gideon offered. "I'm going to begin the feast."

Raven quickly hugged the guardian. "Thank you." The urge to kiss him almost overpowered the fear of how her father would react. Even Gideon's warm, caring expression displayed confusion about what to do next.

The guardian awkwardly pulled away. "You're welcome, I guess. Join us when you're ready," he continued, slowly backing toward the group and avoiding eye contact. "Now, if you'll excuse me, Shorte wants to try some new recipes. I heard it involved boar meat or deer. Maybe it was a stew." His words became inaudible as he got further away.

"That elf is getting stranger by the season," Eugor laughed. "I've never seen him stumble over words like that."

Do I tell him about Gideon and me? Raven sighed, gathered some internal vigor, wrapped her arm around her father's, and walked toward the wagon. "So—Izarra and I met Astrick at the Cache Tavern." The weight lifted as she described Bernie's discovery of the foul meat, Butch's deformed face, High Priest Carne's holey chest, and Astrick's threatening words. "The images keep coming back. I think they're affecting me being a dependable guardian." Raven wiped the tears from her eyes and then glanced at her father.

Eugor listened silently, and when she finished, he sighed heavily. "I did warn you about this." He glanced at her, a hint of a smile starting. "In a subtle way."

"How?"

"By telling you all the horror stories about things I went through," her father replied. "And that's not even the worst of it. If I told you everything, you'd probably still be hiding in your bed chamber."

"How can I be a guardian if I can't handle the fact that life can be dangerous?"

"You put the safety of others before yours, and the ability will come naturally."

"May I ask what it was like? Death?"

"I'm still haunted by the demon's sword swinging for my neck. So, I empathize with your vision. But you can't let that fear control you. You *face* it, learn from it. You *control* it!" He closed his eyes as if searching for something in his mind. "But as for death, I don't remember the Astral Realm, so it's like falling asleep and not waking. I struggled for a bit after opening my eyes at your uncle's infirmary. Even then, I wasn't sure because your mother hovered over me like a personal guardian, and Ausharz performed every herbal and magic healing imaginable. I would wake screaming from the night terrors and pain resonating from my neck. It was weeks until my body was fully healed. While I have a physical scar, my mental pain still exists." Eugor paused, rubbed his throat, and took a deep breath. "I cheated death, and I still don't know how."

This must be hard for him. Raven placed her hand on her father's shoulder. "Did they ever confirm it was directly related to eating the dragon's egg?"

"It was a theory, but most people say it's all due to Blade and being lucky. But no matter the reason, I learned to appreciate the second chance."

"You met Mother," Raven said quietly, comforting him.

"I'd met her before because your uncle was a realm trainee, too. But it wasn't until I saw her caring nature and how she was always there for—"

"Wait, wait, go back—Uncle Ausharz attended Gideon's camp?"

"It's where he met your Aunt Stacia."

Raven sighed and mumbled, "The camp seems to be a magical spot for relationships."

"What's that dear?"

Raven bit her lip. "Jarz and Izarra—I was thinking about Jarz and Izarra."

"Ah, yes." Her father's face beamed, reminiscing. "The Class of 1140 was a special one. Your brother, Blade. The Plunkett Brothers, Buzz'diir and Ray'diir. It's where your Uncle Ausharz met your Aunt Stacia. You're the first group in thirty-some years that Gideon decided to train after my incident. He carried tremendous guilt for a long time. But I had a lot of support from my friends, and of course, Gideon helped me fulfill my retirement dream of operating an inn."

"So don't be afraid to rely on friends," Raven responded. "Is that what you're suggesting?"

Her father placed his arm around her. "No matter how much training or studying you do to prepare, friends and family will always be your biggest strength."

"Even Carya?"

Her father nodded, playfully gripping her shoulder. "Especially your sister." Eugor stood and offered his hand as Raven sprang up, embracing him, putting as much love as she could into that simple gesture. "If you decide to return home, no one will think any less of you. We understand."

Raven pulled back. "What?! And miss out on telling my children all my horror stories one day? And the epic tales of Night Breeze? But If I'm going to help others, I need to help myself."

Eugor gleamed. "That's my girl—Nightbird."

CHAPTER TWENTY-FOUR

SHADY DIALOGUE

The thunderous roar of the water in the distance stirred Gideon. It had been a long time since he had a more traditional sleep, so he stretched his tight body. Raven stayed later than usual, cuddling as they listened to the downpour pelting the roof. When the rain receded and she dashed out to her tent, he didn't bother to fight the fatigue.

He squinted as a beam of sunlight escaped the dark clouds, piercing his window as he filled a mug with Kaffa. He grumbled, noticing his supply of blackberries was running low for his tea. Dumping his spell material out of his component pouch, he slid two flat stones inside. *I hope she likes them.*

Dressed casually, Gideon slid the gauntlet on his right arm after securing his pouch to his belt, then grabbed his mug. "Cessis Nar." His left hand's skin faded to red, radiating heat as he warmed his drink using the trick Raven had shown him. Using spells for everyday tasks wasn't his specialty.

The guardian opened the back door while taking a sip, then glanced at the calendar before stepping out—*the Fifth of Vrrar, 1176. Oh, how time flies in the Mortal Realm.*

Noticing the eerily deserted camp, the guardian spotted the group on the banks of the lake, staring across the water. Last night's storm had boosted the flow of the waterfall. Gideon walked up, wrapping his arms around Raven and whispering in her ear. "What's going on?" Avalann shot them a disapproving look while Shorte sat only in his braies, sadly sorting through pebbles.

Raven placed her hands on Gideon's arms and whispered, "Jarz is honoring his brother's birthday."

They watched as Jarz pushed off the ring of flowers into the choppy water. The young swordmage knelt and dropped his head. His back trembled as he wept silently.

Izarra lingered over him, caressing his shoulders, trying to comfort him as she muttered, "ᴀqua ᴛɛmpɛro," to help the flowers drift past the small, angry waves that rushed the beach.

Gideon sighed. "I'm glad Jarz has Izarra to get through this."

"I think it was love at first sight," Raven said softly. "She won't admit it, but she pretty much ditched me for him on our first day here." She turned to face Gideon. "I guess some of us needed a bit more time."

How much more time do we need to inform her parents? "How was the trip to Thistlebane?"

"Amazing. Thank you for allowing us to celebrate Izarra's twentieth birthday there." She quickly gave him a peck on the lips. "We all thought you were joking since her birthday falls on Trickster Day."

"Tell everyone they may have the morning off. We will convene at midday," Gideon said as he turned toward the wagon.

Raven grabbed his arm, almost spilling his drink. "Are you all right?"

"Now isn't the time nor place," Gideon replied. "Be with your friends, and we can discuss it later this evening."

The two were interrupted when the group stood at attention and shouted, "Ready for today's lesson!"

Gideon sighed. "I've just informed Raven that you should take the day off. Jarz, please allow yourself some grieving time."

"I've grieved long enough, sir," Jarz stated, pulling himself together.

Gideon paused. "Very well, we can use this time to review Cenergy," he said, pointing to the logs. The group rushed to take their seats around the fire as Raven gave him a quick kiss and joined her friends. He placed his cup on the steps of his wagon and returned. "In the beginning, there was darkness." Gideon muttered, "ᴛɛnɛbris," encircling them all in a Darkness spell. He barely made out their silhouettes. "The source fractured into existence, creating the first realm. Which was?"

"Astral Realm," Jarz answered first.

"Correct." Gideon smiled and continued, "But I assume you learned all this at Waterfront."

"That would be correct," Jarz replied.

"Maybe we should let the others answer," Gideon responded.

Shorte coughed. "I learned all of this at the church. So—"

Gideon huffed and faced Izarra, who responded, "Mother."

"They teach us elves very early," Avalann stated. "What do they teach you over at the rogue camp?"

"My father taught me," Raven replied. "The Realm Wheel."

Avalann snickered. "That's the children's version."

Gideon noticed Raven staring daggers at his niece and then intervened. "Let's go over the course as intended. Jarz, please stand," he instructed, casting a blue light over him. "You are the Astral Realm."

"So heavenly," Izarra blurted, making the swordmage blush.

"From the Astral Realm, Natus was the first humanoid created by the water of life and the Realm Artifacts. All the tools he needed to create realms for the source."

Shorte shot up from his seat proudly. "I'm the Abyss."

Gideon cast a red glow around the dwarf and continued. "With the artifacts, Natus created the Abyss Realm with five elemental planes: Hydro, Inferno, Metallic, Petra, and Sylvan."

"Everything a perfect realm would need," Avalann stated.

"But to build the perfect realm, he needed workers," Gideon resumed. "Solas was the first female humanoid created."

"The goddess of energy," Raven quickly added.

"Natus and Solas, with the aid of the Artifact of Souls and Water of Life, created demons. As you can imagine, they weren't exactly the most obedient workers. So, they tried again, creating dwarves."

Shorte grunted. "We always fix other people's shite."

Gideon pointed to Izarra, and she stood. He cast her in a beautiful green light. "They decided to create the Fey Realm—the perfect realm."

The swordmage blushed again. "Not as perfect as you, dear."

"He does learn quickly," Avalann snickered.

Gideon continued. "They realized they needed a way to transport the elements from the Abyss to form the new Fey Realm. So together, they created Draconia, the goddess of dragons."

Izarra got excited. "Like Omlett's fall festival play!"

Gideon cast another spell, and miniature dragons flew around the darkness. "The goddess created her creatures to deliver the material. Once they finished, the dragons retired to the Fey Realm."

"So, they became the first inhabitants of the new realm?" Raven asked.

"Yes. Natus and Solas created the fey-elves and fairies to inhabit their perfect world. This moment is when the universe discovered love. Natus fell in love with Ammorra, a fairy, and they had twins: a demigoddess of fertility and love, Fharla, and a demigod of chaos, Felix."

"This is where it gets good," Shorte chimed in.

"In Fey, the days are three-quarters daylight and one-quarter night. Most of the creatures in this realm preferred it that way. However, while bored one day, Felix discovered his father's book of instructions and created his dark realm."

Raven quickly rose, beating Avalann. "I'll be the Shadow Realm."

Avalann sat down and mumbled, "That's very roguish of you."

Gideon covered Raven in a silvery light. "But it was the opposite of the Fey Realm—three-quarters of darkness and only a quarter of daylight. Natus didn't take it well and banished his son to the newly formed realm, while Fharla was restricted to the Fey. But of course, the brother and sister missed each other and decided to create a middle realm."

"You would think they would have learned the first time," Izarra commented.

Avalann huffed and said, "I guess I can be the Mortal Realm." A golden light covered her.

"The twins created a world with perfect balance—all that was beautiful in the Fey and Shadow Realms," Gideon continued.

"That's why the Mortal Realm has an even amount of daylight and darkness," Jarz stated.

"Indeed," Gideon replied.

"I have so many questions," Raven replied. "What happened to the twins?"

"Natus again banished them to their respective realms and created the High Council, preventing any more realm breaches."

"Weren't the dragons banished to the Mortal Realm to keep them from creating new realms?" Izarra asked.

"Yes," Gideon answered, noticing his red gem begin to glow as a bat appeared, flapping around his wagon. "We can discuss more details about the fate of the dragons in a later session. Meanwhile, please gear up. We're going on a field trip."

Everyone glanced around in excitement as Gideon returned to his wagon.

Raven stopped him as everyone else dashed for their tents. "Please—" was all she said to get him to talk to her.

Gideon took a deep breath. "We should inform your parents about our relationship. It's been a year and a half."

"We will," Raven responded. "I promise."

"But your father—"

"Will understand. We didn't plan this." She reached up and kissed his lips softly before Gideon pulled away.

"Finish getting ready."

"Yes, sir," Raven said playfully.

Gideon walked to his wagon and smiled, acknowledging the bat. "Thank you, Warwick." He created a red portal to return his friend's familiar, then summoned his gold armor. Gideon went into a trance and focused telepathically to reach the Shadow Realm's Guardian. *Are you ready, Krut?*

Yes, Gideon. Thank you! And Allus is waiting.

Thank you!

Good luck with your mate.

After dismissing the vision, Gideon extended his wings, patted the stones in the secured component pouch, and returned to the campfire. The group gathered in their battle gear, excited. "We all ready?" Everyone nodded as he cast a red portal.

A tall half-orc with white wings, wearing gold armor, popped out. The group gasped, raising weapons as Gideon and the stranger glanced at them, laughing.

Krut spoke in common. "I'll be quick."

"No rush, my friend," Gideon responded as they gripped each other's forearms. "Take as much time as you need."

The half-orc cast a blue portal and stepped through.

Gideon eyed his trainees. "Let's go." They formed a line and stepped through, looking nervous. He snickered, then whispered, "Truly embarrassing."

The portal led them to a stone church in a quaint little town at night. The sky was like a bag containing infinite stars, highlighting the full moon. Gideon had forgotten how the Shadow Realm's sky seemed more extensive than the Mortal Realm's.

"Is this—" Jarz began.

"Welcome to the Shadow Realm," Gideon stated. "This is the Temple of the Chaotic Shadow."

Jarz glanced back. "If the High Council—"

Gideon laughed. "I won't snitch if you won't."

"Gideon," Raven said nervously.

"We'll be fine," Gideon responded. "Krut and I are switching realms while he visits sick family in the Mortal Realm."

Izarra hesitated. "Gid—"

"Listen," Gideon quickly interrupted as the group faced him, "I appreciate all the concern, but it's a guardian thing." He glanced around the town. A moonbeam stretched toward them as an image began to form. A tall, lanky, dark-skinned moon-elf with shoulder-length silver hair walked toward the group.

"What do you want us to do?" Shorte whispered, pulling out his weapon.

"Welcome to HallowMorr," the moon-elf said, grinning as he gripped Gideon's forearm.

"Thank you, Allus," Gideon replied.

"Giddy, it's been ages," the demigod gleamed. "You haven't changed a bit."

Shorte snickered, glancing at the perplexed group. "As in the demigod of moons?"

"In the flesh," Allus responded. "The citizens should be on their best behavior with me here."

"Thank you again," Gideon said, watching the group frozen in bewilderment. "Go explore," he encouraged.

Shorte tried his best to stealthily slide closer to Avalann as they walked side by side, and Izarra wrapped her arm tightly around Jarz.

"No need to be fearful, my friends," Allus reassured them. "We only bite unwelcomed guests."

"This is Raven," Gideon said, introducing her.

The moon-elf demigod kissed her hand. "A pleasure."

"Is *it* ready?" Gideon inquired.

"Of course, Giddy," Allus responded. "What kind of host would I be if not punctual?"

Raven glanced at Gideon. "Is *what* ready?"

"Just follow the main road down to the marsh," Allus instructed. "And don't worry about the dire-crocs." Raven's eyes widened as he continued, "Krut penned them before he left."

The demigod rushed to follow the others into the town's heart. "To the left is the local blood bank for the vampiris," Allus said as he pointed to a windowless obsidian-constructed building with a gothic iron double door. The protectors continued walking through the streets of HallowMorr, passing structures created primarily of dark stones with quartz or calcite trimming. In the windows of most buildings, candles glowed dimly, outlining the ledges.

The moonlight cast a soft, white aura, creating shadows across the public square as tiny fireflies drifted in the breeze, making their own star field.

The others continued the tour as Raven and Gideon split off toward the outskirts of town, where the gravel road sloped toward a marsh.

"Vampiris . . ." Raven mumbled, gripping Gideon's arm and gradually gazing up at him. "You mean vampires?"

"There are all types of shadow creatures in this realm. Vampires, lycanthropes, shades, moon elves."

"And dire-crocodiles?"

"I'm sure he was jesting," Gideon replied suspiciously.

"But the others—"

"They are perfectly safe with Allus. No one would dare cross a demigod. Now come," Gideon replied, taking her hand. "I have something to show you."

At the bank of the marsh was a small boat with a lantern attached to the bow. Gideon lifted Raven before trudging through the water. He sat her inside the ship, then lifted himself on.

As the craft tipped, Raven leaned forward, gripping his hand. "This isn't exactly the most romantic trip."

Gideon half-grinned, realizing she was trying to lighten the mood. "I'm sure you were disappointed I didn't gift you anything for your twentieth birthday last fall."

Raven gripped his hand tighter. "Being with you is a gift I wouldn't trade for all of Euphrasia."

Reaching into his leather component pouch, Gideon pulled out two gray, flat stones and handed them to her. "Happy belated birthday."

"You risked the trip to the Shadow Realm for rocks?" Raven said as she inspected them.

"I thought you knew me by now?" Gideon smirked, holding one up. He cast a spell, "Noctis Avem Sermo Porta," lighting the flat stones up and activating a small portal-like opening. He held the small portal up to his face and nodded for her to do the same.

Raven's face appeared in the portal-like space. "What the spell?"

"It's a set of ancient portal receivers used for cross-realm communications. Remember how Natus separated Fharla and Felix? Well, they used these to communicate about the creation of the Mortal Realm."

Raven returned hers to him. "Gideon, these artifacts belong somewhere like Waterfront."

He shut down the comm stone and handed it back to her. "They had more than one set. These were spares, according to Blade."

"My half-brother," Raven replied in disbelief. "He gave you these."

"Yes, we talk occasionally at the High Council," Gideon responded. "I had to talk about us with *someone*."

Raven dove to the other side of the boat, hugging him. "I don't know what to say."

"I take it you like them," Gideon whispered.

"Of course, but why the Shadow Realm?"

"I knew we were coming here to help Krut. He needed to visit family in Zuhgan, and I thought this would be a unique way to give you the stones. So I sent a message to Blade for Allus to help set this up."

"What am I going to do with you, Mister Grindal?" Raven asked, leaning in for a kiss. As they pulled their heads back, he noticed that even in the dark, the lantern light had a way of reflecting off her purple eyes. After a long day, his nerves finally settled.

Gideon slid the stone into an empty socket on his gauntlet next to the red gem, saying, "Got to love Mug and his ingenuity."

Raven stared at her coin pouch. "I hate to put it in here," she said as she safely stowed the stone. "It deserves better. Maybe I need Mug to create something for me."

Gideon rocked the boat as he hopped out, making a splash. "Let's go find the others."

When he reached for her, she leaned into his arms as he lifted her to dry ground. They walked hand in hand up the path to explore more of HallowMorr.

They reached the blood bank as a red portal opened, and Krut dashed out. *That was a quick trip.* Gideon noticed the Shadow Realm Guardian's concerned look. "What's wrong?"

With sad eyes, Krut finally managed to say, "My family is missing, and skeletal remains and bloated-belly vultures litter my hometown of Zuhgan."

Gideon's urge to portal to Zuhgan halted as the High Council's warning echoed in his mind: *Gideon Grindal if you interfere again, there will be no voting.*

CHAPTER TWENTY-FIVE

OMLETT'S TWENTY-FIFTH ANNIVERSARY

R aven sat sharpening her daggers by the extinguished campfire. There was no need for a fire on this hot summer day. Beads of sweat clung to her skin, and combined with the humidity, she felt like a basted turkey. She glanced toward the lake, debating whether to jump in since there was no breeze to carry the mist over from the falls.

Izarra lay nude, while Jarz, wrapped in a groin cloth, was sprawled out on a blanket at the beach, soaking in the sun's rays. Shorte sat in the shade at the forest's edge as Avalann continued adding a sky view in her tree hut.

Fall can't get here fast enough.

Avalann's yell echoed throughout the alcove. Raven's gaze turned toward the elf and then the road. She spotted Pixie on his packed wagon of goodies. It was another delivery. *I wonder if anyone wrote.*

Jarz slipped on his robe and helped Izarra stand, placing a robe around her before giving her a quick kiss. Everyone gathered around to collect their packages and letters. Shorte received a couple of scrolls and a medium-sized box. Pixie handed Jarz a scroll and some books, then helped Izarra.

The half-water nymph giggled as she fumbled the packages. "I'm not dressed for this."

Shorte scoffed. "I'm surprised you're dressed at all."

"It's been a hot summer," Izarra replied, tightening the robe.

Shorte mumbled under his breath, turning toward his tent. "You can say that again."

Pixie handed Raven two small boxes and two scrolls as Avalann hopped off the back, holding a container. Raven, being nosy, peeked around the back of the wagon. "Anything for Gideon?"

"No," Pixie answered, "sorry."

It'd been six months, and he still hadn't received anything: no correspondence, packages, or anything. "Wait here a moment," Raven instructed as she returned to her tent.

"Make it quick, Princess! I still have deliveries for Brindell," Pixie called out irritably.

Raven dropped the boxes and scrolls, then grabbed a blank parchment. Chills dominated her sweaty skin. *I can't believe I'm writing this.* She cast Illusory Script on it, creating an invisible message. Her hands shook as she rolled it up and tied it with the ribbon from her small box. She returned it to Pixie. "Deliver this to Gideon . . . please," implored Raven. "Please!"

Pixie shot her an exasperated look. "Sure," he uttered, taking the scroll from her.

Raven sighed. "And don't tell him who it's from."

"As you wish, Princess," Pixie replied. "But you *owe* me, Princess."

Raven's heart raced as Astrick's voice rang in her mind as she envisioned running down the path toward home. "*You owe me, Princess!*" She watched from behind Pixie's wagon as the dwarf knocked on Gideon's door. The guardian answered eventually, allowing her to study Pixie's movement. *Where the spell is he? Will Gideon know if it's an impostor?*

"What are you doing?" Jarz asked as he stacked the ration crates.

"Shh, nothing," Raven replied impatiently, waving him away. She overheard Pixie telling Gideon there was a message. The guardian glanced around curiously as he accepted the scroll.

Jarz glimpsed back and chuckled before walking away. "Women."

"It's done, Princess," Pixie stated, dusting off his hands.

As her hands trembled, she opened the coin pouch at her waist, flipping him a SIP, then pulling him in for a hug. "Thank you," she said gratefully.

"Keep it," Pixie said, handing back the silver coin. "I was jesting."

"No, you keep it," Raven insisted, feeling slightly guilty. "What you delivered was priceless."

Pixie shrugged, pocketed the silver piece, closed the back of his wagon, and left for his next destination.

Relieved, Raven skipped back to her tent, focusing on Gideon's wagon, but he never reappeared. Having waited long enough, she opened her parcels. First, she chose a small box. After removing the ribbon, a familiar smell hit her. It was two bars of her mother's homemade lavender soap, just in time to replace the current one, about the size of a pebble. The second box contained another familiar and welcome smell: sugar cookies.

"I smell cookies!" Shorte yelled. Suddenly, he appeared at the opening of her tent.

Raven pulled one out of the box. "Make sure you share with everyone else."

"Yes, ma'am," Shorte said enthusiastically, snatching the sugary treats and wandering out. "Anyone want a cookie?"

Raven read the first message.

I hope you enjoy the soap and cookies. Can you make it home for Omlett's twenty-fifth-anniversary celebration? I can't believe it's been twenty-five years. It seems like we just built this place.
Love, your Mother and Father.

Raven rolled up the scroll and untied the second one that read:

Hey, ogre poop,
Is my necklace protecting you and bringing you all the luck in Euphrasia? I would love to see you at the Omlett celebration. We have so much to catch up on. The rolling in flowerbeds and the sunshine dances aren't the same without you. You also have a swamp to clean so we can return to our secret sister spot, but I have good news!
I miss you and love you.
Always,
Carya

Even her parchment smelled like sunshine. *I wonder what her good news is.* She rolled up the scrolls and carefully placed them in her backpack.

Jarz swung by her tent, tossing in a scroll. "It's from Brugg. Not sure why Pixie gave this to me."

"Thanks," Raven replied anxiously, opening the scroll. It read:

You can't hide at camp forever. I'll see you tonight.

Why would Jarz give me this? It's not in Orcish or from Brugg. She pulled out the other parchment and matched the handwriting. *It's by the same author. Was*

Pixie really Astrick in disguise? Did he refrain from revealing himself? She stuffed the scrolls into her backpack, rushed to Gideon's wagon, and knocked.

The guardian swung open the top half of his wagon door, greeting her with a smile. "Raven."

Has he read my message? "When is Omlett's anniversary celebration?" Raven asked. "I know it has to be soon."

"I do believe today is the fourth of Vakil, so most likely tonight."

"You weren't going to tell me?" Raven asked, crossing her arms.

Gideon laughed. "Actually, I was just about to. As a matter of fact, we're all going."

"Really?" Raven grinned, hugging and kissing him on the lips. "I'll tell the others."

"That's fine." When she didn't leave, he asked, "Is there something else?"

"No, no, that's it," she responded, disappointed.

"Make sure everyone is ready to be teleported at nightfall."

"You're teleporting us?"

"No, *you* are," Gideon declared. He opened the bottom half of the door, and she stepped inside. It was still organized and clean compared to the squalor in her tent. He opened an ornate cabinet stacked with rolled-up parchments. "Those are all portal scrolls to Omlett."

"There are hundreds of them."

"I know. My favorite city."

"What about Suttiir? It seems like Avalann missed you."

"Avalann was always busy with some type of schooling or training."

"Trying to impress you."

Gideon paused for a moment in thought. "Do you think I should speak to her?"

"I think she would love that."

"I promise I will. For now, please inform the rest of the gang. We don't have much time before we have to leave."

Raven couldn't hold it in anymore. "Did you receive a scroll today?"

"Yes, from Pixie."

"And?"

"It was a blank parchment," he responded, looking around to spot where he had placed it. "I was about to use it to create a portal scroll."

Raven dropped her head and sighed. "Did you test it to see if it was magical?"

"No," Gideon replied, raising his eyebrows. "Should I have?"

Raven picked it up from the table. "This one?"

"Yes."

Raven placed it in a drawer. "Promise you won't read it till after the celebration." She murmured, "Securus," casting the Arcane Lock spell on the drawer.

Gideon smirked. "You know I have ten other spells to retrieve that."

"True," Raven chided. "But you have nothing stronger than your promise."

"Yes, Princess," Gideon teased. "I promise."

She gently placed her palm on his cheek, caressing it. "Good."

Gideon guided her hand, closing his eyes as if to enjoy her touch. As they reopened, his gaze was mesmerizing. He leaned in and gently kissed her lips, then slowly trailed kisses around her cheek and onto her neck, just like the stories of the vampiris in the Shadow Realm. Only he wasn't draining her life; it was triggering something inside. Like his touch was teasing her nerve endings.

Raven's pulse quickened as electrical tingles shot from her neck, traversing her entire spine. She ran her hands through his hair, guiding him as her soul levitated.

His mouth massaged her earlobe, stopping to whisper, "We should be getting ready."

"No!" she managed to squeal as he continued kissing her neck, enjoying the unexpected pleasure. She felt Gideon pull away as she opened her eyes in disappointment. Her pulse continued racing as she straightened her ponytail. "I guess I should get ready for the party."

"I shall see you at sundown," Gideon responded, kissing her on the cheek one last time before she returned to her tent.

Raven grabbed her bathing supplies, dropped them off on the beach, and dove into the calm water. The cool, refreshing lake water dropped her body's temperature. *I'm unsure if it was the heat of the sun or Gideon.* She caught herself blushing as she finished bathing. Slipping on her black robe, she headed straight to Izarra's tent.

The half-nymph finished getting ready, looking gorgeous in the light blue dress she bought at the outfitters. She was applying dust to her face in front of her copper mirror.

"What are you doing?" Raven asked.

"It's crushed dyed powder. Bards use it in theatrical performances." She glanced over at Raven, who was frowning. "Raven Naelo, that's not attire for a princess. Blade must be watching over you because I remembered yours, too." She opened a box and pulled out a backless purple satin dress. "I've had this since that first day I met you."

"That's why you didn't have coins for the drink?"

Izarra laid it out carefully on her cot. "I've been saving it for a special occasion."

Raven giggled as her eyes teared up.

"No, no," Izarra commanded, rushing over with a cloth. "No puffy eyes. We will fix this, Princess."

"Thank you," Raven said gratefully, sitting in front of the mirror.

"Don't thank me yet." Izarra applied some powder to the rogue's face and removed the band that held Raven's hair in a ponytail. "We don't even know if it fits yet. Now, let's put those spells to good use. Do that hand-burning spell," she instructed, separating Raven's hair into strips. "Not too hot! We don't want your hair to catch fire."

Raven nervously cast Cessis Nar as Izarra handled the strips of wet hair.

"Press your hands and run them downward." Once dry, Izarra ran a brush through Raven's hair. "Now you can get dressed."

The rogue stood, slipping on her gown. The material clung to her skin as she kept tugging at it. "I don't know, Izarra. This feels more uncomfortable than any armor."

"Stop! Now, pick out a pair of shoes." Izarra opened a chest beside her backpack.

"I'm not sure . . . I feel like I'm going to rip this."

Izarra shook her head. "Try these," she suggested, pulling out a pair of purple slippers.

Raven pulled up the dress to slip her foot into one, grimacing. "They're too small."

"Don't worry." Izarra pulled out a thin board in the shape of a foot. "Place your foot on this." She tapped it twice, and, to Raven's amazement, the board conformed to her foot. Izarra removed the contraption, tapped it once, and watched it shrink. She then placed the device in the small shoe, tapped it twice, and the shoe reshaped itself around the board. Izarra repeated the process with the second shoe. "Now try."

"They fit perfectly!" Raven exclaimed, walking around in a circle. "Where did you find that?"

"Mizzendale," Izarra replied, giving Raven a final inspection. "You'll find the most exotic shops there."

"Maybe one day."

Their heads spun toward the tent's opening when Gideon yelled, "Everyone ready?"

Izarra grinned and grasped the rogue's hand. "Let's go knock 'em dead."

Withdrawing her arm, Raven anxiously whispered, "I can't."

"How about I go first," Izarra declared. "Then follow me, but I swear on my father, if Avalann says anything remotely insulting, I'll drown her."

Raven's eyes widened as Izarra winked, then dashed out, throwing her arms up, spinning around, and showing off. The gasp from the group amplified Raven's nerves.

"You look amazing," Jarz complimented as Shorte and Avalann flattered her.

Everyone's out there. That means all eyes will be on me.

Izarra shouted in a playful distress call, "Help, Raven! There's a bugbear out here!"

Before she could change her mind, Raven forced herself to step out of the tent. The laughing ceased as every noise at camp disappeared. Izarra grinned, clapping enthusiastically, thrilled with her creation. "Wow," Gideon uttered under his breath.

Gideon's white and gold trim, long-tailed tunic contrasted with the dark settings of camp. *I have always loved the design of Elven Garb.* His blond hair was pulled into a stylish bun, exposing the collar's edge that ended just above his neck. It was like an invitation to one of her favorite places to kiss him. The dark blue undertunic highlighted the ice blue of his eyes. His white breeches with the same gold trim clung to his muscular legs as they tucked into his matching knee-high boots. The crystal buckle on his golden belt had a magical dark yellow sparkle as if he had captured fireflies to dance around it. *If he had a crown, he could pass for a king.* They locked eyes, and for a moment, she wanted to whisk him away to dance around in the stardust of the Astral Realm until a familiar voice broke the silence.

"Don't just stand there." Izarra nudged the guardian. "Go get her."

Gideon approached Raven, offering his arm, and she accepted it as they walked toward the camp center.

Shorte and Jarz bowed. "Princess," they said in unison as Avalann smiled, tilting her head respectfully.

"Raven," Gideon said, mesmerized, "I don't think I've ever seen your hair styled this way." He brushed it aside. "I love it."

"You look very handsome tonight. It's always nice to see you out of your celestial armor," Raven innocently said as Shorte snickered. "You know what I mean," she clarified, blushing.

"Well, let's go. I'm starving," Shorte said as he extended his arm for Avalann.

"Remember, folks," Gideon instructed, "your camp graduation ceremony is in two days, so don't do anything stupid. Try to be"—he eyed Shorte—"somewhat professional."

"Hey!" exclaimed Shorte, feigning offense.

"I'll take care of the portal," Jarz offered, opening the scroll.

"Thank goodness," Avalann teased. "Raven's so nervous we would probably end up in the middle of the Suttiir River."

"Should I drown her," Izarra whispered to Raven, "now or later?"

Raven flashed a smirk, shaking her head.

"They don't work like that," Gideon chimed in, gently patting Raven's hand.

"I was jesting," Avalann snapped.

Gideon smirked. "Our lower halves would be here, and our top halves would be in the middle of the river." The group laughed as the blue portal appeared.

Jarz and Izarra were the first to step through, followed by Avalann and Shorte. Raven took a deep breath, and Gideon whispered, "Nothing to worry about. I'll be by your side."

Once through the portal, a familiar sight greeted them—*home sweet home*. She noticed the reconstructed church. *Someone did a great job*. The new stained-glass windows were breathtaking as candlelight highlighted the colors as the stars began to consume the night sky.

Raven felt Gideon's arm move around her protectively. She leaned into him momentarily, then quickly separated, glancing around to see if anyone had caught her.

Gideon snickered, shaking his head. "We have to inform your parents."

"I know . . . let's just enjoy the festivities. If we see them and the time feels right, we can tell them then." She accepted his extended arm and moved closer to him, stealing a quick kiss. "Don't pout."

Loud laughter and applause came from outside Maggie's Magic Shop. Maggie was dressed in a black wizard robe and top hat, entertaining a group of children by levitating a bunny out of another cap. Headmaster Taiker stood tall, clad in a colorful robe and wearing an amused expression as if actually enjoying himself. *I wonder if he's making sure Maggie doesn't break any Waterfront regulations.*

The headmaster's gaze grew intense as he noticed Raven. She glanced back as they walked north, following the prison road as Taiker's eyes locked on them. The blacksmith and his wife were handing out metal charms. A shop across from them had a young bard in a bright orange costume juggling a set of knives. People crowded the road as they moved from vendor to vendor. Further down, in the central market area, they saw Izarra and Jarz sharing a bag of sweets, focusing on a performer spitting fire.

As they moved down the road further, a group of gypsy belly dancers outside of Suttiir Jewelers began playing another song. The nomads had a camp on the city's outskirts called Gypsy's Corner. *Carya and I used to love visiting them. We always returned home with scarves and jewelry. The fortune readings were always fun, too.*

"A personal reading for the lovers?" asked an old gypsy wearing a yellow robe. She had a wrinkled face and held a crystal ball in her hands.

Gideon laughed, shaking his head. "No thank you. I bet it gets better for every coin we pay."

The gypsy's eyebrow lifted and moved closer. "Do I know you?"

Raven extended her hand. "I'm—"

The woman rudely brushed the rogue aside and stared at Gideon. "Not you, him. I feel like I know you." Without warning, the gypsy dropped her crystal ball and grabbed his hand.

Gideon pleaded, "Ma'am, I must insist—"

"Power," the gypsy spat, grasping his hand tighter, then flipping it over to read his palm.

Raven tried tugging Gideon's other hand. "We really must be going."

The gypsy traced the lines on his palm and recited. "Long life—loneliness."

"Feels like it," Gideon teased.

The gypsy closed her eyes. "A true love—"

Gideon flashed a smile as Raven blushed.

"Maybe," the fortune teller continued, "death—"

"Everyone dies eventually."

"You will be mourned but be reborn royalty." The elderly gypsy woman pouted. "You will anger the gods."

"Now it's just getting weird." Gideon removed his hand and presented her with a gold piece. "Thank you for the reading—please take this." The gypsy stuffed the GOP in her pocket.

Raven wrapped her fingers around Gideon's, trying to cross the road to the food vendors, but the older woman stepped in front and bowed. "All hail! The King of Suttiir!"

Gideon sighed deeply. "No, ma'am, sorry to disappoint you. But I'm not King Luhnar."

The crowd of dancers had stopped, noticing their elder kneeling. As the others crowded around, Raven and Gideon rushed away. They glanced back as the elder pointed their way.

"What the spell was that all about?" Raven asked. *My thoughts about him looking like a king were spot on.*

"A wonderful performance, that's all." Gideon smiled. "Are you hungry?"

"A little"—she paused to curtsy—"your majesty."

As they came to the end of the road, the air filled with the aroma of roasting boar. Chefs from the Meat and Greet Eatery had built a fire pit in the middle of the grass area. Raven witnessed Shorte devouring a giant turkey leg and a tankard of what she assumed was ale. The Fish and Ships Eatery had a stand selling shrimp skewers. The long road in front of the prison was dark, an area undisturbed by the festivities.

Gideon cast a spell, Unicornis Spirituus, to summon a phantom white unicorn.

"No spell can beat Ghost," Raven whispered as he smiled coyly, unsummoning the magical steed and sweeping her off her feet. "You aren't going to carry me all the way there."

Gideon murmured, "Gravitas Separatus," casting the Sever Gravity spell. "Hold on," he said playfully.

Raven held on for dear life as Gideon laughed. She snuggled her head against his shoulder as the force of the wind blew against her. Flying on the dragon at her eighteenth birthday party had nothing on the real thing. It wasn't long before they'd arrived at the main platform across the road from the Omlett Inn. He landed by the stables to keep from drawing too much attention. She ran her fingers through her hair to straighten it. "That was a close second," she teased. "Still can't beat Ghost."

Gideon smirked. "I tried."

Gary sold slices of melon and bowls of berries, and Miss Crinkly had a stand of baked sweets by the makeshift dance floor near the amphitheater. They bought two sweet rolls with icing. Gideon handed her one and bit into his as the icing coated his fingers. He licked them as she stifled a laugh.

"Raven?" Miss Crinkly said uncertainly. "Raven!" The elderly gnome dashed around the stand, hugging her. "I didn't recognize you with your hair down."

Raven grinned. "It's been three years."

Miss Crinkly nudged the rogue's hip. "Who's your companion?"

"That would be Mister Grindal," Raven replied.

"What?" Gideon asked innocently, still trying to clean his hand. "You would think they would supply something to wipe this off."

Miss Crinkly handed him a wet cloth. "You remind me of my dear Chuck. Adorable but just a star too far."

"Was I just insulted?" Gideon replied as Raven sucked in her lips.

"It's all right, dear," Miss Crinkly said, "we understand."

Coating the tip of her finger with icing, she dabbed some on his nose. "You have some on your face."

He shook his head, wiping it off. "That was very *sweet* of you."

"May I get a honey bun?" a patron asked.

"Slow your roll," Miss Crinkly snapped, holding her hand up and whispering to Raven, "Baker jokes." She waddled back. "I'm coming." As she settled behind the counter, she glanced over. "Well, your parents are out there dancing somewhere, dear."

"Thank you, Betty." Together, she and Gideon moved toward the dance floor.

Couples danced on the platform as Cyndi's band played at the north end of the stage. Raven spotted her parents on the dance floor, wearing their royal attire. Her mother's gold dress gracefully flowed with her as she moved. Her father looked positively regal in his crimson tunic and dark pants.

"Follow me," Raven said, taking Gideon's hand. She wrapped her arms around his neck, shrouded her face behind them as she surveyed the dance floor, and slowly danced closer to her parents as they laughed and whispered conspiratorially. The loud music stopped her from eavesdropping as the band transitioned to a slow folk song.

Gideon pulled Raven closer, swaying to the music. "The ass marks the spot," he blurted out, catching her off guard as she playfully stared into his ice-blue eyes. "Punchline for the donkey and pirate joke. You know, they walk into a tavern."

Raven laughed heartily, drawing gazes from everyone around them. "You're full of surprises tonight, Mister Grindal," she said, composing herself.

"I believe Celestial Guardian rule number one is never to let them see you nervous," he explained.

"And what does the Celestial Guardian of the Mortal Realm have to be nervous about?" Raven asked flirtatiously. *It was as if the Fates had heard the question.*

"Gideon?" Eugor asked, puzzled as Raven, dancing in Gideon's arms, glanced back at them.

Mara gleamed over at them. "Raven!"

They all stopped and hugged. Eugor vigorously shook Gideon's hand. "Glad you could make it," her father said, as her parents' eyes stayed fixated on their daughter.

"You are beauteous," Mara said lovingly, "and you're in a dress!"

"I know," Raven mocked with a frown. "It's a special occasion."

"It sure is," her father agreed excitedly.

"Where's Carya?" Raven asked.

"You mean Cleric Naelo," Mara replied with glee.

"She was promoted?" Raven asked.

"Yes, and it's High Priest Stone-Prayer now," Eugor answered, eyeing the crowd.

"I'm sure Shorte will be pleased to hear this news," Raven responded.

"Little sis!" Carya called out as she came running over in her lovely white gown to hug her sister. Thomas, in his formal attire, followed close behind.

I forgot how handsome he was. Raven guiltily glanced at Gideon, reassuring herself that she made the right decision.

"You look wonderful," said Thomas, kissing her hand.

"You didn't tell her, did you?" Carya asked her parents as Mara shook her head.

"That your Cleric Naelo now?" Raven replied, baffled.

"Besides that." Carya grabbed Thomas's arm and announced, "We're betrothed."

Raven's eyes widened, staring at them. "What?" As if she misheard her sister. "That's wonderful." She gripped her sister tightly. "Congratulations! I'm happy for you both."

Gideon enthusiastically shook Thomas's hand and then hugged Carya, quickly giving her a peck on the cheek.

Raven's mind raced momentarily, and finally, she asked, "So when's the exciting day?"

"We're thinking this winter," Carya announced, practically glowing.

Raven glanced at her parents, who were beaming at their eldest daughter.

"You're graduating in a couple of days, aren't you?" asked Eugor, turning to Raven. "They waited until after graduation to ensure you would be there."

Do I tell them about Gideon?

"Who said she passed?" Gideon joked. "I might have to hold her back a year."

Maybe not.

The song ended. "It's time," Eugor said mysteriously. He walked toward a patch of land in the middle of the road, just south of the stage, where something large sat with a cloth draped over it.

"Time for what?" Raven asked.

"You'll see," answered Mara. "Your father has wanted this for Omlett for a very long time."

Eugor cleared his throat and began speaking loudly to ensure he had every-one's attention. "I want to thank my wife, Mara; my best friend, Gideon; and my partner, Mug; for making my dream come true. My dreams would have died if it hadn't been for the rare dragon egg. So, in honor of the genesis of this beauteous city, I present Omlett with this marble statue that will stand here in the center square." He pulled off the cloth to reveal a giant black dragon sitting on its egg. "For Omlett, the Heart and Soul of Euphrasia for twenty-five years and to eternity," he said, reading the plaque.

Raven approached Thomas while Carya talked with her father. "It's terrific to see you again," Thomas said. "You look like you're doing well."

"Couldn't be better," Raven replied confidently, noticing Gideon eyeing Thomas. "I'm happy for you and my sister."

"Thank you," Thomas responded appreciatively.

"I'll come after you if you hurt her, you know. But I know you won't—Mis-ter Do-Gooder."

"I'm sure you will find someone," Thomas said, placing his arm around her.

Raven pulled away and announced, "I already have." She slid up to Gideon, gently taking his hand. Thomas appeared stunned as Eugor's grin faded.

"What's this?" Eugor asked as everyone around them stared.

"What's what?" Raven asked defiantly.

"Eugor," Gideon began hesitantly, "I wanted to tell you, but Raven wanted to wait."

Eugor momentarily paused to absorb the shock as his expression became emotionless. "After everything we've been through together, Gideon. She's just a child."

"I'm not a child," Raven bristled, offended.

"Eugor," Mara said softly. "She's a young woman. Can you imagine anyone else who would care for our daughter better than Gideon?"

Her father looked bewildered, trying to formulate his thoughts, but gave up, storming off. Mara called out to him as Gideon chased after his best friend.

Raven went to follow them, but a hand gripped her shoulder.

"Your father will come around," Mara explained, removing her hand. "I think it just caught him off guard."

Raven's heart dropped as she witnessed her father and Gideon arguing out-side the Inn. Eugor vanished into the crowd as the guardian lowered his head in defeat. Raven's eyes followed as she saw Headmaster Taiker staring directly at her.

"Since when do you like old guys?" Mug joked as the group glared at him, causing Raven to turn for a brief moment. "But seriously, I'm happy for you."

The rogue glanced back into the crowd, but the headmaster was gone. *He still gives me the creeps—or is he really Astrick?* Vulnerability washed over her, realizing she didn't have—

"Gideon, hunh?" Carya mused. "Who would have thought that?"

"I called it years ago," Thomas declared, smiling proudly. "In the courtyard."

"You should have written to me," Carya said, disappointed.

"It's not like you sent me any information on your relationship status," Raven snapped. *This isn't Carya's fault.* "I'm sorry."

Carya embraced her little sister as Thomas explained, "We wanted to tell you in person." After an awkward pause, he asked, "How does that work with the High Council?"

"I don't think it matters," Raven said, distracted by surveying the crowd. *Where are they?* She pulled nervously on the straps of her dress. A melon-sized knot formed in her stomach. "I mean, I'm guessing it doesn't matter."

"I knew Gideon liked you more than me," Carya teased. "Now I understand how much more."

Raven stared daggers at Carya. "This wasn't planned," she explained, holding back her temper. "It developed over time."

"Raven, stop worrying," Mara consoled. "I couldn't be happier for you. Gideon has always been a part of this family, and as I said, your father will come around."

"We're going to go dance," Carya told Raven. "Would you care to join us?"

Raven shook her head, glancing back at the Inn. Tears formed in her eyes. *I've ruined everything.* Avalann's voice yelled out as she and Shorte threw axes, trying to win a prize. The archer seemed to be losing, which gave Raven a moment of satisfaction. She heard her mother call out. "Gideon!"

The guardian joined them at the statue. "I couldn't find him. I lost him near the bakery."

"I'll talk to him," Mara promised, taking both their hands. "I'm truly happy for you." Then she walked toward the Inn.

"I want to return to camp," Raven said, folding herself into Gideon's arms.

"As you wish," Gideon agreed as he cast a portal. "Castra Porta."

"You're going to get in trouble," Raven said nervously. "Don't you need a scroll?"

"I'd rather be in trouble with the council than your father."

Raven stepped through the portal, and when Gideon appeared beside her, she threw herself into his arms. "I'm so sorry. I don't know why I did that." He rubbed her back, and she rested her chin on his shoulder, trying not to cry. "My father is going to hate us."

"Your father could never and would never hate you. He loves you and Carya more than anything in this world."

"Then he'll be angry with you."

"Perhaps, but Eugor and I have a long history. He knows in his heart that I would never do anything to hurt you or your family. And if I say I love you—I do, with all my being."

Raven pulled away, surprised at the words. *He just said he loves me.* "Come with me." She guided him to the wagon and retrieved the scroll from the drawer.

Gideon looked at her suspiciously and unrolled the paper.

"Go ahead."

"Verbum Revelare," As the words appeared on the parchment, he read out loud, "*I love you.* Aw, Pixie loves me." He dropped the note onto the bed, pulling her in for a kiss, whispering, "I love you, too."

"I mean it, Gideon," Raven replied as her voice trembled. "I do love you."

CHAPTER TWENTY-SIX

FAMILY HEIRLOOMS

Gideon beamed as the vision's purple hue changed to a dark blue. A sign that morning arrived. He exited his meditation as the birds chirped. Sunlight penetrated the small windows of the wagon. He glanced down at a sleeping Raven. *I could get used to this.* He placed his arm around her and snuggled into his loft bed beside her.

His mind recalled the events of last night, holding her in his arms, kissing her passionately. The conversations about becoming a guardian, her fascination with magic, the time she accidentally misplaced her father's lucky dagger, and the crazy adventures he and her father got into when they were young.

He even recalled the brief argument with Eugor last night before losing him in the crowded streets. Gideon wanted to make sure Eugor understood that it was something new, that his feelings for her overwhelmed him after the attack at the church. *Please, Eugor, be happy for us.*

Gideon tugged on the blanket covering his princess. *I better check on the others to see if they've returned.*

After kissing her on the forehead, Gideon exited his wagon. The camp was empty. *Where is everybody?* He muttered, "Ignis Projectum," fire streamed from his fingertips to start the campfire. A blue portal appeared, and Avalann stepped through.

"Morning, Uncle," she said as she headed for her tree fort.

"Morning, Avalann," he responded with a smile. The thought of Raven's conversation suddenly struck him. He stopped his niece, pulling her in for a hug. "I'm so proud of you . . . always have been."

"Thank you," Avalann said, caught off guard. She hugged him tighter. "That means a lot." She pulled away and grabbed her vine, climbing to her sanctuary as another portal appeared behind Gideon.

Jarz and Izarra stepped out. "Sorry, Gideon," the swordmage apologized, gesturing toward Izarra. "She wanted to find Raven."

"Raven's here," Gideon responded.

"Oh, good," Izarra said, rushing to Raven's tent.

Gideon pointed to his wagon. "Miss Lyte."

Izarra smiled with delight, raising her eyebrows and placing her hand over her mouth.

"Gideon!" Jarz nudged him with a goofy grin.

"Nothing happened," Gideon clarified. "We talked. That's all."

"Is that what the High Council calls it?" Jarz asked as Gideon shot him a dirty look. "I'm jesting, I'm jesting."

Raven pulled Gideon's blanket around her shoulders as she exited the wagon, yawning. "Morning, all."

Izarra skipped over, hugging her friend. "Girl gossip," she said gleefully, pulling Raven toward her tent. Raven smiled apologetically to Gideon as the girls walked past.

The guardian couldn't help noticing Jarz's expression. "What is it?"

"Nothing," the swordmage replied, sucking in his lips, clearly lying. "We just talked."

A moment passed before Jarz blurted. "Well, Izarra and I *talked* at the Inn all night . . . very enthusiastically, I might add."

Gideon shook his head. "If you need to gloat, my friend, I'll be here all day."

"At least we know what they'll be talking about," Jarz joked.

"I'm sure, so I hope you provided one spell of a performance." Gideon patted the swordmage on the back as Jarz's eyes widened in terror. "Where's Mister Stone-Grin?"

Jarz shrugged. "I haven't seen Shorte."

A rare, orange sorcery portal appeared as Shorte rolled out, laughing. Three gypsy ladies blew kisses as the gateway closed. The dwarf stood, brushing himself off, noticing Jarz and Gideon watching. Shorte's expression shifted to more of a serious demeanor. He cleared his throat, walking past them toward his tent. "Professionalism, gentlemen."

Gideon and Jarz laughed as the guardian patted the swordmage on the shoulder again, then returned to his wagon. He sat on his bed and closed his eyes, meditating, searching the realm for any dangers. Everything seemed quiet, so he allowed his conscience to return to the wagon.

Rays beamed through his sky view, indicating the sun was higher. His stomach growled. Grabbing a jar of preserved pears, he downed the sweet snacks quickly. *I wonder if Mara talked any sense into Eugor yet.* Placing the empty container on the counter, he inspected the gifts he planned to give the trainees tomorrow night at graduation. He ensured the cover was secure over the longbow Eugor had given him as a special gift for Avalann.

Gorr-et! The guardian cursed in his mind as he summoned his celestial armor and portaled to Eugor's work chamber.

Eugor was reading a scroll at his desk when the guardian appeared through the portal. He glanced up. "That's not proper portal protocol according to Waterfront."

The guardian approached his friend as the portal closed. "Eugor."

"Gideon," he replied curtly as he read the parchment. "Do I need to remind you of the article pertaining to portals?"

He's definitely still upset. "I wanted to tell you—"

Eugor slammed down the scroll. "Yes, so you've already stated. But instead, you left it up to my daughter."

"I'm sorry. I should have told you how I felt before this happened."

"You're like a brother to me. To keep a secret like this"—Eugor stood, gathering his belongings—"it's unforgivable."

Those simple words pierced Gideon's heart. "But I love her," he whispered. "Raven's an incredible woman."

"She's turning twenty-one. She's just becoming a woman."

"I'm equivalent to a twenty-one-year-old human."

"That may be. But you have over three hundred years in this world."

"So I'm more experienced."

"Stop with the jokes!"

"How many relationships have I been in?" Gideon asked, holding back his temper as Eugor eyed him. "None in over a century. Do you think I planned this? Fall for the daughter of my best friend? Risk alienating myself from the one person I would die for in this realm?"

Eugor slammed his fists on his desk. "I *did* die for *you!*"

Gideon paused as his heart sank to his gut. "You still got to marry and have children, but I—"

"You chose that when you became a Celestial Guardian," Eugor reminded him. "And when you still haven't aged when Raven is old and gray? What happens then?"

"Is this about Celeste?"

Eugor's face reddened. "It was her choice to leave me when she was promoted to Celestial Guardian—I know that."

"And keeping the secret of Blade's birth from the High Council was the hardest thing she had ever done."

"Yet she chose the High Council over her own family."

"You're worried I'd do that to Raven? I would never hurt her, Eugor."

Eugor rose again, eyes glued to his desk. "You helped save my life, Gideon, and as a result, I fell in love with Mara. And I'm grateful for both of those things."

"And Mara is human. If you hadn't had the resurrection, you would still be aging like an elf. So what would you have done? Because you would have outlived her, too."

Eugor remained silent.

"Please, Night Breeze, tell me what you would have done. If you would have walked away, I will walk away."

"I would have cherished every moment with her," Eugor whispered.

"I love her, Eugor. Since the church incident, her lying there hurt—my feelings for her grew, changed . . . something I can't explain. And I *want* your blessing."

Eugor watched his friend closely. "You would take good care of her. There is no doubt in my mind."

"I'm going to be here," Gideon said with sadness, "when everyone else around me has gone, so let me . . . let *us* . . . cherish this moment."

"And the High Council?"

"We're not breaking any laws being together. There is only one rule about relationships—we're not allowed to produce offspring—but you already know that."

"And Raven is fine with that restriction?"

"Slow down, Eugor. We aren't there—yet."

Eugor sighed deeply, reaching out his hand. "You have my blessing, but Raven will be a handful."

"No doubt."

"Mara kept reminding me all last evening. It's going to take someone special to keep her grounded."

"I think we both know Raven is meant to soar."

"Go on now!" Eugor proclaimed. "I must deal with a madman at the prison."

"Anything serious?"

"He keeps rambling about seeing the dead roaming the Zorn Mountains."

"Necromancy?"

"Probably inhaled too much of that druidic cannabis."

"I have to return and finish preparing their graduation ceremony."

"Ah, I remember that day like yesterday." Eugor sighed. "Do you mind if I drop in?"

"Not at all." Gideon grinned, opening a portal to camp. He returned to his wagon to find Raven waiting inside.

She hugged him. "Where were you?"

"I had a chat with your father."

"And you're still alive? That's a good sign."

Gideon chuckled. "I'm immortal, remember?"

"I thought you knew my father. He would find a way."

"He's attending graduation."

Raven's eyes widened.

"So you might want to look your best." He twined his fingers with Raven's as they exited the wagon. The only sounds were the rushing of the waterfall and Shorte's snores echoing off the cliffs.

"Your friends had a late night . . . Wait!" Gideon said mischievously, releasing her hand. "Stay here." He uttered a spell that created a sizeable grizzly bear illusion, which charged out of the woods, growling.

The first to awaken was Avalann, who immediately reached for her bow. She shot a few arrows that went right through the beast. Jarz and Izarra emerged from Jarz's tent. She wore his tunic, and he was only in his trousers. *They must be talking again!* The swordmage cast his magical sword and shield while Izarra summoned her twin water elementals.

Shorte stumbled out of his tent, half asleep. "G-Ma?" He saw the bear heading straight for him and dove back into his tent as the enormous creature charged. "That's NOT G-MA!" He returned outside, wielding his mace and shield.

Raven watched the chaos from behind Gideon, her hands resting on his shoulders, laughing hysterically.

Gideon chanted again, and the bear disappeared as he smiled broadly. "Good day, everyone. Now that I've got your attention, I have some chores for you to complete before graduation." The protectors groaned. "I expect your armor to outshine the sun and your weapons to be sharper than Shorte's wit."

"That won't take much," Avalann yelled from her fort.

Shorte tilted his head toward the tree fort and yelled, "I dare you to say that down here, tree hugger!"

Avalann grinned.

"Avalann," Gideon interrupted, "have them in formation for inspection by dawn." He was pleased to see how happy she was at receiving some authority.

Gideon retreated inside his wagon to continue his midday meditation. Luckily, all was calm and quiet in the realm. *Thank Blade! Now I can spend more time with Raven.* Her birthday was in a few months, and he wondered if she'd stay with him until then. *What can I do to top all the other birthdays?* he mused as he continued surveying the realm. *Celeste!*

The sound of the door opening and the vibrations in the yellow aura brought him out of his meditation as he saw Raven waiting.

"Have you finished your chores already, Miss Naelo?" he asked.

"No, sir, I needed another piece of parchment," she said as she slid past him, her hand brushing his arm. The smell of lavender intoxicated him and his heart pounded as she stared up at him seductively. *Breathe.* He leaned in for a kiss.

"Princess!" Avalann yelled, causing them to jump and ruin the moment. "Get out here! No fraternizing with the chief."

Raven laughed. "She's so bossy. I wonder who she gets that from." She smiled and left. He could hear her respond, "Yes, ma'am."

Gideon changed his clothes, then polished his armor. His wagon grew darker, and he glanced out the window to see the sun setting when a knock came at his door.

Avalann stood at attention, clad in her dark green leather armor. "We're ready, sir," she said, saluting him.

Gideon stepped out and saw his other students in formation near the water. Avalann dashed over to stand next to Jarz. Gideon walked the line, inspecting them. "Avalann, your armor is impeccable. Great job." He reached for her longbow. "Your string has some slack in it. Make sure you tighten it."

Avalann inspected her longbow. "*Gorr-et,*" she cursed under her breath as Gideon moved on to the next student.

"Shorte, you missed a spot of dirt on the back side of your armor."

The dwarf looked like a wolf pup chasing its tail as he turned around in circles, trying to see his back.

Gideon continued down the line. Jarz's armor was spotless, so the guardian nodded at the swordmage and moved on to Izarra.

He took a whiff. "Your armor smells like fresh leather."

"It arrived yesterday," Izarra answered sheepishly. "My old one was out of season, sir."

Gideon shook his head and tried to remain serious as he approached Raven, back straight, standing at attention. "Miss Naelo, may I see your daggers, please?"

"Yes, sir," she responded as she handed them to him.

He inspected them thoroughly. "The hilts have a lot of unnecessary gems."

"You can never have too many gems," Raven replied. Izarra giggled.

He walked around her, pacing slowly, surveying every inch of her. "Nice armor."

"Do I pass, sir?" Raven asked playfully. Avalann rolled her eyes as Izarra giggled again.

"Indeed. You all look very professional, and you're all dismissed. Enjoy the evening."

He left, returning to his wagon. A familiar knock sounded on the door as he gathered ingredients for the evening's stew. "Raven."

"I was hoping we could do something together," she said sweetly, wrapping her arms around him.

"I'm glad you offered," he said, handing her a bowl of carrots. "You can help me clean these." She pulled a carrot out of the bowl and threw it at him. He picked up a sack of potatoes and a bowl of meat cubes, then headed toward the campfire.

Once settled to prepare the meal, Raven sliced the carrots. "Do you know why my father is coming tomorrow?"

"I'm not sure. Eugor asked if he could attend, and I couldn't say no."

"Keeping my father happy would help our situation," she agreed, handing him a handful of chopped carrots.

"Indeed," Gideon replied as he dumped all the ingredients into the cauldron. He sat on the ground with his back against a log, watching the pot heat as Raven positioned herself between his legs, leaning against him. He put his arms around her, kissing the top of her head. They sat quietly, watching the fire and the group. The stars above seemed to twinkle brighter as if Fate gave its approval.

Izarra and Avalann played fetch with Oslo, who had grown into an adult these last two years, while Shorte and Jarz laughed near the boulders.

"I think the gypsies predicted an exciting future for Shorte," Raven stated as they watched the dwarf's hand gestures that mimicked looking into a crystal ball.

"Filled with food, females, and foes."

"Speaking of future predictions, could you envision yourself as a king?"

"Not really my style," Gideon responded. "Too much responsibility."

"And protecting an entire realm from a dimensional beast, isn't?"

"That's different. I don't have to ensure Bob's cows stay off John's property."

"Point taken. I've seen plenty of squabbles brought forth to my father."

"What about you? A queen?"

"No, thank you—it involves too many ceremonial dresses."

"Your mother?"

"No, Brugg," she teased. "Of course, watching my *mother* attend different events."

"I don't understand—you were absolutely breathtaking in your purple dress."

She pulled him in for a kiss. "Thank you."

Gideon pulled her closer, resting his head on hers. "Well, if it's any consolation, you would make a wonderful queen." Moments like this were all he wanted, but they were running out of time. *Graduation is tomorrow!* "I wanted to ask you something."

"Anything," she said coyly, rubbing her hand gently on his thigh.

"Tomorrow after graduation, will you stay here with me? We can have some quiet time together. Your father will be disappointed, but we'll ensure you're home for your birthday." Her lips were soft when she kissed him, and as he pulled back a little and stared into her purple eyes. "Can I take that as a yes?"

"Of course," she replied as the others finally joined them at the campfire.

The excitement about tomorrow's graduation filled the air. The group all teamed up, convincing Gideon to reveal what he planned to present to them at the ceremony. "You will know soon enough," the guardian replied.

"I'm going to turn in," Raven said to everyone. "Tent or wagon?" she whispered in Gideon's ear.

"Wagon," he whispered back, thrilled she'd suggested it.

Raven stretched while standing up. "Good night, all."

They watched as she headed for Gideon's wagon. Shorte's one eyebrow shot up as he eyed the guardian and grinned. "I suppose you have to retire, too."

"Not yet, Master Dwarf," Gideon replied casually, sitting up straighter against the log.

The fire began to die out, and most of the stew was gone when Shorte, in his creepiest voice, said, "Before we all retire for the night, has anyone heard about the legend of the wizard and the coin pouch?"

Avalann shook her head. "A ghost story? Really, Shorte?"

"I haven't heard it," Izarra responded, inching closer to Jarz, who shook his head.

"It took place here at this lake over five centuries ago," Shorte began. "I believe Gideon was still on his mother's milk then."

The guardian chuckled. "I'm not that old."

Shorte continued as Izarra curled her feet under herself, holding Jarz tightly. Avalann stroked Oslo's head, who was asleep on her lap. The only sounds were the roar of the waterfall and the owls hooting in the trees. "It involved a black dragon named Rax. The dragon held its breath under the water for a week straight. It lay at the bottom and waited to ambush adventurers. A group of elven travelers—"

"They were humans," Avalann interrupted.

"My story," Shorte grumbled. "They were elves."

"Does it matter?" Izarra asked.

"They die," Avalann responded, "so he's purposely making it elves."

"Thank you." Shorte scowled. "You just ruined the story."

Izarra appeared confused. "But what about the wizard and the coin pouch?"

"Continue, Mister Stone-Grin," Gideon said. "Avalann, hush. It doesn't matter who the adventurers were."

"Thank you, Gideon," Shorte responded. "Now, where was I? Oh yeah, a group of elves approached the lake to set up camp. It was getting dark, so they decided to build a campfire in this exact spot. As they began to doze off by the fire, they heard a gigantic splash, as if the water gods themselves were angry. The water doused the campfire, and something enormous landed in the middle of the camp."

"Rax, the black dragon?" Izarra asked anxiously.

"Yes," whispered Shorte. "The mighty dragon cast a Darkness spell so that not even the moonlight could guide them to safety. They ran around blind as the black dragon spewed acid on them, melting the poor humans—er, elves—"

Avalann snorted. "Told you."

They all laughed as Shorte continued. "Their bodies melted into flesh puddles. The dragon was headed for the children's tent when a wizard, who had somehow been able to see in the dark, brought out a treasure chest from a wagon and pulled it over to the lake. The sound of the coins drew the dragon's attention to the wizard, who cast a Levitation spell on the chest and sent it to the middle of the lake. Once the levitation wore off, the chest dropped and sank to the bottom. The wizard rattled a coin pouch just as the dragon went to dive in after it. The dragon quickly bit down on the old man, but he vanished into a gaseous form. Once he heard the dragon splash into the lake, he reappeared in his elf form."

Izarra gasped in horror. "In the dragon's stomach?"

"Yes," Shorte answered gleefully.

"No way," Izarra said. "The dragon would digest him."

Avalann snickered. "And become dragon poop."

"He had cast a protective shield, or whatever wizards do," Shorte said irritably before continuing. "He heard the chest blown apart by the dragon and then felt the dragon swim upward, so he rattled the coin pouch again. The noise stopped the dragon, who dove back toward its new treasure because it thought someone was stealing it. Every time the dragon would start to swim up, the wizard would rattle the coins. He continued this until his family and the rest of the elves had escaped. If you listen very carefully by the water, you can still hear the rattling of the coin pouch."

Everyone sat still, straining to hear.

"I don't hear—" Izarra began as a coin pouch loudly rattled beside her, causing everyone but Shorte to jump from their seats and shout. It had even caught Gideon by surprise. Raven had cast Invisibility and returned with her coin pouch, waiting for the right opportunity. She and Shorte howled with laughter at their prank.

"Not funny," Avalann said, storming off to her tree fort.

"I thought we were friends!" Izarra scolded Raven. Jarz grasped the angry half-nymph's hand, and the two left for their tents as he tried to comfort her. Gideon shook his head; they'd gotten him again. Raven danced her way over and high-fived Shorte.

Raven laughed. "We've planned this since we returned from the kobolds."

"Well," Shorte chimed in, "it's been fun, but this dwarf needs his beauty sleep."

"Good night," Raven replied, as they both chuckled again.

Shaking his head, Gideon eyed the rogue, now dancing toward him. "What am I going to do with you?"

"Have to stay sharp around me, Mister Grindal." Raven leaned in for a kiss.

Avalann yelled from her window, "Can you *please* not do that in public."

Gideon swept Raven off her feet and into his arms, holding her close to his chest. Shivers ran down his spine as her breath brushed his skin. He mumbled, "Ianua-Aperta," and the wagon door flew open.

Raven whispered, "You make that sound so . . . what's the elf word . . . *sexui*."

"*Sexui ere Cin*." He navigated the steps, maneuvering them both inside. "Ianua-Clausus." The door slammed shut.

"Impressive," Raven laughed, "even with your hands full."

Gideon gently set her down as she called off her armor. It magically re-formed in the corner as he removed her circlet.

Gideon guided her to the edge of the loft bed as she wrapped her legs around him. His nerves kept him from any rational thought as his hormones raged like an out-of-control fireball. Raising his arms, she pulled his tunic over his head before tossing it on the floor. She ran her hands across his biceps as her lips traced the outline of his abs. The touch was soft and cold against his bare chest. As she glanced up at him with those innocent purple eyes, his blood rushed to his lower extremity, producing a bulge in his breeches. Leaning down, passionately kissing her, she quickly yanked her tunic off. Her dark hair cascaded over her shoulders as she released it from her ponytail tie, causing the lockpick to clatter to the floor.

Gideon brushed her hair to the side as he cupped her breasts. She closed her eyes and softly moaned as she guided his hands. Pushing his hand down her chest to her belly, she leaned back. He felt a nervous twitch in his voice. "Raven—"

Shooting upright, she kissed him. "No more talking." She pulled her knees up underneath her on the bed to be the same height as him. "We've already wasted too much time."

A tsunami of tingles washed over his body as she pressed her bare chest against his, hugging him. Gideon ran his hands under her lengthy hair, caressing her back. "I know, but—" Her hands slid down his breeches. "It's been a long time since—"

"And it's my first time," Raven interrupted as he stepped out of his pants. "As I've said before, we'll figure it out." Leaning back against the wall, she pulled him forward. "Now help me."

Gideon slowly removed her breeches, tossing them with the other articles of clothing, shifting to the side, and placing her head on a pillow. He gazed at her as if the Astral Realm was no longer the most beautiful thing in the universe.

"You can see the stars," Raven said excitedly, bringing him out of the trance.

Gideon fought to transfer his gaze to the skylight in the ceiling as he lay next to her in bed. "I count them every night."

Flashing him a smile, she ran her hand over his hip. "Touch me."

He didn't hesitate to place his hand on her hip as she rotated toward him. His fingers traced the crevices of her groin as she closed her eyes again. If any more blood rushed from the rest of his body, he would faint. Laying on her back, she brought him on top of her. Wrapping her legs around him, he settled between them like a missing puzzle piece. They kissed deeply, then stared at each other with great anticipation. At first, she grimaced with discomfort. *Should I stop?* But then he felt her eyes pierce his soul as the overwhelming feeling of pleasure struck them as they continued to be one.

In the morning, the light streamed in through Gideon's windows, and sunbeams fell on Raven's sleeping body, her skin glistening in the sunlight. He leaned down, kissing her.

"Rise and shine," Gideon whispered. "Your father will be arriving soon."

Raven sat up and yawned as her dark hair cascaded down her naked body. "We don't want him seeing me like this, now do we?" she asked, kissing his lips. "I'm going to the lake to bathe." She ransacked one of his closets, donning an oversized wizard robe. Gideon chuckled as she lowered her voice, mocking the headmaster of Waterfront. "That *is* unauthorized use of spells." She glimpsed back before exiting. "Mister Grindal, please clean up this pigsty."

Gideon heard Shorte teasing as she walked by. "Rough night, Princess?"

Maybe I should join her? The thought immediately vanished as the outline of a blue portal formed. *That was close.* He threw on his clothes and greeted his friend, who conversed with Shorte and Izarra.

"Welcome back, Eugor," Gideon greeted his friend, leaving the door open. "Would you care for some Kaffa or some breakfast?" Gideon glanced back after the invitation, noticing Raven's armor. He quickly closed the door.

"No, thank you, I just ate. I hate using portals with an empty stomach." Eugor glanced around. "Where's my daughter?"

"Raven's bathing in the lake," Shorte responded. "She got a little dirty last night."

Izarra pinched the dwarf, making him yelp.

"Would you like a tour?" Gideon asked Eugor, trying to move him away from the group.

"That's an impressive dwelling, Avalann," Eugor complimented as she slid down her vine. "How long did it take you to build it?"

"Thank you," the archer blushed. "A few months, sir."

"Avalann, please have everyone in formation by midday," Gideon ordered.

"Yes, Uncle," she replied.

"I'm so excited!" Izarra clapped. "I'll go get Jarz." Then she sprinted away.

"Father!" Raven called, returning from the lake in the old wizard robe. Her hands fidgeted, holding the robe closed.

"How was the lake?" Eugor asked. "Shorte mentioned something about getting dirty?"

Gideon eyed Raven, who glanced back at him as his cheeks flushed. "A late-night exercise," the guardian replied.

Raven cleared her throat. "So what brings you to the graduation?"

Eugor glanced around the camp. "I have a few things to take care of."

"But are you being nice?" she questioned accusingly.

"Yes, my dear. Gideon and I spoke yesterday. I'm sorry for my behavior at the anniversary festival. It was a bit of a shock. I'm still trying to get used to my best friend courting my daughter—but I know he will always protect you."

She hugged him tightly. "Thank you, Father."

"Raven, you need to prepare for graduation," Gideon said sweetly. She stared at him, slightly moving toward the wagon before coughing. *What is she doing?*

Eugor watched them with amusement. "She wants to know if it's all right to get her armor from your wagon since I'm standing right here." They eyed Eugor with alarm. "What? I noticed it when Gideon came out."

Raven smirked. "Always be aware of your surroundings. But thank you for understanding," she said sheepishly, kissing her father on the cheek and then kissing Gideon on the lips.

"I guess I have to get used to it," Eugor grumbled as he watched her enter Gideon's wagon. "If you don't mind, I have something to present to Raven and Izarra during the ceremony."

"Of course," Gideon replied as the two friends walked toward the campfire.

"So, are your new students ready?"

"I believe so. This class has grown so much. Izarra has more confidence with her water spells and has helped Jarz escape his shell. He used to be quiet and reserved."

"Like his mother," Eugor stated.

"I miss them, Ausharz and Stacia."

"Has Raven already changed you to Mister Emotional now?"

Gideon snickered, ignoring his friend. "Avalann has learned the importance of friends and being part of a team. Shorte—well, he's Shorte, always jumping into the fire to help his friends."

"And Raven?"

Gideon paused for a moment, trying to formulate the right words. "She's becoming a leader—fearless, overcoming that wizard's attack, training harder than any others."

"What about . . ." Eugor glanced around then whispered, "her other . . . abilities."

"Holding her breath for long periods underwater . . . so far," Gideon replied. "Other than that, nothing unusual. No darkness, no acid. Thank Blade because my jaw—"

"Stop! Don't go there."

They stared at the fire pit momentarily before Eugor finally cackled, holding up his scarred hands. "Do you remember that quest you sent me to retrieve the Lost Pearl?"

"In the Arctic Straight," Gideon recalled.

"It was freezing."

"Well . . . hence the Arctic."

"I recklessly dove into a body of ice-cold water searching for that pearl," Eugor reminisced. "I was cocky, arrogant, wanting to show you and Celeste that I was unbreakable, that I could hang with Celestials. Poor Mug shivered the entire trip, leading him to discover the ice-making contraption."

"You two were young."

"And I failed. Now I'm worried that Raven is too much like me."

Gideon chuckled as Eugor glanced at him. "You don't have to worry. Raven isn't gullible enough to search for something that never existed."

"What?!"

"It wasn't real. I wanted to test if you would take the Arctic plunge. Celeste and I had a wager. She paid me with silkworms from the Fey Realm. If I lost— well, I didn't."

Eugor turned red. "*Gorr-et!*"

"I do have one regret," Gideon mumbled as Eugor eyed him with concern. "I should have never sent you and Mug to retrieve the Artifact of Stolen Souls. It's my fault that you were intercepted by the balor and lost your head and are now aging and dying faster than you should be."

"My friend, stop. It was my fate to be there. To be resurrected and meet the love of my life. It allowed me to create a city where everyone has a home and be blessed with the two most beautiful daughters. I regret nothing."

I'm so thankful to have Night Breeze in my life. Gideon nodded, then faced the beach. The sun shone across the lake, creating a rainbow in the waterfall's mist.

"Avalann," Eugor stated as Gideon eyed his niece.

"We're ready," the archer reported, then walked back toward the wagon, where the others stood at attention in a row.

"Let's go induct the new class of guardians," Gideon said, placing his arm around his friend. "But we all know which class was the best."

Eugor lifted a brow. "No one likes a bootlicker."

The two grabbed the gifts from the wagon and placed them on a table before the disciplined mortal guardians.

Gideon approached Avalann while Eugor followed close behind, holding a sizable object covered by a piece of fabric. The guardian removed the cloth, exposing a black longbow from ebony tree bark.

When Raven saw her half-brother's weapon, she stumbled backward into Shorte, who helped her regain her footing. It had hung in Eugor's work chamber at the Omlett Inn for decades. Now, it was being presented to Gideon's niece. A tear rolled down Raven's cheek as Eugor left the guardian's side to comfort her.

"I present to you," Gideon said to Avalann, "Blade Naelo's magical longbow, the bow he created before ascending into the heavens. It changes color depending on the enemy and creates a magical arrow as you pull back the drawstring." He also handed her a ring inlaid with the same red jewel as was in his gauntlet. "This is a guardian oath ring. Keep it with you at all times."

Eugor peered down the line. "Don't worry, Avalann. I have the parchment that explains the color correlation with everything it pertains too. But if it ever turns red, run! Run your arse off."

Avalann appeared concerned, nodding at Gideon as he moved down the line, taking a sneak peek at Raven and mouthing, "Are you all right?"

The rogue responded with a nod as Eugor wrapped an arm around her.

Gideon now faced the swordmage. "I present to you the Bracer of Elements, which creates a shield of any element you desire." He handed Jarz the same ring that Avalann received.

After lifting a trident from the table, he approached Izarra. "I present to you the Tidal Trident of Thistlebane. I'm sure you've heard of it."

Izarra gasped, nodding with her mouth agape.

"It allows you to cast the spells I taught you, but without a water source or speaking any incantations."

Quickly taking Gideon's place in front of Izarra, Eugor held up a medal. "I present this medal to you, Izarra Lyte of Thistlebane, for your father's bravery and sacrifice that helped make Omlett a safer place for all." He placed the medal around her neck as tears streamed down her face.

"I don't remember this many weeping at my graduation," Eugor quipped.

"I cried when you left," Gideon whispered to his old friend, "on the inside." Then, proceeded to present Izarra with a ring before moving on to Shorte.

"I present the Guardian Mace and Shield of Iron Cliff to you."

Lost for words, Shorte gazed at the weapon set and accepted the mace and shield.

"Tap the mace onto the shield twice and it will cast iron skin on you," Gideon instructed.

Shorte grinned. "I'll be a walking golem."

After presenting Shorte with a ring, Gideon moved to Raven. She stared at him with her tear-filled, bright purple eyes, and he forced himself to remember where he was. "I present to you the Black Dragon Staff of Rax."

Raven grinned as the others smiled. "You made that up," she said, wiping tears. "That's a raven on top."

"Guilty," he admitted, handing her a long black staff. "The staff can split into two daggers," he said, twisting the weapon. "Place the dagger hilts together, and the blades will reform the staff." He chanted, "Vita Corvus," and the raven came to life. "Your very own familiar. If you split the staff, it will unsummon the raven, and it will vanish."

Raven's eyes widened, and mouth dropped open. "The bird is speaking to me."

"I have the familiar linked to your circlet," Gideon responded. "You can give it orders and messages using telepathy or unsummon it at will. I know the daggers aren't as fancy as your gem-hilted ones, but—"

"I love it." She shook her head in disbelief before hugging him tightly.

Eugor gently pushed Gideon aside. "I, my dear, present to you"—he paused—"the Razor Wire of Eugor." Raven cried again while the others applauded, and Eugor pulled her close. The gift Gideon had given Eugor upon graduation was now being passed down.

Even the great Celestial Guardian felt the water build up in his eyes, and he had to clear his throat as he nodded to his niece.

"Mortal Guardians," Avalann shouted, "Class of 1176, you're dismissed!"

The group cheered as Shorte ran to the beach, dropped to his back, and made a sand angel as the others gathered to show off their new weapons. Izarra held up the medal and thanked Eugor.

Avalann approached Raven. "I'll cherish this as long as it's in my possession."

Gideon spread his wings and floated above the group. "The rings I presented to you are for emergencies. They'll allow you to cast a portal to camp when they glow red. You must immediately stop whatever you're doing and report back here." He descended to the ground to shake hands with the graduates, then dismissed them to clear out the camp.

"Avalann, leave your tree fort," Gideon said. "I would like you to visit me more often."

Avalann beamed, nodding enthusiastically. "Of course, Uncle."

Gideon approached Raven's tent, where Eugor instructed her on how to store the wire.

The guardian overheard Raven say, "I promise I'll be home soon. I want to spend some time with him alone."

Eugor spotted Gideon. "Fine. We expect to see you on your birthday." He hugged her and shook Gideon's hand. "Take good care of her."

"Always," Gideon promised.

"Shorte, are you ready? I'm about to portal, so you'd better come along before I change my mind," Eugor joked.

Shorte finished saying farewell to everyone, then ran up with his knapsack flopping against his back. He continued to shake the sand out of his armor. "I don't remember bringing all this stuff," he complained, short of breath. "Why aren't you packed, Princess?"

"I'm staying for a bit." Raven blushed, putting her arm around Gideon.

Shorte glanced at Eugor with surprise. "Are you getting soft in your old age?"

Eugor scowled at the dwarf and used a scroll to cast a blue portal.

"Farewell, Princess," Shorte said, saluting her before following Eugor.

Izarra and Jarz strolled up, holding hands. "Gideon, Jarz is accompanying me to Thistlebane."

"It's been a pleasure training you both," Gideon replied as he shook their hands.

Izarra faced Raven before embracing her. "I'll see you at Carya's wedding. I'm going to miss you."

"I'll miss you, too," Raven replied affectionately. "Take care of her, Jarz."

Jarz nodded and patted Raven's arm. "Of course, cousin."

It's nice to know he's getting more comfortable with his immediate family.

"I finally get to use it," Izarra joked, creating a portal from her Thistlebane scroll, and then the couple walked through.

With Blade's bow around her torso, Avalann rode up on Krit with Oslo trailing behind.

"Do you need a portal scroll to Suttiir?" Gideon asked, but Avalann shook her head.

"It's a long trip by horse," Raven stated.

Avalann offered a slight nod. "I look forward to the ride, Princess."

"But not the bugs," Raven teased.

Avalann cracked a half grin. "Not the bugs."

"Are you sure you can't attend my sister's wedding?"

"We shall see. I'm unsure my temperament can handle a houseful of Naelos." She nodded again and rode off toward the only trail out.

Raven faced Gideon, amused. "We're all alone," she said flirtatiously, wrapping her arms around him.

Gideon grinned. "Finally."

CHAPTER TWENTY-SEVEN

THE DRACOMBIE TRIAL

"**S**hite!" Raven groaned as three glowing, light blue magic darts impacted her chest, knocking her flat on her back. *This is not how I wanted to spend my morning.* With her entire body aching, she stared at the cloudy sky *again*. "At what point is this considered abuse?" The treetops waved in the breeze as if warning her to stay down. She tried to sit up, but the leather training gear bogged her down, growing heavier after each journey to the ground. Sweat ran down her forehead. *And the brutal summer sun hasn't even reached midday yet.*

"Again," Gideon sternly replied as she sat with her arms wrapped around her knees.

Raven grunted, slowly rolling onto all fours as her leg and arm muscles protested. *I'm going to need an ice bath.* Back on her feet, she dusted off her gear and adjusted the pungent padded helmet to see her opponent better. "This isn't fair. I can't even tell you're casting a spell."

"You're focusing on everything that you shouldn't," Gideon responded as she picked up her staff. "I'll let you in on the secret. Every caster, even me, must focus. Watch the eyes. You'll always have a sliver of a moment to react."

"How will I counter your spell if you cast first?"

"Trust the spell, my dear, just like the Shield spell I taught you. However, realize your counter may fail under certain circumstances."

"I'd still like to see Astrick cast that magic projectile shite at me now." Raven gripped her staff and focused on him pacing. *Watch the eyes. Trust the spell.* The bird songs from the tree line vanished as if spectating the duel. The waterfall's roar diminished as she fixated on the guardian's face as he paced like a dire-wolf stalking its prey.

"Some spells may be too powerful." Gideon quickly paused, and his playful smile disappeared as his eyes squinted. "For a rogue."

The intentional insult briefly broke Raven's concentration, but she quickly stuck her hand out and shouted, "Contra Magia!" and then closed her eyes, waiting for the unexpected impact. She raised an eyelid to see him clapping. *I did it?*

"Remember, for that spell, you don't have to shout it. But well done."

Raven's face soured. "For a rogue, you mean."

Gideon held out his arms. "It was a distraction tactic."

"And it almost worked." She waddled over, trying to jump up on him, but the thick leather training gear made maneuvering difficult. Instead, she balanced herself on her tiptoes, lips pursed, and settled for a kiss. "Thank you."

Pulling her closer by the leather chest strap, he kissed her again. "You're welcome."

"Are these spells authorized?"

"Of course. I submit all spell lessons to Waterfront. It's a requirement."

"Why?"

"Magic in the wrong hands can be a perilous weapon, and they keep a close eye on who wields it."

The stiff armor created another obstacle as she struggled to grab her canteen. "Like Astrick."

"I had a colleague, Mister Owens, do some research. Astrick Fake attended Waterfront in the year 1163 at the age of eighteen. He attended for three years until barred for misconduct."

Raven gulped half the canteen, then wiped her mouth. "I can see why."

"I'm glad you've overcome the church attack. I've been worried since the obstacle course."

"I'm a guardian now. I need to be at peak performance. She paused to take another sip. "It also helps to have therapy sessions with my father and Izarra. I miss my friends."

"Well, you're about to see them very soon."

Raven stopped mid-sip. Her heart danced with her eyes widening, "Really?"

Gideon grabbed her hands with a stern look. "And please take me seriously when I say this—"

"I swear, Gideon, If you say I need a bath, I'll—"

"No." He paused. "Prepare yourself for a challenging encounter, then meet me back at the campfire."

What does that mean?

They nodded at each other, then kissed before she parted for his wagon. Raven leaned her staff against the cart; she couldn't strip out of the damp undergarments and gross armor fast enough, leaving it piled just outside the door. Even in the buff, the stagnant summer air didn't help her cool off. She glanced at the misty waterfall. *I wish I had time for a bath.*

She entered and rushed for the washbasin, peering into the still water. Her reflection revealed a smooth face—*no more black and blue eyes. My lip healed. No deformities.* The thought immediately raised her throwing hand, exposing the scar. *Aim higher.* Taking a cloth and bar of lavender soap, she washed her body as quickly as possible, counting the healing bruises. She eased up around her chest, which was still sensitive from the impact of the magic missiles. After applying aloe lotion, she threw on fresh undergarments before slipping on her worn-out magical boots and summoning her dragon armor. She rubbed and tucked the blade necklace under her chest plate.

Raven clasped her purple cloak around her neck after placing an onyx circlet on her head. She wiggled the lockpick into her elastic band that formed a ponytail. Attaching the clip of the disarm-trap kit to her belt opposite her coin pouch, she surveyed the room. *Am I forgetting anything? Ah, my razor wire.* Taking a deep breath, she secured the clip of the leather compartment to the rear of her belt and exited the wagon. The door slammed shut behind her after grabbing the staff. While practicing verbal spell incantations, she strolled over to Gideon by the campfire.

He tapped his gauntlet when she arrived. The guardians' rings activated the opening of four portals. Clad in green leather armor with Blade's longbow at the ready, Avalann was the first to enter. Sitting at his desk in his Waterfront chamber with ink and quill, Jarz inscribed something on a piece of parchment. Izarra's mother wandered through, mouth agape, while in another portal, Shorte, with breeches around his ankles, sat on the privy with his hand covering his forehead in embarrassment.

"We need to discuss the range of these portals," Shorte snapped. "Do you want to help or—"

Gideon quickly waved his hand for Shorte's portal to close as Izarra called out, "Mother!"

The half-nymph tossed her backpack through the portal and stepped through in her midnight blue leather armor. "What did I tell you about entering strange portals?!"

"But look, dear, it's Jarz," Dawn responded, waving to the mage standing by his equipment.

Jarz laid down the quill and gathered his gear. "Greetings, Misses Lyte."

"We miss you," Dawn shouted, blowing him a kiss as Izarra guided her mother through the gateway.

Gideon closed the portals after the swordmage stepped through, kissing the half-nymph. The guardian tried opening Shorte's portal again to see the dwarf still on the privy.

Shorte huffed. "It's going to be a bit. G-Ma's stew surprise."

Waving his hand again, Gideon closed the latrine gateway. "I need to adjust the portals."

Raven hugged Izarra as Jarz shook Gideon's hand. *I didn't realize just how much I missed my friends.*

Before standing next to her uncle, Avalann gently nudged Raven. "What's the emergency? Did Miss Naelo lose her daggers again?"

But I don't miss that.

"No and no emergency," Gideon responded as Raven grinned. "It's the last day of summer, and I need to test the rings. You had a couple of weeks with your new weapons. It's a trial for everything—spells, armaments."

"A trial?" Raven stated, "You never mentioned another trial."

"Let's just call it a sparring session to keep the rust off," Gideon replied. "Just follow me." Once at the shoreline, he chanted a spell as the water crystalized into an ice bridge that formed across the lake to the waterfall. "Don't slip."

Avalann proceeded to go first, followed by Jarz and Izarra.

Raven placed her boot on the bridge and then pivoted, searching Gideon's face for clues. "What's going on?"

"You'll see," Gideon answered as he waved his hand again, opening a portal on the beach. Shorte stumbled through with his shield attached to his back, dragging his mace while fixing his belt.

"What did I miss?" Shorte called out, dropping his weapon as the belt didn't fasten securely. "Is it dead already?" He glanced around, securing his belt, then picked up his mace.

Gideon's face dropped as the cleric rushed past him, trying to catch the others at the waterfall. "Slow down, Mister Stone-Grin, you're going to—" The dwarf did an awkward split at the edge. "Slip."

After regaining his balance, Shorte shuffled more toward the waterfall. "Of all the bridges. An ice one, Jarz?"

"Wasn't me!" the swordmage called out from under the cascade as Shorte glanced back at the guardian.

"I'm glad you could join us," Gideon responded as he eyed Raven, trying not to laugh. "After you, milady."

Raven carefully stepped on the frosted bridge, grabbing the smooth half wall, hoping not to slip. Glancing down, she could see through the glass-like floor at the water below, noticing the fish swimming. A hand pressed on the back of her armor as Gideon whispered, "Trust your spells." She made it to the end of the ice, stepping onto a rock ledge. The raw power of the falls caused the ground to rumble under her feet as she raised her face, allowing the mist to cool her skin.

Gideon tugged her hand, leading her to the back side of the water. The group huddled under a magical shield Jarz appeared to have summoned from his bracer.

"It's a dead end," Avalann said, shivering.

"Follow me," Gideon responded, walking through the side of the cliff.

"An illusion wall." Jarz snickered. "I should have known."

They followed Gideon through a tight corridor. The stone passage was dark and smelled of rotting fish. Jarz pulled a light orb, similar to the one in the secret sister spot, from a pouch and lit up the space. The group walked silently, footsteps echoing off the rock as they finally reached an enormous cavern. Mysteriously, the torches ignited around the cave.

The cave's interior was cool and damp, the air thick with an earthy moss scent. Mist danced around the tomb, catching light from the flames. Glistening stalactites and stalagmites, formed over eons by the endless flows of the tributaries, adorned the cave walls while the vaulted ceiling hosted dancing shadows. Trickling streams of water carved intricate channels through the rock. The crystal-clear waters that cascaded from above formed a natural pool by the northern side of the cave. A smaller cavern opening contained three stone tombs, the largest of which were atop the V-shaped formation. The smallest sat to the left and the medium to the right—the old tombs etched with an unrecognizable language. The bottom end of each tomb had an identical copper insignia fastened to it.

"Please don't ask me to flood this place," Izarra whispered to Raven.

Raven shook her head. *There's a sense of honor here.*

Facing the group, Gideon opened his arms. "Welcome to the heart of my camp."

A feeling of disappointment washed over Raven—*Why didn't he show me this when we were alone?*—but then her body tingled. *What the spell?* A language she couldn't translate whispered in her mind, something she only ever felt when she'd toured Waterfront with her father. *It's a beauteous language even if I can't translate it.*

Shorte gasped. "This reminds me of—"

"A dragon's lair," Raven interrupted as if something was still trying to communicate telepathically. A name entered her mind.

"Yes," Gideon said, "and it's the home of—"

"Bakahrrato," Raven blurted out.

"Raven, you're freaking me out," Izarra said, grabbing Jarz's hand.

"Interesting," Jarz stated as Gideon appeared amused. "Anything else?"

Raven closed her eyes as the warmth of the magic in the cave wrapped around her like an inviting hug. "It's a language I never heard before." With her eyes still closed, she waited for the strong guttural voice to continue. "Wait, wait, now it's in Elvish. He sounds sad. He trapped himself here to protect something for a very long time, but he's fond of you, Gideon." She gasped as the chilly cavern air replaced the cozy welcome. "But he wants to kill the rest of us!"

Walking over to the three tombs, Gideon smirked as he laid his hand on the largest. "Knock it off, Baka." The group gasped as a loud, hallowed laugh echoed throughout the cavern. "You have to appreciate a copper dragon's sense of humor."

Gripping his mace and shield tighter as the bellow ceased, Shorte grimaced. "I'm not laughing."

Izarra gulped. "You want us . . . to fight a dragon?"

"Not exactly, Izarra," Gideon replied.

Raven snuck closer to study the resting places, noticing an ancient symbol with text carved on the granite covers. *Something tells me I should know this.*

"Careful," Gideon warned, grabbing her attention as he cast Levitate on the stone slab of the smaller tomb. The guardian glanced at the group as the heavy lid hit the ground. "This challenge has a combat rating of fifteen."

"Fifteen what?" Izarra asked, glancing around to see if someone else knew the answer.

Jarz sighed. "Waterfront has a scale for combat ratings, the WFCS, or often pronounced WiffKaas. The higher the number, the more difficult."

Raven approached the others. "What's the max?"

"Thirty," Avalann responded, testing the tension of her drawstring. "I've been training my life knowing that threat level is out there."

Shorte snorted. "Eating my G-ma's fruit cake is definitely a thirty." A forceful bellow resonated in the tavern again. "I'm starting to like this Baka."

"We won't see that kind of threat from the creatures of the Mortal Realm," Jarz replied, casting the Sword and Board spell. "I would think maybe a twelve would be the highest if we were to go against the headmaster of Waterfront or even Gideon."

Raven began, "So when we fought the kobolds and bugbears—"

"It was based on their low WiffKaas," Gideon responded.

"How low?" Izarra asked.

Jarz shrugged. "Two, maybe three tops."

Raven shook her head. "That seems low."

An out-of-place giggle came from Avalann as everyone eyed her. "Add two if Raven assists you." Raven glared at the archer, waiting for a retort. *Oh, how I didn't miss that.*

"Well, it was your first mission, but enough about that. Baka, don't take it easy on them." Gideon cast a blue portal. "May Blade watch over you, and if you're defeated, I'll revive you in the morning." As Gideon stepped through the portal, Baka's playful laughter altered to a sinister snicker.

"He's jesting, right?" Izarra asked.

Raven twisted her staff to form the daggers. "Do we have to find—" The deep voice chanted the mystery language in her head as a gray swirl of smoke formed. Bones levitated over the lidless tomb as the mist in the cavern thickened. The sizeable foot bones bonded on the ground, stitched with dark magical cords. Then, the bony legs formed after.

"I think it's starting," Avalann called out. The spine linked together for the rest of the framework to connect. Two sets of facile wings expanded from the ten-foot adolescent skeletal dragon as the back part of the skull connected and locked into the round tip of the spine. Its creepy, glowing green eyes lit the haze as the skeletal structure stretched its ten-foot spider-web-filled wingspan. The long, rigid tail flailed wildly as it took flight. The archer waved her hand, casting Hunter's Mark. "I'm going to mark it and set up a flanking position. Jarz set up on the high ground behind the creature. Shorte, clank it at the cave's center."

"What? I'm no dragon fodder." He tapped his mace against his shield, forming iron skin, then huffed. "But if I must!"

Raven cast Invisibility, then hugged the back wall near the entrance, watching for Baka's first move. Avalann moved in the distance, touching her skin to the texture of pine tree bark.

Water spouted from Izarra's trident as she spun it, forming a giant water golem. "Go get it, Baby." She stuck out her weapon in a defensive stance as Jarz severed gravity and landed on a rocky ledge about twenty feet high.

The skeletal dragon finally dove down to the middle of the cavern to meet the iron dwarf as he raised his shield. The dragon bounced side to side, toying with him, pretending to strike. "What are you?" the dwarf yelled.

"It has to be undead!" Avalann shouted. "My bow has a gray glow."

"An undead dragon." Shorte grinned and pointed his mace at the creature. "C'mon, Dracombie! How about a serving of Searing Light?

Praemium-Mortuus." A ray of light blasted the beast. But the skeletal figure remained in the air before him when the brightness diminished. "Did I hurt it?"

Raven raised a dagger, aiming at the creature, but a loud bellow echoed again as the cavern floor shook. Shorte braced himself as Izarra forced the butt of her trident into the ground to help her steady. Five body-length pointy stones protruded from the ground; one ended up just tipping the iron rear of the dwarf. Avalann cried out as the pointy rock grazed her bark skin.

Shorte groaned. "I guess he didn't like that?!"

Two magic arrows flew from Avalann's bow, hitting the target in the side of the head and chest, causing the creature to spin around, shrieking. A firebolt blasted it in the face, ending its angry scream as a second blast from Jarz silenced it for good.

Raven sprinted around a stone spike to set up behind the creature—a ring of dark mist shot from the creature, blasting her. It surrounded Shorte, who hid behind his shield as Izarra ran off screaming once the mist hit her, but Baby continued charging the monster.

Jarz called out to Izarra as he and Avalann lingered outside the tainted area. "I think it's a fear ability or spell."

After waiting a moment, Raven dashed toward the flying creature and stabbed it in the backside, where the tail met the back. Her daggers shanked off the bone as the creature squealed.

The bony tail lifted and struck Shorte's shield, knocking the dwarf prone. The beast fixated on the now-visible rogue as Baby slammed its giant water hands into the bony creature, drenching it.

A floating, green spectral hammer materialized after Shorte called out something intangible from the flat of his back. The magical weapon slammed into the target, blasting green sparks. Mud formed under the cleric as the creature spun back around. Panicking as he sank, he called out a high-pitched, "HELP!"

Avalann shouted, "Augmento Spica." Creeping plants sprouted around the center of the cavern. Shorte grabbed a vine, avoiding the thorns as Raven and Izarra evaded the spikes that quickly spread across the rocks.

"Raven!" Jarz called out as he projected a fireball at the flying creature. "Duck!"

The rogue plunged toward the ground, and her chin almost scraped a thorn as a blast of fire burned above her head.

The beast swooped out of the fire radius as Raven rolled out of the way of the creature's tail attack, causing it to glance off her dragon armor. She placed her daggers together, forming a staff. "Nissre Nar." Her electrified hand grabbed the bottom of the wet, bone-tipped tail. The creature remained unphased as an electrical current traveled its bony frame. *Did it even do anything?* As she studied the reaction, the creature flapped its wings, whipping up a strong gust that slammed Raven into the cavern wall, knocking the wind out of her. She lay on all fours, clinging to her staff, gasping for air.

Returning to the battle, Izarra thrust her trident and slammed it with three eldritch blasts of water. The three streams of force knocked the weapon toward Raven as Baby attacked the creature again with a powerful hydro-fist.

Pulling himself from the mud, Shorte grasped his amulet. A golden glow with heavenly figures surrounded him, catching the skeletal figure in its radius. The summoned spirits struck the creature as the dwarf's green hammer slammed into the target once more before the magical weapon dissipated.

The creature's spine cascaded green as it rushed toward Raven, still hunched over. *This can't be good.* She tried to roll, but the breath attack from the magical cords running through the mouth blasted her. Closing her eyes as a gooey fluid clung to her armor and skin, her teammates gasped in disbelief. When she opened her eyes, greenish-bright slime hissed and smoked on her skin but left no permanent damage, no pain. Burning holes filled her cloak as it dangled by threads, but it protected her gear on her belt. The lockpick in her hair sizzled away, leaving behind a melted, waxy layer—an *acid attack.*

A deep, husky voice entered her head, speaking Elvish. *"My apologies, Lady Krea."*

Krea, as in the first dragon, Krea?

As the skeleton floated, mesmerized, Avalann shot two magical arrows, striking its head with precision. Shorte raised his shield to take cover as Izarra raced up misty clouds to flee the thick, grayish stormcloud that Jarz summoned.

The creature flew over Raven, spreading out its skeletal features. Ice shards pounded the skeletal frame, slipping through the space. The rogue cast a lesser gaseous form and floated over to Izarra, watching the storm finish before reforming. *Did the beast try to protect me?*

Izarra expelled three more streams from her trident, hitting the creature and pushing it back toward Avalann and Jarz as Baby rushed into the beast again, knocking it back further.

Shorte glanced back, holding up his mace. "You ladies all right?" Raven and Izarra nodded. "All right then. Ðivinus Beneficium." He waddled around the mud pit as he charged toward the enemy with his radiant weapon.

The creature spun and flapped his wings toward Avalann and Jarz. The archer braced herself, but the swordmage bounced off the back wall, falling off the edge. Before hitting the ground, he teleported to Izarra. When a magical arrow hit the target, it created a hail of thorns that clattered off the bones.

"I think that thing tried to protect me," Raven stated. "I don't know if I can—"

"It's already dead," Jarz responded. "We destroy it, it will—" His face lit up. "Izarra, go to the tomb and search for a phylactery."

"A what?" Izarra asked.

Jarz inhaled deeply. "Anything magical that looks like it would store a soul."

"Sure," Izarra responded.

A loud bellow echoed again as Avalann shouted, "A little help over here!" The ground shook as the creature summoned stone spikes around the archer and Shorte's area.

Raven gave Jarz a quick nod and split her staff into two daggers again. Her body tingled as her limbs and torso enlarged along with her equipment. After shaking off the dizziness, she slammed the double-sized daggers into its lower back, trying to stop the green cascade as it hovered over Shorte. The brief hesitation made her late, and bright green acid covered Shorte's shield.

The dwarf frantically dropped his shield as it sizzled. He tried scraping the little bit that singed his facial hair. "Not the beard! Not the beard!"

Holding up a glass prism attached to a copper chain, Izarra called out from the smaller tomb, "Is this it?" The skeletal figure froze, glaring toward the half-nymph.

Izarra! Still enlarged, Raven dropped her daggers, grabbed the creature by the tail, and planted her feet against one of the stone spears. As the beast twisted toward her, snapping its jaw, the glow in its eyes pulsated with the radiance of the phylactery. Raven grunted, swinging the creature toward the mud hole with the help of Avalann's Gust of Wind spell. "This thing is strong for not having muscles." *It's like pulling Ghost for horseshoe replacements.* The rogue gritted her teeth, holding on for dear life, noticing the skull rotating on the ball joint connection at the top of the spine.

As Izarra created a swirling mass of water to keep the grounded creature at bay, Raven reached for the pouch on the back of her belt. The beast beat its wings, but she secured the razor wire around the connection point before it could take flight. She clenched the leather handles, sawing back and forth. The more the creature struggled, the easier it was to cut into the bone. The greenish color cascaded up the spine again. *Oh no, acid!* Dust clouded her vision, intensifying as Raven sawed faster. The skull filled with acidic fluid before snapping from the spine and dropping into the twirling pool below.

As Izarra dispelled the whirlpool, Raven noticed two topaz crystals shined in the eye sockets. *It was already dead.* She raised her head as Baka's laughter filled the cavern again. The skeletal body dropped to the floor, releasing a green gas from its back end.

Dropping his mace, Shorte bent over, pointing and howling. "He just released Mother Nature's laughing gas."

Raven shrunk to her normal size, hitting her knees on the ground as an uncontrollable giggle escaped. "Look, my cloak has more holes then Shorte's underpants." *Did Baka poison us?* Jarz and Izarra bent over in fits of laughter.

Shorte slapped his knee laughing, "She is a true rogue . . . cause she stole my joke!"

"What's so funny?" Avalann asked.

Jarz, hunched over, lifted his head and chuckled, "Why aren't . . . you affected?"

"She has no sense of humor!" Izarra stated, pointing to the archer. She continued to titter as the other three cackled.

Avalann huffed. "I can't help but think that my mind is more resilient."

"Look, she's bleeding sap." Raven pointed at the archer's wounded leg.

The group wailed again as Avalann dispelled Bark Skin. "Funny, Princess, but where are your daggers?"

Damn it!

Shorte snorted, wiping away tears. His laughter eased. "I think . . . I rusted my armor," he announced from the flat of his back. "In other words, I think I pissed myself!" The comment flew like a humorous arrow, critically striking Avalann's funny bone as the archer laughed along with Baka's thunderous howl.

A blue portal appeared, and Gideon stepped through. "I see everyone is still in one piece." The group's laughter ceased as they stared down the guardian. "What? I told him not to take it easy on you." The guardian seized the skull and placed it in the open tomb.

"You have much explaining to do," Izarra said, dismissing her water minion as Raven retrieved the daggers and formed the staff.

"I really want to know Baka's story," Shorte said as his skin turned normal.

Gideon approached the half-nymph with his hand out. "I'll explain everything back at camp." Izarra wrapped the copper chain and placed the clear, triangular prism in his hand. He cast levitation, returning the rest of the bones to the smaller tomb. After stowing the magical pendant inside, he cast levitation on the granite cover. Once he completed the work, he reverently placed his palm on the enormous tomb. "Thank you, my friend. But next time, we'll try WiffKaas twenty."

The group gasped. *Is he serious?*

"*And* we'll hide the phylactery." Baka left out one last howl as Gideon opened a blue portal. "Avalann, your leadership is improving, but you didn't give Raven or Izarra any guidance."

Avalann began, "But—"

"Whether you feel they would listen or not, you still lead. It's on them."

"Yes, sir," Avalann replied.

"But your shots and spellcasting were impeccable." Gideon hugged Avalann. "We'll talk more at camp." He tilted his head, signaling her to enter the blue gateway as Jarz stepped up. "Jarz, great thinking about the phylactery, but you need to watch your area of effect spells."

Jarz lowered his head, "I almost pelted Raven and Shorte with my ice shards."

"Exactly, but overall, great job," Gideon complimented as Jarz exited. "And watch out for those heights."

Shorte approached the guardian, shaking his shield. "I don't think I did too well. Even with the iron skin, it hurt like—"

"You did well for what do you call it?" Gideon asked. "Clanking."

"Just a term Avalann and I use for being a meat shield. I take all the abuse while they whack away. I'm a cleric with the armor of an alchemist chemical tank. Clank for short."

Gideon nodded. "I see, but you can't always rely on the Iron Skin ability, but you kept the creature's attention for most of the battle."

Shorte grinned and whispered, "How do I get this goo off my shield?"

"I'll help back at camp."

Shorte eyed Raven, "Oh, I see, cause you have to help clean her off too."

Gideon pushed the dwarf through the portal. "Next!"

Izarra slouched toward the portal, dragging her trident. "So you watched me run off?"

Gideon bobbed his head. "But I also watched you return with a vengeance. Baka has a lair effect that can bring fear out in creatures, so you fled, but not by choice." Izarra glanced at Raven with a smile. "Your spells were on point, and you found the source of the creature's power."

Izarra struggled with the word. "The fill-actor-ory?"

"Yes, the phylactery. Job well done."

Izarra smiled and skipped through the portal. Raven followed her, and before she could enter, Gideon grabbed her arm.

"Not so fast. Are you all right?" Gideon asked, his hand rummaging through her thick, matted hair, picking at the melted lock pick.

"Exhausted." She pressed her head against his chest, trying to suppress a grin as he struggled to find a spot not coated in the slimy green stuff to wrap his arms around.

"Are you sure you returned to normal size?" Gideon asked. "You seem taller."

"So, how did I do?" Raven asked.

"You never hesitated. Quick thinking saved you from Jarz's ice shards. You severed a skull from the spine."

"But it's officially confirmed, I'm immune to acid attacks. I'm glad the armor you gave me has acid immunity properties, too."

"I'll need to research, but we'll figure it out."

"I don't understand how you could put us in danger like that, though."

"As long as you believed you were in danger, Baka did his job. But you keep letting distractions easily break your focus."

Raven exhaled. "But he called me Krea."

"Krea? Well, Baka is ancient. But still—"

Raven rested her chin on his chest and eyed him. "You had us battle a senile dragon?" She shook her head. "Do you have any other secrets I should know about?"

He flashed a guilty grin. "There is another, but I'm saving that for a special occasion."

She scowled.

"But let's get you cleaned up. It appears as if Baka sneezed on you."

CHAPTER TWENTY-EIGHT

FAIRY TALE

R aven consumed a honey roll off the plate. It was part of the birthday breakfast Gideon had prepared before claiming he had to retrieve more firewood, but she knew he was on a secret birthday mission. She sat on the bed, leaning against the wooden wall of Gideon's wagon, and pulled her knees to her chest as she ate the tasty treat. *The last three months alone with him have been blissful.*

She stifled a yawn. *I can't believe I'm twenty-one.* Yesterday's visit with her family in Omlett had left her exhausted. She glanced at the new purple cloak her mother crafted for her, then gazed out the small window above the bed, watching the morning sunlight become brighter. *Where could he be,* she wondered, licking the last remaining honey from her fingers. She glanced around the wagon, realizing that it was no longer as tidy as it had been before she had moved in. *It's my fault.* Jumping down from the loft, she began to straighten up. She collected the dirty dishes, placing them in a bucket to take to the lake later.

The red glow from a portal flashed through the windows, and Gideon opened the back door. "What are you doing?" he asked quizzically.

"Tidying up," she answered. "I've made such a mess."

"Leave it," he replied, taking the bucket out of her hands and setting it on the floor. "It's your birthday. Besides, I think we need to expand our living area."

Raven wrapped her arms around him. "I don't. I like bumping into you every time I turn around."

Gideon smiled. "I would stay here with you for eternity. But I think you'll enjoy this." He kissed her hand and sat her on the bench, then pulled out an oversized spell book and sat beside her.

"Oh no, the big book of spells," Raven said playfully, sliding the bucket under the bed and securing it. "It must be a doozy."

Gideon waved his hands in a circular motion. "You ready?"

"I'm only wearing a robe, so I hope it's not somewhere too public."

"You might want to hold on to something," he instructed, "and don't worry, your closet is coming with us."

Raven gripped his arm. "Should I be nervous?"

Gideon chanted, "Fey Domus Porta."

Red sparks whirled around the small windows as the wagon shook. The light show faded as soon as it began, and everything settled to a calm stillness. Raven paused, making sure it was safe. "I've always wondered why I've never seen horses pulling this thing."

Gideon held his hand out as Raven gently grasped it, following him through the wagon door. They had landed next to a bridge upon which a modest white cob cottage sat, a grass-covered roof adding to its charm. Tall, green grass peppered with exotic purple and yellow flowers surrounded the cabin, and small butterfly-like creatures skimmed the surface of the blooms, gathering and eating pollen.

In place of a backyard, there was a crystal blue waterfall that emptied into a small pond that flowed under the bridge and house. Her eyes followed the stream and saw horse-like creatures drinking from the pond. "Are those unicorns?"

"Yes, we're in the Fey Realm." He glanced around and commented, "It seems like it's the spring solstice here."

Raven shot Gideon a worried expression. "Will we get in trouble?" But as soon as she finished her question, a blue portal appeared. "I spoke too soon."

A female elf with white wings and long, braided blond hair stepped through, dressed in the gold Celestial Guardian armor. Gideon extended his arm to her in greeting. The female elf grasped his forearm with her hand.

"Thank you, Celeste," Gideon said, "for permitting me to bring her here."

"Any time, Gideon," Celeste responded. "I owe you." She glanced at the surprised rogue. "This must be Raven Naelo." The elf extended her arm. "The resemblance to your father is indisputable."

She could be Gideon's twin. Raven gripped Celeste's arm as she'd seen done by other guardians. The Fey Guardian appeared precisely as the portrait in her father's work chamber.

Celeste pulled Raven closer. "I heard about the legendary purple eyes," she teased, taking a closer look. "I'll be giant-stomped."

Raven couldn't help but notice the elf's ice-blue eyes. *I'm not here to be studied like some alchemist experiment.*

"I like her," Celeste whispered to Gideon as she motioned to Raven. "Enjoy your stay, Princess." A blue portal appeared again. "Please let me know if you need anything, and give my regards to your father."

Gideon bowed as the female elf nodded, entering the portal.

"Well, she's more attractive in person," Raven said with a twinge of jealousy.

Gideon grabbed her by the waist, whispering, "Not as beautiful as you. The Fey Realm will be jealous."

Raven blushed. "Show me your home!"

Hand in hand, they walked up the earthen steps carved into the side of the small hill that led to the bridge. When he opened the front door, Raven gasped as she entered a vast living area with a stone fireplace on the right and a white leather chaise longue in the middle. The room opened into a small kitchen area, but what drew Raven's attention were the sliding glass doors at the rear of the house. It was a magnificent view of the waterfall.

"It's—"

"Beauteous," Gideon said, grinning.

"Took the word right out of my mouth. What is this place?"

"I live here when I'm not teleporting around in my cabin on wheels."

"What does the High Council think about it?"

"I allow Celeste to have a home in Suttiir in the Mortal Realm, and in exchange, she allows me to live here. It's a guardian thing," he explained smugly.

Raven slid open the glass door and leaned over the bridge's stone wall. The waterfall's cool mist washed over her, causing her skin to glisten in the sunlight. Down in the water, yellow and orange sprites swam under the surface.

Gideon embraced her from behind, resting his head on her shoulder. "Most guardians are close since we can relate to each other's struggles."

"Most?"

"Meliae, a wood nymph from the Fey Realm who watches over the Astral Realm, and Krut, the half-orc guardian who watches over the Shadow Realm, tend to keep to themselves."

"Krut, the Horck with the sick family that you helped?"

"Yes," Gideon answered. "Another elf guardian, Tier, watches over the Abyss Realm, but Celeste and I haven't heard from him for almost a decade. When we ask the council, they tell us he's busy but doing well."

"But maybe he's just busy?" Raven interjected.

"Celeste and Tier are a couple . . . well, *were* a couple. She entered the Abyss Realm twice, searching for him, but Tessk, the Abyss representative, kept sending her back. She doesn't believe he would leave her without an explanation. The High Council grounded her in the Fey Realm, putting her on probation. She'll lose her wings and celestial status if she enters the Abyss again."

"That must be hard on her," Raven said sympathetically. "If you disappeared, I'd rip that realm upside down."

"You get used to following orders. Even I'm on probation."

"*You*?!"

"The latest mark against me was when I entered the Abyss to help Celeste find Tier," Gideon explained. "The first was when I had your father and Mug recover an artifact for me."

"The Artifact of the Stolen Souls."

"It would have been different if I'd known the artifact was from the Abyss Realm. I would have retrieved it myself. I never meant to get your father hurt."

"He never held you responsible, Gideon." Raven hugged him. "He's always said to be careful what you wish for because he had wished for an early retirement."

Gideon smiled, but she saw sadness in his eyes.

"Can you show me more of the Fey Realm?" she asked.

"Certainly. Let's take a stroll to the cliffs."

They left the bridge and walked along a dirt path that led to the clifftop. Tall, lush trees covered in vibrant pink flowers reached the sky. Hand in hand, they strolled upward, occasionally stopping so Raven could admire the surroundings. Nestled in a bush were three baby owl-bears.

"They are so cute." Raven giggled as she reached down to pet them. One snapped at her with its little beak as the other two scurried to the back of the bush.

Gideon laughed as she pulled her hand back. "Wait till Mama gets back."

Finally, they reached the top of the cliffs. Raven approached the edge, noticing the wagon and cottage far below. The thunderous roar of the rapids drowned out the various chirps, whines and hisses of the wildlife. Gideon's protective arms wrapped around her. In the distance, a rainbow of colors danced across the treetops. A deep sense of peace overcame her; she wanted this moment to last forever. Unfortunately, her stomach protested, growling loudly.

"Are you hungry?" Gideon asked.

"A little," she said, embarrassed that he'd heard.

Gideon lifted her and whispered in her ear, "Hold on," as he flew them off the cliff. It reminded her of the first time he'd flown with her during Omlett's twenty-fifth anniversary celebration.

They returned to the cottage, and Raven walked onto the back deck while Gideon prepared their dinner. The sun slowly set over the waterfall as she enjoyed the last moments of daylight. The water was the clearest she had ever seen, and she could look straight to the bottom of the pool, where colorful fish swam.

Little flash bugs awoke as the evening grew darker, filling the grass with specks of colored lights. The story was that these insects glowed their emotions. *Watch out for the red ones.* In the distance, she heard the calls of animals that reminded her of wolves. A gentle breeze constantly brought the sweet scent of exotic fruit from the trees that lined the perimeter of the shore. She inhaled deeply. *Pears? Strawberries?*

Gideon leaned against the doorjamb and took a deep whiff. "Dragonfruit."

"Dragonfruit?"

"It was one of the first edible plants created here and named after the creatures that planted it."

Raven's stomach growled again as if an alarm went off.

"You're in luck," Gideon said. "Dinners ready."

She kissed him quickly and brushed past, reaching a small, ornate table near the fireplace. He followed, pulling her chair out. A small pot filled with bubbling stew sat in the middle.

Raven tried to make room for her bowl. "This is cozy."

"I don't get much company here. Celeste and I usually throw a blanket out in the field for a quick picnic."

They ate their stew as Gideon told her about the other lands in the Fey Realm and the Fey capital city of Fharlix.

After dinner, they tidied up and moseyed onto the back deck as the moon brightened. The stars appeared in the night sky, more bountiful than in the Mortal Realm. Gideon gestured toward a mounted telescope, inviting her to look. She hunched over, squinting to peer through the eyepiece.

Raven moved the optical tube around and muttered, "It's beauteous."

"It's the Astral Realm."

Raven lifted her head. "What? How's that possible?"

"It's like an umbilical cord to all the realms. What you're seeing is just a fraction of the Astral Realm."

"The High Council is there?"

"Yes," Gideon answered as she glanced through the scope again.

"I can't even imagine what it must be like to walk among the creation of the universe."

Gideon pulled her away. "There are no words." Bringing her to his chest, he passionately kissed her. "Being with you is the closest way I can describe it."

As she ran her hands through his hair, she pressed her lips against his. "Flattery can only get you so far."

Gideon pulled away, taking her by the hand and guiding her into the bedroom. A mahogany four-poster bed with ethereal blue sheets and curtains was in the middle of the room. The bedroom shared a flue with the living area fireplace.

Raven noticed the night sky filled the area where the ceiling should have been. "There's a fireplace, a bed, but no—"

"It's invisible." Gideon pulled her closer.

Raven giggled nervously. "People could peep on us from the cliff."

"Did you notice it when we were on the cliff?" asked Gideon, amused. "Besides, this isn't the Mortal Realm," he explained, lighting the fireplace and activating a couple of light orbs around the room.

"I don't have any clean outfits here," Raven remembered, knowing her clothes were still in the wagon.

Gideon removed his breeches and tunic. "You don't need them," he said seductively.

"This isn't the Mortal Realm," Raven mimicked, disrobing.

Gideon slowly walked to her and picked her up. She wrapped her legs around his waist and kissed his neck as he carried her to the bed.

"Look at that night sky," she whispered as Gideon kissed her neck. "Beauteous." She moaned as he moved his body between her legs.

"We have plenty of time to count the stars . . . together."

Raven rolled him over and straddled him. "You can count them now."

"Stars?" He ran his hands down her body. "What stars?"

The evening faded as the couple made love. Sometime after the witching phase of the night, Raven felt Gideon breathing softly beside her. She stared into the night sky. *Another fabulous birthday gift.* She rolled over and cuddled into his arms, falling fast asleep.

The morning sun woke her as it beamed onto the bedroom wall. She threw off the covers and glanced up at the top of the cliff. Of course, there were no onlookers. *This isn't the Mortal Realm.*

Raven noticed a nude Gideon in meditation beside the other side of the bed. *I hope the Mortal Realm didn't fall into chaos because he took one night off.* She slipped on her robe and walked into the living area, stretching her tight muscles.

It's been a few days since I've done any training. I'm going soft.

She entered the small kitchen, poured a glass of water, and picked up an apple. Instinctively, she pivoted, whipping the red fruit at the bedroom doorway. Gideon snatched it before it hit his forehead.

"A rogue has to stay sharp," Raven snickered, "even in intimate circumstances."

Gideon laughed. "Remind me never to make you angry."

"How's the Mortal Realm doing?" she asked, slicing an orange with a small dagger she pulled from the wooden knife block.

"It's still there," Gideon said, crunching on the apple. "Nothing out of the ordinary. You didn't need to dress."

Raven shrugged. "Habit. I do need a bath, though."

Gideon walked out the back door and leaped off the bridge. After dropping her orange, she removed her robe and jumped in after him, swimming downward and exploring the vastness of the ravine. She approached the waterfall and swam under it to rinse her hair.

"I'm still baffled at how long you can hold your breath! I get nervous when you don't come up for so long."

"There's nothing to worry about. Carya and I have been doing it for years." She splashed Gideon as he swam closer. "You know that."

She pulled him under the falls, kissing him as their bodies entwined. When he pushed her against the rock wall, a soft patch of moss pressed against her backside, their caresses became more passionate as they made love under the waterfall.

Later, they lay contentedly on the pond's banks, allowing the sun to dry their skin.

"I don't want to go back," Raven sighed, rolling over him. "It's almost too good to be true, like a dream."

"What about Omlett? Your parents and sister?"

Raven stared at him thoughtfully. "You already have a stockpile of scrolls to teleport to Omlett. I can visit whenever I get homesick."

"What about your crew? The Mortal Guardians, is it?"

Raven laughed. "It was either that or Shorte's recommendation, Nature's Gas Guardians."

"I can't believe we've already been together for two years. Time has slipped away."

"It's been like a fairy tale," Raven fondly mused as she traced her finger around his chest. *I wonder if everyone loves with this much passion.*

"Would you like to live here . . . with me?" he asked hesitantly.

Her eyes shot up to meet his. *He just asked me to live with him.* Raven bit her lip, trying to find the word. "But what about Baka? And watching over his lair."

"I can still check in on him from time to time."

"Then yes!" She leaned in for a kiss to seal the deal.

"I'll talk to Celeste and see what we can work out because the longer you're here, the greater the chance Celeste and I could get in trouble."

Raven's smile abruptly disappeared. "Oh. Well, I couldn't live with myself if I got either of you into trouble."

"Don't worry. Us guardians like to live dangerously." A couple of sprites flew past their heads, making a cute buzzing sound. The smaller purple spirit sat on Raven's shoulder, and the yellow fairy sat on Gideon's.

Gideon chuckled. "They're just being nosy." The sprites chirped a few times and buzzed off under the bridge toward the pond. When Gideon and Raven swam after the small, winged creatures, they found three unicorns drinking from the pond.

"Ghost would love it here," Raven said softly. "She would be home again." She had an idea. "Gideon, where are the discarded unicorns located?"

"I'm not sure you want to see that," Gideon warned. "Not everything in the Fey Realm is—"

"I want to see it."

He stared at her for a moment and sighed. "If you insist."

They went to the wagon so Raven could dress and retrieve her circlet and dragon armor while Gideon donned his celestial armor and activated his wings. Once he summoned a magical steed, they rode off. It wasn't long before Raven noticed the once-green grass had turned dry and withered, and the trees were sick with rot. Their dirt path was dusty as if it had not rained in years. They approached a group of white unicorns attacking a gray one, pushing it toward a bottomless pit. The gray unicorn, missing half its horn, couldn't defend itself.

"What the spell?" Raven growled, jumping off the magical mount and screaming at the herd, trying to scatter them.

"Raven!" Gideon yelled in a panic. But by the time she'd gotten there, the group had already pushed the injured unicorn into the pit. Raven glanced down into the hole as the unicorn struggled to stand among the pile of bones. She tried to push back the horrifying thought that her beloved Ghost had gone through this.

"Gideon, we have to help," Raven implored.

"Raven, it will still die," Gideon said sadly.

"Not like this," Raven whispered, tears welling in her eyes. "Please."

Gideon sighed. "Levo Unicornis," he said, casting a Levitation spell on the unicorn in the pit. "Remember—it's still wild. It took me weeks to break in Ghost."

Raven slowly approached the injured unicorn, which reminded her so much of Ghost. "Hey, girl," she whispered, gradually offering her hand. Surprisingly, the unicorn didn't move. Raven touched its head gently, but it backed up.

"Raven!" Gideon called out in warning.

Hooves beat the ground as the white unicorns rushed toward Raven, and she quickly cast Invisibility on the gray unicorn. The herd stopped, pawed at the ground, and then returned to the grassland. She activated True Seeing on her circlet and watched the unicorn as it approached, nuzzling her. "Easy, girl," she said, stroking its coat and glancing at the guardian. "Gideon."

Gideon cast a Levitation spell on Raven to raise her onto the back of the gray unicorn. "Now that's a sight," he chuckled as he watched her sitting on what appeared to be nothing.

"It's all right, girl," Raven softly patted its neck. "Aerica. I'll call you Aerica." She did her best to calm the injured unicorn as they returned home. "We need to build a stable, maybe fence off this area to keep the healthy unicorns from attacking her."

"Yes, ma'am," Gideon agreed obediently. "Anything else?"

"When I retire, I want to create a sanctuary to care for them. I wonder if this is how my father felt when he realized he wanted to own a tavern."

"I do see the same desire in your eyes that your father had for the tavern, but not at the age of twenty-one. I believe he was in his late two hundreds! That's like fortyish in human years."

Raven tied Aerica to the wagon. "She can stay nearby until we build the stable, right?"

"This is that important to you?"

Raven nodded, flashing her passion-filled eyes. *This could have happened to Ghost!*

Gideon cast a portal. "I'll be right back."

"Gideon?" Raven tried to stop him before he disappeared. Once he was gone, she returned to the house, grabbed a handful of carrots, and fed Aerica.

What is that elf up to? She found a rope and looped it loosely around Aerica's neck, walking the unicorn to the stream to see if the line would reach. Aerica gulped water as if she hadn't drunk for days. "Once we fence off this area, we can let you off this leash."

Suddenly, a blue portal opened, and twenty small humanoid creatures resembling elves mixed with beavers poured out. They were about the size of dwarves, as thin as elves, buck-toothed, and covered with hair. One of the creatures summoned a table while another threw down some parchment papers. Gideon brought up the rear. "They drive a hard bargain."

"Who are they?" Raven asked.

"Castoridaens—the best builders in the Fey Realm. They know all the requirements for handling the trees. They will replant every tree they cut down."

Raven watched the creatures move as one organized unit. "What did you offer them?"

"A wagon full of ebony trees from the Mortal Realm."

"Like the tree in the magical painting?"

"The very same. The trees grow near Koport."

Koport sounds familiar. Koport, Koport, Koport. Raven gasped.

"What's wrong?"

"The mage who attacked me—Astrick? He mentioned Koport."

"Are you sure?" Gideon asked. "It's been years."

"I'm sure. Maybe we never found him because we didn't look far enough to the east."

"I could go searching for him."

"As you said," she replied, "it's been years. Astrick might not even be there."

Gideon kissed her hand. "I just want you to feel safe."

As she watched Gideon's gallant gesture, the red gem in his gauntlet began to blink, then transitioned to a solid glow.

"Gideon, look," she whispered. His face soured, and she knew he had to leave.

"I need to check it out."

"Of course," Raven agreed, trying to hide her disappointment. Suddenly, a blue portal opened.

"Gideon!" Celeste exclaimed, concern etched into her brow. "The High Council has summoned you."

"Is it about me being here?" Raven asked, worried.

Celeste shrugged. "I'm not sure. They just sent the message. I was meditating when it came through."

Gideon frowned. "Don't worry, Celeste, I'll take the full blame."

"Raven, don't fret," Celeste replied. "I'll watch over him."

"Thank you," Raven said gratefully.

Gideon paused to stare into her eyes, then kissed her. "I'm sure it's nothing." He used his gauntlet to cast a portal to the High Council. "After you,

Celeste." Once Celeste entered the portal, Gideon took Raven's hand. "Don't forget, there are portal scrolls to Omlett in the wagon."

She nodded and let his hand slip through hers. "I love you."

"Don't worry, we'll be counting the stars tonight." He beamed. "Together."

Raven watched as Gideon flashed his familiar twinkle look as he vanished through the portal. *Please, Blade—watch over him! He'll need all the luck.*

CHAPTER TWENTY-NINE

WHISPERS OF WAR

Gideon exited the portal while Celeste waited outside the golden doors. "Stay in the rear," he suggested. "I may need you to return to Raven and give her a report."

Celeste furrowed her brows, and her lips quivered. "Absolutely."

Gideon entered, walking to the middle of the chamber. Behind him, Celeste immediately ducked to the rear, sitting on a high-back leather chair. The High Council members were already seated at the bench, Blade with his hands tightly clenched and elbows on the counter, avoiding eye contact as Elora sprung up, banging her gavel.

"Mister Grindal," Elora announced, "welcome back to the High Council Chamber."

"Thank you, but I assume this isn't a social call."

"No, I wish it were." She paused. "Where to begin—"

"How about getting straight to the point?"

"As you wish," Elora replied. "Guards!" Four High Council guards entered the chamber through the rear doors.

Gideon eyed the guards. "What is this?"

"We have reports of a great war between orcs, gnomes, and dwarves in the Mortal Realm."

"That's absurd! I would know if a war were happening in my realm."

"Perhaps your attentions have been focused elsewhere," a fairy representing the Fey interjected.

"That's enough, Ellie," Elora scolded angrily. "Gideon, the war is about to affect the city of Omlett."

"What?" Gideon asked in disbelief.

"We know how much you care for that particular city," Elora stated. "However, we cannot allow you to take things into your own hands. We are, therefore, detaining you until the war is over."

"You can't! If this is the case, I promise I won't interfere."

"I'm sorry, Gideon, but the council voted, and you lost four to one." Elora frowned and banged her gavel.

A blue forcefield surrounded Gideon as he floated upward. His wings disappeared, followed by his celestial armor. When his feet hit the ground, he was left standing in his cloth tunic and breeches. The magical shield dropped as two guards approached, each grabbing an arm.

"This is only temporary," Elora assured him. "Just until the war is over."

"Blade!" Gideon called out in alarm. He tried telepathically connecting with his friend. *If it's true, your father must be warned!*

Blade frowned.

With Celeste following, the guards escorted Gideon to the holding cells from the chamber and down the Great Hall. They placed the guardian in a cell and touched a crystal stone to the entrance, creating an invisible door. Gideon tried to cast a spell, but the magic fizzled.

"It must be a Dead Magic Zone," Celeste said helplessly.

Gideon walked to the invisible wall. "I need you to tell Raven about this."

"I will. I'm sorry, Gideon."

"For what?"

"I can't get you out of there."

"You will be a great help if you deliver the message to Raven."

Footsteps approached. When the door opened, Elora entered the foyer outside the cells. Celeste nodded at Gideon and then at Elora before she tried to leave. Two guards stood menacingly at the outer door.

"Take her to the other cell block. I'll be there shortly," Elora ordered. When the guards escorted Celeste from the room, Elora fixated on Gideon. "She's a dedicated guardian."

Gideon sat on the extended bench, the only seat in the cell. "Finally, something we agree on."

"Dedicated enough to leave her child behind," added Elora, shaking her head as Gideon stared at her in shock. "Yes, I know about Blade, but he's been such a tremendous asset to the High Council that I chose to ignore the breaking of our one golden rule."

Gideon stood speechless. *She knows!?*

"It's a shame she has two marks against her."

"I don't blame her," Gideon seethed angrily. "All she wants is to know Tier's whereabouts."

"We must hold her for a couple of days."

"Why? She has nothing to do with this."

"She also has an emotional attachment to Omlett. I'm sorry, Gideon, but you both have two marks against you, and I won't let either of you destroy your guardian careers over a petty war."

"A petty war? I'm telling you—there *is* no war."

"I have proof."

Gideon walked over to her, his stomach in knots.

"Believe it or not, I still have personal contacts in the Mortal Realm," she said. "The report says that the orcs destroyed all the gnomes and dwarf villages south of Omlett. Now they're marching toward your city."

"But I've seen no signs of any war," Gideon pleaded, perplexed.

"Is there anything I should know that would distract you from your duties?"

He could tell she already knew the answer. "There are no laws about relationships."

"You are correct," she nodded. "Maybe we should change that. Relationships have caused two of our best guardians to incur two marks against them."

"You change it, and you can keep my wings," declared Gideon vehemently.

"Now relax, Mister Grindal," Elora said calmly. "I said *maybe*. Besides, the council would have to vote on it."

"You take out relationships, you might as well select your guardians from the Shadow or Abyss Realms," Gideon snarled.

"Not all mortals or fey need a relationship. Not the ones dedicated to the cause."

"I've been dedicated for over one hundred and fifty-five years. Maybe I'm long overdue for a little happiness."

"I remember when those wings and celestial armor gave you all the happiness in the universe," she responded, watching his reaction. Gideon stared at her coldly as she continued. "But you'll have some time to think about it. And don't worry, each day here equates to two weeks in the Mortal Realm, so the war will end faster than you realize."

Gideon's face drained of color as he realized he'd forgotten to tell Raven about the time differences between realms. *Each day I'm here, Raven will be in the Fey Realm for a week.* His stomach dropped at the thought.

"But don't worry," Elora whispered, interrupting his thoughts as she glanced around. "King Naelo did receive an anonymous message about the incoming danger."

Relieved, Gideon replied, "Thank you."

Elora nodded and left.

All he could do now was think about how he'd left Raven behind in the Fey Realm, waiting for him to return. Or worse—maybe she'd returned to Omlett and teleported into the middle of a battle.

How did I not see this war and the destruction of so many cities? Maybe Elora is right.

He sat in his meditation pose to find out if he still had his vision and was relieved to see that he did. Apparently, they had only stripped him of his armor and wings.

He focused on the Mortal Realm. Everything was still in a calm, dark-blue hue with light blue teleport spots here and there. The vision did not indicate any internal wars. If there had been a war, the battles would have had an abnormal number of portals from cities by those trying to escape. *I could at least watch for this sign.* The hard part about being in a cell was that there were no indications of how much time had passed other than when guards brought him a clean set of clothes.

The foyer door opened, pulling him from his meditation. Celeste entered and slouched outside his cell with fizzy hair. The bags under her ice-blue eyes made them pop even more.

I'm afraid to ask. "Did you speak with Raven?"

"They just released me." Celeste frowned. "They interrogated me for four miserable days."

"We've been here for four days?! That means Raven has either been in the Fey Realm for a month or she teleported back to Omlett, where it's been almost two months."

"I came by to tell you I'm returning to the Fey Realm to check on her."

Gideon placed his palm on the invisible wall in gratitude. "Thank you, Celeste."

She forced a half-smile and trudged out to the hall.

Gideon couldn't believe the council had detained him for four days, helpless. The small room adjoining his cell was his privy. He knew magic was allowed because it disposed of all the collected waste, though there was still a foul smell. He stared down the dark, smelly hole, contemplating his escape.

Gideon resumed meditating, watching for any signs of battle. A red light blinked into view west of Suttiir, disappearing as quickly as it appeared. As Raven would say, *What the spell?!*

CHAPTER THIRTY

THE RED GIVE AWAY

Thomas changed out the burnt candles in the wrought iron chandelier, alternating new red and gold ones, as High Priest Stone-Prayer was perched at the altar, preparing his ceremony. Today was the twenty-sixth of IrJiil, so the big day was two days away, and he wanted everything perfect for Carya. But the two guards standing in the foyer made it difficult. They shivered next to the newly installed fireplace, attempting to warm up after rotating shifts with the other guards posted outside.

Three years had passed since they'd met, and it still felt like he'd heard her joyous laugh the first day. *I'm marrying the most beautiful girl in the city.* Flashbacks entered his mind: their time together, the horse rides through the meadows, the hand-in-hand strolls around town, the private moments at the lake. An image of Raven, nude, slowly walking out of the watering hole, diverted his thoughts, and guilt burned his cheeks.

Carya startled him as she reviewed the long to-do list. "It must have been a good one." His warm cheeks must have turned rosy, giving him away. "You were daydreaming again." The smell of lavender in her hair wafted over as she hugged him. "Was it good?"

He cleared his throat. "How was the dress fitting?" he asked, quickly changing the subject.

Carya checked off something on the parchment. "Perfect. Miss Gwaelon did a wonderful job."

"And the cake?"

Carya checked off another thing on the list. "Mother is taking care of that right now with Miss Crinkly."

"I've always loved her pastries," Thomas said, licking his lips as Carya glanced at the giant chandelier and giggled. "What's so funny?"

"That's a lot of candles, and we'll still need more." They glanced at the remaining two chandeliers that still hung from the ceiling. "If you want, I could always get Brugg to lift you."

Stone-Prayer chimed in, "I have more in the back. I'll find someone to send them out." The high priest scuttled toward the storage room.

Flashing her a smirk, Thomas took the opportunity to hold Carya in his arms. "Break time," he whispered, kissing her.

"Are you sure we're doing the right thing?" she asked with a sulky pout.

"Your father insisted he has everything under control." Thomas tilted her chin. "One thing I learned after three years is not to argue with him. He gave me a speech on how armies won't attack during the winter because it's hard to maintain troop morale." Guiding her luscious lips to his, they felt soft and gentle as he pulled her closer.

Mara cleared her throat as the guards closed the front doors, startling the couple apart. "I have a habit of walking in on you two. This church must be magical." She brushed snow from her coat as a guard set down a basket. "Thank you," she whispered to the guard who returned to his post. "It's only midmorning, and the snow is already sticking."

Thomas removed the basket lid, inspecting its contents as Mara resumed talking. "Here are the flowers and garland for the archway and pews. They need to be hung. Miss Crinkly shared a sample of the cake, too." She placed various items near the altar. "And the King and Queen of Suttiir just arrived at the Omlett Inn. They're staying in the Royal Suite."

Thomas secured the strands of silver garland to the archway before stepping back to view his handy work.

"They need to be higher." Carya glanced at her mother, who nodded. "Are you sure you don't need Brugg?"

Thomas's shoulders dropped in defeat. "I'll pass. But I think there's a step ladder in the training room."

"Speaking of Brugg," Mara interjected, "you may want to do something nice for him. He's been upset about all the extra people staying at the Inn."

"Why?" Carya asked.

"It means more messy privies," Mara answered.

Thomas chuckled. "That stinks."

Carya nudged him. "Stop—I'll make sure to thank Brugg."

"I could teach him some spells to make the job easier," Thomas offered. "I told you I had that job in the Paladin Guild. It's a shite job, but a man's got to do what a man's got to do."

Carya grabbed his arm and whispered sweetly, "And that's why I love you." She faced her mother. "Have you heard from Raven?"

"Yes," Mara answered. "Raven and Gideon will be arriving sometime tomorrow."

"Gideon and Raven," Thomas said, nodding his head.

"We know . . . you predicted it," Carya mocked as she deepened her voice. "In the courtyard."

Thomas snickered. "Give me a crystal ball and call me a gypsy."

"Izarra and Jarz arrived yesterday from Thistlebane," Mara added. "I can't wait to speak to him again."

Carya handed Thomas more flowers. "I can't wait to meet my cousin."

"He's grown so much. I only wish I had known he was alive. I could have helped." Mara stopped, turning away to retrieve a cloth from her beaded bag.

Thomas moved toward his soon-to-be mother-in-law and gently touched her shoulder. "It's a blessing that you found each other now."

Mara lifted her tear-stained cheeks. "Thank you," she whispered, cupping his face.

They heard a wagon pull up, and Eugor called, "We could use another hand, son!"

Thomas opened the front doors as Mara and Carya followed. The cold air was a relief, cooling him down from the morning's work. The flurries continued to fall as the fluffy snow covered the dirt roads.

Brugg hopped down from the wagon as Mug unstrapped something in the back.

Eugor jumped from the coachman's side, rushed to Mara, and embraced her as if he knew she was upset.

Thomas felt his heart melt on that cold wintery day. *That's true love.*

"What's this?" Carya asked.

Mug grinned as he uncovered the sculpture. "A masterpiece—I chiseled this for the wedding." Stray beams of sunlight bounced off and created a brilliant rainbow.

Thomas ran his hand over it. "It looks and feels like an ice sculpture."

Mug slapped Thomas's arm. "Don't touch it, genius. Your fingerprints will block some light prisms.

"Mug, it's gorgeous!" Carya exclaimed.

Thomas shook the gnome's hand. "It's angelic, just like Carya."

Mug slid it to the wagon's edge as Brugg lifted it. "Careful, Brugg," the gnome said with alarm. Carrying the cover, Mara followed Brugg to the courtyard.

Eugor joined the others. "I received a message from Mister Plunkett. Half of the Suttiir Army arrived with their king. We stationed them at the barracks for now. They're rotating shifts with the Omlett Army."

Carya frowned. "Are you sure we shouldn't postpone the wedding?"

"The city is under threat," Thomas added. "We would understand, sir."

"We will have no more talk about canceling," Eugor ordered. "Every road entrance into Omlett is under guard, and we have scouts out on patrol. Reports show no signs of any army within a two-day ride." He kissed Carya on the cheek. "I need to get back to the Inn. We will see you both for dinner later this evening." Mara and Brugg returned, climbing onto the wagon as it departed for the Inn.

"Speaking of food," Thomas said, watching them ride off in the distance, "I'm famished."

He grabbed Carya's hand and walked arm-in-arm through town toward the meat stand. Along the way, a suspicious older man wearing a frayed hooded cloak asked Bernie the whereabouts of the purple-eyed princess.

Carya glanced up at Thomas. "Are you reading auras?"

"It's red—"

"No more auras," she said, directing him toward the market. "We can't kick out everyone who has a red aura."

"There aren't many people with red auras," Thomas explained. "Maybe I should at least question him."

Carya elbowed him. "Stop. My father and Buzz have everything under control."

Despite Carya tugging Thomas away to buy dried figs, a loaf of bread, goat cheese, and assorted meat skewers, the paladin eyed the stranger.

"May we go back to the Inn to eat?" Carya asked. "We have all day tomorrow to finish."

The long walk was quiet as the stranger paced through Thomas's thoughts. *What did he want with Raven?* They retrieved Grail, still hitched in front of the church, then dashed off to the Inn.

As they arrived, the tavern was chaotic with elf guards. Carya pulled out a blanket from Grail's saddle, and then they pushed their way through the crowd toward the banquet room. Thomas laid out their picnic spread as Carya cast the Illusion Ball to show a meadow by a river.

"I'm going to *try* to get us drinks," Thomas offered, walking toward the bar. Two elven guards were preoccupied with the magical *Ebony Tree* painting as he squeezed past people trying to check-in. Lilly frantically rushed by with an empty tray, attempting to keep up with orders.

"Cyndi—two ales, please," Thomas ordered, pressing tightly against the counter.

"Sure thing, Pally." The bard took a moment to find clean mugs. After filling them, she said, "You know this is your fault! Between the threat and your wedding," Cyndi joked as Thomas reached for his coin pouch. "Consider it an early gift."

"Thank you," Thomas replied, carefully swinging the two mugs around as another elven guard rushed past him, spilling the drinks. The paladin's pulse quickened when the elf's determined green eyes locked with his.

The guard's eyes widened as if about to trigger a trap. "Watch it, ass," he mumbled in the common language, continuing toward the pantry hall.

"What's wrong?" Cyndi asked. "You've gone pale there, Pally. Like you seen a ghost."

He sat the drinks on the counter. "I'll be right back for these."

"I'll fill'em up again for ya!"

Thomas followed the elf guard down the hall past Brugg's and Cyndi's quarters. Ducking behind a column, Thomas watched the elf glance back before tiptoeing up the stairs.

"Thomas?" Mara's voice came from behind him at the edge of the hall near the bar.

"Mara, I need your help," Thomas whispered. "Can you come with me?"

Mara nodded, joining him as they crept up the stairs. "What's going on?"

"A guard walked past me—his aura was red. I know for a fact that all royal guards are screened before they're accepted in that position."

At the top of the stairs, they overheard the King of Suttiir say, "What's this? I didn't summon you."

Thomas and Mara had just reached the landing as red sparks flew from the guard's hand. The man's illusion instantly disappeared, and Thomas recognized the wizard.

Mara didn't hesitate—"Somus Signum." She cast Symbol of Sleep, which slumbered the threat.

King Luhnar stepped into the corridor, followed by Queen Baela. "What's the meaning of this?"

"He was about to kill you," Thomas warned. "He's the demon that attacked Princess Raven."

"I'll find Eugor," Mara said, hurrying down the steps.

Thomas straddled Astrick. "Your Majesties, it might be safer to retire to your room and lock the door until security arrives."

They nodded and went back into their suite.

Mara returned shortly after with Eugor. "It was a good thing you spotted him."

"I sent a messenger to the prison for Buzz," Eugor said as Brugg scooped the unconscious man onto his shoulder.

"He'll be out for a while," Mara said, walking to Eugor's work chamber where Brugg placed the man on the floor and stood guard.

"I'm pretty confident this is the man who attacked Raven," Thomas said.

Eugor studied the unconscious man. "He has some explaining to do."

Buzz'diir arrived, conjuring magic cuffs and a tongue gag on the stranger as he awoke. Three dwarves from his security force restrained the mage, escorting him to the wagon.

Thomas heard Carya call his name as they left the Inn.

"Where did you go? I've been waiting," she fumed.

"I'll explain later, but I must go with your father and Buzz."

"Of course," Carya responded with curiosity in her voice.

Thomas pecked her cheek, then hurried to catch up with the guards.

Once at the prison, Buzz'diir removed the prisoner's tongue gag and cuffs as he locked the cell.

Astrick tried to cast a spell, but it fizzled out. "DMZ," he groaned.

"A Dead Magic Zone? Not quite," Eugor snarled as he stepped toward the bars. "But there has been a spell cast on the cell."

"What's your name?" Thomas inquired of the prisoner.

"Astrick Fake," the man blurted out. "What the hell?"

"Where are you from?" Eugor asked, scowling.

"Koport," Astrick answered, laughing. "The cell has a zone of truth. Impressive."

"Why did you attack the king?" Buzz'diir asked.

Astrick went silent, and the veins in his head swelled as he fell to his knees, fighting the spell. "I thought he would be an easy target with all the chaos going on," he finally answered, "with everyone distracted by the wedding." His pain subsided. "I thought the High Council banned this type of torture."

"Tell the truth, and it won't hurt," Eugor sneered, "but I pray to Blade that you keep trying to lie."

"You attacked his daughter," Thomas said, "three years ago at the church."

Astrick remained silent, trying to recall the memory. "Oh, I remember her. The princess elf that killed all my men. She should be locked up, too."

"I'm sure you asked for it," Eugor sneered. "When will Omlett be attacked?"

"After Suttiir, it was supposed to be next." Astrick laughed. "But the King and Queen of Suttiir and half its army arrived here. All for what? A spoiled princess's wedding. Oh, by the way, she looked great while trying on all the wedding dresses. I personally liked the low-cut one. It perks up her bosom."

An image of Astrick dragging Carya's body like he did Raven's made Thomas tremble with anger as he advanced, hands balled into fists. His face burned red with rage. "We need to warn Suttiir," he said through clenched teeth.

Eugor stepped before the paladin, keeping him from attacking the monster. "So, you've been spying on us?"

"For a while." Astrick flashed a wicked smile. "You know, reporting the weak spots, strong areas. But when the elves arrived, it was like tying a ribbon around Suttiir for us."

"Us?" Eugor asked. "You're working with the orcs?"

Astrick laughed again. "At first, but then with the gnomes and dwarves."

"That makes no sense!" Buzz'diir interrupted.

"It will all make sense soon. Now, the elves will join our ranks," Astrick said maliciously.

"How did you summon an Abyss creature?" Thomas asked. "The dretch."

"No, don't ask me that," Astrick pleaded, beginning to feel the pain again. He fell over, clutching his gut. "I'm . . . word . . . cursed."

"By whom?" Thomas demanded.

Astrick rolled over into the fetal position. "I . . . can't . . . say." The tough guy now had tears streaming down his face as his body convulsed.

"By whom?" Thomas insisted.

Eugor smirked. "Don't answer—I'm enjoying this."

"Courtlynn!" Astrick screamed, looking up at the ceiling before emitting a creepy laugh. "You just killed me." A patch of red sores formed on his face, and he screamed as the rest of his skin blistered, forming a fleshy puddle.

"Buzz? I thought this was a Dead Magic Zone?" Eugor asked with alarm as they frantically opened the cell. Buzz'diir poked the fleshy ooze, still clinging to the skeletal corpse.

"It was a mental spell that triggered inside him," Thomas said. "I only know of a couple of creatures that can do that. He said a female name. She may have visited him while he was unconscious."

"Well?" Buzz'diir asked with anticipation.

"A succubus. Demons from the Abyss that like to play with men's minds," Thomas explained. "She would have to enter the realm in her physical form—but why would a succubus want to send a man to his death with the sound of her name?"

"To hide something," Buzz'diir offered. "Do you think she's leading the orcs?"

"Possibly, with the help of other subjugates. My bigger concern is even the High Council has no way of detecting them when they visit the minds of men," Thomas said.

"If she's involved, we can receive help from Gideon," Eugor realized. "Son, we must go back to speak with King Luhnar."

Thomas followed as they hurried along the snow-filled roads. Once inside the Inn, they went to the bar, where Mug and Cyndi chatted.

"Mug," Eugor called out, tilting his head to get the gnome to follow. The three proceeded to the Royal Suite, where they knocked on the door. No one answered.

"The man who tried to take your life is dead," Eugor announced.

The door opened to show the king wielding a dagger. He set it down when he realized it was Eugor.

"The enemy bypassed Omlett and marched to Suttiir," Eugor explained.

"We must go," insisted the elven king.

Eugor nodded. "Agreed, and I will accompany you. I will gather the Omlett Army and march with you. Mug, we may need your golems."

"It will take me a bit to prepare them, but I'll be right behind you," Mug promised.

"We will destroy them or die trying," King Luhnar declared.

"You're welcome to stay here," Eugor offered the elven queen.

"I will not hide while my city is being attacked," responded Queen Baela, "but thank you, King Naelo, for the kind gesture." She bowed her head in gratitude.

"Carya," Thomas blurted. "She'll understand postponing the wedding. I'll meet you out front shortly."

Thomas trotted downstairs to the bar area. "Cyndi, where's Carya?"

"She went home with her mother," the bard responded. "You need those drinks?"

"You know what?" Thomas stated deliberately. "I *am* going to need them."

Cyndi handed him two freshly poured drinks.

"Thanks." He quickly dashed outside, holding the drinks steady. Trying to control his shivers, he high-stepped in the snow to the front door of the Naelo home, where he knocked lightly.

Mara let him in. "Thomas, what's going on?"

When Carya came in from the kitchen, the paladin handed Carya a drink and explained the situation. "I'm sorry, my love, about postponing our wedding," he said remorsefully, holding her in his arms. "But we can't let Suttiir suffer."

Eugor entered, geared up in his black leather armor. "I'm not sure how long we will be," he said to Mara, holding her hand. "I've left a quarter of our army and Mister Plunkett's security force here to protect Omlett. You will be safe."

"Of course I will because I'll be with you," Mara replied sternly.

"As will I," Carya added firmly.

Thomas's heart pounded as a sudden tightness spread in his chest. "Carya—" he began, but Eugor put his hand on the paladin's shoulder.

"Son—don't even try."

Thomas finally understood where Carya had gotten her stubbornness.

"You'll need healers, Eugor," Mara said.

Eugor nodded. "I know. I'm not arguing. Get Brugg to load the family tent in the wagon. You can use that for the infirmary."

Mara and Carya scurried around, gathering herbs and bandages.

Eugor shook his head and glanced at Thomas. "Marriage is like war—you must choose your battles wisely."

Thomas crossed his arms in defiance, scowling. *I may have to disagree with this decision.*

"I'm just as concerned for their safety," assured Eugor, as if Thomas's face snitched on him. "We'll set up the tent far from the battle."

This battle I won't win.

Eugor patted the paladin's shoulder. "Now go and get your gear. We'll meet you back here in front of the Inn. I also sent a message to Gideon telling him what's going on."

The flurries speckled the elven army's armor as they lined up in five rows in the middle of the road, stretching from the center of the Inn to the first shop to the north.

Soon afterward, Thomas, clad in his armor, joined them outside. The Omlett Army lined up behind Eugor, and a small space separated the two formations. *What an impressive sight.* Familiar faces awaited on mounts in front of the Omlett Army.

"Shorte, Izarra, Jarz—what are you doing here?" Thomas asked.

"What does it look like, dragon fodder? I'm wearing my best for this wedding . . . I mean this war," Shorte boasted.

"We're the Mortal Guardians," Jarz stated. "We have a duty to protect this realm."

Izarra nodded in agreement. "Raven will be angry she's missing a war."

"She's better off with Gideon," Eugor said, "and I wish the three of you would stay here to protect Omlett."

"If Mara is going, I'm going," Shorte growled. "What kind of reputation would I have if a queen went to war, and I sat back and watched Brugg clean the privies?"

"Fair point, Shorte," Eugor agreed. "For your reputation, then. Let's go." He waved his rapier as King Luhnar waved his in return. The Suttiir Army began marching.

"Here we go," Shorte said excitedly. "I just wish the elves were in the rear."

Jarz joked, "There will be plenty left for you, Shorte."

The travel to Suttiir seemed to take no time at all. They marched double-time for a day straight before coming across the open field south of Suttiir. As the sun set, everything seemed calm. Mara and Carya chose a site for the infirmary, unloading the tent with the help of some soldiers.

"The Mortal Guardians will stay with me and the main force. Thomas, you will oversee the security perimeter," Eugor ordered. "I will dismiss the army for some well-deserved rest." King Naelo was about to shout the order when a red-haired female elf on a black horse dashed across the open field.

"Avalann!" Shorte exclaimed.

"Avalann, my dear. We had word that an army was marching here. Have you seen any signs of it?" asked King Luhnar.

"Nothing, sir," Avalann replied. "I spotted your army and came to investigate. *But* then I got a whiff of Shorte and knew our armies were massing."

"Ha!" Shorte howled.

Avalann gawked at the dwarf before pointing toward the field. "We could set the armies up in the middle of—"

A massive explosion rocked the city. With mouths agape, they remained still as the shock of the heatwave warmed their bodies. Screams mixed with the blasts filled the chilled evening air as a vast army emerged from the woods west of the open field.

King Luhnar, his shaking hands gripping the reins, hastily rode to Eugor and Thomas. "King Naelo . . . we aren't ready . . . and our armies are weary."

"I'll send half of my units toward the west tree line to flank," Eugor responded calmly. "We need to make haste on those infirmaries."

"Be careful, though—the cemetery for the Earthist is there," King Luhnar stated. "We need to respect the dead."

"Of course," Eugor responded.

"Earthist?" Thomas questioned.

Carya placed her hand on Thomas's leg. "An elven tradition to be buried in the dirt to become one with the land. I should know—"

"Carya! Help unload the infirmaries! *Now!*" Eugor ordered.

Thomas caressed her hand as she ran it across his thigh. While watching her rejoin Mara, something caught his eye. It was a figure he couldn't make out, but the aura was unmistakable—blood-red swirled with dark green. *A necromancer!* The menacing figure sat on a fiery black horse. *A Nightmare?* The leader unsheathed his long sword and then pointed it forward for his forces to attack.

Thomas hastily pulled a spyglass from Grail's saddlebag, focusing on the intruders. The soldiers' movements were slow and jerky as if weighed down by heavy chains. Their skin was grayish and rotten. The wretched horde stumbled together in unison, their heads bowed and bodies twitching. Thomas noticed the fighters were all different races: dwarves, humans, gnomes, and orcs. "Oh no!" Thomas shouted in shock.

"What is it?" Eugor asked.

Thomas gulped. "They're undead."

"Time to shine, clerics!" exclaimed Shorte. "We like to blow undead shite up."

"Should be easy," Avalann declared, flexing her bow's drawstring. "Look how slow they move."

Thomas adjusted the spyglass again, focusing on more details and scanning for their weaknesses. Some of the corpses sported fresh signs of sliced throats and evidence of explosions, but the others' features were a gruesome sight. Rotting flesh hung from their bones, burnt cloth melted into their skin, eyes dangled from their sockets, limbs trailed by thin tendons.

I don't feel well.

The dark figure raised his arms, and his hands emitted a cloud of dark purple, blue, and black. Instantly, the undead army emitted a blood-curdling scream. The agony and pain in their cries echoed across the snowy grassland, and Thomas's skin crawled as the Suttiir and Omlett Armies panicked.

"Easy!" Eugor shouted, bringing his horse around to face his army, "Stay focused!"

The enemies' worn-out sponge bodies transformed into chiseled barbarian warriors. Sizable claws protruded from their hands and feet as the horde's snail pace changed to that of a pack of cheetahs. Limbs fell off some as they charged.

Thomas glanced over at Shorte, who was wide-eyed with fear. They both cursed in unison.

"Oh, shite . . ."

CHAPTER THIRTY-ONE

THE BATTLE OF SUTHIR

The thoughts of cozying up to Gideon on the cold wintery days or listening to the pounding of the rain against the wagon's roof while they lay together made her blush. *Just another beauteous day in the Fey. Oh, how I miss the inclement weather.* Raven grabbed a pitchfork and tossed hay into the new stable as Aerica and another gray unicorn ate. After hanging the tool, her thoughts turned to Brugg. *I wonder what he's doing?* She sighed. *I wonder what they're all doing?*

Folding her arms on the new white picket fence, she gazed toward the water. The pen did an excellent job protecting the gray unicorns from the healthy ones. Aerica trotted over, nuzzling her. "Hey, girl." Caring for the rescued animals still couldn't distract her from the constant worry about Gideon's absence. *Where are you?*

Countless times, she'd packed her belongings, staring at the Omlett portal scrolls, contemplating returning home. *I have to stay for the unicorns' sake. Or am I using this place as a haven?* Over the years, Gideon would be away for months and then portal to Omlett, telling her parents of his adventures. *I hope the High Council needs him for something urgent.*

Raven grabbed her staff and wandered toward the back of the stable, where she had converted an area into a rogue training facility, using scarecrows as target practice. *It's no Gideon obstacle course, but it will do.* A red portal caught her eye on the way there, and Celeste appeared. Raven's spirits rose, holding her breath as she watched anxiously, hoping Gideon followed close behind. When the gateway closed, her lungful of air deflated. "Where the spell is Gideon?"

"The High Council detained us," Celeste answered wearily.

Raven noticed the guardian's weary appearance. The frazzled hair, bags under the eyes. "Detained as in—"

"A holding cell."

"Why? Because we're in the Fey Realm ?"

"No." Celeste paused momentarily. "There's a war in the Mortal Realm."

Raven gasped, then clasped a hand over her mouth.

"They feared he would interfere since he has many personal connections."

Raven lowered her hand. "Is my family safe?"

"I don't know."

Raven's heart dropped to the pit of her stomach. "Oh, no!" *I need to find out.* Images of the Inn and the city on fire raced through her mind as she ran to the wagon, Celeste close behind. After quickly packing, she grabbed one of the portal scrolls from the shelf. "I don't understand. Our rings didn't blink to warn us."

"The guards confiscated everything from him. His ring, armor, sword, gauntlet. He had no time to activate it."

"But he's all right?"

Celeste nodded. "He'll be fine."

"When will he be released?"

"Most likely, after the war."

Please, Blade, let everyone be safe. Raven placed her circlet on and summoned her dragon armor. She glanced up at the Fey Guardian. "Celeste, I would appreciate it if you could care for the unicorns until Gideon or I return."

"I'll assign a guard to the premises. But there's something else you need to know," Celeste said with an uneasy tone.

Raven slid on her backpack, then paused. *Now what?*

"You've been here for almost a month."

"Yes, I know," Raven snapped. "I have twenty-six notches on the fireplace." *I wonder how long they have been fighting for.*

The Fey Guardian continued, "It's no longer the month of IrIr in the Mortal Realm. It's closer to the end of IrJiil."

"The war *may* already be over."

Raven grabbed her weapon. "I guess I'll find out." Using the portal scroll, she summoned a red gateway to Omlett. "If Gideon returns, tell him I love him."

As Raven stepped through, the chill of Western Euphrasia's winter welcomed her home as her feet landed in a couple of inches of snow. A red wave washed over her armor as her body warmed, even though her face still felt the sting of the cold breeze. *Gideon didn't tell me this armor had temperature control.* Glancing toward the decorated church, she gasped when she noticed it was eerily empty. *Where is everyone?*

A *clip-clop* echoed through the deserted streets, and she spotted two horses trotting toward her. Two dwarves, members of Buzz's security force, approached with caution.

"Princess Naelo," greeted one of the dwarves.

"Where is everyone?" Raven asked.

The dwarves glanced at each other. "You don't know?" asked the second dwarf.

Raven's patience snapped. "If I knew, would I be asking?"

"The Omlett and the Suttiir Armies marched for Suttiir about two days ago," responded the first dwarf.

"So did the entire wedding party," the second dwarf added. "Everyone thought we were next, but the enemy traveled north through Grey-Holg, then around to Suttiir."

"I need to get to Suttiir," Raven said with urgency.

The dwarves scoffed. "That's a day's travel on horseback if you ride through the night. The battle will probably already be over. Stay here, Princess—help us protect Omlett."

Raven glanced around as the new shift of patrol squads roamed the empty street. "Sorry, gentlemen—I must go."

"Do you need a mount?" asked one of the dwarves.

Raven shook her head and ran toward Maggie's Magic Shop. She picked up a rock and was about to throw it through the window when she thought it was too severe. Instead, she pulled out the new lockpick wedged in her ponytail and fidgeted with the door's keyhole. *Success!*

Casting the Burning Hands spell, she lit a candle to search for the portal scrolls. Aged parchments rolled up, tied with leather twine, or dabbed with melted wax to seal them were piled in a giant stack. Setting down the candle, she rummaged through the bin, searching for a Suttiir portal. She grabbed a scroll with a snowflake symbol.

I need to be careful. I don't want to end up portaling to the Arctic.

Placing it down, Raven finally recognized one with a tree indentation in the wax. She carefully pulled the seal off, recited the incantation, and cast the portal, stepping through and landing outside Suttiir behind an old Druid camp converted into an infirmary.

In the distance, shrill screams, clattering weapons, and utter chaos reached her. Black smoke billowed to the north over Suttiir. The stench of burnt flesh wafted over, causing her to dry heave.

Thank Blade, I haven't eaten yet!

A familiar neigh drew her attention to the larger tent as she noticed her mount tied to a hitching post. "Ghost! This is no place for a unicorn," she said, stroking Ghost's snout.

Raven pushed aside the tent flaps, entering the makeshift infirmary. She froze in terror as clerics scurried between cots filled with people with burns, shrapnel wounds, and deep lacerations. Shouts of "Vulnus Percuro" filled the tent as clerics tended to wounds. *Shorte practiced the spell right before graduating camp.* High Priest Stone-Prayer stood in the center for the most critical patients. Lillianna's mother lay on the stone table, bleeding out. *Yulnea.* Carya pressed a cloth to the woman's open wounds. Mara was nearby, attending to someone at another table.

Carya quickly turned her head as blood squirted from another of Yulnea's wounds. "Raven!" she exclaimed after opening her eyes, placing the cloth atop the gash to stop the bloodstream. "What are you doing here?"

Raven grabbed a cloth from a nearby table and pressed it to another wound on Yulnea's abdomen. "I'm supposed to be here . . ." she began, but the deep claw marks on the woman's body shocked her. ". . . for a wedding."

"Out of the way! I know that tone," said a familiar voice from the table where Mara was stationed. The elf ranger pushed a cleric to the side. "Raven!"

"Avalann!" Raven exclaimed as the high priest cast cure wounds on Yulnea.

"You may go, child," Stone-Prayer told Raven as he touched the patient.

Carya nodded. "Go on—we've got this."

Avalann grimaced as the rogue walked toward her. "You're late. I needed that gaseous form, and you weren't there."

"What? Shorte didn't supply you any of his nature's laughing gas?" Raven joked half-heartedly, still watching the clerics tending to Lilly's mother.

Avalann snickered, then winced in pain as she held her side. "Ouch, that hurt."

Raven held her hand. "Where's everyone else?"

"On the battlefield." Avalann's face became serious. "Our first line of defense fell, so we're regrouping near the midpoint of Suttiir."

Raven noticed Stone-Prayer shake his head as Carya pulled a blanket over Yulnea's face. A soldier ran up to the High Priest, whispering something. Stone-Prayer glanced around, grimacing. "Find a healer and start a final resting area out back."

Raven dropped Avalann's hand and whispered, "I'll be right back." She headed to the western entrance of the tent, where the flaps remained closed. "Why is the battle in the open field instead of the city?"

Avalann frowned. "Suttiir is destroyed. But Raven, before you—"

Raven opened the flap and assessed the situation. Her last ounces of half-hearted humor drained like the blood from her face. The sight of the red-stained snow stuck out as bodies littered the cold ground. Some of the scattered figures wailed in pain, while others slowly rose with missing limbs, and many remained dead. *What the spell?*

"It's as bad as it looks," Avalann said sincerely. "A group of undead at the city's west end—"

"Undead?" Raven repeated, still fixated on the carnage.

"Those monsters are trying to push through the fiery debris to kill the remaining survivors. Shorte led a small unit to help the children and elderly evacuate safely."

When you put others' safety first, converting her fear and anger into adrenaline, Raven exited the opposite side of the tent and leaped onto Ghost, charging into the city.

The undead scouts consisted of reanimated orcs, dwarves, elves, gnomes, and humans. In the distance, blue energy appeared over a Suttiir Royal Guard, who lay lifeless—lifeless, that is, for only a moment. The soulless elf guard with a missing arm rose and began to charge, only to explode as suddenly as he had become reanimated.

A familiar husky voice called out, "Gideon never told me Searing Light would leave a bloody mess."

Raven glanced back at Shorte, profoundly relieved to see him, just as an undead gnome broke off from the pack and charged him. The hideous creature clung to Shorte's shield as the dwarf whipped his mace around, crushing the enemy's head. She directed Ghost toward her fellow protector as the rest of the undead pack closed in.

Shorte prepared to hit another creature with the Searing Light spell. "Good to see you again, Princess."

Raven dismounted and cringed as an undead orc exploded near her, painting the snow-covered ground around them with blood and body parts. The contrast of the blood on the snow was as startling as the first time she saw it outside the infirmary.

Shorte laughed. "That never gets old," he said, jerking his shield back and forth, shaking the creature's entrails off it.

Raven drew her daggers and steadied herself as an undead elf charged. She pierced it through the chest and dodged another swing before stabbing it in the knee. "Why won't it stay down?"

Shorte grimaced. "Remember the creature lessons! Aim for the cranium," he called out as Raven withdrew the dagger and drove it through the undead elf's temple. "Efficient, but not as fun as exploding them."

Raven combat-rolled between two undead gnomes, stopping with one knee on the ground before she thrust her daggers into both of their heads simultaneously.

"Now you're just showing off," Shorte grumbled. "At least your stomach is holding it together."

The two fighters whirled, ready to return the way they'd come, only to see a handful of undead blocking their path. They glanced at each other as the horde approached. *There are too many!* Raven froze, gauging the scene as the sea of monsters closed in. Their deformed bodies twitched as they charged.

Shorte hit his magical shield with his mace. "Let's go, Princess." He activated Iron Skin, screaming as he stormed the threat. The undead surrounded him, scratching and biting at his armored exterior.

Raven cast Arcane Step and gracefully strode next to an undead orc, stabbing it through the back of the skull. She vanished from behind a reanimated elf only to reappear in front of him. *Shite!* She swiped his leg, making him fall on top of an undead gnome, then pierced them each with a dagger as they clawed at her. Her hands trembled as she studied her latest victims. The older gnome's uncanny appearance reminded her of Gus. *Is it murder if they're already dead?* When she glanced up, two dwarves held Shorte against the ground while clawing at his shield.

Her friend got off one good blow with his mace, making one undead stumble into her as she rushed over, holding her bloody daggers. She jabbed the off-balance, undead dwarf in the eye as the other grabbed her from behind, his teeth cracking off on her armor. She turned to pierce the creature's temple as Shorte screamed, "Praemium-Mortuus," casting Searing Light. Pressure from the body's explosion pushed her back while pieces rained down.

"What the spell, Shorte?" she yelled, wiping fragments of the burst dwarf from her face and spitting out a remnant. "Wait till I'm not in bathing distance."

"Sorry, Princess," he responded as Iron Skin wore off. "I see we had the same battle plan, but going in swinging won't work. There are just too many of them."

"Agreed," Raven responded. "We should fall back and join the rest of the army."

Shorte groaned. "What's left of it."

The sound of crumbling rubble made Raven glance toward the collapsed food silo. Six elf corpses crawled out. Most of them had various burns and lacerations. One had a severed arm, while another had a chunk of his skull missing.

Shorte huffed. "Oh, come *on!*" The duo inched back-to-back, preparing to fight again.

As half of the newly formed horde charged toward the arriving couple, Jarz strode into view atop his magical water steed, Kelpie. Izarra yelled into the fray, "Shorte! Raven!" The mount vanished as Jarz summoned his magical ice sword and activated an ice shield from his bracer. Izarra wielded her trident, summoning two medium-sized water golems. She sprayed the ground with a water geyser, turning the snowy landscape to mud, power-spraying the feet off some undead while others became stuck. Jarz picked off the stuck creatures by inserting his ice sword through their heads.

The other half charged Raven and Shorte. He blew up one undead elf before it got any closer. She raised her daggers as another approached.

Raven's heart sank, and her eyes shot straight to the smoke-covered stars. *Please, Blade, guide his soul.* Pacing anxiously as the creature slowly approached, her mind cried. *It's only a child.* But in one swift move, she pierced his temple, then bent over, vomiting.

Shorte swung his mace, pounding the other undead skulls. "And there goes the stomach."

Two newly formed undead elves crawled from under more rubble and then charged Raven. Still hunched over with her daggers pressed against her thighs, stomach still locked, she tilted her head up, panting. *This is never-ending.* She raised her daggers as they got within arm's length when arrows pierced the last two in the back of their heads.

"Avalann!" Raven yelled.

The archer arrived on Krit, holding her bow with one hand and her side with the other as she grimaced. "I can't let you have all the fun."

"You should be resting! We're going back," Raven ordered.

Avalann frowned. "I just got here."

"You're going back to the infirmary."

Avalann rolled her eyes. "You're lucky I'm injured."

The sound of splashing caught the group's attention. Two undead elves chased the water golems around in circles until Jarz strolled over and finished them.

After everything settled, the protectors moved quickly and returned to the opening of the field. Raven spotted her father on his horse, trampling and stabbing the undead, only to have more rise. The Suttiir and Omlett Armies were being pushed back closer and closer to the infirmary, giving up ground to the armies of the undead.

"They're rising as fast as we can kill them," Jarz stated, alarmed. "Someone is turning our own dead against us."

"We need to evacuate the infirmary," Raven ordered. "We're about to be overrun."

"To where?" Izarra asked.

"We could head south toward Omlett," Jarz recommended. "Mug's golems should arrive soon."

"Brilliant!" Raven agreed. *It must be serious if Mug is marching his golems.* They returned to the infirmary tent, where Mara was tending to the injured inside. "Mother, we need to evacuate."

Mara's eyes widened, her jaw clenched, beads of sweat already glistened off her forehead. "I don't know if there are enough wagons for all the injured."

"I've got an idea." Raven ran out to Ghost's saddle, where a pouch held her portal scroll to Omlett. Returning to the tent, she waved the rolled-up parchment. "Home should always be a scroll away!" She unrolled the paper and chanted, "Omlett Porta," to cast a blue portal inside the tent. "We'll defend it as long as possible, but we can't let the undead through."

"I can help you," Carya offered as she approached Raven.

"No, we need you to help the injured to evacuate," Mara replied.

Carya pleaded, "But Thomas is out there!"

Raven hugged her sister. "We'll help him, I promise." As she hurried out of the tent, she witnessed the second line of defense retreating. Shorte tapped his shield twice with his mace, turning his skin to iron, then shuffled his way back toward the heart of the battle. Several undead creatures tried clawing at him, their fingernails ripping off at the contact. The dwarf ignited the Searing Light spell again, splashing body parts all over the field.

Raven mounted Ghost, surveying the chaos, when she finally spotted Thomas's armor in the distance, as he had lost his shield. As it clattered to the ground, more corpses closed in. *He's too far out.* She hesitated, glancing back as Izarra and Jarz helped with the evacuation.

"Go, Raven." Izarra's voice broke the thought as she helped someone through the portal. "We can handle this."

Snapping the reins, Raven raced to Thomas's aid. Sliding off the saddle and combining her two daggers to create a staff, she swung it around in giant arcs. She fought through the horde, clearing a space for Thomas to retrieve his shield.

"Thank you!" Thomas called out, breathing heavily.

The undead and living armies continued fighting around her, but Raven heard a familiar voice shouting above the battle noises. A white warhorse charged toward them. *Grail!* The stallion must have injured his front legs because it collapsed halfway between the infirmary and them, tossing Carya. Still, her sister caught her balance and began casting Searing Light to explode the undead.

Raven's mount bucked and neighed, then raced toward where Carya and Grail were in trouble. "Ghost!" The unicorn trampled some undead and speared an enemy orc, leaving its head dangling from her broken horn as Grail escaped.

Raven and Thomas dashed toward her sister, away from the main undead horde. "Carya is several yards from us toward the infirmary," she said as Shorte rendezvoused with them. They had a clear route as her sister locked eyes with them, but the enemy creatures quickly closed in. Raven transformed her staff into daggers and lashed out at everything in her path. As they moved forward, one by one, the nearest fighting corpses exploded, victims of Shorte's and Thomas's spells. Pieces of flesh, muscle, bone, and brains rained down on them as the trio fended off deadlier and deadlier attacks.

As Carya limped toward them, Raven gasped with relief. *She's still alive.* A pair of hands grabbed the rogue's shoulders, pulling her backward. When she turned, Raven faced an undead human inches from her face. Twisting away, Shorte dropped the creature by slamming his mace into the kneecap as she jammed her dagger into the top of its skull. She glanced over again to see Carya's eyes widen when swarmed by a wave of undead Omlett soldiers that had risen.

Carya swung a jeweled mace as the shield was ripped away from her. "Hurry!" she screamed, shoving an undead gnome out of the way.

"We're almost—" Raven lost balance as her boot slid on a blood patch. Forming her staff again, she forced it into the ground, stabilizing herself. She lifted her weapon, smacking another creature in the head, causing it to crumble. Carya's ear-piecing scream a few yards away drew Raven's attention as creatures tackled her sister to the ground. "No!" Raven thrust her daggers into the enemy's temples, trying to reach her fallen sister. Shorte swung his mace wildly as Thomas used his sword and shield, trying to clear the battlefield.

I've trained on land, air, and water, but this sea of bodies is a terrain I never expected to encounter. Raven's heart ached as she forced herself to ignore the pleas of fallen soldiers calling out, "Help, Princess!" *I can't help them all.* She tried to focus, clearing her mind and blocking out the screams. She high-stepped over the dying while avoiding the immobilized undead still clawing with their upper torso.

"Stay strong," Thomas blurted out as if reading her mind. "We can't help her if we're dead."

It still doesn't make me feel any better.

Shorte huffed as his mace crushed the head of a snarling undead half-orc. "Something we can finally agree on."

Thomas desperately called out, "I can't see her," as Shorte collapsed.

Raven faced Shorte, fighting off an undead torso that tripped him. Thomas still marched forward. *What do I do?*

"Keep going!" Shorte called out, trying to poke his mace at the creature buried under another body. "Get to Carya."

Raven took a deep breath, slapping her daggers together to form her staff. She swung, crushing the skull of another undead elf, trying to take advantage of Shorte's fall.

The half-body that gripped Shorte exploded as Thomas peered over her shoulder and said, "Let's keep moving."

Shorte quickly rose, wiping off remnants. "So that's what it feels like," he mumbled before following them again.

When they finally reached Carya, Raven stabbed the two undead Omlett soldiers who had tackled her sister to the ground. As she took her sister's head into her arms, Raven spotted deep cuts and scratches that had sliced her sister's stomach. Blood poured from the four bite marks that pierced her throat. Carya gargled on blood, trying to talk. "Shhhh, shh." Raven used her cloak to apply pressure to her sister's neck. "Save your strength."

Shorte dropped his mace and shield, then fell to his knees, placing both hands around Carya's head, repeating, "Vulnus Pereuro."

Thomas pushed the energy-drained dwarf to the side and touched Carya's forehead. He closed his eyes, concentrating on something as Carya's blank blue eyes stared skyward. "Carya! Stay with us. Stay with me."

Shorte cried out, "May the gods be damned!"

With puffy, tear-filled eyes, Thomas shook his head as he gripped Raven's shoulder.

The sounds of the battle went silent as Raven closed her sister's eyes and wiped away the matted hair from her face. Raven pulled the limp body closer to her, then gasped as shimmering blue energy left Carya's body. It hovered momentarily, then floated away across the battlefield toward the necromancer.

"No, no, no," she cried. "Thomas!"

The paladin moved closer, lifting Carya into his arms as Raven stepped up, bashing an undead female elf in the skull. The undead creature fell over, and the rogue continued to slam her weapon into the side of its head as Shorte sat with his arms cradled around his knees, mumbling about not knowing how to revivify yet.

"Shorte!" Raven turned, swiping the legs out from another undead soldier. Before she could swing again, a horse's hoof stomped on its skull, making it splatter. Glancing up to see Ghost with Jarz and Izarra, she yelled, pointing to her sister. "We have to get her to the tent!"

Jarz dismounted the unicorn. "There's still time."

Using her trident, Izarra penetrated the skulls of any undead charging the group, then reached for Raven's hand, helping her mount Ghost. Thomas hoisted Carya's body over the mane as the guardians quickly retreated.

"We could use Haste right about now," Raven yelled to Jarz.

The swordmage nodded in agreement and cast the Haste spell on Ghost. Even with the spell, Raven pushed Ghost to the limit as Izarra held on for dear life.

Ghost burst through the tent, ripping the flaps. "MOTHER!" Raven screamed as she leaped off. Izarra helped to lower Carya into Raven's arms. Her sister's weight made her knees buckle. *I've got you.* She tried to hoist the body over her shoulder but felt a hand on her back, steadying her balance.

"Give her to me!" High Priest Stone-Prayer demanded, taking Carya into his arms. He carried her to the table where Avalann had been lying. Mara rushed in through the back side of the tent.

"My baby!" Mara cried out, helping to lay Carya's body on the padded stone table.

Raven touched her sister's hand and whispered, "Hang on."

"Cleric Naelo," Stone-Prayer uttered, feeling her wrist. "Carya."

Raven heard screams from people outside, where small pockets of soldiers were under attack. She kissed her sister's forehead. "Mother will take good care of you. You're going to be all right."

Raven tore down the dangling tent flaps and spotted Thomas, Shorte, and Jarz, joined by Eugor, fighting their way back to the infirmary using all the weapons and spells they had.

Hatred filled Raven's heart, her blood boiled, and her senses heightened. A second wind rushed her depleted body as she dug for the last remnants of energy. Stabbing a pair of undead Suttiir soldiers in the head gave her a sensation of satisfaction. She welcomed the other creatures with the same fate as they charged her, then another, and another as she recklessly swung her daggers.

Raven aimed and threw a dagger, piercing her target, the head of an undead Horck. She raised her throwing hand and cast Cessis Nar. Her hand grew red as she pressed her palm on the forehead of an undead dwarf. Its grotesque teeth chomped at her as she continued applying the pressure of the sizzling hand through his melting skin. The smell no longer phased her as puddles of flesh oozed across the creature's face until she gripped the hardness of its skull. She forced the other dagger through his temple.

Her father appeared beside her, pulling her arm from the undead dwarf. "You've got to stop. This rage won't help your sister," Eugor said as Raven stared desperately at him, tears in her eyes as her hand cooled. "It's only going to get you hurt. We must think now—we should close the portal to protect Omlett. We need to protect the last group."

Raven collected her daggers, still lodged in the skulls, then returned to the infirmary. She peered inside to see Carya lying on the table as High Priest Stone-Prayer chanted an incantation over her while applying a mustard-colored paste.

Raven's muscles tensed, her skin tingled in response to every air particle, and her heart raced as a surge of energy left her body. It was the same feeling she'd had three years ago on the black dragon ride at her eighteenth birthday celebration. "Everyone! Create a chain to the portal!" she instructed as everyone paused inside the tent, eyeing her, confused. "Just do it!" The blackness of the spell covered the tent area. Pinpricks of light from the torches extinguished one by one. "Hurry!"

Mara and the other clerics formed a chain, Eugor at the portal's opening, as the sky turned pitch black. Raven activated her circlet, watching her father guide the injured through the portal. "I'm doing this to give us a chance!"

Eugor shouted, "How long can you maintain the darkness?"

"Till my dying breath," Raven yelled confidently as she stabbed two figures who wandered in front of her, sniffing for fresh flesh. The undead gnomes toppled to the ground. The satisfaction fueled her adrenaline, so she Arcane Stepped through the darkness like a whirlwind, killing any unlucky creature unfortunate enough to be close to her and the tent.

"Mug should soon be here," Eugor yelled, holding his arms out for the next injured person.

Raven watched the undead regroup outside the darkness bubble, shambling menacingly around the edges. Her enchantment began to fade. "Focus, focus!" she hissed, trying to force the darkness to remain. Despite her efforts, the ability fizzled out.

The sound of metal echoed through the camp as the remaining forces of the Suttiir and Omlett Armies drew their weapons, realizing they were losing cover. She doubled over, breathless and exhausted, as the portal closed and the darkness bubble disappeared.

The undead charged the remaining survivors.

Blood oozed from Raven's nose as she gripped her daggers for what she thought might be the last time. An undead orc loomed over her, and for a moment, the orc reminded her of Brugg and his crooked grin as he formed his arms into the orc swing. The simple memory cost her the edge against the invading enemy as the figure reached out to seize her. *One last swing, Carya?*

Raven dipped her head and closed her eyes when she heard a thud. When she opened them, the undead orc dropped to the ground, an iron bolt piercing his skull.

Raven's head swung back to watch Mug's clockwork iron golems advance, equipped with rotating crossbows. The metal army drew the attention of the undead army, which lashed out with teeth and claws but couldn't penetrate the iron golems.

Thirty yards away, she noticed the setting sun highlighting a dark figure in armor atop a fiery horse, surveying the outcome. The necromancer who had brought this terror called out orders as blue energy escaped through a red portal behind him.

Raven gripped her daggers tightly. *One last swing!* And with her last remaining power, she cast Arcane Step. One by one, she killed the corpses, carving a path to their leader.

Raven blinked beside him, and the evil knight caught her by the throat. Her daggers dropped onto the snowy field as he applied more pressure to her throat, lifting her higher. Unable to breathe, she clutched his hand and tried to pry herself loose, but his grip was too tight to chant a spell or pry his fingers away.

Instinctively, she spat acid on the front of his helmet, nearly hitting his eyes. The right side of his helmet formed tiny bubbles, releasing white smoke as it sizzled, but even the deformation wasn't enough for him to decrease his grip. Her eyes locked on a pulsating red glow from a stone pendant around his neck. His hand tightened around her throat as she kicked his shin and clawed at his chest, but she managed to grab hold of the charm, feeling it dig into her palm. She locked on to his only visible eye. *Watch the eyes!* It squinted. *Contra Magia!*

The necromancer tilted his head as if waiting for something to happen. "What are you?" he sneered, squeezing her windpipe harder. He angled his head in case of a second round of chemical saliva, but Raven held tightly to the stone with one hand and tried frantically to pry his fingers away. Her vision began to blur, but before she lost consciousness, a magical arrow impaled the melted, softened part of his helmet. The necromancer dropped her to the frozen ground.

"Raven!" Avalann's voice cried out.

The rogue glanced up as the archer loosed another arrow, grazing the other side of the necromancer's helmet. He called for his army to retreat as he rode off on his fiery horse, followed by his undead army and the golems that pursued them.

Raven's body trembled as she pushed herself onto her knees; pain radiated from her esophagus as she sucked in the air.

"Are you all right, Princess?" Avalann asked, clutching her wounded left side.

Raven tried to speak, but it hurt. The constricting pressure on her throat, combined with the acid, made her temporarily unable to communicate. She nodded, adjusting her cloak. *I'm not all right.*

Her body ached and her ears rang as she used her cloak to wipe the blood dripping from her nose. Realizing she used the section covered in Carya's dried blood, she continued.

Mug's golems created a perimeter, protecting Raven as Avalann helped her onto Krit. They returned to the infirmary while the metal guards were alerted to more danger.

Raven dismounted the black horse and entered the tent. Mara and Eugor, arms around his wife, sobbed together beside Carya's mangled body. Thomas held his love's hand, pressing his forehead against hers.

Raven paused motionless, watching happier moments pass in a blur: Carya laughing, cooking breakfast for Shorte and Izarra, swooning over Thomas and dancing at the festival, helping the injured, and riding out to assist Thomas in battle.

Raven tore off her necklace, a gift from Carya, and gently wrapped it around her sister's cold hands. "Blade," she rasped, "watch over her." She stormed out to stand under the night sky. The silence of the forest was frightening. All the creatures still alive had abandoned this land of death. Her hands shook—from cold or anger, she wasn't sure. Her muscles spasmed as pain shot up and down her sides. She tried to focus on the landscape to keep herself from passing out from exhaustion and grief.

In through the nose, out through the mouth. Raven attempted deep breaths, forming white clouds in the cold air. Pain around her throat made it feel like swallowing glass. Moonlight sparkled off the abandoned swords and shields of the fallen, and the usual serenity of the snow that filled Suttiir Forest was now littered with blood and corpses. The remaining Suttiir and Omlett soldiers searched for survivors, leaving muddy footprints in the snow.

Jarz carried a female elf child who cried out for her brother as Izarra tried to calm her. He placed the child on a table for High Priest Stone-Prayer and then cautiously approached Raven. "I'll take the rest of the survivors to Omlett. Then we should have Mug set up a golem perimeter around the town."

Raven nodded.

A small group of golems from the western woodline returned, Mug leading them back. Someone at camp explained that the others were still tracking down the army and destroying as many undead as possible.

Feeling numb, Raven cracked her neck, trying to release some tension. *What kind of monster would do this? Killing mothers, children . . . Carya.*

Avalann joined Raven, wincing as she adjusted her bow. "Moments like these are why I despise the High Council's rule about interfering. My uncle could have turned the tide of this battle. Where is he anyway?"

Raven realized that no one besides Celeste knew that the Council had Gideon locked away because of his love for family and friends. *Avalann has a point. Do I tell her that Gideon's in a holding cell?* Raven responded with a shrug.

Avalann shot her a quizzical look. "All right then." The archer returned to help with the recovery effort.

Raven reached into her coin pouch, pulling out her comm-stone. "Gideon, I need you," she whispered. No response. Stowing the stone back in her pouch, she untied Ghost as snowflakes fell; *The victims' bodies would soon be covered in snow.* A spark flared inside her, reigniting her rage as she mounted Ghost. *I swear on Blade, I will find that necro!*

Izarra rushed up to her. "Wait!"

Raven ignored her friend, snapped the reins, and dashed south toward Omlett.

CHAPTER THIRTY-TWO

RETREAT, RECOVER, REVENGE

Aushade glanced back, making sure the iron golems no longer pursued him. His deformed helmet limited his vision to one eye. His only company was the undead minions struggling behind him.

The exhausted necromancer nearly dropped an unadorned silver box as it began to slip from his hand. He tightened his grip, pulling the makeshift phylactery up for inspection. It contained the only soul he'd stolen for himself during the battle. The bright blue light seeped through the gap between the box and the lid. "Can't lose this," he mumbled, finding comfort in talking to himself during the long trip back, "but I need the body for this to work."

Do I go back?

The potential power of this soul was tempting, but the thought of returning to Suttiir quickly faded as he approached Grey-Holg. The memory of his partner abandoning him when they arrived here flooded back. *Damn it, Astrick—if I find you, I'll kill you.*

Defeat nipped at him as much as the cold air. When he dismounted from his magical mount, the Nightmare faded. The snow and wind still swirled relentlessly, as it had throughout his two-day travel. He cast a spell, Grey-Holg Circuitus, for his remaining undead minions to patrol the city.

He struggled to maneuver up the short steps, but his annoyance subsided, soon replaced by relief as he touched the black, splintered door of the Grey-Holg Inn. After shaking off the snow, he entered, kicking in a sleeping room door.

Once inside, he gently placed the phylactery on the rusted iron bed beside his tattered leather duffel bag.

"Astrick?!" Silence.

He attempted to pry his helmet off, but the metal had adhered to his skin, and he ripped away flesh. "Son of a—" he cussed as he yanked it off. Blood ran down his cheek, dripping off his chin.

He grabbed a cloth with his empty hand and approached a cracked copper mirror. "The elf spat acid," Aushade huffed after inspecting the damage. He slammed his once pristine helmet against the wall.

Out of habit, he reached up to remove the artifact from around his neck and laughed. "The bitch took the artifact, too." Shaking his head, he released his chest plate and threw it against the wall beside his helmet.

After undressing, he lit the fireplace, then slid down against the wall, moaning. The vision of the metal golems ripping through his army, making them retreat, and losing the battle made his blood boil. He'd done enough fighting—for now. His eyes grew heavy and he surrendered to fatigue.

The image of holding the female elf by the throat came into focus. "What are you?" Aushade repeated multiple times. He focused on her, seeking to recognize anything about her. The black onyx on her circlet caught his attention. "Who are you?"

"I'm jealous. I thought I was the only woman of your dreams," a feminine voice whispered in his ear as ivory arms wrapped around his waist. "Who is she?"

He released the elf to rest his dark arms on Courtlynn's. "I don't know," Aushade answered, staring more intently at the image of the enigma. "She can spit acid."

"I like her," the succubus giggled.

"I'm talking about some dragon-level acid shite."

"I like her even more."

"But she took the artifact."

"I'll kill her," Courtlynn spat, pushing him away.

He turned to face the seething succubus as the elf's image dissolved.

"How could you let a child beat you, the Great Aushade."

"Trust me—she's not some mere child."

"Let's just hope my master's demon army is ready," Courtlynn warned, facing back toward him, "because he's preparing to march them against the Second Layer."

Aushade clenched his jaw and fist. *She still has a master.* "And where is that jester of a wizard?"

"Astrick? Authorities detained him in Omlett. I had to kill him so he wouldn't talk."

Aushade shook his head. "The lunatic became deranged with madness after the attack on the dwarves."

Courtlynn placed her delicate hands on his chest. "It's over anyway. You don't have the artifact. Your services are no longer required."

"But the fox has one tail remaining. Let me use him against Omlett."

"It's over—"

As he awoke, severe pain in his cheek caused his eyes to swell. He opened them wide with rage. Reaching up to touch his aching face, he felt a bandage. He glanced to his side and found Courtlynn sitting beside him with an herbal ointment.

She dropped it and moved closer, wrapping her arms around him and placing her head on his shoulder. She smelled flowery for a demon, as if she'd arrived straight from the Fey Realm instead of the Abyss.

The aroma of roasting meat made him glance at the fireplace. A wild boar carcass hung from the spit as Floxy slept on the rug. "So my services are no longer needed?"

"Yes," she responded with a look of desire. Aushade leaned in and kissed her, pulling her body closer. He leaned back, gazing into her dark eyes that reflected the fire.

"I should be thankful you're not an assassin," he said with a groggy smile, "or I would be on my way to the Astral Realm."

"I can only portal to someone with an intimate connection," Courtlynn whispered. "But the Abyss is better."

"I'll take your word for it," he responded, standing up and fighting the tingles in his legs. The succubus stayed kneeling, glancing up at him as he reached down to rub the demon fox behind its ear. "I don't need Floxy."

As she stood, she mocked his words under her breath, which compelled him to laugh. He walked over to his bulky duffel bag, removed some worn-out, homemade blue wings, and gently placed them on the bed.

"Did you cut them off a fairy?" she asked as he kept rummaging through the sack. The question didn't even merit an answer as he pulled out a thick spell book that had seen better days. Wear and tear marred the pages after years of traveling.

"I'll cast a Rust Metal spell on my minions to defeat those damned golems." Aushade grinned, then snapped the spell book shut before she could get a peek. "It was my father's," he explained before the nosy succubus could ask anything as she glanced back at the wings. "My brother's." He was unsure why the overwhelming urge to open up to her hit him, but he was too exhausted to fight it. "He loved the guardians' wings when we were kids."

She huffed at the mention of guardians.

"I crafted those for him." The look of surprise on her face forced him to go silent.

"That's"—she struggled to find the right word—"sweet."

"We were kids. I'd just celebrated my fifteenth birthday when the war orcs attacked us." The wings crunched under his grip. "He had these on that day."

"Now I understand why you despise the orcs so much." She wrapped her arms around him.

"The wings were the only thing I found left of him," he said, stuffing the spell book back into the sack. "I was in the courtyard studying my father's spell book when the green menaces sieged the castle."

"And your father?"

"He saved my life," Aushade responded, picking up the wings.

She gripped him tighter. "He died saving your life?"

He responded with a chuckle.

"What?"

Aushade's grin faded. "He was already dead. I did the unforgivable. I raised his bloody corpse to protect me while I escaped with the wings and spell book. Then the castle became ashes and a burnt ruin."

Courtlynn released her grip. "I thought my childhood was rough."

He opened the duffel bag to place the wings in, but the thought of her as a child brought his guard down for a brief second.

She rushed to grab a metal box beside his bag. "What's this?" Blue light shimmered through the small opening.

Aushade quickly grabbed it, securing the lid as she shot him a stern look.

"That appears to be a phylactery."

"Yes."

"You plan on becoming a lich?"

"No, it's not for me."

"You're stealing souls from my master?"

"Once I collected all the souls, I realized spell casters have a slightly lighter blue color," he answered, trying to read her facial expression. "I know a way to create liches."

"Your spell book?" she asked furiously.

"Yes," he answered. "I knew Suttiir was full of elven wizards, but I could only collect one special soul from that mess."

Courtlynn huffed as if she was at a loss for words.

"Will you teleport me east of the Suttiir Bridge?" he asked, facing the risk of rejection.

She nodded with a frown.

"They won't expect me to approach them from that direction."

"So . . ." the succubus hesitated, "what are your plans for after?"

"I'm not sure," he shrugged. "I can't live in the Abyss, and you can't reside here . . . but why does it matter? Aren't you still tied to your master?" He approached her as she lowered her head with what looked like a tear forming. Wrapping his arms around her, she returned the embrace. "I promise, after this, I'll return to Fellswar's Claim and we can figure something out."

She glanced up at him with her dark, teary eyes.

"The helmet is useless, and I'll never block you from my dream world again."

"Promise?"

"Promise," he responded, raising her head and wiping a tear away.

Courtlynn gathered her composure before spinning around and pushing him onto the bed. She straddled him, pinning him down, kissing his neck.

He whispered in her ear with concern. "The guardian?"

Courtlynn hushed him with her finger on his lips. Running her long fingernail from his chin to his chest, she leaned down for a kiss. As their lips locked, his pulse sped up. Aushade's mind shut down for the first time in a long time. *What's this feeling?* It was as if time halted as her lips touched his like someone had cast a Time Stop spell upon him. It was intoxicating. *Is she trying to kill me? After all, she is a succubus.*

His mind raced with doubt, but the pleasure overruled all rationale. He carefully moved his fingers down her back, tracing the base of her wings, which seemed sensitive and pleasurable. They continued kissing, but she had a way of making it feel like they were back in the dream world.

The morning sun pierced the windows; the fire barely burned, and the half-eaten, charred boar stilled on the spit. It was the most peaceful sleep he'd had in a long time. A warm breath touched his cheek. He sat up. Courtlynn was sleeping on her side, her curls a mess. He brushed the hair off her face and ran his hand over her horns.

Peering out the window, a thin layer of snow covered the ground, reflecting the morning rays and making them brighter. The silhouettes of his soldiers still limped about the city.

Her yawn and stretch caught his attention. Courtlynn spent the night with no guardian appearing. "Do you realize this is the longest I've physically stayed in the Mortal Realm?" She sat up and kissed the middle of his back. "I could get used to it."

Aushade huffed. "You know you can't. I'm surprised the guardian hasn't knocked down the door yet."

"Will you stop worrying about him!" she moaned, removing the blanket and standing along the bed. "The guardian, the guardian," Courtlynn mocked as she dressed, "that's all you worry about." She struck a pose. "Am I not worth the risk?"

He didn't respond.

"Fine," she said, grabbing his helmet and casting a red portal to the Abyss. "I'll be back in a few days to execute your plan."

"Courtlynn." Aushade frowned as she ignored him.

After she left, he gathered some of the remaining undead minions and cast Rust Metal. Their skin turned a copper color as he commanded half of them to march toward Omlett to attack from the west. *They should reach their destination by the time we portal there.*

The next few days of the New Year's cycle passed in a blur of anger, drinks, and longing for revenge.

"I don't lose."

Aushade woke to a raven squawking outside his window on the morning of his planned attack. "An omen?" he whispered as he stared at the figure of the bird through the dirty window. He glanced at the year 1177 circular parchment, where he had marked the Sixth of Ir with his blood from his injury.

A red portal appeared out of the corner of his eye, and Courtlynn exited. A horde of undead soldiers followed her. After adding his armor, he rushed to open the door.

The succubus walked in smiling.

"I missed you," he whispered, which made her cheeks as red as her hair.

"I thought you might need reinforcements," she said playfully, nodding toward the recruits still pouring through. "I stopped by Fellswar's Claim and baited them to chase me here."

"More is good."

"And this," she stated, handing him his repaired helmet.

He grinned as he inspected it. "But how?"

"A very handsome young blacksmith," Courtlynn whimsically answered as Aushade shot her a look. "Don't be jealous. I only seduced him with an enormous bag of gold."

He ordered his soldiers into formation. "Rost-Metallum," he called out, casting Rust Metal on the army. "That should destroy the golems."

She smiled evilly. "There is a portal receiver just east of the Suttiir Bridge."

"You've been busy," Aushade mused.

Courtlynn handed him a portal scroll. "There you go, my dark pally. Finish this now!" She kissed him swiftly on his cheek and turned to Floxy, rubbing the fox's head before kissing it on its forehead.

As he cast the blue portal, Aushade realized this would be the last time she would see Floxy.

They appeared on the bridge's east side. Aushade summoned his Nightmare and mounted it. As Floxy sat beside him, they watched the rest of the undead troops funnel through, advancing toward Omlett.

The army marched across the Suttiir Bridge as something in his satchel vibrated. He retrieved the phylactery box, which pulsated with a blue glow. The eerie sound of a female voice moaning in pain echoed from the metal prison. *Her body is nearby.* He frantically searched for a tombstone or graveyard. After returning the box, he grinned menacingly. "Elevare Mortuus." He raised the undead across all the final resting areas in the vicinity.

"Revenge."

CHAPTER THIRTY-THREE

REACHING OUT TO FAMILY

Four days had passed since Carya's funeral, and Raven's eyes were swollen and sore from crying. She sat hunched over at the bar in the Cache Tavern. Hiding her head under the hood of her cloak, she finished her third ale, spinning the magical stone Gideon had given her, waiting for him to activate the comm-stone.

This is a shite way to start the new year.

Rusty was good company because he left her to drink. But no drink would ever fill the emptiness of losing Carya. Raven recalled her father weeping, not only over the loss of his eldest daughter but to hear his parents had died as well. Ever since Raven's return, strangers would stop her in the streets to express how sorry they were for her loss.

How do they know how I feel? They weren't there to watch the massacre.

Raven closed her eyes, hoping it would make the room stop spinning. The memory of the reanimated elf child, lifeless at her feet, made her ill. *How many families lost loved ones?* She wiped away a tear as a stranger approached the bar.

"Why are there golems surrounding the city?" he asked Rusty. "It took me forever to get through the checkpoint."

"The city is on high alert," Rusty explained as Raven closed her eyes, slowly inhaling while trying to ignore the bartender. A hand rested on her shoulder, and her eyes flew open to find Izarra sitting beside her.

"Rusty, may I please get a glass of mulberry wine," Izarra ordered, then turned to Raven. "You look like—"

"Ogre poop," Raven mumbled, gulping down the last of the ale. "Another," she slurred at Rusty, knocking over the mug.

"I think you've had plenty, Princess," he responded gently.

Raven glared at him and then at Izarra.

I'm not a child.

"Avalann returned—she's off finding Shorte and Jarz. We're meeting at the Omlett Inn to discuss the Mortal Guardians' status. We haven't heard from Gideon, so we need to plan something. Will you be there? Because we need you."

"I'm really not in the mood," Raven responded, tossing the comm-stone into her coin pouch. "I'm one ale away from storming the High Council."

Izarra placed her hand on Raven's shoulder again. "Don't do anything crazy. Maybe we can go shopping at Maggie's?"

Raven rose haphazardly, nearly knocking over the drink Rusty had reluctantly supplied. She downed the ale and tossed her coin pouch at Rusty. "Excuse me, but I need some fresh air." She left, and Izarra followed, holding the coin pouch Rusty had tossed back.

"I could come with you," Izarra said enthusiastically.

Raven shook her head. "I need to be alone." She untied Ghost, turning back to her friend. "Please, Izarra, just return to the others. I'll be home soon."

Raven mounted Ghost and trotted off toward the church, where Thomas had isolated himself since the funeral. Even Mara had tried to speak with him, but High Priest Stone-Prayer relayed the message that the paladin didn't want to talk to anyone. Once at the church, Raven sat staring at the entrance. Though the memories of Astrick seemed like a lifetime ago, they still haunted her.

Maybe I'm not ready to talk either.

Raven decided to continue to the Omlett Inn, but the ride was blurry. She replayed all the painful moments that had plagued her dreams. Carya's lifeless body sprawled on the table, hearing her parents weeping in their bed chamber. Brugg and Mug stripped away all the wedding decorations, replacing them with preparations for a funeral. Izarra and Jarz were sitting with a comatose Shorte, comforting him. Thomas kneeling next to Carya's body, refusing to release her hand for High Priest Stone-Prayer to lay her in the ground. *She always wanted an Earthist druidic burial—not the elven pyre burning.*

Raven arrived at Omlett Inn, tying Ghost in front of the stables. She staggered to the front of her house, quietly pushing the door open. No one seemed home, so she slowly descended the stairs, tripping on the last step and falling. *Shite.* She got to her knees and stared at Carya's flowery-decorated door. After briefly hesitating, she rose to her feet, pushing it open.

Raven entered the room, approaching a rosewood vanity table. Carya's trinket box sat open, spilling out all the diamonds and gold jewelry. When Raven sat on a small stool, looking into the copper mirror, a stranger's reflection stared back with dark bags and greasy hair. The musky smell that percolated from her contrasted with the honeydew scent of her sister's room.

Maybe I should bathe.

She rolled off her hair tie, pulled apart her ponytail, and reached for Carya's brush. Each stroke painfully snagged her knots, but it was a temporary relief from all the mental anguish. Her fingers traced the jeweled brush backing as she closed her eyes. The memory of Carya fighting with her to sit still while trying to groom her hair made her grip the handle tighter with rage. Raven slammed down the brush and hastily put her hair back into a ponytail.

She pushed herself away from the vanity table, moving to the stack of books on the nightstand where a book on poisonous plants waited on the top. Lying across the bed was Carya's wedding gown. Her sister had chosen an intricately designed white dress. Flower patterns made from crystals were sewn into the bodice, complementing the flowy lace bell sleeves—*typical Carya.* Part of the garment hung over the sides of the bed, touching the dusty floor. Raven lifted it gently, placing the sleeves back on the bed. *Carya would have looked like an actual princess.* Tears formed as she left, slamming the door behind her.

I need more ale.

Raven stomped downstairs to the kitchen and through the secret passage that brought her to her father's work chamber. Her parents were nowhere to be found. She headed to the bar, where she was surprised to see Thomas sitting on a stool, hands cupped around a mug of ale.

"Thomas," she said cautiously.

"Hello, Purple Eyes." His hair was messy, and it looked like he hadn't shaved in days.

Raven sat beside him. "I'm surprised to see you."

"Your father insisted I leave the church for a bit. I've learned not to argue with him."

"Wise man."

He glanced at her. "Are you all right?"

"Not really." She wiped her eyes.

"Yeah," he said, taking another sip. "I know the feeling." He swirled the liquid before gulping down the last of his drink. Raven ordered an ale as Cyndi hesitated to pour one. "Raven, I'm leaving Omlett," he blurted out, staring morosely into his empty mug.

"Why?"

Thomas slammed his glass on the counter. "I'm going to hunt him down and kill him. I don't care how long it takes. I'll probably lose my paladin status and knighthood, but I don't care. I won't stop until he's dead . . . or until I join Carya in the Astral Realm."

Raven put her hand lightly on his shoulder. "I'll join you. I want revenge."

Suddenly, a barefoot Gideon, wearing what looked like rags, stumbled through the front door. Raven and Thomas watched with shock as the guardian tried to compose himself. Every emotion hit her at once, but anger prevailed. Thomas had looked rough, but Gideon appeared as if he had gone through the nine layers of the Abyss.

"Now you show up," Raven said, furious.

Thomas wrinkled his nose. "You smell like shite. Like an overflowing privy."

"We need to talk outside," Gideon said urgently.

"Where were you when I needed you?" Raven sternly asked as Thomas turned to focus on his drink. "In Suttiir or at Carya's funeral?"

"I was held—"

"I know where you were," Raven interrupted. "Maybe you should try listening closer. "Where were *you* when *I* needed you?"

"Oh shite," Thomas gargled with his face buried in his mug.

Gideon sighed. "Can we have a private conversation, please? I don't have much time. They're probably searching for me as we speak."

"Fine." She placed her hand on Thomas's shoulder. "I'll see you later." Raven rushed past the paladin as he lifted his mug in response.

Gideon chased her out the front door, catching up. "They held me for days in a Dead Magic Zone cell."

"Days?" Raven mocked. "It's been months for me."

"I know. I'm very sorry for that," Gideon said remorsefully. "I'm not used to having company there."

"Why didn't you just quit?" Raven grilled him. "Join us as a mortal again."

"That's not fair."

"Fair? Do you want to know how much death and horror I witnessed? Loved ones were maimed and brought back to murder their own families and friends. Fair? When their life force is sucked into, only Blade knows where. Fair? When a necromancer has Bull Strength, and you're dangling by the neck. I thought I knew what evil was, but apparently, I still have much to learn."

Gideon paused in silence for a moment. "I don't know what to say."

"But no, I'm off in the Fey Realm playing house with unicorns and fairies. Ask me if I would give up everything if I asked you to."

He hesitated as if walking into a trap. "Would you—"

"Yes," she responded without hesitation. "If I had to choose between you and everything else. But I know you, Gideon—my family means as much to you as they do to me." She stared at him as he remained silent. "It's the High Council. Will they be there if you need a hug or a laugh? A shoulder to cry on? Of course not. They'll replace you the day you decide to give up your wings."

"I've been doing this job for almost two hundred years. It's all I know."

"Well then, maybe having a courtship won't work," she blurted out, not knowing if she meant it.

"Maybe you're right," Gideon agreed, lowering his head.

Shocked by his response, Raven silently watched him cast a blue portal. "How did you escape the High Council?" she asked before he stepped through.

"Through the privy," he answered dejectedly before disappearing.

Raven, alone, stared at the space where he'd vanished. She wrapped her arms around herself, trying to keep the pain inside. Her body convulsed as she screamed at the top of her lungs—no words, just a guttural sound of heartbreak. Tears flowed along her face, the taste of salt on her lips. *I don't know how much more my heart can take.* Raven wiped her eyes and tried to catch her breath. Once she felt under control of her emotions, she returned to the bar.

"That was quick," Thomas mumbled, hunched over his mug.

Raven said nothing as she searched for her coin pouch before remembering she didn't have it.

"Don't worry about it, Raven," Cyndi whispered.

Thomas sprung up from the bar stool, slamming down his coin pouch. "Drinks for everyone, on me!"

Cyndi rushed to Thomas and hid his currency under the bar. Then yelled over at a human patron wearing white fur armor who was celebrating the news. "You'll be paying for your *own* ale." The bartender glanced at Raven and signaled that she was cutting the paladin off from any more alcohol.

Thomas slumped over, burying his head in his arms as Raven patted his back, trying to comfort him, but she couldn't contain her grief anymore. She rushed for the secret tunnel, crying. The light from the sconce torches blurred as she raced down the familiar stone passage, and grief ate away at her soul. As her pace quickened, every footstep echoed the names—Carya—Gideon. She stumbled through her kitchen door, spotting a note on the counter. It was in her father's handwriting. Without reading it, she tossed it aside and dashed to her bedroom.

When she opened the door, an elf resembling a younger version of her father was there, placing a set of golden armor on a stand. She rubbed her swollen eyes, verifying it wasn't Eugor. Raven reached for her daggers. "Who are you? FATHER!"

"*Our* father is on his way to Suttiir," the strange male elf said calmly, "which you would know from the note in the kitchen."

"Blade?" Raven asked incredulously as she squinted through her puffy eyes. He bowed. "In the flesh."

Raven ran to her bureau and equipped her circlet to cast True Seeing. *He's real?! But it's not good enough.* "Prove to me you're telling the truth."

"Our father was decapitated and resurrected where he met your mother," Blade answered, smiling.

"Everyone knows that story," Raven replied, still suspicious. "Tell me something I know, but only a demigod would also know."

The stranger thought for a moment. "I know our father ate a black dragon's egg, and now you display the characteristics of a black dragon." He glanced at her as she slowly sat on her bed, trying to absorb what he was telling her. "You're immune to acid, you spit acid, you can hold your breath underwater for long periods, you can turn pools of water into swamp water, and you can cast Darkness." He paused. "Am I missing anything? Oh, and you enjoy carrying a coin pouch because the sound of coins is soothing."

"How could you know that? I only told Gideon and my father."

"Gideon and I talk often at the High Council."

"I'm turning into a dragon?" *Is this happening now, after everything else I've been through?*

"You're not turning into a dragon."

"You said—"

"I said you're displaying *traits*—but that isn't why I'm here."

"Now what—"

"I brought Gideon's armor and bought him some time by appearing as him in his cell."

"He told me he was in a DMZ."

"Dead Magic Zone, yes, he was, but want to guess who's in charge of the holding cells at the High Council?" Using his hand, he gestured to himself. "Can you believe he escaped through the privy tank, the one place in the cell still an active magic area?"

"He was telling the truth," Raven mumbled to herself.

"All he wanted was to get to you," Blade said, smiling. "Anyone who loves my sister that much has earned my respect. But—"

"But?"

"I'm here for something even more important. Your sister's soul never reached the Astral Realm."

Raven's jaw dropped in shock.

"When the council voted to hold Gideon during this war, I decided, without the High Council's knowledge, to investigate incoming souls from the Mortal Realm. For a war, hardly any new souls were arriving, which I thought was strange."

Raven sat back on her bed. "It means they're going somewhere else."

"Exactly."

"But where?" she asked. "It's like they're being stolen!" She walked to the stone fireplace, removing a hollow stone and dumping a necklace with a cone-shaped pendant. "I think it has something to do with this."

"The Artifact of the Souls," Blade whispered, shocked at the sight. Raven held it out for Blade to take, but he refused, shaking his head. "I don't trust the council currently. Keep it for now."

"Isn't it dangerous? They'll be looking for it."

Blade took the necklace, casting a spell to hide its aura. Then he cast another that made it look like a typical Blade charm worn by many. "You should be safe now. I'll do what I must up there, and you do your part down here. We'll figure this out."

"If you see Gideon—"

"I'd have to escort him back to the High Council, so—"

"Understood."

Before leaving, Blade returned the artifact to Raven. "Your sister didn't remember me gifting one of these to her because she was too young then, but when this is solved, I will give you a real luck charm."

"Thank you, Blade."

He cast a red portal. "Give our father and your mother my love," he said, stepping through, leaving her alone in wonder.

Raven put on the necklace and sat momentarily, trying to absorb everything she had just learned: the black dragon traits, no souls arriving from the war, meeting her demigod half-brother, and the love of her life on the run from the High Council. And now she sat wearing the artifact that had gotten her father killed.

Raven left the house and crossed the garden to Carya's grave near the bridge. She knelt and spoke to the headstone. "I'm so sorry I couldn't protect you. I would have been there longer if I hadn't gone to the Fey Realm with Gideon. But I knew you were happy—you had Thomas in your life." Her eyes stung, and her heart felt like it had been ripped from her body.

Raven collapsed onto her hands and knees, sobbing at Carya's grave. The hardened dirt cut into her palms, and she welcomed the physical pain—anything to stop the aching in her heart and mind. She sat back on her feet, trying to catch her breath.

Crossing her legs at the foot of the freshly dug spot, Raven sat. The frozen earth had slashed open her palm, where the old knife-throwing scar was. *Damn it.* After watching the drops of blood run down her hand, she ripped off a piece of her tunic and wrapped the wound. She stared motionlessly at her sister's headstone. The words "beloved daughter," "gone too soon," and "will be loved forever" burned into her eyes. She glanced away before allowing the tears to start again. A cold winter wind was blowing through the trees across the river. Raven curled in on herself and placed her head on her knees. *I'm going to kill the necromancer who did this.*

Her eyelids closed as exhaustion took over her body, taking deep breaths. On an inhale, a strong odor made her gag. *What is that smell?* Raising her injured hand to her nose, she sniffed it, ensuring she hadn't laid her hand in shite or something that would infect it later. *The battlefield!* The scent of decaying flesh. Even the fresh flowers couldn't camouflage the stench.

Screams from the south rang through the city, causing her to perk up. Confused, she glanced around and watched a group of townsfolk frantically dashing from the pier. Bile filled her mouth when she saw the creatures that were chasing them. *The undead!* Before she could stand, the ground beneath her shook as Carya's cold, stiff hand broke through the dirt and grabbed her wrist.

Raven screamed and pried the hand loose, falling backward. The roar of the creatures came from behind her. She spun around as the necromancer and a small group of his undead crossed the Suttiir Bridge. She scrambled to her feet as the dirt below finally broke away, and the corpse of Carya pulled free. Raven frantically got to her feet as Carya's dead eyes stared at her blankly. Two hands grabbed the rogue from behind as she swung in defense.

Izarra ducked before the fist hit her. "Raven! It's me."

The two girls hurried into the street toward the Dragon and Egg statue. The other Mortal Guardians were gathered around it, trying to protect the people.

Raven watched in horror as the necromancer stopped at the bridge entrance, an undead Carya by his side. There was something different about the way she moved and reacted. The reanimated version moved with purpose and control, unlike the puppets of flesh that the necromancer used to destroy the city.

"She's a lich," Jarz whispered, surprised.

"Oh, Shite," Shorte replied, grasping his mace. "How? She's no wizard!"

Raven's eyesight blurred as her stomach tightened. Her heart raced, and the world spun as she tried to control her breathing. "I can't . . . I can't do it . . . I can't destroy my sister."

"I will if I have to," Avalann responded as Raven eyed her with resentment.

The necromancer commanded his undead army to form a half-circle around the Mortal Guardians as a sizeable red demon fox charged past the group.

"What in the Abyss is that thing?" Izarra yelled as they watched the fox dart toward the city's center.

Raven's ears blocked out all the commotion as her mind fixated on how that vile monster had turned her beloved sister into a lich. *Will she still remember me?* A bright light suddenly appeared overhead, and she defeatedly closed her eyes.

I can't take it anymore! I'm ready for the Astral Realm!

CHAPTER THIRTY-FOUR

THE LAST STAND

"I've been doing this job for almost two hundred years," Gideon replied defensively. "It's all I know."

"Well then, maybe having a courtship won't work," Raven retorted.

Gideon's heart ached. *Is she serious? Or is she acting tough?* "Maybe you're right," he agreed, lowering his head and creating a blue portal.

"How did you escape the High Council?"

He hesitated before answering. "Through the privy." He stepped through the opening. Wanting to stay near Raven, the portal opened before the Naelos' home.

Hungry, smelly, and exhausted, he went over to a newly placed tombstone, noticing the loosely piled dirt that looked freshly dug. *Carya got her wish. To be buried so her body would become part of the Earth.* He bowed his head in respect. "I'm sorry, Princess Carya," he whispered as Raven's face appeared in his mind. *Can I blame her for being that upset?* He regained his composure. "May Blade welcome your soul, Princess."

Gideon glanced down the road. *Raven must have returned to the Inn.* He gave the grave one last nod, continued across the muddy yard, and entered the Naelo residence. The home felt like he did—cold and empty. As he wandered into the kitchen, he noticed a parchment on the counter.

Raven,

Ensure you secure the Inn at night, feed the horses, and keep the kitchen clean while your mother and I visit Suttiir.

Love, Father

Gideon grabbed some of Mara's homemade lavender soap. The smell of the flower-filled bar consumed his senses as he closed his eyes, bringing his thoughts back to his love. A basket of honey rolls caught his attention as he was leaving. *Raven would pin my hand down with a dagger for taking one.* He chuckled at the thought, but his stomach made him take the risk.

Gideon finished the honey roll by the time he reached the Suttiir River. After undressing, he tossed his filthy white tunic and pants along the riverbank. Shivering, he stepped into the chilly waters, keeping close to the bridge to stay out of sight.

After scrubbing the grime from his skin, he ducked under the water to rinse off. Resurfacing, he noticed Raven approaching Carya's grave. *She either doesn't see me, or she's intentionally ignoring me.*

After three hundred years, he'd found someone he wanted to share his life with. The other faces and names were just distractions to help make his immortal life feel normal. But with Raven, things were different. She sparked something inside him, making him feel alive—a speck of pure happiness in a long lifetime.

He counted the blessings of having her in his life. Every morning, he couldn't wait to hear her voice; every evening, she fell asleep in his arms. She'd become his stargazing partner, helping to chart all the constellations. He recalled all the tricks she played on him and the others. She always asked a million questions about his adventures, and he loved her stubbornness when they argued that she couldn't learn the impossible Wish spell.

He'd never felt true love before, and the thought of losing all that or her crushed his soul. "It wasn't even my fault," he muttered miserably.

Gideon spotted movement coming from the eastern tree line. He could barely hear the faint sounds of the tree branches snapping in the woods over the bubbling river. A horde of undead creatures approached the Suttiir Bridge. Gideon watched a knight in dark gray armor slowly cross the bridge astride a fiery black horse, casting spells over the undead creatures.

A Nightmare? In this realm? He instinctively glanced at his wrist for the red gem and cursed under his breath, remembering he no longer had the gauntlet. Gideon quickly spun his head toward the cemetery. Raven was gone, but a white figure lingered atop Carya's grave.

Gideon held his breath and dove underwater, swimming as fast as he could to reach the riverbank. He dashed through the lawn, naked and soaking wet, bursting through the Naelos' front door in a panic.

"Raven!" Gideon shouted.

Brugg stared at him with a bewildered look, stopping mid-sweep. "You," the orc stated, pointing at the guardian's private area, "nude."

Gideon grabbed a throw blanket from the leather chair, wrapping it around his waist. "The city is under attack. Get to safety."

Brugg snapped his broomstick in half, tossing the straw hairs but keeping the pointy end. "Me . . . safe now."

The guardian shrugged. "Stay here in case Raven returns."

The orc nodded in agreement.

Gideon rushed up the stairs and knocked on her bedroom door before forcing it open. He stopped, staring at the corner of her room where an armor stand held his bright gold armor, the gauntlet, and his vorpal sword. It was a sight for sore eyes. The thought of how Raven possessed them entered his mind fleetingly as he summoned the armor and the white wings extended from his back.

Glancing down at his gauntlet, he noticed the red gem wasn't glowing. *How's that possible? How are they blocking the gem's scry ability? Perhaps the Nightmare is just an illusion.*

Gideon cast a blue portal and stepped through, arriving behind the necromancer's undead army on the bridge's west end. The remaining undead soldiers halted by their master as a red fox dashed toward the center of town.

A flox—here? He watched the creature run, its single tail bouncing with each step. *Oh no!*

Gideon flapped his white wings, flying over the horde of undead that marched across the bridge. From his vantage point, he observed the creatures penetrating the city from all angles. A group of at least two hundred undead streamed chaotically from the west, the flox's destination.

The residents of Omlett sought shelter in their homes as Buzz's security rallied to protect the city. Gideon's skin tingled when he saw Raven and the Mortal Guardians hovering around the Black Dragon statue, preparing to fight the horde.

Descending toward them, he cast the Time Stop spell just as Raven tilted her head toward the sky. A bright white light lit his hand as he landed beside her.

Everyone in Omlett City froze. In a single moment, he studied his guardians. Shorte, clad in his cleric gear, mid-shout, wielding his mace and shield. Avalann, with her bowstring drawn, a magical arrow notched as she eyed the evil on the bridge. Izarra, with her trident, pointed as water stilled at the bridge's height. Jarz was protecting Izarra with his shield and sword at the ready. Raven, eyes closed, as if welcoming death.

His heart ached. *My love.* He leaned in to kiss her cheek, then turned toward the attackers.

Anger boiled inside as he walked toward the undead, several yards from the statue, but he knew there were too many for the group to handle. The light in his left hand pulsed, marking the time left in the spell.

Gideon stretched out his right hand and shouted, "Mortem Immortuos Indu," casting Undeath to Death, emitting a black aura over the army. A horde of the undead soldiers' heads exploded near the necromancer. Gideon repeated the spell several more times, with every pulse of the orb, enjoying the fireworks of cranium explosions until the light faded.

"I'll return for you later!" Gideon growled, eyeing the necromancer. *What can I do?* The guardian mischievously grinned as he cast a spell, turning the knight's Nightmare into a cow. Gideon surveyed the square, confident that his apprentices could manage the remaining undead. As soon as the white light vanished, he felt a hand on his shoulder as Raven turned toward him. They both smiled.

"Gideon!" Izarra screamed, losing control of her wave as the water receded under the bridge.

The guardian nodded as he flew off. Locating the determined fox, he zoomed into the center of town. "Two can play that game." He cast a spell, Scutum Exitium, creating a protective shield around the fox, knowing what would come. He landed next to the demon fox as it stopped at the church, a horde of undead ready to charge him.

Gideon used his vorpal sword to pierce some through the skull as he watched another group of undead elves trying to bite and claw at the fox's tail. But they detonated into ashes every time one of them hit the red energy barrier.

In his head, Gideon prepared to alter his blunt magic missiles, then stuck his vorpal sword out, launching a barrage of piercing projectiles that penetrated the enemy skulls. The red demon fox turned and snarled.

A red portal appeared next to the beast, and a curvy demon stepped through, waving at Gideon as the demon fox escaped. The red gem in his gauntlet became bright red, catching his attention. *The flox.* He glanced up at the sneering succubus.

"The mighty Mortal Realm Guardian," she smirked. "Gideon, is it?"

He shot her a surprised look. "You have me at a disadvantage. And you are?"

"Courtlynn," she replied, approaching him. "I must say . . . it's about time."

"Excuse me?"

"That you help your realm." Courtlynn put her hand on his shoulder. She was about to walk around him when his wings expanded to block her. Her hand went from his shoulder to touch his wing, but he retracted them. "I have them, too," the succubus boasted, flexing her blood-red wings, "but no one will take them from me if I'm a bad girl."

"You seem to know a lot about me."

"Typical guardian stuff." She flashed him an evil look. "How does it feel to see your realm in chaos as we pillage it?"

"We?" he repeated, trying to keep his temper. "I'll report this to the High Council."

"My sources say the High Council wants *you*. Escaping through the fecal compartment?" She pinched her nose. "Clever but stinky."

"Enough of the shite jokes—I've heard plenty."

Courtlynn giggled. "It's because of a woman, isn't it?" The guardian stayed silent. "It is! But don't worry about it, sweetheart—I can distract and seduce the most powerful men."

"Then I'm fortunate to be an elf."

Courtlynn offered a seductive look. "You're still a male with needs."

A piercing scream drew his attention toward the shops, but as he turned back, the portal closed, and the bright red gem ceased to glow.

A succubus and a flox. Gideon had proof that the attack was coming from the Abyss. *Finally, I can protect my friends, family, and our realm.*

Gideon patrolled the streets west toward the Cache Tavern, searching for anyone in trouble. Maggie was leaning out her top window, casting a Binding spell on each creature as her unseen servant used a dagger to put the creatures down permanently as they passed her shop. Gideon hurried further down the road and found an undead elven soldier pinning down one of the security dwarves.

The young guard cried out, pushing the creature's head away with the handle of a battle axe. "Laiex! It's me . . . Horith. Stop!"

Gideon swung his vorpal sword as the undead soldier bobbed up, slicing the top of the creature's head in half. The dome piece splattered over the dwarven guard.

Horith sobbed. "Laiex."

"I'm sorry," Gideon replied compassionately, "but that wasn't your friend." He helped the guard to his feet. "Are you injured?"

The young dwarf shook his head.

"Can you still fight?"

The dwarf nodded, gripping his battle axe.

"The city needs you."

"Look out!" Horith yelled, raising his weapon. A loud snarl grew louder as an undead orc ambushed them, grabbing the guardian by the arm and biting down on his gold armor. The security dwarf bounced anxiously, lining up a good swing.

Gideon stuck his vorpal sword through the creature's torso, letting go. He grabbed the undead orc by the hair, then cast Uanescere, a Disintegrate spell, as the beast turned to gray dust. The guardian quickly grabbed his sword before it fell to the ground. Horith hunched it over with his mouth ajar. Gideon nodded to the side, signaling for the security dwarf to go, then continued west, casting Undeath to Death at the undead enemies, shattering their skulls. Finally, he reached the Cache Tavern, where a small group of undead clawed at the front door. The horde noticed him and charged. Raising his vorpal sword, Gideon sliced the heads of the three attackers in half.

One creature remained on the porch, trying to claw into the bar. As Gideon approached, his heart sank. "Pixie," he muttered.

The undead dwarf, eyes glazed with murderous intent, hissed at the guardian. Before the creature could move, Gideon cast Levitation and had Pixie floating mid-air. Pixie snarled and clawed at the air as it slowly spun in a circle.

The front door cracked open, and Rusty dashed out, stabbing his undead cousin in the temple with a corkscrew. Gideon lowered Pixie slowly as Rusty sat on the stoop. The tearful dwarf guided his cousin's bloody head to his lap.

The guardian tried to say something comforting but remained silent. *I've never seen a dwarf cry before.* "I'm sorry, Mister Keggs," he murmured, bowing in condolence. After looking at his fallen friend one last time, Gideon flew back toward the Omlett Inn.

Raven opened her teary eyes. Gideon stood there in his gold armor and white wings. They both smiled. *It wasn't the Astral Realm. It was better.* Instinctively, she grabbed him by the shoulder, and for that moment, she forgot about all the evil surrounding them.

"Gideon!" Izarra screamed. The guardian nodded and flew off.

Raven watched him depart as the sound of mooing snapped her attention back to the undead army near the bridge. The Nightmare steed had turned into a cow.

"Ha!" Shorte huffed. "Gideon!"

After dismissing his altered mount, the dark knight dropped to the dirt amid the bloody mess the guardian left. Half of the undead army lay headless on the ground. Carya's corpse, however, had survived the massive onslaught and lingered beside the vile monster.

"Gideon leveled the playing field," Jarz snickered as he summoned his magical ice sword and an ice shield from his bracer. "I think he's going after that fox." Blue, watery wings formed behind him.

"You and those damned battle wings," the dwarf laughed, tapping his mace against his shield to create iron skin.

"You and your damned alter ego," Jarz replied.

"I am"—Shorte clanked his solid chest—"Iron Dwarf."

Avalann drew back the string of Blade's bow, creating a magical arrow as Izarra spun her trident like a bard performance.

With the staff still in her bedroom, Raven drew her gem-encrusted daggers.

"What is this dragon fodder waiting for?" Shorte asked, growing impatient. But the dwarf wasn't the only one—the necromancer cast a spell after the comment, and the undead roared as they charged.

Thomas barged out the front doors of the Omlett Inn at that exact moment with no armor or weapons. He grabbed the head of one of the undead, smashing it into the stone wall before punching another in the face and knocking it down. He straddled the creature and began wailing on it, punch after punch.

"What the spell?" Raven asked in disbelief. "Thomas!" She tried to draw his attention, then broke off from the group to help her drunken pal.

"Look, Purple Eyes," he slurred, covered in blood. "I got two of those bastards." He tried to stand, but an undead gnome tackled him.

Raven recognized the creature wrestling with the intoxicated paladin.

"Hey, look, it's Gary," Thomas confirmed from the flat of his back. *He's correct. It was indeed Gary the garden gnome, another victim of the undead.*

Vines quickly grew around the undead creature, gripping him tighter and tighter. She wrapped her razor wire around the gnome's neck—*I'm sorry, Gary*—then pulled tight, severing the head.

A female warrior in white fur armor pierced the animated head with her axe. The paladin wobbled to his feet as the warrior struggled to remove her axe from the skull.

"Thank you," Raven said as the warrior nodded in response.

A shout came from the stables. "Ash!"

"That would be me," the warrior confirmed, shaking her axe off and splattering blood on her white fur. "Damn, that's not coming out."

"Ashley!" the voice shouted again.

"Be right there, Gobs," Ash yelled, running toward the stables as a petite female elf wearing brown fur armor held the reins of Krit, Ghost, and Grail, pulling them away.

Are they stealing them? Raven noticed the corpses tangled in vines around the stable, indicating that the pair had defended the animals.

Thomas ran past, pursuing the stranger as Raven cursed under her breath.

As Raven followed Thomas, she pulled her other dagger from her belt and forced it into his hand. While she was wary of giving him a weapon, she had no choice as they charged another horde.

Ashley butchered a sizable undead orc with dual battle axes while Thomas stabbed several undead gnome warriors through their eye sockets with the dagger.

Raven tightened the razor wire around the neck of a dwarf while Gobs watched over the four-legged animals. Some of the other horses in the stable weren't as fortunate.

Once the chaos died down at the stable, Raven checked on Ghost. The rogue stroked the unicorn's muzzle, trying to calm her. "Easy, girl." Another scream came from the direction of the statue.

"Come on, Raven!" Thomas yelled, raising the dagger, but he stumbled against the warrior who held him upright as he vomited into the grass.

"Watch the fur!" Ash barked, stepping back and glancing at the rogue. "Go—we'll look after him."

Raven nodded, casting Arcane Step to pierce undead creatures with her dagger as she raced back to the guardians. A blue portal appeared as Carya's shell and a group of undead forced Jarz through.

The necromancer glanced back at the guardians as he followed his allies through the portal, leaving a wall of undead behind him. The guardians did quick work against the remaining undead as Raven returned to the group.

Izarra cried hysterically, shoving the rogue. "It's your fault! You left us to chase after a guy."

Raven regained her balance. "Izarra?"

"The undead surrounded us, and you left! Afraid you'll lose another guy?"

Shorte placed his hand on the half-nymph's back, trying to calm her.

"He was defenseless," Raven pleaded.

Izarra whipped around, wrapping her arms around Shorte's head, smothering his face into her bosom. The dwarf huffed with a confused look as he patted her back clumsily. "Easy, Izz. I haven't undone my Iron Skin yet. You'll rust me,"

Shorte joked, adjusting his helmet, trying to cheer her up. The half-nymph just cried harder.

Frustrated, Raven turned to Avalann. "What happened?"

The elf-ranger scowled. "Izarra was in trouble, and Jarz tried to help, then he just collapsed as Shorte and I tried fighting off dozens of crazed cannibals."

Izarra glared. "I couldn't cast my water spells fast enough, and those creatures swarmed me."

"I saw Carya cast a dark spell at Jarz," Shorte moaned, still patting the sobbing half-nymph. "I wanted to save him, but that type of spell scared the shite out of me. It's not natural."

"Carya cast a dark spell?" Raven muttered. "But how?"

"Not sure," Shorte responded. "Maybe she's truly a lich."

"We failed," Izarra uttered, wiping her eyes and stepping away from the dwarf.

Raven moved to her tearful friend, entwining their hands. "I'm sorry I wasn't there to help you. I promise we'll find him."

Izarra abruptly pulled away. "I'll be fine." She glared at the rogue seething. "We don't need to rely on you. Gideon's back." The half-nymph stormed off to the spot at the bridge where Jarz disappeared.

Avalann followed the half-nymph and placed her hand on Izarra's shoulder. "They captured him alive, unlike most of his victims." The archer's eyes widened as Raven shot her an annoyed look, and Izarra choked back more tears. "What did I say? It's not my fault you left us."

Raven's heart sank watching her distressed friend drop to her knees, crying. *Izarra's upset that Jarz is gone. But she's right, Gideon's returned! Should I—*The thought vanished when she heard the cries from family members hovering over the corpses of their loved ones, now littering the roads of Omlett. The smell of death now overtook the sweet and savory aromas the city had always offered.

Raven gripped her head as a sharp pain ricocheted around like an arrow hitting an obsidian boulder. She cleared her throat and gulped as if swallowing her pride. The group gazed at her. "Listen—"

"Are you all right?" Shorte asked, walking toward her. "You look paler than usual."

Raven's heartbeat raced as her headache grew. A cold sweat ran down her back, making her shiver, which was odd because a fever ignited inside her. An acidic taste flooded her mouth, dropping her to her knees. She held her hand out to stop Shorte from advancing further as she braced herself with her hands. Her stomach erupted, and her vomit sizzled the grass away.

"Your hands!" Avalann called out.

Raven raised them to see the bile that splashed, attempting to melt the skin on the back of her hands. *No pain or burns. Ugh! the smell!* Butch's face flooded her memories. The remaining patches of grass near her wilted as puddles of melted snow dried into thicker mud.

She gasped in horror as the uncontrollable darkness slowly swallowed her friends. Extending her hands, she tried to concentrate on dispelling the Darkness ability. *I can't stop it.* She frantically searched for her circlet. *Shite!*

A blond man collapsed in front of her with her dagger protruding from his forehead. *Stop. Stop. It's not real!* Images of the bugbears drowning flashed around in the darkness. As she glanced up, arrows flew overhead. Following them with her eyes, she watched as they rained down, piercing a group of kobolds. A scream made her turn her head quickly as she watched Carya get tackled by the undead. *So much death!*

All the images replayed again but spun around her until she finally collapsed. She lay there, exhausted, as the pictures faded, bringing a sense of peace. A bright light broke through the darkness.

Am I going to the Astral Realm?

ACKNOWLEDGMENTS

The authors would like to thank the following for their contributions to this work:

Raven Motes (preliminary creative and line editor), Allyson Thomas (creator of the Euphrasia and Omlett Maps and the Naelo coat-of-arms), Kevin Fritsch (alpha and beta reader), Kerry Wentz (beta reader), Sarah Peachey (developmental, line, and copy editor), and Crystal Devine (book designer).

ABOUT THE AUTHORS

Rachel Ann Fischer, an author from Harrisburg, PA.
After serving time in the US Army, she attended technical school for Auto-Cad and Interior Design. Her creativity began at an early age when she discovered the world of fantasy role-playing games. This sparked Rachel's imagination and passion for creating worlds and characters. She wrote two play scripts that a

local drama department produced. The process made her fall in love with writing dialogue and helped her develop the confidence to write this novel. The story is based on a role-playing campaign that began many years ago in her cousin Kevin's kitchen.

AnnMarie Knorr-Fischer, an author from Harrisburg, PA.
Her love of the arts began at a very young age. The first memories of writing that she can recall are from elementary school, where she wrote short poems and stories. Ann's love for the written word progressed over the years as she wrote for school literary publications and a full-length movie script her senior year in college. Working with Rachel, AnnMarie directed and produced two plays. Currently, she works as an entertainment consultant in Hershey, PA.

R.A.Fischer Authors

www.rafischerauthors.com

Omlett City

1. Omlett Inn
2. Secret Sister spot
3. Crinkly's Bakery
4. Gary's Garden Hub
5. Wally's Wagon Shop
6. Miley's Book Shop
7. Lumber Yard
8. Soldiers' Barracks
9. Omlett Prison
10. Meat & Greet Eatery
11. Iron Vale Jewelers
12. Omlett Outfitters

13. Cocke Tavern
14. Bernie's Butcher Shop
15. Apothecary
16. Wicked Weapons
17. Blacksmith
18. Maggie's Magic Shop
19. Blade's Church
20. Mag's Golem Factory
21. Amphitheatre
22. Black Dragon Monument
23. Fish & Ships Eatery
24. Gypsy Corner
25. Fischer's Dock
26. Starlight Orphanage

www.ingramcontent.com/pod-product-compliance
Lightning Source LLC
Chambersburg PA
CBHW060426030726
47495CB00003B/755